WALL STREET JOURNAL AND USA TODAY BESTSELLING AUTHOR

AVELYN PAIGE

All The Pretty Little Lies © 2024 Avelyn Paige

Cover Designer: Simply Defined Art

Editor: Breathless Lit

Page Edge Designs by Painted Wings Publishing

This is a work of fiction. Names, places, characters and incidents are either the product of the author's imagination or are used fictitiously, and any resemblance to any actual persons, living or dead, organizations, events or locales is entirely coincidental.

Dedication

To the ones who love their romance with shadows and sharp edges. This one's for you—because sometimes, happily ever after comes with bloodstains and lots of trigger warnings.

Trigger Warnings

Buckle up, because in this wild ride of morally ambiguous lovers and untamed hearts, you'll find enough twists, turns, and "Did that really just happen?" moments to make a rollercoaster look tame.

Content Warnings (or should we say *Welcome to Mafia Land Survival Kit*):

• Anxiety? Check. Just remember to breathe.

• Blood and Gore? Oh, you'll need more than a wet wipe.

• Body Horror? Yep, you'll definitely cringe (and probably peek through your fingers).

• Kidnapping, Forced Marriage, Torture? Just a day in the life of our darkly charming antiheroes!

• Needles and Non-Con Medical Procedures? Let's just say these guys don't believe in bedside manners.

• Organized Crime? You'd better believe it.

So if you've ever wondered what it's like to be swept off your feet by men who don't mind getting their hands dirty (like, *really* dirty), this book is for you. Just make sure you've got your therapist on speed dial—and maybe a stress ball or two. Happy reading! 🖤

Full List of Content Warnings

    Anxiety and Anxiety Attacks

    Blood and Gore

    Body Horror

    Captivity and Confinement

    Car Accident

    Death

    Dismemberment

    Drugging

    Emotional Abuse

    Forced Marriage

    Infertility

    Involuntary Pregnancy

    Kidnapping

    Loss of Autonomy

    Murder

    Needles

    Non-Con Medical Procedures

    Organized Crime

Post Traumatic Stress Disorder
Pregnancy
Sex Trafficking
Sexual Assault
Sexual Harassment
Torture

Play List

"Addicted" - Saving Abel
"Say This Sober" - Archers
"Next Contestant" - Nickelback
"Sound of Madness" - Shinedown
"Just Pretend" - Bad Omens
"Bodies" - Drowning Pool
"Pain" - Three Days Grace
"Daughters of Darkness" - Halestorm
"Shame on Me - Catch Your Breath
"Broken (feat. Amy Lee) - Seether
"Silhouettes" - Smile Emmy Soul
"Always" - Saliva
"Boots and Blood - Five Finger Death Punch
"Zombie" - The Cranberries

Rossi Family Tree

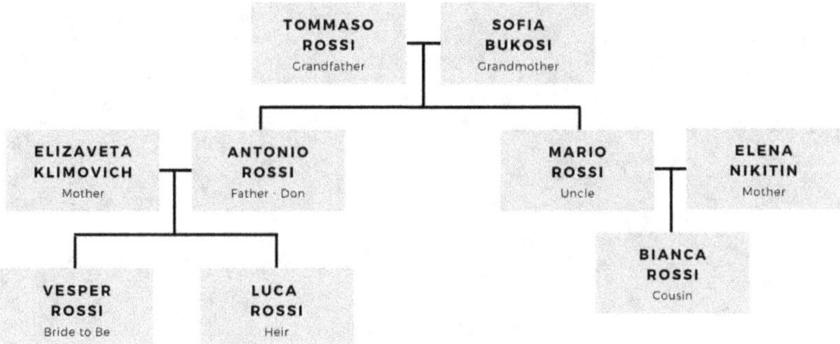

Petrov Family Tree

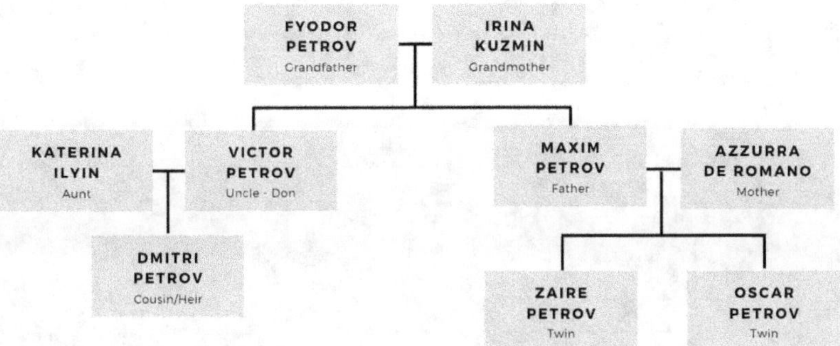

Chapter 1

EVERYONE ASSUMES that being a spoiled little rich girl is the path to Easy Street. Designer clothes. Fancy cars. Exotic vacations to faraway places that most people only see in magazines and coffee table books.

Let me be the first to tell you.

It's all bullshit.

It's a facade that the uber rich of the world put out there to elevate themselves over the hard-working people who dream about the world I was born into. A world so dark and depraved that all those little fairy tale dreams of a worry-free little girl are nothing more than pastel painted nightmares. While most girls had pretty dolls, I had etiquette lessons. Play dates? No. I had dinner parties where my parents brought me out to show off, dangling me in front of the shark infested waters of their circle of friends, chumming the water to whet their appetites. I was trained to understand that my role was to seal alliances and provide heirs. My virginity and womb would be sold off to the highest bidder amongst the mafia families of the world. An arranged marriage to a stranger. My life was always on a specific path, one that was predetermined from the moment I took my first breath as the eldest daughter of the most powerful syndicate in the United States.

In the Rossi family, what lies between your legs decides your fate. The men automatically join the family business, like my younger brother Luca, who is next in line for succession. But for me, things were different. Instead of fairy tales and white picket fences, my future held a *different* kind of family obligations - one tied with blood and loyalty.

My father, Antonio Rossi, saw me solely as a bargaining chip to gain more power outside of the U.S. I was the first-born daughter in the Rossi family in two generations. Every mafia family, according to my father, is salivating to get a taste of the advantages that an alliance can bring. It's the kind of thing every daughter wants their father to tell her at my age. The only thing that is useful about me is my ability to look pretty and make babies.

As soon as I turned eighteen, my final year of freedom, our house became a revolving door for potential suitors. Old. Young. Suitors that barely spoke English. A modern-day marriage market for the rich and powerful. Except, I was the only one on the market. I mean, there were plenty of other mafia princesses in the sea, but none of them carried my name or legacy. Other than my seventeen-year-old cousin, Bianca, I *am* the ultimate prize. Another family's way into my father's empire.

While my peers were living out the teenage dream of parties, boyfriends, and friends, I was trapped within the confines of our family compound. My parents, determined to protect my virtue, kept me tightly sequestered. And when I wasn't attending my prestigious private school for the children of the rich and ruthless, I was confined to my luxurious yet lonely prison cell - my bedroom. My once cozy sanctuary now felt suffocating, a reminder of all the experiences I was missing. The hours I had wasted staring out my bedroom window, like I am now, a sad reminder of just how little control I have over my own life.

Only the sound of a quiet knock at my bedroom door before the click and clack of heels draws me away from my daydreaming of a better life. As I turn towards the door, my heart quickens with dread. The familiar scent of my mother's expensive perfume wafts into my room choking me before she even speaks a word.

"Vesper, darling, your father would like to see you in his study. He has news to share with you," she announces in a tone that leaves no room for argument. Normally, her Russian accent is well hidden, but not today. Something has rattled her to let her tight grip on her accent slip. My father had once told me that when his marriage was arranged to my mother that the first thing, he changed about her was her accent. If she were to be a Rossi, she'd speak as one.

Her cold, calculating gaze scrutinizes my disheveled appearance. "Is it so difficult for you to look presentable, Vesper? Your father despises sloppiness. You are a Rossi. Act like one." She huffed disapprovingly before disappearing into my walk-in closet. My eyes fall to the soft pink sweater and white leggings on my body, and I sigh. Unlike my mother, I prefer comfort over appearance.

Minutes later, she emerges with a designer white sweater, pale pink trousers, and matching heels, which she neatly lays out on my bed.

"If I had known you were in this state, I would have intervened sooner. Now get changed and tidy up your hair. Show some pride in yourself."

I mutter a defeated "yes, mother" as I reluctantly leave the comfort of the windowsill. My heart races with anxiety; my mother's standards for appearance are unyielding and unforgiving. Growing up in a mafia family has its challenges, but having a former supermodel for a mother only adds to the pressure. Unlike most mafia princesses who are married off at an early age, my maternal grandfather allowed my mother to remain unmarried until she was twenty-one. It's a luxury I wish I had been granted. All the women in our world were married off as soon as they turned eighteen. Marriages of convenience and strategy. Bianca, being the only other Rossi princess, would be next on the market after

I'm married if Uncle Mario's bragging to my father is to be believed. Unlike me, Bianca loved the attention. She thrives in it, really. She is the social butterfly at every party whereas I would much prefer to be left alone.

Taking the clothes, I slip into my bathroom and change. The soft, cashmere feels like pricking needles against my skin.

"Hurry up," she demands from the other side of the door. I run my brush through my long, blonde hair twice before pulling it back into a low ponytail. Reluctantly, I leave the safety of my bathroom and step back into my bedroom back into my mother's hard gaze.

"This will have to do." Without another word, she turns on her designer heels and gracefully glides out of my bedroom door. I follow her out of my room and down the elaborate staircase of the Rossi mansion. The grand chandelier above us casts a soft glow on the polished marble floors as we make our way to the opulent sitting room where my fate is sealed over and over again.

As we enter the room, I notice a man standing with his back to us, staring out of the floor-to-ceiling windows that overlook the sprawling estate. His broad shoulders are tense under his fitted suit jacket, betraying the calm demeanor he is trying to exude. My mother clears her throat, causing him to turn around slowly. What I see takes my breath away - piercing blue eyes that seem to see right through me, a strong jawline dusted with a hint of stubble, and an air of confidence that makes my pulse race.

"Oscar?" I blurt out in surprise.

I'd never formally met him or his twin brother, Zaire, but I'd have to be blind to have not noticed either of them at school. No one at my school was overtly unattractive, but Oscar and Zaire are like two tall, dark, and handsome gods who allowed us to be in their presence. Every female gaze lingered on them no matter where they went. They were members of the Petrov family. The Rossi equivalent in Russia. Powerful, and as wealthy as my family. He gives me a small smile, one that doesn't quite reach his eyes.

"Miss Rossi," he greets me, his voice smooth like velvet. His Russian accent is rich and melodic.

"Please take a seat, Oscar. My husband will be with us shortly," my mother offers.

The tension in the room is palpable as my mother gestures for us to sit across from each other on the plush sofas. As we both take our seats, I can't help but steal glances at him. His presence brings an unexpected comfort, even amidst the suffocating atmosphere of inevitability that hangs over me. I'd never been this close to him or any man my age that isn't related to me. I can't help but steal glances in his direction.

His eyes, a striking shade of blue like the winter sky, hold a depth that seem to hide countless secrets. His features sharp and chiseled, every line and angle perfectly complementing each other. His dark hair ends just below his ears. There is a quiet strength in the way he holds himself, a confidence that exudes power without needing to be spoken. As we sit in silence, the only sound filling the room is the ticking of the ornate grandfather clock in the corner. Each passing second feels like an eternity, stretching the tension between us until it is almost tangible.

Before either of us can breach the suffocating silence that envelopes us, the heavy mahogany door creaks open, revealing my father's imposing figure as he enters the room. His sharp gaze sweeps over us before settling on Oscar with a calculating glint in his eyes, who rises from his seat and extends his hand towards my father.

My father accepts the handshake with a curt nod, his expression unreadable. "Oscar Petrov, welcome to my home," he states, his tone laced with a thinly veiled hint of suspicion.

"It's an honor to meet you, Mr. Rossi," Oscar replies smoothly, his posture remaining composed despite the palpable tension in the room. "Please accept my uncle's apology for not being here in person today."

"When business calls, these things can't be helped," my father smirks. "It's the way of things for families such as ours, is it not?"

Oscar only offers a polite nod.

I observe the exchange between them, feeling like a mere spectator in my own life. The weight of my family's expectations hangs heavy on my shoulders, suffocating any semblance of choice or autonomy. I steal a glance at Oscar, wondering what thoughts are running through his mind.

My father gestures for Oscar to take a seat once more, his piercing gaze never leaving him.

"Let's get straight to the point. Your uncle, Victor, and I have been working towards an agreement that would be mutually beneficial to both the Rossi's and the Petrov's."

I feel a knot form in the pit of my stomach as I anticipate the direction this conversation is heading. My fate is slipping further out of my control with each passing moment. I struggle to keep my emotions in check, my heart racing as the weight of my father's words begin to crush me. If Oscar is here, it means only one thing. My Father has chosen a Petrov as my husband. Only one comes to mind, and the thought terrifies me.

Oscar's expression remains unreadable, his eyes briefly meet mine before returning to my father. His silence speaks volumes, a veil of mystery shrouding his thoughts and intentions.

"This arrangement will solidify the bond between our families for generations to come."

Oscar nods in understanding, though a flicker of something unreadable crosses his eyes. "I am here to honor my family's commitments." His voice is steady, betraying none of his thoughts swirling beneath the surface.

My father's gaze lingers on Oscar for a moment before he turns to me, a glint of expectation in his eyes. "And you, Vesper. Do you understand the significance of this union and what it means for our family?"

I swallow hard, steeling myself against the overwhelming tide of emotions threatening to consume me. "Yes, Father. I understand," I reply. "I accept my duty."

A heavy silence descends upon the room once more, punctuated only by the rhythmic ticking of the clock. The weight of my impending future hangs over me like a shroud, snuffing out any semblance of control I had over my life.

"Good," he smiles. "With the Rossi's and Petrovs in alliance, no one will be able to touch us. This alliance will solidify both sides of the world with a single vow." My father nearly glows with his delight. Everything that he has wanted will be at his fingertips the second he binds me to the Petrovs. His dream becomes my nightmare.

"When is the wedding?" my mother asks from behind us. "Preparations will need to be made for the ceremony."

"A week," he answers flatly. "Out of respect for your education, your future father-in-law has allowed you until your graduation day to fulfill your obligation."

A gasp escapes my lips. My father's eyes narrow in the rare break of my calm outward demure. A break that I may pay for later.

A week? That's all that I am allowed to come to terms with this arrangement. That's all the time I'm given until my life as I know it ends.

The words hang heavy in the air, sealing my fate with an irrevocable finality that sends a chill down my spine. I glance at Oscar and catch a brief glimpse of the whirlwind of emotions raging behind his cool facade. His eyes meet mine for a fleeting moment, a silent understanding passing between us.

"A week isn't much time," my mother remarks. "There's much to do."

"I'm sure you'll figure it out," he flatly answers.

"Father, am I permitted to ask a question?"

"Ask," he declares.

"Why is Oscar here instead of Dmitri?"

"As Dmitri is still abroad, and will be until your wedding day, his father has appointed Oscar and his brother, Zaire, to be your guardians until you are handed off to your husband. They will also be joining your security detail at school."

I steel myself against the tide of emotions threatening to overwhelm me, forcing a mask of stoicism over my features. With a barely perceptible nod, I acknowledge my father's decree, knowing that resistance would be futile. My destiny has been written in stone, and I am but a puppet.

Chapter 2

VESPER

AFTER MY FATHER escorts Oscar away to celebrate with a cigar, my mother immediately ushers me back into the confines of my room where I am to wait for further instructions. The door closes behind her with a resounding thud, and I slump against it, forcing back the tears until I can no longer hear my mother's heels echoing in the distance.

I can't breathe. *I can't fucking breathe.*

I force myself from the floor. Without a second thought, I rush towards my balcony door, throwing it open, and feel the cool night air kiss my skin. My lungs heave, as I rest my arms on the balcony railing, gazing out into the darkness that surrounds the vast estate like a dense fog, desperately trying to focus on my breathing. The stars above me twinkle and mock my situation with their effortless beauty. They have no worries about where to go or what to wear, they simply shine day and night until their light eventually fades away in a dazzling finale. To be free like that, be able to glimmer in the night sky without a care in the world, seems like an impossible dream. Yet, it's one I would give anything to have at this moment.

Dmitri Petrov is not only dangerous, but he is also my future husband. Any morsel of hope I had that my own father would protect me has now dissipated like smoke in the wind. Of all the families to shackle me to, he picked the one person on the entire planet that absolutely terrifies me.

I'd seen him only a few times at the academy. Much like his cousin, Dmitri is tall. His muscled body a weapon. His face, while handsome, holds something more sinister behind the beautiful facade. Rumors follow him everywhere. The sons of rival families have a way of disappearing when he is present. That is, until Dmitri was sent back to Russia after our Freshman year. The reason was never leaked, but about the time he left, so did one of the female members of an Irish family. Like Dmitri, she never returned. Luca had his suspicions, but he, of course, never bothered to share those with me other than to tell me that Dmitri being abroad was safer for everyone, including myself. Now, it wouldn't matter where he was because in a week, I would be by his side.

The thought of being tied to him makes my stomach

churn, souring more with each passing moment. The heavy weight of tradition and duty crushes me. I'd been trained for this, to endure for the sake of my family. Endure a loveless, arranged marriage to a dangerous man in a foreign country, far away from any lifeline I might still have after I said my vows.

Dmitri will control everything about my life. What I eat, when I sleep, how often I spread my legs, and bear him heirs. I knew this was my fate, but the reality is finally settling in. I am drowning without water, being dragged so far down into the depths that my body chills with each passing second. I force myself to focus on breathing. In and out until warmth finally returns to my limbs. I stare off in the distance below, letting myself settle back into my skin when a sudden movement in the shadows below catches my eye, and I strain to see through the inky blackness. A figure emerges from the darkness, moving with a grace and stealth that belies their presence. As they draw closer, the dim light from the moon reveals a familiar silhouette - Oscar. His eyes meet mine, studying me from his position in my mother's lavish garden. He's so still that had I not seen him move before, I would have thought he was a figment of my imagination.

What is he doing in the garden? He should still be with my Father. Surely, he's not starting his guard duty tonight. I consider calling down to him, but a voice comes from behind me.

"Not thinking about jumping, are you?"

I practically jump out of my skin at the sound of the voice, spinning around to see Luca leaning against the door frame leading into my room. Where my parents are cold and ruthless, Luca is the sunshine in my life. The only true joy that I have within our family. My ally in everything. "It looks like you've seen a ghost," Luca teases, a smirk playing on his lips as he saunters closer to me on the balcony. Despite the lightness in his voice, I can see concern flicker in his eyes before he masks it with humor.

Taking a deep breath to steady myself, I shoot him a look of mock annoyance. "Very funny, Luca. You scared the life out of me."

Luca chuckles, but there's a warmth in his gaze that tells me he's genuinely relieved to see me unharmed. "Sorry about that. Couldn't resist giving you a start. So, who were you expecting to find down there? A secret admirer perhaps? An escape route?"

I shake my head with a wry smile, "I take it you've heard who Father has selected for me."

"I have." Luca's expression turns serious at the mention of Dmitri, his playful demeanor fading away as he steps closer to me. "You know you don't have to go through with this, right? There are other options, other paths you can take."

I sigh, knowing Luca means well, but also understanding the constraints of our family's expectations. "I appreciate your concern, Luca, but you know as well as I do that there's nothing you or I can do. It's settled. After graduation, I'll be shipped off to Russia to marry Dmitri."

Luca's jaw tightens at the thought, his worry evident. "He's a dangerous man, Vesper. I fear for you. I fear what he will do to you. I fear," he sighs. "I fear that you will end up just like our mother."

"It's not like that hasn't been the plan for me since the day I was born. I'm not like you. I'm the means to a powerful alliance. You're the future of this family."

"Fuck our family. It doesn't have to be the plan. You could leave. I have enough cash that you could get away and live a good life."

I look at Luca, his offer tempting me with the promise of freedom and a life of my choosing. The idea of leaving everything behind, including my family's expectations, and the looming shadow of Dmitri Petrov, fills me with a mixture of fear and excitement. Could I really walk away from everything I've ever known? Could I turn my back on tradition and duty in search of a life that is truly mine?

The sound of my own heartbeat fills the silence that stretches between Luca and me, each thud a reminder of the choice that lies before me. Taking a deep breath, I meet Luca's gaze, seeing the hope and worry etched in his eyes.

"Luca, running away is a tempting prospect, I won't deny that," I begin softly, weighing my words carefully. "But you know as well as I do that it's not that simple. Our family would never stop looking for me. And Dmitri, he would consider it an even greater challenge to hunt me down."

Luca nods, his jaw clenching with frustration. "I know it's risky. But staying here, marrying him. It's not just risky, Vesper. It's dangerous. He's a killer."

I reach out to grasp Luca's hand, needing the comfort of his touch in this moment of uncertainty. "Believe me, the thought of being bound to him terrifies me more than anything else in this world, but if I leave, the Petrovs will take their revenge. It would put our entire family at risk. While I may not care what happens to everyone, I care about what happens to you."

"Don't worry about me, Ves. I can take care of myself once I know you're safe."

"Even if I entertained trying to leave, you know as well as I do that escaping isn't that simple. Where would I go? How would I survive on my own? And what about you? The Petrovs will not stand for an alliance of this magnitude to be broken. You'll be the one in their crosshairs."

Luca's gaze softens, a mix of resignation and determination flickering in his eyes. "I'll figure something out. Your safety is worth any consequence. You're all I have left, Vesper."

Tears threaten to spill from my eyes at his words, at the unconditional love and loyalty he shows me when everyone else has turned their backs. He's right - Luca is all I have in this world, the one person who has never wavered in his support for me.

I squeeze his hand tightly, drawing strength from his unwavering presence. "Thank you, Luca. For everything. I don't know what I'd do without you, but you know there is nothing either of us can do. My die has been cast."

He offers me a small, sad smile before pulling me into a tight embrace, as if trying to shield me from the storm that looms on the horizon. We stand there in silence for a long moment, the weight of our unspoken fears and hopes hanging heavy in the air between us.

"Just give me time, Ves. I'll figure something out."

As I pull away from Luca's comforting embrace, a sense of foreboding settles in the pit of my stomach. I can't escape the feeling of being trapped, like a bird with clipped wings expected to soar. Deep down, I know that time will not change anything. The reality of my situation is a heavy weight pressing down on me, suffocating me with its grim certainty. I have to marry Dmitri. There is no other option. I just have to figure out how to survive it.

Chapter 3

AS OUR CHAUFFEURED car glides along the same route as yesterday, I can't help but notice the new addition to my hand: a sparkling ring with a vibrant red diamond at its center. The rock is massive, and the band is encrusted with dozens of smaller diamonds, creating a blinding effect in the sunlight. My mother, who prides herself on her knowledge of designer items, estimates its value in the millions. A shocking amount to sit upon my finger.

"Looks like someone is overcompensating," Luca mutters under his breath.

"More like trying to buy my affection or pliability."

"I'm surprised it didn't come with its own armed

guard." Luca barely glances up from his phone. Since our talk last night, he seems more preoccupied than usual.

"It did."

Luca's gaze snaps up from his phone.

"Dmitri's father assigned Oscar and Zaire Petrov to my security detail. Oscar was there on behalf of the Petrov family to accept the marriage contract."

"Why didn't you mention that last night?"

I shift to stare out the window, trying to let the rolling hills of central Massachusetts cull the storm inside of me. Our school, Saint Jude Academy, lingers in the distance. It's ironic, really, that our school is named after the Patron Saint of Lost Causes, considering within its walls are the heirs and descendants of some of the world's most dangerous people. The children of killers, thieves, and mercenaries. The fledglings of the underbelly of society. Saint Jude's teaches men how to serve their respective families and the women how to be picture perfect wives and mothers.

"I asked you a question, Ves. Why did you leave that part out of our conversation last night?"

"It slipped my mind," I offer.

"Slipped your mind?" Luca retorts. He shifts in his seat to see if the driver is listening to us before lowering his voice. "I'm trying to get you out of this, Ves. Our guards are one thing. But Oscar and Zaire are a complication we don't fucking need." He throws his back against the leather seat of the limo hard enough that I hear the leather creak under his weight.

"I'm sorry," I mutter.

Our driver comes to a stop outside the entrance of the school and exits the car to open our doors.

"We'll talk about this later," Luca warns me before exiting his open door. He disappears around the car, and up the steps before the driver opens my door. I offer a polite thank you as I step out.

As soon as I step out of the car, Bianca comes running towards me, her long, black hair bouncing with each step. Her eyes narrow as they land on the ring, glinting on my finger.

"I knew it! Father wouldn't say a word about why Uncle Antonio came to see him last night, but I had a feeling. Who is it? Do we know him? Is he handsome?" Bianca's words spill out in a rush, her envy thinly veiling her curiosity. "How much money does he have?"

"It's Dmitri Petrov."

Bianca's eyes grow wide. "You don't mean the Dmitri Petrov, who may or may not have offed his Irish mob girl-friend, right? Son and heir of the largest mafia family in the Western hemisphere? That Dmitri Petrov?"

"The one and only," I shrug.

"Well, well, well," she says, a mischievous grin spreading across her face. "Looks like things just got a whole lot more interesting around here."

I shoot her a warning look. "Bianca, please. This isn't some scandalous gossip for you to spread around the school."

Her grin widens. "Oh, Ves, you know me better than that. I'm not going to spill your secrets. But this? This changes everything. Besides, the Petrovs marrying into the Rossi family is front page news. It won't take long for every mafia family on the planet to hear about the two largest families merging together in unholy matrimony."

I sigh, knowing she's right. Being engaged to Dmitri Petrov would undoubtedly change everything, not just for me but for everyone connected to us. More power only brings more problems.

"I mean, is Dmitri an ideal husband? No, but think of the power you'll wield, Ves. You'll be the most powerful woman in both families. And as the only other unmarried Rossi princess, it means my own prospects just got better."

I laugh at her suggestion. The only power I will have is broodmare, producing Rossi-Petrov heirs until my uterus dries up.

Bianca chatters on about our wedding, sharing with me how she envisions her wedding, including a Petrov groom of her own. Only instead of Dmitri, her eyes are set on Oscar or his twin brother, Zaire.

As we make our way into the school, the whispers begin. Students turn to stare, their eyes lingering on the ring on my finger before darting away when they realize I've caught them looking. I can practically hear the rumors starting to swirl around us like a gathering storm. I can feel the weight of all the eyes on me. The whispers and sidelong glances confirm what I already knew - news of my engagement to

Dmitri Petrov has spread like wildfire. Students and staff alike watch me with a mix of curiosity and wariness as if they expect me to suddenly sprout horns and a forked tail.

It's a reminder of the burden I now carry - the legacy of the Rossi family, intertwined with the formidable Petrovs, has become my future. And with it comes a whole new set of rules, alliances, and dangers.

Luca catches up to me as Bianca drifts off towards her own group of friends, his expression troubled. "We need to figure out how to manage Oscar and Zaire," he says.

"Did I hear my name?" a low, familiar voice rumbles from behind us. I turn, only to find Oscar's looming presence. He wearing our school uniform, though it's clear his has been tailored to fit him well.

Luca tenses beside me, his jaw clenched as he glares up at Oscar. He puts himself between us, but I take a step forward, meeting Oscar's gaze with a determined stare of my own.

"What do you want, Oscar?" Luca asks.

Oscar smirks, still eyeing Luca, the corners of his lips curling up in a way that sets me on edge. "My business isn't with you, Luca. I'm here for your sister."

Luca's protective instinct flares up, his body tensing even more as he steps closer to me. "My sister doesn't need anything from you," he retorts, his voice low and dangerous. "She's not Petrov property for seven more days."

"Six by my count." Oscar's smirk only widens at Luca's reaction. "Relax, Rossi. I'm not here to cause trouble," he says, his tone mocking. "I just need a word with the future Mrs. Petrov."

I shoot Luca a quick glance, silently urging him to let me manage this. "What could you possibly want to talk to me about?" I ask, trying to feign confidence.

Oscar takes a step closer, his towering frame casting a shadow over me. "Just a little chat between future family members," he says smoothly, but there's an underlying edge to his words that sets off warning bells in my mind.

Without giving me a chance to respond, Zaire materializes beside Oscar, his face betraying no emotion. "Let's not create a commotion in the sacred halls of Saint Jude Academy," he murmurs, his voice as smooth and silky like the finest fabric. His piercing gaze briefly grazes over Luca and I, before settling on Oscar.

It's almost startling to realize just how alike the two brothers are in appearance - both tall and well-built, with sharp jawlines and piercing eyes. The only contrast is Zaire's heavily tattooed arms and his sleek, dark hair that falls just above his pierced ears.

Zaire's presence adds a layer of tension to the already charged atmosphere. He exudes a quiet confidence that draws attention, much like his brother Oscar, but there's a subtle difference in the way he carries himself - a sense of control that hints at the hidden depths beneath the surface.

Luca narrows his eyes at the Petrov brothers, his stance protective and wary. "Whatever you have to say to her, you can say in front of me," he demands, his voice sharp with suspicion.

Oscar's smirk falters for a split second before he regains his composure. "No need to get your briefs in a twist," he replies casually, tension lacing his tone.

Zaire speaks up, his voice smooth as silk but holding a steely edge. "We merely wanted to offer our congratulations on your engagement," he says, his eyes never leaving mine. "And formally introduce ourselves to our future cousin in law, considering she will be seeing a lot more of us until the wedding."

"Thank you," I say, keeping my tone polite but guarded. "It's kind of you to offer your congratulations."

Oscar's smile widens at my response, seemingly pleased with himself. "It's the least we could do for the family," he says, his words laced with an unspoken threat.

Zaire steps forward, reaching out to take my hand in a gesture that appears almost friendly. "We look forward to getting to know you better," he says smoothly, his touch cool and firm. "After all, family is everything."

I force a smile; their presence feels suffocating. "Of course," I reply, trying to maintain an air of composure. I can sense Luca bristling beside me, his protective instincts on high alert. But I place a hand on his arm, silently signaling for him to remain calm. The last thing we need is to create a scene in the middle of the school hallway. "We appreciate the gesture," I say diplomatically, trying to navigate the delicate dance of interactions with the Petrov brothers. "I'm sure there will be plenty of opportunities for us to get to know each other better in the future."

Zaire nods once, his expression inscrutable. "Indeed," he replies simply before turning to walk away, Oscar falling into step beside him.

As they disappear into the throng of students, I let out a slow breath I didn't realize I was holding. Luca turns to me, his eyes filled with concern. "Are you alright?" he asks quietly.

I offer him a small smile, though it doesn't quite reach my eyes. "I will be," I say, though uncertainty gnaws at my insides.

Luca wraps an arm around my shoulders, guiding me towards our homeroom period. The only class we have together since he's a year younger than me. After first period, I'll be on my own until the end of the day. "We'll figure this out, Ves," he says softly, his voice a comforting presence amidst the chaos that threatens to engulf us. "We always do."

I lean into his side, drawing strength from his unwavering support. Despite the challenges that lay ahead, I know that as long as Luca is by my side, we can face whatever obstacles come our way, but with less than a week of freedom left, a reprieve seems impossible.

As we step into the classroom, the chatter of students fades into background noise. I take a seat, and the lesson begins almost immediately, but my thoughts drift back to Oscar hiding in our garden last night. The teacher's voice becomes a distant echo as my mind replays the image of Oscar's intense gaze in the moonlight.

His gaze had been unnerving, and I couldn't shake the feeling of being under scrutiny. It was as if he was trying to unravel the layers, I kept hidden, to uncover secrets I hadn't even whispered to the wind. But deep down, I know that the encounter with the Petrov brothers is just the beginning. Their sudden interest in our lives, in my life, raises questions that demand answers. And I can't shake off the feeling that there are dark secrets lurking beneath their polished exteriors.

The bell rings, signaling the end of the lesson, and I gather my things preparing to head to our next class. Once outside, I find Luca waiting for me in the hallway. But before we can move, my phone vibrates in my pocket. I retrieve it, only to find a text from an unknown number.

Soon you'll be mine, Printsessa.

My heart skips a beat as I read the ominous message, the words sending a chill down my spine.

"Ves, what is it?" Luca's voice breaks through my racing thoughts, his eyes searching mine for answers.

I quickly show him the text, watching as his expression darkens in response. "Dmitri."

Chapter 4

VESPER

THE REMAINING hours of the school day felt like trudging through waist-deep snow. Luca, always playing the role of my overprotective brother, stuck to my side between classes. His dark eyes constantly scanning the halls for any sign of danger, his presence almost suffocating me. I could see the tension in his jaw and the tight fists at his sides.

Finally, the final bell rang, signaling the end of the day. Dread formed a knot in my stomach as I headed from my last class, knowing that Luca would be waiting outside for me. As expected, when I stepped out of the classroom, he was there with an even deeper scowl on his face. Without a word, he grabbed my arm and marched me towards the exit.

As we weave through the crowded hallways, I feel Luca's grip on my arm tightening.

"What's wrong?"

"We need to get home," he growls under his breath. He tries to cut down the side hallways, but it's just as crowded as the main hallway. "Fuck," he snarls. He tries another one, but it too is blocked with a throng of students gathering their belongings to head home for the weekend.

"Where are you going, Rossi? I hope you don't think our little one on one this morning was the end of the conversation." I peer away from my brother and notice that Oscar and Zaire are waiting ahead of us with two other guys with them. On one side stood Talon St. James, known as the golden boy of our school and the bastard son of the leader of the British mob. His perfectly styled brown hair was pulled back into a man bun at the crown of his head. To his right stood Alexander Rafnar, a recent transfer from Iceland and member of one of Europe's biggest drug smuggling families. While the Petrov twins and Talon exuded effortless confidence and tanned skin worthy of Gods, Alexander's pale blonde hair, lean frame, and towering height set him apart like a beacon amongst darkness.

"If shit goes south, I want you to run to the car and call Father."

"Wait, why would it go south?"

"Just listen to me, Vesper. Run and call Father. Do you understand me?"

Luca pushes me behind him, his stance defensive and strong. I can see the tension in his muscles as he prepares for whatever may come next. His action must be amusing to them because Talon laughs aloud at Luca's reaction.

"Little Luca playing protector for his sister. Remind me, that's our job, isn't it, brother?" Oscar sneers. He stands with his arms crossed, a smirk playing on his lips and daggers in his gaze as he stares down Luca and me.

"Yes, it is." Zaire steps forward, a sinister glint in his eye. "It's cute that you think you can keep her safe from us. Adorable, really, considering in what, six days, she'll be a Petrov, too."

A surge of fear rushes through me as I stand behind Luca. The tension between our two groups crackles like electricity on a stormy night, the air thick with hostility. Luca stands tall and unwavering, his jaw clenched and his eyes blazing with determination. "She'll be a Petrov over my dead body," he growls, his voice low and dangerous. His words are a promise of protection, and I can feel shivers run down my spine at the strength in his stance.

Zaire sneers and examines his nails with a smug smile, goading Luca further. "That can be arranged," he taunts. "The world could use one less Rossi." His words hit Luca like a slap in the face, stoking the fire of anger within him.

Luca's fists clench tightly at his sides as he locks eyes with

Zaire, their gazes filled with silent defiance. A tense energy radiates from both of them, threatening to erupt into chaos at any moment. But instead of backing down, Zaire only laughs cruelly, his arrogance fueling Luca's temper. The hallway walls seem to tremble with the force of their animosity.

"What are you going to do, Luca? Cry for mommy and daddy to come save you?" Zaire taunts, dripping with scorn. "Not even your father would be stupid enough to let this kind of alliance slip through his fingers because his heir objected."

"There's always another heir to take your place," Talon chimes in. "Oh, wait. I guess there isn't in your case."

"You'd know all about that, wouldn't you, Talon? How many bastards has your father sired?" my brother fires back.

"You say that I should care about being his heir. I'm not daft enough to want the title. You, on the other hand, relish it. That title defines your very existence. Without it, you'd be nothing more than a low-level lackey for your father. A role that would suit you better now that I think about it."

My heart races in my chest as I frantically plead with Luca to halt, but it's already too late. With a guttural snarl, he charges at Zaire, his body tense and ready to attack like a predator stalking its prey. Zaire's eyes widen in surprise at Luca, but he quickly regains his composure, his own stance shifting into one of deadly readiness.

The sound of their fists colliding echoing through the now silent hallway of other students. Zaire's eyes narrow in determination, his stance firm as he meets Luca head-on, each blow exchanged with ferocity.

"Luca!" I bellow out, but he doesn't hear me.

I watch in horror as Luca fights with all the pent-up rage and frustration he has carried for so long, his muscles strain with every powerful strike he delivers. Zaire, no stranger to combat, matches him blow for blow, his face a mask of grim determination as he defends himself against Luca's relentless onslaught.

"Run, Vesper!" Luca's voice cuts through the chaos of battle, his words a desperate plea that tug at my heart. But I am rooted to the spot, unable to tear my gaze away from the brutal spectacle unfolding before me.

Zaire stumbles back after taking a punch from Luca, blood trickling down his face from a split lip. He wipes it away casually, flashing a twisted grin. He seems almost feral, driven by a primal urge to dominate and destroy.

"Didn't know you had that in you, Rossi," he taunts my brother, which only enrages him further. "Figured your sister would have more of a right hook than you would."

Luca charges toward Zaire again. His attention is so focused on him that he doesn't notice Alexander moving behind him."

"Luca!" I bellow. "Watch out!"

Luca swings wide and falls back against Alex. Both tumbling back in my direction. Suddenly, a hand reaches out and grasps mine, pulling me away from the chaos. I turn to see Oscar, his face a mask of determination as he yanks me out of harm's way.

"Delivering damaged goods is not on my death wish list, solnishko. I'm not taking shit for you getting banged up for being too close to a fight."

"Let go of me. I have to help my brother."

Oscar's grip tightens on my arm, his eyes pleading with mine. "Can't do that, solnishko. It's better for us both if you're away from the fray. Well, better for me."

"I'm not going to leave my brother like that."

"Yes, you are." Before I can register his movements, he effortlessly lifts me off the ground and tosses me over his shoulder as if I were weightless.

"Where are you taking me?" I shout, my legs flailing against his solid stomach with no effect. My heart pounds in my chest as I try to make sense of what is happening.

"Somewhere safe," Oscar replies, his voice surprisingly gentle compared to the chaos raging behind us. He leads me through a maze of hallways, the sound of the ongoing scuffle fading into the distance as we move further away.

"I don't need your protection," I say defiantly, my voice laced with resentment. "I can take care of myself."

Oscar chuckles softly. "Oh, I have no doubt about that." His words catch me off guard. We finally come to a stop in a secluded classroom far away from the chaos of the fight. Oscar puts me back on my feet and turns to face me, his gaze searching mine. I reach for my phone in my pocket, but Oscar plucks it from my hand before I can even unlock the screen.

"You won't be needing this." He shoves it in his back pocket. "Now, where were we?"

"Take me back to my brother. Let me go."

"Can't do that, solnishko. We need to talk without an audience."

I narrow my eyes, wariness creeping back into my heart. "I have nothing to say to you."

"Are you so sure about that?"

I hesitate, unsure of what to make of his unexpected statement. "What do you want from me?"

Oscar stills in front of me. As I stand there staring at him, a mixture of confusion and fear swirling within me, Oscar's eyes seem to pierce into my soul. He moves closer to me until the wall is at my back, the only barrier separating us. His eyes blaze with intensity, and I can feel the danger emanating from him.

"I don't think my fiancé would like you being this close to me."

"No, he wouldn't, but I don't see him around."

"What do you want from me?"

A predatory smile forms on his lips. "Everything."

"You don't know anything about me," I whisper, my voice barely audible.

"Oh, but I do," he replies, leaning in even closer. "You've spent your entire life locked in your family's cage. The Rossi's prized pretty little princess whose unspoiled pussy everyone has been salivating to get a chance to taste. I wonder if it's as sweet as we've been led to believe."

I gulp at his words. "You wouldn't dare touch me. Do you know what my father would do to you and your entire family?"

"Your father is no concern of mine," he chuckles. "It's a shame that my uncle chose you for my sick bastard of a cousin. Dmitri will take no pleasure in ruining another expensive toy, whereas I would relish watching you break in front of me." His words are like a cold slap to the face, and I feel myself trembling under his intense gaze. "The things I would do to you, solnishko."

I swallow hard at the thought.

He runs a finger down the side of my face before his hand wraps lightly around my throat. Black inks his irises as his grip tightens like he's considering his next move very carefully. I force myself to remain still. Fighting back is pointless. Oscar could overpower me without even breaking a sweat. The only way I am getting out of this unscathed is to fake it. Playing along and living seems like a much better option than defying and dying.

"If you defile me, my father will kill you."

"Might be worth it," he shrugs.

"I'm not worth dying for," I mutter. The darkness around his eyes recedes at my words.

"Whoever told you that is a fool, solnishko. There are three things in our world that matter. Power, money, and heirs. Without all three, you're nothing. You have more power and worth than you realize."

"Is that what you're doing? Seizing your chance for more power?"

"Power only matters to those who need it. I have it in spades. If I wanted to defile you, as you so eloquently said, I could for nothing more than my own pleasure, and yours, of course."

I feel my face pale.

"You're afraid of me," he declares flatly, cocking his head slightly. "Interesting."

"You...you don't scare me," I manage to say, trying to keep my voice steady. But inside, my fear is growing with every passing moment. No one has ever dared to be this close to me or talk to me in such a vulgar manner for fear of my father's wrath. Even the hint that my virginity is threatened would incite a war from the Rossi's. If any of my father's men happen to stumble into this room, and see us this close, Oscar would be dead on the spot. No questions asked. "The contract has been signed. I belong to your cousin."

"You belong to no one." Oscar's eyes narrow, his expression darkening. "Dmitri will not be just your husband; he is your captor, your warden, your tormentor. He will break you, Vesper, and not even your family will be able to save you. Your father has set wheels into motion that will not stop. Try as he might, your brother cannot stop the inevitable hell coming your way under the guise of this marriage alliance."

I try to pull away from him, but he holds me in place, his hand tightens against my throat. His touch is suffocating, and I can barely breathe under his dominance.

"I know what life is like for women in my position. I see it every day in the face of my mother."

Oscar shakes his head, a bitter smile playing on his lips. "You have no idea what true suffering is, Vesper. Your father treats your mother far better than most wives in her position. In the brief time I was in your home, it didn't take me long to ascertain that information. You, on the other hand, will be lucky to feel the sunshine on your skin again once your feet touch down on Russian soil."

"You say that like I have a choice in the matter. You said so yourself: the wheels are in motion. My fate is sealed. Luca's trying…," I blurt out before I stop myself from revealing my brother's plans any further. Oscar is a Petrov. For all I know, this could be nothing more than a test from his uncle. A test of my loyalty to my future husband.

"So that's why he's suddenly following you around campus. Your brother is trying to save you." Oscar smirks, the corner of his lips curling up in satisfaction. "That's adorable. Misguided but adorable. What is his grand plan? To hand you cash and help you disappear into the night?"

I try to stop, but my face flushes instantly.

"He really thinks that will work. Luca is dumber than he lets on," he mutters to himself. "He's brave for attempting to go against your father. I will credit him for that, but it won't work. You'd be better off with my alternative."

My heart races in my chest, unsure of what he could mean. "An alternative to what?" I ask.

Oscar's intensity doesn't waver. "An alternative to being a pawn in your family's twisted games. Being a prize for Dmitri to claim." His eyes bore into mine, challenging me in a way I've never been challenged before. "An alternative to being locked away, controlled."

My breath catches in my throat. "What do you want from me?" I ask again.

He leans in closer still, his face mere inches from mine. "I told you, Vesper. I want everything," he repeats, his voice a low rumble.

"You mean you want to take his place."

"You think that's why you're here with me, isn't it?" he laughs. "Don't be as foolish as your brother, Vesper. It's beneath you."

"Then what do you want?"

"For you to not marry my cousin."

"You say that like you can snap your fingers and make it happen."

"What if I can?" He releases his grasp from my neck, drawing his hand up between us. "What if with a snap of my fingers," he snaps them, "I could not only free you from your poor excuse of a marriage but give you what you've always wanted. A *choice*."

The idea of leaving everything behind, of escaping the

life that has been chosen for me, is both exhilarating and terrifying. I've never known anything outside of the life that has been forced upon me. The pressures of being a Rossi, the suffocating expectations and duties that come with the family name. But to have a chance at true freedom, at making my own choices and following my own path. It's too much to comprehend.

"What if I want it?" I dare to ask, feeling some sort of rebellious streak rising within me. "What would you do?"

Oscar's smile widens ever so slightly as if he knows exactly what he's capable of igniting within me. "That," he says, leaning in until his lips are just barely brushing against my ear, "is a question better left unanswered until you're sure."

As I stand there, lost in thought, trying to decipher what this all means and what I want, the door bursts open, and Talon runs into the room. "Time's up. Cavalry is here. We've got to move. We can't risk getting caught." His urgent voice snaps me out of my trance.

Oscar steps back, his eyes never leaving mine. "Think about it. There is a choice beyond the fate your family has laid out for you. I'll be in touch." He shoves away from me and joins Talon at the door. With just a wink, he disappears into the hallway. As the sound of footsteps fades into the distance, I'm left alone in the room with my thoughts. My head spins with possibilities and consequences, swirling like a tempest in my mind.

My chest tightens as the weight of Oscar's words settles

upon me. The room suddenly feels smaller, the walls closing in like a vice around my trembling form. I gasp for air, but it's as if all the oxygen has been sucked out, leaving me dizzy and disoriented. Images flash before my eyes: my father's stern face, Dmitri's cold smile, and the suffocating future that awaits me as a pawn in their power games. But now, interwoven with these familiar nightmares, are new visions - Oscar's intense gaze, Talon's roguish wink, and the tantalizing promise of freedom they represent.

The enormity of the choice before me crashes down like a tidal wave. Loyalty to my family or a chance at true happiness? The safety of the known or the terrifying allure of the unknown? My mind races through countless scenarios.

I take a deep breath, trying to steady my racing heart. The idea of leaving everything behind - my family, my life as I know it - is both thrilling and petrifying. But the thought of having a choice, of having the power to control my own destiny, is intoxicating.

I've always been told what to do, who to marry, and how to behave. But Oscar...Oscar represents something different. Something wild and free. And the idea that there might be a way out - a way to escape the life that's been chosen for me - is almost too much to bear.

I can't think about that now. I need to find Luca. I need to make sure he's okay. I head for the door. A voice calling my name echoes through the hallway, jolting me out of my hiding spot. I quickly step into the open, trying to find where the sound is coming from. As soon as I'm out in the hallway, one of my father's guards appears before me, his gun poised at his side. He grabs my arm, muttering a response in his earpiece. He leads me towards where I last saw my brother fighting with Zaire, Talon, and Alexander.

My vision blurs as we reach the center of the hallway, my heart sinking at the sight before me. My brother Luca lies on the ground, his head a bloody mess from a brutal beating. I struggle against the guard's grip, my body shaking with fear and anger. With every step towards Luca, the blood splatters on the ground stains my light-colored tights. But I don't care. All I care about is my brother's life. "Luca," I scream, but he doesn't respond. Desperation takes over as I turn to the guard, pleading and begging for him to call for help. But he just stands there with a blank expression, ignoring my desperate pleas. In a fit of frustration and rage, I shout at him once more to call 9-1-1.

Suddenly, heavy footsteps approach us, and the guard quickly straightens up, fear evident in his eyes. A commanding voice orders him to take my brother outside. My heart drops as I look up and see my father standing before me with a cold, angry expression on his face.

"Get moving to the car, Vesper," he repeats sternly, disappointment laced in his voice.

As my father grabs me harshly by the arm, I resist the urge to cry. This isn't the first time I've seen Luca hurt, and it won't be the last. We walk out of the hallway, my blood-stained tights catching the attention of a few passersby who quickly look away as soon as they make eye contact with my father. In the car, the tension is unbearable. My father doesn't say a word as he rides next to me. Luca lies motionless in the backseat of my father's limo. His guard sits quietly next to Father's driver in the front.

As we pull into our driveway, I can feel my heart breaking at the sight of Luca's battered body. My father shoves me out of the car before we're even stopped by the front door.

"Go clean yourself up. Come to my office when you're done," he orders coldly as he slams the door behind me.

Chapter 5

I ASCEND THE GRAND STAIRCASE, my heels clicking against the polished marble, echoing through the large foyer of the Rossi mansion. The opulent surroundings, with their gilded frames and crystal chandeliers, feel suffocating as I make my way to my room, my mind racing with the events of the evening.

Once inside my sanctuary, I shed my school uniform, peeling the blood-soaked tights from my body and gather them up in my hands, tossing them in my bathroom trash bin. I move to my expansive walk-in closet, my fingers trailing over the array of designer labels before selecting a crisp white blouse and tailored black trousers. After cleaning the now dried blood from my legs, I dress in new clothes, and my eyes catch my reflection in the full-length mirror. The woman staring back at me looks composed, but I can see the storm brewing behind my own emerald gaze. My father's wrath is not something I've experienced directly, and to be honest, I have no idea what to expect now that it seems to be directed at me. With a deep breath, I steel myself and make my way back downstairs, each step feeling heavier than the last. The dark mahogany door of my father's study looms before me, and I knock with a steady hand that belies my inner turmoil.

"Enter," comes the gruff response from within.

I step into the room, the scent of leather and cigars enveloping me. My father sits behind his imposing desk, his weathered face set in hard lines.

"Vesper," he begins, his voice low and controlled, "explain to me why your brother was fighting with Zaire Petrov."

I meet his gaze unflinchingly. "It was a misunderstanding, Father. You know how hot-headed Luca can be sometimes."

Father's eyes narrow. "A misunderstanding? That's all you have to offer?"

I shrug elegantly, careful to keep my expression neutral. "Boys will be boys, as they say. I'm sure it was nothing of consequence." The lie tastes like acid as it spills so easily from my lips. If my father found out the real reason behind

Luca's clash with Zaire, I shudder to think of the consequences.

My father's fist comes down hard on the desk, causing
the crystal decanter to rattle. "Nothing of consequence? Do
you have any idea how important this alliance is to our
family?"

I remain silent as my father continues, his voice rising
with each word. "Your brother was reckless, provoking Zaire
into a fight. Do you understand the delicate nature of our
negotiations with the Petrovs? One wrong move and years
of careful planning could crumble! Until you're married to
Dmitri, it's imperative that we do not provoke them to
change their mind about the alliance." I watch as he rises
from his chair, pacing the length of the study. The firelight
casts long shadows across the room, making my father's
imposing figure seem even more menacing. "Your idiot
brother will be punished for his actions," Father declares, his
tone brooking no argument. "He needs to learn that his
impulsiveness has consequences. And you, Vesper," he turns
to face me, his eyes boring into mine, "I expect better from
you. Maybe allowing your mother to raise you instead of
sending you off to an all-girls boarding school was a mistake
after all. I just hope that this mistake will be the only one
you make until you're no longer my problem."

I feel a chill run down my spine, knowing that I'm the
reason this happened. I'm the reason he felt the need to
fight, to protect and defend me. My heart sinks at my
father's words, the weight of my guilt pressing down on me

like a lead blanket. I struggle to maintain my composure, but I can feel my carefully constructed facade beginning to crack.

"Father, may I see Luca? Perhaps I could speak with him, make him understand the gravity of his actions."

My father's laugh is cold and humorless, sending a shiver down my spine. "See him? Oh no, my dear. Your brother isn't here to coddle or console. He can lick his wounds under someone else's roof until I decide what to do with him."

The room spins around me, the furnishings blurring into a mixture of guilt and fear. I grip the edge of my father's desk, steadying myself as I process his words. Luca, my fierce protector, my confidant, is gone. And it's all because of me.

I can still see the determination in Luca's eyes earlier today, the way his jaw clenched when Zaire made that crude comment about me. I should have stopped him then, should have pulled him away before things escalated. But a part of me, a selfish, prideful part, had relished seeing Zaire put in his place.

Now, as I stand before my father, I realize the full cost of that moment of satisfaction. Luca is suffering, cast out and alone, while I remain in the comfort of our family home. The injustice of it all threatens to overwhelm me.

"Where is he?" I ask, my voice stronger now, fueled by desperation. "Please, Father, at least tell me he's safe."

My father's eyes narrow, assessing me with a coldness that makes me want to shrink away. "Your brother is where he needs to be, learning a valuable lesson about loyalty and obedience. You would do well to learn from his mistakes, Vesper."

I nod, swallowing hard against the lump in my throat. The ornate clock on the mantel ticks away the seconds, each one feeling like an eternity as I stand there, trapped between my duty to my family and the love for my brother.

"Father, please," I implore. "I need to see him, to make sure he's alright. Luca is—"

"Enough!" Father's voice cracks like a whip, silencing me instantly. His eyes, dark and flinty, bore into mine with an intensity that makes me want to look away. But I force myself to meet his gaze, summoning every ounce of strength I possess.

"You disappoint me, Vesper," he says, his voice low and measured. "I expected better from you. How could you allow this to happen? Your brother may be impulsive, but you're supposed to be the levelheaded one. The one who understands what's at stake."

I feel each word like a physical blow, my chest tightening with a mixture of shame and indignation. "I didn't know he was going to—."

"It doesn't matter what you knew or didn't know," he interrupts, turning to face me. The fading sunlight casts half his face in shadow, making him look more menacing than ever. "You're about to become a Petrov. Do you under-stand what that means? The responsibilities that come with it?"

I nod mutely, my throat constricting around words I dare not speak.

"You are expected to be a lady, Vesper. To carry yourself with grace and dignity at all times. To be a good wife to Dmitri." He pauses, his eyes narrowing. "And most importantly, to be loyal to your new family. The Petrovs will not tolerate any hint of divided loyalties."

The mention of Dmitri and my impending marriage sends a wave of nausea through me. I can feel the bile rising in my throat, bitter and acrid. The thought of being bound to a man I barely know, of leaving behind everything and everyone I love, makes my stomach churn violently.

I clench my fists at my sides, digging my nails into my palms until I feel the sharp sting of pain. It grounds me, helps me maintain my composure even as my insides rebel against the future that's been mapped out for me.

"I understand, Father," I manage to say, my voice steadier than I feel. "I won't disappoint you again."

My father's lips curl into a cold smile, one that doesn't reach his eyes. "Oh, my dear Vesper," he says, his voice dripping with a mixture of condescension and finality, "you won't have the opportunity to disappoint me again."

A chill runs down my spine as he continues, each word falling like a hammer blow. "I've spoken with your headmaster. He assures me that despite missing the last four days of classes, you will graduate. Your academic record is impressive enough to warrant this special consideration."

The room seems to tilt on its axis as the implications of

his words sink in. The antique globe on his desk, becomes the focal point of my blurring vision.

"I...I don't understand," I stammer, my usual composure deserting me. "What about my final exams? My graduation ceremony?"

Father waves his hand dismissively, the light catching on his heavy gold signet ring. "Inconsequential details, my dear. Your true education begins now."

He moves to the liquor cabinet, a beautiful Art Deco piece that has stood in this study for generations. The crystal decanter clinks against a tumbler as he pours himself a measure of amber liquid. The scent of aged scotch fills the air, mingling with the lingering aroma of leather and cigar smoke.

"You won't be returning to school," he states, taking a sip of his drink. "The next five days will be spent preparing for your wedding. Your mother has already begun making arrangements. Dress fittings, etiquette refreshers, briefings on the Petrov family history, and business interests. Every minute will be utilized to ensure you are the perfect bride for Dmitri."

The weight of his words press down on me, making it difficult to breathe. The ornate wallpaper, with its intricate patterns of golden leaves and crimson flowers, seems to close in around me. I feel trapped, like a butterfly pinned to a board, my wings uselessly fluttering against the inevitable.

"But Father, I had plans. There were people I wanted to say goodbye to, things I wanted to do before..."

"Before what, Vesper?" he interrupts, his voice sharp. "Before you fulfilled your duty to this family? Before you took your rightful place in securing our future?"

He sets down his glass with a decisive thud and turns to face me fully. "You've been indulged for far too long," he continues, his tone brooking no argument. "It's time for you to embrace your responsibilities. The Petrovs are expecting a refined, educated young woman who understands her place in this world. Not a spoiled little bitch who cares more about friends and walking across the stage for a piece of paper that means nothing in the end."

My father's words hang in the air, heavy and suffocating. I stand there, frozen, as the full weight of my situation crashes down upon me. The ornate grandfather clock in the corner ticks away the seconds, each one feeling like a nail in the coffin of my former life.

"You may go," my father says dismissively, turning back to the window. "Your mother will brief you on tomorrow's schedule."

I nod mutely, unable to form words, and turn to leave. As I reach for the doorknob, my father's voice stops me once more.

"And Vesper," he says, his tone cold and final, "do not disappoint me again."

I step out into the hallway, closing the door behind me with trembling hands. The long corridor stretches before me, the plush carpet muffling my footsteps as I make my way back to my room. Family portraits line the walls, generations of Rossis staring down at me with eyes that seem to judge and condemn.

As I enter my bedroom, I'm struck by how foreign it suddenly feels. The pastel walls, the delicate white furniture, the bookshelf filled with my favorite novels – it all seems like it belongs to someone else now. A girl who had dreams.

I sink onto my bed, my fingers clutching at the silk comforter. The room spins around me, and I struggle to catch my breath. How did everything change so quickly? Now I'm a bride-to-be, my future mapped out in precise detail by parents who see me as nothing more than a pawn in their grand game of power and influence.

As I sit on my bed, surrounded by the remnants of my former life, Oscar's offer echoes in my mind. The memory of his earnest face, his whispered promise of help, now feels like a lifeline I foolishly let slip through my fingers. If only I had been braver, less hesitant to accept the risks that came with his offer.

But it's too late now. There's no escaping this hell.

Chapter 6

VESPER

I STORM out onto the balcony, the sting of my father's declaration still prickling against me. The declaration that ripped what little freedom I had left away from me because of my brother's fight. My brother is hurt, and God knows where my father chose to dump him to lick his wounds. My brother's absence gnaws at me, a constant ache in my chest. Where is he? Is he safe? The uncertainty is almost worse than knowing he was in danger. Almost. My father won't kill Luca, but he would certainly use this to teach him a hard lesson unless something were to happen to the marriage alliance as the result of his actions. I can't be positive about what will come of my brother if this union fails.

"Luca, if you're out there, I hope you're safe," I whisper into the breeze. "I hope my sacrifice keeps you safe."

A flicker of movement in the garden below catches my eye, pulling me from my brooding thoughts. I lean forward, my keen gaze scanning the shadowy landscape. There – a figure moves between the carefully pruned topiaries, pausing beneath my balcony. I recognize the hulking form at once: Oscar.

Our eyes meet across the distance, and even in the dim light, I can see the determination etched on his face. Without a word, he approaches the flower-covered trellis on the wall beneath my balcony. With the grace of a cat, he begins to scale the wooden lattice, the fragrant blooms quivering with his ascent.

My heart races as I watch him climb, a mix of exhilaration and worry coursing through my veins. When Oscar finally pulls himself over the balcony railing, I can see he is slightly out of breath, a sheen of sweat glistening on his brow.

"Fuck, that was harder than I thought. That looked easier in movies," he comments slightly out of breath.

"Oscar," I hiss, glancing nervously at my bedroom door. "What are you doing here?"

He flashes me a roguish grin, reaching into his pocket. "Bringing you this," he says, producing my smartphone. "Figured you might want it back."

My eyes widened as I take it, my fingers brushing against

his, emitting a short electric jolt between us. "Thank you," I mutter, staring down at it.

"You really shouldn't thank me, solnishko. I did take it from you," he smiles down at me. Oscar pauses, studying me for a moment. "You've been crying."

I quickly wipe at my eyes, embarrassed by my show of weakness. "It's nothing," I lie, but Oscar's piercing gaze tells me he doesn't believe me for a second.

He takes a step closer, his voice softening. "It's not nothing. What happened?"

"What hasn't happened?" I blurt out. "Luca's fight with your brother, for starters. I have no idea where my brother is, if he's hurt, or if I'll see him again before I get shipped off to Russia to become your cousin's property."

"Zaire can be a bit of a hot head, and when he finds a chance to goad someone, he takes it. Your brother was an easy target," he tries to explain. "It's not an excuse for what happened, but it wasn't entirely Zaire's fault either. I have to take the blame for part of it."

I peer up at him in confusion. "How would it be your fault? You didn't throw a single punch."

"I asked Zaire to start it," he admits casually. "I needed to talk to you alone, and your brother was hovering around you like a fucking moth."

"You did this?" I hiss as I feel the anger boiling inside of me again. "My brother is gone because of you. I am trapped in this house because of you. The last few days of my freedom are gone because of *you*."

Oscar's face falls, a flicker of regret passing through his eyes. "I didn't mean for it to go this far," he says, his voice low and urgent. "I just wanted a moment alone with you. I never thought your father would—"

"Would what?" I snap, cutting him off. "React exactly how he always does? You may not have meant for this to happen, but you should have known better."

I turn away from him, gripping the balcony railing so tightly my knuckles turn white. The cool night air does little to soothe the fire burning inside me.

"Listen," Oscar says, moving to stand beside me. "I know I fucked up. But I'm here now, and I want to help. Tell me what I can do to make this right."

I laugh bitterly. "Unless you can magically undo this arranged marriage and bring my brother back, there's nothing you can do."

Oscar is quiet for a moment, and when he speaks again, his voice is filled with a determined resolve. "My alternative still stands, Vesper. I can get you out of this."

I turn to face Oscar, my eyes narrowing in disbelief. The moonlight casts shadows across his face, accentuating the sharp angles of his jaw and the intensity in his dark eyes. For a moment, I allow myself to entertain the wild notion that he could actually help me escape this gilded cage.

But reality crashes back like a tidal wave, drowning out that fleeting hope. I shake my head, a bitter laugh escaping my lips. "And why would you do that, Oscar? What could you possibly gain from helping me?"

I step closer to him, my voice dropping to a dangerous whisper. "My marriage to Dmitri benefits your family. It strengthens the ties between the Petrovs and the Rossis. It expands your influence, your power." I gesture broadly to the opulent gardens below, the sprawling estate that represents just a fraction of our families' combined wealth and influence. "This union is a masterpiece of strategy, crafted by minds far more cunning than ours. And you expect me to believe you'd risk it all for what? Some misplaced sense of chivalry?"

Oscar opens his mouth to speak, but I press on, my words sharp and cutting. "No, I don't believe you. This is just another game, isn't it? Another ploy to manipulate me, to keep me off balance." I pace the length of the balcony. "Perhaps you think if you can gain my trust, you can use me as a pawn in some larger scheme. Is that it?"

I stop and face him again, my green eyes flashing with a mixture of anger and pain. "Or maybe this is just amusement for you. The thrill of playing with fire, of seeing how close you can get to the forbidden fruit without getting burned."

The night air grows heavy around us, thick with tension and unspoken words. In the distance, I hear the faint sound of a car engine, probably one of my father's men patrolling the grounds. It serves as a stark reminder of the invisible bars that surround me.

"You don't understand," Oscar begins, his voice low and urgent. "This isn't about—"

"No," I cut him off, holding up a hand. "I understand perfectly. I've been raised in this world, Oscar. I know how it works. Every move, every word, every seemingly kind gesture is calculated. There are no selfless acts here, only carefully disguised self-interest."

I turn away from him, gazing out over the moonlit gardens. The roses my mother so lovingly tended now seem to mock me with their beauty, their freedom to bloom and wither as nature intended. "Your offer of help is either a lie or a trap. Either way, I can't afford to believe you."

The silence stretches between us, filled with the soft chirping of crickets and the distant rustle of leaves. When I finally turn back to Oscar, I school my features into a mask of cold indifference, the one I've perfected over years of navigating this treacherous world.

"You should go," I say, my voice steady and devoid of emotion. "If you're caught here, it will only make things worse for everyone."

Oscar doesn't move immediately. He stands there, his dark eyes searching my face as if trying to decipher some hidden message in my expression. For a fleeting moment, I see something flicker in his gaze – hurt, perhaps, or frustration. But it's gone as quickly as it appeared, replaced by a hardness that mirrors my own.

"You're right," he says finally, his tone matching mine in its detachment. "I shouldn't have come. It was impulsive."

He moves towards the balcony railing, preparing to

make his descent. But before he swings his leg over, he pauses and turns back to me.

"Vesper," he says, his voice softer now. "I know you have no reason to trust me. But I meant what I said. If you change your mind, if you decide you want out, I'll be there. No strings attached."

I say nothing, maintaining my stony facade. Oscar nods once, accepting my silence as an answer. With the same feline grace he displayed in his ascent, he begins to climb down the trellis.

As I watch him disappear into the shadows of the garden, I feel a pang of something. Regret? Longing? I push the feeling aside, burying it deep where it can't touch me. I can't afford such weakness, not now.

I turn back to my room, closing the balcony doors behind me. The opulent space suddenly feels suffocating, every gilded surface and silk drape a reminder of the cage I'm trapped in. I move to my vanity, catching sight of my reflection in the ornate mirror.

The woman staring back at me looks composed, regal even. But I can see the cracks in the facade, the fear and uncertainty lurking just beneath the surface. I take a deep breath, steeling myself for what's to come.

As I prepare for bed, my mind races with thoughts of Luca, of the impending marriage, of Oscar's offer. But I push them all aside. I can't afford to dwell on what-ifs and maybes. I need to focus on the reality of my situation, on finding a way to navigate this treacherous path without losing myself in the process.

Tomorrow, I'll begin preparations for my new life as Dmitri Petrov's wife. I'll play the role expected of me, the dutiful daughter cementing a powerful alliance. But beneath it all, I'll be watching, waiting, looking for any opportunity to assert control over my own destiny.

As I slip under the silk sheets of my bed, I whisper a quiet promise to myself. "This isn't over. I won't let them dictate my fate. One way or another...I'll find a way out of this all on my own."

As I lay in bed, sleep eludes me. My mind keeps replaying Oscar's visit, his words echoing in my head. Despite my outward rejection, a tiny part of me wonders if I've made a mistake in dismissing his offer so quickly. But no, I can't afford to entertain such dangerous thoughts.

The soft buzz of my newly returned phone startles me from my ruminations. I reach for it, half expecting to see a message from Oscar. Instead, it's an unknown number. My heart races as I open the text:

> I'm okay. Don't worry. Stay strong. - L

Luca. Relief washes over me, followed quickly by a surge of questions. Where is he? How did he get this number? Is he truly safe?

I type out a rapid response:

> Where are you? Are you hurt?

Minutes pass with no reply. I stare at the screen, willing another message to appear. Nothing comes.

Frustrated, I toss the phone aside and sink back into my pillows. At least I know Luca's alive. It's not much, but it's something to hold onto in the chaos of uncertainty surrounding me.

Chapter 7

I STAND on the pedestal in my mother's expansive closet, surrounded by mirrors that reflect my discontent from every angle. The white gown clings to my body like a straitjacket, its intricate lace and beading a poor disguise for the prison it represents. My mother circles me like a vulture, her critical gaze dissecting every curve and line of my figure.

"The waist needs to be taken in further," she instructs the harried dressmaker, who nods obediently, pins clenched between her teeth. "And see if you can add some padding to the bust. We can't have her looking like a boy on her wedding day."

I bite my tongue, tasting the metallic hint of blood as I

force back the retort that threatens to escape. Two days have passed since my father's decision to remove me from school, and I feel as if I'm sinking further into some surreal nightmare. The groom, the dress, the venue, the guest list - all of it decided without my input or consent. I am merely a puppet, strings pulled taut by the expectations of two powerful families.

The dressmaker's hands flutter around me, adjusting and pinning, as my mother continues her litany of critiques. "Perhaps we should consider a corset. Vesper, darling, you really should have watched your diet more closely these past months. What will the Petrovs think?"

I meet my own gaze in the mirror, green eyes blazing with a defiance I dare not voice. The reflection staring back at me is a stranger - a porcelain doll version of myself, stripped of agency and dressed up for display. The delicate veil cascades down my back, its gossamer threads a mockery of the web I'm entangled in.

As the fitting drags on, I let my mind wander, searching for any possible escape from this gilded cage. But the Rossi name is both my legacy and my burden, and I know that the tentacles of family obligation reach far and wide. Even as I stand here, being molded into someone else's vision of a perfect bride, I can feel the walls closing in.

The dressmaker steps back, admiring her handiwork with a satisfied smile. "There, Mrs. Rossi. I think we've achieved the perfect silhouette."

My mother claps her hands together, her eyes

gleaming with triumph. "Oh, it's magnificent! Vesper, you'll be the most stunning bride the families have ever seen."

I force my lips into a semblance of a smile, the effort making my cheeks ache. "Thank you, Mother," I manage, the lie leaves a sour aftertaste in my mouth. As I step down from the pedestal, my legs wobble beneath the weight of the gown. The layers of tulle and satin swirl around my ankles, creating a treacherous landscape of fabric. I try to take a careful step forward, but my foot catches on the hem, and I lurch forward, arms flailing wildly as I struggle to maintain my balance.

"Vesper!" My mother's shrill voice cuts through the air like a whip. "For heaven's sake, child! Where is your grace? Your poise?"

I manage to right myself, cheeks burning with embarrassment and frustration. The dressmaker hovers nearby, her hands twitching as if she wants to reach out and steady me but doesn't quite dare.

"I'm sorry, Mother," I mutter, smoothing down the front of the dress. "There's so much fabric."

My mother's lips purse into a thin line of disapproval. "A true lady knows how to move in any attire with elegance and dignity. Perhaps we should have enrolled you in more etiquette classes instead of indulging your academic pursuits."

The barb stings, but I swallow my retort. Instead, I try to steer the conversation in a different direction. "Mother, about the wedding. I was wondering if we could discuss some of the details. The guest list, perhaps, or the menu?"

Her eyebrows arch so high they nearly disappear into her hairline. "Oh, Vesper," she says, her tone dripping with condescension. "You're far too young to concern yourself with such matters. Leave the planning to those who know what is proper and befitting of our station."

Too young to plan my own wedding, I think bitterly, but old enough to be married off like a prized mare. The irony is not lost on me, but it seems to have sailed right over my parents' heads.

"But, it's my wedding," I fire back. The insubordination slips from my mouth before I can stop it. "Father has chosen my intended groom. You're choosing everything else. Where is *my* choice in all of this?" My hands tug at the gown on my body. The delicate lace twisting around me like a vice, squeezing me from the outside in. "Can I have at least one choice before Father sells me off?"

"Now," my mother continues, gesturing imperiously to the dressmaker, "let's get you out of this gown before you manage to tear it. Honestly, Vesper, you must learn to be more careful."

"I hate this dress," I spit back.

My mother's eyes flash with anger, but she quickly plasters on a saccharine smile for the dressmaker's benefit. "Vesper, darling, you're just overwhelmed. This is all so exciting, isn't it?"

The rage building inside me threatens to burst forth like

a volcano. I can feel my cheeks burning, my fists clenching at my sides. The lace of the dress suddenly feels like it's suffocating me, each intricate pattern a reminder of the cage they're forcing me into.

"Exciting?" I seethe, my voice low and dangerous. "You think being stripped of every choice and every decision about my own life is exciting?"

The dressmaker's eyes widen, darting between my mother and me. She takes a hesitant step back, clearly sensing the tension in the air.

My mother's smile becomes strained, her eyes silently pleading with me to stop. But I can't. The dam has broken, and years of pent-up frustration come flooding out.

"I don't want this dress. I don't want this wedding. I don't want to be married to Dmitri fucking Petrov!" My voice rises with each word, echoing off the dressing room's mirrored walls.

"Vesper!" My mother hisses, her composure slipping. "That's quite enough!"

But I'm beyond caring. I reach behind me, fumbling for the zipper of the dress. "I'm done being your perfect, obedient daughter. I'm done pretending this is what I want!"

With a satisfying rip, I tear the delicate lace sleeve, the sound like music to my ears. My mother gasps in horror, while the dressmaker lets out a strangled cry. I rip, and twist until the dress falls free from my body in a pool at my feet. The silk slip underneath feels like a rush of freedom.

"Miss Rossi, please!" The dressmaker pleads, her hands outstretched as if to stop me. "That gown is worth—"

"I don't care what it's worth!" I shout, yanking at the bodice. Another rip, and I feel a surge of twisted satisfaction. "It's not worth my freedom!"

My mother lunges forward, grabbing my wrists. "Stop this at once!" She turns to the shell-shocked dressmaker, her voice sickly sweet. "I'm so sorry, she's just nervous about the big day. Wedding jitters, you know how it is."

I wrench my hands free, stumbling backward. "Don't touch me! And stop lying! This isn't about wedding jitters. This is about you and Father treating me like a pawn in your sick games!"

Tears of frustration sting my eyes, but I blink them back furiously. I won't give them the satisfaction of seeing me cry.

"I want one choice," I say, my voice dropping to a dangerous whisper. "Just one. Is that really too much to ask?"

My mother's eyes narrow, a storm brewing behind her carefully composed features. She grabs my arm with surprising strength, her manicured nails digging into my skin as she drags me away from the bewildered dressmaker and into the main portion of her private bedroom.

The air around us feels thick with tension, the scent of expensive perfume and freshly steamed fabric suddenly cloying. Crystal chandeliers tinkle softly overhead, their delicate light catching on the sequins of nearby gowns only heightens my sense of disorientation.

"Vesper Alessandra Rossi," my mother hisses, her voice low and venomous. "You will cease this childish tantrum immediately. Your little act of rebellion won't change a thing. Your father set this in motion, and nothing you do or say will stop it."

I open my mouth to protest, but she cuts me off with a sharp gesture. "It's high time you grew up and faced reality. The world isn't some fairy tale where you get to choose your own path. There are obligations, alliances to be made and maintained. Your silly dreams of independence and choice? Those are luxuries we can't afford. You were born to marry a connected, wealthy man, and that's what you'll do. This is your duty to this family."

Her words cut deep, each syllable another nail in the coffin of my hopes. But the fire inside me refuses to be extinguished. "And what about my happiness?" I challenge, my voice quivering with emotion. "Does that mean nothing to you and Father?"

My mother's face contorts with a mixture of frustration and something that might be pity. "Happiness is a fleeting thing. Power, security, those are what truly matter."

"But at what cost?" I argue back, my voice rising despite my efforts to keep it down. "My freedom? My future? My very self? You may have allowed your father to force you to marry Father, and give up everything you had, but to put your own daughter through the same thing? You're just as much of a monster as he is."

The slap comes out of nowhere, the crack of palm

against cheek echoing in the small space. My head snaps to the side, the sting of the blow bringing tears to my eyes. I raise a trembling hand to my face, feeling the heat rising beneath my fingertips.

Shock ripples through me, followed quickly by a wave of humiliation as I realize the dressmaker has witnessed this entire exchange. The poor woman stands frozen, her mouth agape, pins still clutched uselessly in her hand.

My mother's voice is ice cold when she speaks again. "Go to your room, Vesper. We'll discuss your behavior when your father returns home."

I stand there for a moment, my cheek throbbing, torn between the urge to fight back and the crushing weight of defeat. In the end, it's the pity in the dressmaker's eyes that breaks me. Without another word, I turn and flee, leaving behind a trail of torn lace behind me.

I rush up the stairs, storming into my room, and slamming the door behind me. The moment the door clicks shut, I let out a shuddering breath, burying my face in my hands. Tears threaten to spill, but I furiously blink them back. Crying won't change anything. I need a plan. I need my brother.

I move until I reach my bedside table, where my phone lies untouched since I was dragged out of my bed at an ungodly hour for the fitting. My fingers tremble as I type out a message to Luca, praying that this time he'll answer me.

Where are you? I need you.

The seconds tick by, each one feeling like an eternity. Then, miraculously, three dots appear on the screen. My heart leaps into my throat as I wait for his response.

> It's safer if you don't know, Ves. One of the guards smuggled in a phone for me.

I frown, worry gnawing at my insides. What does he mean, it's not safe? Before I can ask, another message pops up.

> How are you holding up?

> Just had the final fitting. Mother thinks I need more padding in the bust and a smaller waist. Pretty sure she'd prefer it if I could just morph into a living doll. I might have lost my shit on her…she slapped me.

I wait for his reply, hoping for a hint of the sardonic humor we've always shared. Instead, his next message sends a chill down my spine.

> Ves, I'm sorry. I can't stop what's coming. Father knows what I was trying to do.

> How?

> I don't know, but he knows. If he catches you talking to me, we're both dead. Delete these messages. Don't try to contact me again. I'm so sorry.

Tears blur my vision as I read his words over and over. The phone suddenly feels heavy in my hands, as if the weight of my brother's cryptic warnings has made it unbearably dense.

I want to scream, to demand answers, to beg him not to leave me alone. But I know better. If Luca says it's not safe, then it's not safe. He's always been the cautious one, the strategist. If he's telling me to stop communicating, it must be for a good reason.

With shaking hands, I delete our conversation, erasing all evidence of this brief exchange. As I set the phone aside, I catch sight of myself in the mirror once more. The girl staring back at me looks lost, afraid, but there's something else in her eyes now - a spark of determination.

Luca may not be able to help me, but his warning has made one thing clear: I'm on my own now. If I want to escape this fate, I'll have to find a way out myself. A knock startles me from my thoughts, and I shove my phone into the table drawer.

"Miss Vesper?" Sophia's gentle voice calls out. "Your mother asked me to bring you some tea."

I smooth down my slip and take a deep breath,

schooling my features into a mask of calm. "Come in, Sophia."

As she enters with the tea tray, I force a smile onto my face. I mask indifference, but behind the facade my mind is racing. I have four days to figure this out. Sophia sets the tray down and disappears as quickly as she arrived, shutting the door behind her.

I sip the chamomile tea, its warmth spreading through my body. The delicate floral aroma wafts up, usually soothing, but now it seems cloying, almost oppressive. I watch the steam curl up from the porcelain cup, mesmerized by its dance in the soft light filtering through the curtains.

As I drain the last drops, a sudden wave of exhaustion washes over me. My limbs feel heavy, my eyelids drooping against my will. I struggle to focus on the intricate pattern of the wallpaper, the lines blurring and swirling before my eyes. This isn't right, I think hazily. I've never reacted to chamomile like this before.

I try to stand, but my legs wobble beneath me like a newborn fawn's. The room tilts and spins, and I barely manage to stumble to my bed before collapsing onto it. The silk sheets feel cool against my flushed skin, and I find myself sinking into their embrace. As my consciousness begins to slip away, a niggling thought persists something was in that tea.

I'm not sure how long I've been asleep when a soft buzzing rouses me. My head feels stuffed with cotton, my thoughts sluggish and disjointed. I fumble for my phone, squinting at the bright screen in the dimness of my room. An unknown number flashes across the display, followed by a cryptic message:

Have you considered the offer?

My heart rate quickens, cutting through the fog of grogginess. I know instantly who it is: Oscar. I hesitate for a moment, my fingers hovering over the keypad. Throwing caution to the wind, I type back:

We need to talk. In person. It's safer.

The response comes almost at once:

Open the door. I'm on the balcony.

My pulse races as I struggle to my feet. I stumble to the French doors leading to the balcony, my hand trembling as I reach for the latch. Taking a deep breath, I pull back the curtain and peer into the darkness beyond.

As I pull open the door, the cool night air rushes in, bringing with it the scent of jasmine from the garden below. My vision swims, and I blink hard, trying to focus on the two shadowy figures standing before me. Oscar's tall frame is easily recognizable, but as my eyes adjust to the darkness, I realize with a jolt that he's not alone. Zaire stands beside him, his broad shoulders tense, hands shoved deep in his pockets.

"What the hell?" I hiss, my words slurring slightly. The room sways around me, and I grip the doorframe to steady myself. "Zaire, what are you doing here?"

Zaire takes a step forward, concern etched across his face. "You don't look well."

"I'm fine," I snap, even as I struggle to keep my balance.

A wave of nausea washes over me, and I sway danger-ously. Zaire reaches out to steady me, but I flinch away from his touch. "Don't," I warn, my voice low and dangerous despite its unsteadiness.

"Vesper, please," Zaire pleads, his eyes wide with concern. "We can explain everything, but first, let us help you."

The world tilts again, and this time I can't stop myself from stumbling. Zaire catches me before I hit the ground, his strong arms wrapping around me. I want to push him away, to maintain my anger and suspicion, but my body betrays me, sagging against his chest.

"I think they've drugged her," Zaire comments as he holds me up.

"Drugged?" I mumble, my thoughts scattered like leaves in a storm.

"Did you eat or drink anything?"

"The tea…," I point the empty cup on my nightstand. "My mother sent it."

Oscar curses under his breath in Russian, but I have no

idea what he said. He and Oscar go back and forth, talking as if I am not in the room. I try to focus on their words, but they seem to be coming from far away. Zaire's voice rumbles through his chest as he speaks, and despite my anger, I find the sound oddly comforting.

"What are you saying?" I ask, my words still slurring slightly as I struggle to focus on Oscar's face. The world around me seems to pulse and sway, the edges of my vision blurring like watercolors left out in the rain.

Oscar runs a hand through his hair, his usually composed demeanor cracking under the weight of urgency. "It's my uncle," he says, his voice low and tense. "He's changing the plan. There won't be a wedding here in the States, Vesper."

A chill runs down my spine, cutting through the fog of whatever drug is coursing through my system. "What are you talking about?" I demand, trying to push away from Zaire's steadying grip. My legs wobble beneath me like a newborn colt's, and I reluctantly allow him to keep his arm around my waist.

Oscar's eyes meet mine, and the anger in them makes my heart stutter. "He's planning to force your father to send you to Russia tomorrow," he says. "He's threatening to cut the alliance."

The words hit me like a physical blow, and I sway dangerously. Zaire's arm tightens around me, and I can feel the tension radiating from his body. The night air suddenly feels too thin, and I struggle to draw a full breath.

"But...but the wedding," I stammer, my mind reeling.

Oscar shakes his head, his expression grim. "It was all a smokescreen, Vesper. A way to keep you complacent while they finalized the real plan. Our Uncle has far bigger plans than what a political marriage can give him."

I close my eyes, trying to process this information through the haze of drugs and disbelief. The scent of jasmine from the garden below wafts up, a mockery of sweetness in this moment of bitter revelation. When I open my eyes again, the world seems sharper, my senses heightened by the surge of adrenaline coursing through me.

"This doesn't make sense. Why would they do this?"

"They're blaming it on your brother, but it's much more than that."

"My brother?" I say, my voice stronger now.

Zaire and Oscar exchange a look that sends a fresh wave of fear through me. It's Zaire who answers, his voice gentle but laced with tension. "We think he tried to intervene."

The pieces start to fall into place - Luca's cryptic messages, his warning not to contact him again. My brother, always the protector, tried to save me and paid the price. Tears prick at my eyes, but I blink them back furiously. There's no time for weakness now.

"Luca, he texted me. He told me our father found out he was trying to stop the wedding," I admit.

Oscar's eyes widen. "When? What exactly did he say?"

I shake my head, trying to recall the details through the lingering fog. "Just a few hours ago. He said it wasn't safe, that he couldn't stop what was coming. He told me to delete the messages and to not contact him again."

Zaire curses under his breath. "That confirms it. They must have caught him trying to interfere."

"We need to move," Oscar says, his voice tight with urgency. "Vesper, I know this is a lot to take in, but we don't have much time. We have a plan to get you out, but we have to act now."

I look between them, my mind racing. All I have ever wanted is to make my own choices. Maybe it's time I do. A cold resolve settles over me, cutting through the last of the drug's haze. "What do I need to do?"

"Tomorrow, my uncle will force your father's hand. Someone from our family will arrive to collect you to take you to Russia." Oscar's words hang in the air, heavy and ominous.

I feel as if I've been plunged into icy water, my breath catching in my throat. The world around me seems to blur and fade, the gentle rustle of leaves and the distant chirp of crickets muffled by the roaring in my ears. I stare at Oscar, searching his face for any sign that this is some cruel joke, but his expression remains grave.

Oscar cuts in, his voice tight with urgency. "You have to go with them."

"To Russia? Are you insane?" I ask.

Zaire's arm tightens around me, a gesture meant to be reassuring, but it only serves to heighten my nerves. The balcony suddenly feels too small, the night air suddenly becoming too thick.

"I know it sounds crazy," Oscar says, his voice low and urgent. "But it's the only way. If you resist, they'll use force. They'll drug you again, maybe worse this time. But if you go willingly, we can control the situation."

I shake my head vehemently, ignoring the way it makes the world spin. "Control the situation? How? By shipping me off to some frozen wasteland where I'll be at the mercy of your psychotic uncle?"

"Vesper, please," Zaire interjects, his dark eyes pleading. "We have people in place. Your father needs to see you leave, but you will not make it to the plane. I promise you. You will never step foot in Moscow. But we need you to play along, just for a little while."

I push away from Zaire, stumbling slightly as I put distance between us. The cool stone of the balustrade presses against my back, grounding me. "And what about Luca? You expect me to leave while my brother is missing?"

Oscar steps forward, his hands raised in a placating gesture. "We're not asking you to abandon him. Our people are looking for Luca as we speak. But right now, you're the one in immediate danger."

I laugh, a bitter, hollow sound that seems to echo in the still night air. "Immediate danger? I'm standing here in my own home, surrounded by guards who've known me since I was a child. How is that more dangerous than being shipped off to Russia?"

"Because those guards, this home, they're not what you think they are," Oscar says, his voice tight with building frustration. "The moment that plane touches down in Moscow, you'll be married to Dmitri. No ceremony, no guests, just a piece of paper and a signature. And once that happens, you'll be trapped. Everything up until this moment has been orchestrated by our uncle to get you to Russia, and in order to use you as a bargaining chip against your father."

I close my eyes, trying to process this flood of information. When I open them again, I fix Oscar with a steely gaze. "You said you have a plan. Do you promise me it will work? That if I say yes that I'm not trading one jailer for another?"

"Yes," Oscar declares. "It will work. You just have to trust us and let it all play out."

I hesitate, but if they're right, and I wake up tomorrow to a sudden change in plans, I have no choice but to trust them. As much as I don't want to believe this will happen, it's hard to deny the certainty of their words. It leaves me with no choice

"Tell me what I need to do."

Chapter 8

VESPER

I DRIFT off into a hazy sleep, my mind still swirling with the remnants of Oscar and Zaire's visit. The drugged tea lingers in my system, pulling me deeper into unconsciousness. Vivid dreams dance behind my eyelids - snippets of conversations, flashes of concerned faces, and the weight of a decision that will change everything.

When I finally stir, the room is bathed in the soft glow of early morning light. For a moment, I'm disoriented, the memories of last night feeling more like fragments of an elaborate dream than reality. I stretch, my muscles protesting slightly, and reach for my phone on the nightstand.

The screen illuminates, momentarily blinding me. As my eyes adjust, I see a notification that makes my heart skip a beat. A message from Oscar. My fingers tremble slightly as I swipe to open it.

> Be ready. Reset your phone and leave it behind. There's a new one waiting for you in the car.

My heart races as I read Oscar's message. This is it. The moment of truth. I take a deep breath, steadying myself for what's to come. Victor is making his move. Five minutes pass before someone is pounding on my door.

"Vesper! Get up now!" My mother's voice, usually so controlled, carries a note of urgency that sends a chill down my spine.

I scramble out of bed, nearly tripping over the silk nightgown tangled around my legs. "What's going on?" I call back, pretending to have just woken up.

"Get dressed and come to your father's study. Immediately." The sharp click of her heels fade down the hallway, leaving me in a whirlwind of confusion and dread.

My hands shake as I pull on a pair of tailored trousers and a crisp white blouse. I catch a glimpse of myself in the mirror - my blonde hair a wild mess, my green eyes wide with apprehension. I take a deep breath, trying to steel myself. If Oscar and Zaire's warning is right, their uncle issued his ultimatum. I needed to play along. I have to make them believe in this facade.

The house feels different as I make my way to Father's study. The usual hum of activity is muted, replaced by a tense silence that seems to cling to the walls. As I approach the heavy mahogany door, I can hear my father's voice, low and dangerous like a gathering thunderstorm.

"...absolutely unacceptable. That Russian bastard thinks he can dictate terms to me? In my own house?"

I pause, my hand hovering over the doorknob. My father rarely loses his composure like this. Whatever's happening, it's bad.

I push open the door, and the scene before me freezes my blood. Father stands behind his massive desk, his face flushed with rage. Mother perches on the edge of a leather armchair, her perfectly manicured nails digging into the upholstery.

Father's eyes lock onto me the moment I enter. "Vesper," he growls, "pack your bags. You're getting on a plane to Moscow today."

The world tilts beneath my feet with the confirmation that they were right. Oscar and Zaire weren't lying to me. "What? But I thought-"

"Victor Petrov," Father spits the name like a curse, "is demanding your presence, immediately. He says that if you're not there by tonight, the deal's off." He slams his fist on the desk, making me flinch. "This is your brother's fault. Those nephews of his must have spun quite the story."

I stand frozen, my mind reeling as I try to school my reactions. *Play your part, Vesper. They can't know.*

"Antonio, this is absurd! What about the wedding?" My mother rises from her seat, her perfectly coiffed hair bouncing slightly with the sudden movement. I watch as she paces the room, her designer heels clicking against the hardwood floor. Her hands gesticulate wildly, a rare display of emotion from a woman who prides herself on composure. "The expense alone is staggering. Do you have any idea how much we've already invested in this affair?"

Father's face darkens further if that's even possible. "You think I don't know that, Elizaveta? You think I'm happy about this?" He runs a hand through his salt-and-pepper hair, a gesture I've seen a thousand times when he's trying to maintain control. "But we don't have a choice. If we want this alliance to hold, we play by their rules."

I find my voice at last, though it comes out as barely more than a whisper. "And what about what I want?"

Both of my parents turn to look at me as if they'd forgotten I was even in the room. Mother's expression softens slightly. "Oh, darling," she sighs, "You know better than to think you had a choice in this matter. This last minute change is an inconvenience, but it doesn't change anything."

"Inconvenient?" I interrupt, my voice growing stronger. "This isn't just an inconvenience, Mother. This is my life we're talking about!"

Father's gaze hardens. "Your life, Vesper, has always been about more than just you. You've known this since you were a child. The family comes first."

I feel a surge of anger rising within me, hot and fierce. A surge I cannot stamp down. This may be my last chance to say my peace. I can't die on this hill now without a little push back. "The family comes first? Is that why you're shipping me off like some bargaining chip?"

Father's eyes flash dangerously. "Watch your tone, young lady. This isn't up for discussion."

But I'm too far gone now, the words spilling out of me like a dam breaking. "It never is, is it? Not when it comes to what I want. Not when it comes to my future."

Mother steps between us, her hands raised placatingly. "Please, let's all calm down." She turns to Father, her accent thickening as it always does when she's upset. "Antonio, maybe I could speak with Victor. My family has known the Petrovs for generations. Surely he would listen to reason and allow this alliance to precede as planned."

Instead, his expression twists into something ugly. "Your family?" he sneers. "You mean those vodka-soaked has-beens who couldn't keep control of their own territory? The ones who came crawling to me for protection when the Petrovs started muscling in?" He shakes his head dismissively. "No, Elizaveta. Your connections are useless. They'd probably make things worse."

I watch as Mother recoils as if she's been slapped, her usually impeccable composure crumbling. "How dare you," she whispers, her voice trembling with hurt and anger. "My family may have fallen on hard times, but they were once respected. They had honor."

Father scoffs. "Honor doesn't mean shit when you're bleeding money and influence. The Petrovs saw weakness, and they pounced. That's how this world works. Victor has the upper hand right now because your fuck up of a son couldn't control himself for a fucking week."

"You were the one who insisted that our son…," she spits back before my father cuts her off. They trade barbs back and forth, aiming to cut each other down. I stand there, caught between my warring parents, feeling like a child again.

"Stop it!" I shout, surprising even myself with the force of my voice. Both of them turn to look at me, startled. "Just stop. This isn't helping anyone."

I take a deep breath, trying to center myself. I think of Oscar's message, of the escape plan we've been crafting. I think of the life I could have, free from all of this.

"I'll go," I say finally, the words tasting bitter on my tongue. "I'll go to Moscow."

I turn on my heel and march out of the study, not waiting for my father's dismissal. The heavy mahogany door slams behind me, muffling the renewed argument between my parents. Their voices fade as I climb the grand staircase, my fingers trailing along the polished banister.

I return to my room, looking around my gilded cage for the last time. Whether or not Oscar's plan works, I will not be returning here. With a sigh, I walk to my closet and find my suitcase. The one my mother had given to me as a Christmas present years ago. The leather is soft and supple beneath my fingers. It's monogrammed with my name-Vesper Rossi- a constant reminder of the weight of my family name.

I begin to pack, selecting clothes that will be suitable for Moscow's weather. Each item I place in the suitcase feels like another brick in the wall of my prison. Designer labels and luxury fabrics, the wardrobe staples for a mafia princess bound for marriage. As I fold a cashmere sweater, my mind wanders to Oscar and Zaire. Are they watching the house, waiting for their moment? Will they be able to get me out before I'm whisked away to Russia? The uncertainty gnaws at me, making my hands shake as I continue to pack.

I pause at my jewelry box, my fingers hovering over the family heirlooms that have been passed down to me. The Rossi diamond necklace winks at me, a small fortune contained in those perfectly cut stones. For a moment, I consider leaving it behind - a final act of defiance. But practicality wins out. If things go south, I might need something valuable to barter with.

The sound of raised voices drifts up from below, reminding me that time is running short. I quicken my pace, shoving clothes and accessories into the suitcase with less care now. My eyes keep darting to the window, searching for any sign of Oscar or Zaire.

As I zip up the suitcase, my gaze falls on a framed photo on my nightstand. It's from happier a time - my whole family at our villa in Tuscany. Luca and I are laughing, our parents looking at us, smiling. Smiles I haven't seen in a long time. Next to the photo is my phone. I grab it, ready to do what Oscar had instructed. But, I hesitate. I can't erase it just yet. I take a deep breath, steadying myself for what's to come. With trembling fingers, I open a new text to my brother. The words flow from my heart, a bittersweet mix of love and fear.

> Stay safe, Luca Whatever happens, remember that I love you.

I hit send, watching the message disappear. A lump forms in my throat as I navigate to the phone's settings. With a few quick taps, I initiate a factory reset. The screen goes black, and then flashes to life with the startup logo. I place it gently on the nightstand, the final connection to my old life left behind.

My feet sink into the plush carpet as I make my way to the door. The house feels different now, charged with an electric tension that makes the hair on my arms stand on end. As I descend the grand staircase, my father's voice echoes through the halls, a storm of Russian expletives crackling with fury. I catch snippets of his conversation - "incompetent," "disaster," "fix this now" - each word laced with venom.

At the bottom of the stairs, I pause, my hand resting on the cool marble banister. My mother stands by the front door, her usual composure shattered. She opens her mouth to speak, but no sound comes out. Instead, she reaches for me, pulling me into an embrace that feels foreign.

As Mother releases me from her embrace, her eyes lock onto mine, shimmering with unshed tears. "Be strong, my darling," she whispers, her voice barely audible over the gentle hum of the arriving town car. "Russia is not easy for women, but you are a Rossi. You will endure. Just like I do."

Her words settle over me like a heavy cloak, a mix of expectation and comfort that I've known all my life. I nod, not trusting my voice to remain steady if I speak. The weight of the moment, the finality of it all, threatens to overwhelm me.

"Do as you're told," Mother continues, her fingers gently smoothing my hair, a gesture so achingly familiar it makes my heart clench. "Everything will be okay if you just follow their lead. Remember, this is for the family. Do not disappoint your father. Do your duty. Give them an heir. It's easier after that."

The town car gleams in the morning sun. The driver, a stone-faced man I don't recognize, steps out and approaches us with fluid efficiency. He reaches for my bag, and I relinquish it without protest, feeling oddly detached from the whole process.

Mother's hand rests on the small of my back, guiding me towards the vehicle. Each step feels like I'm moving through molasses, my legs heavy with reluctance and fear. I scan the windows of our sprawling mansion, searching for any sign of Father, but he's nowhere to be seen. His absence speaks volumes, a silent declaration of his expectations.

As we reach the car, Mother turns me to face her one

last time. Her eyes roam over my face as if committing every detail to memory. "You are stronger than you know, Vesper," she says, her voice thick with emotion. "Never forget that."

She ushers me into the back seat, the leather cool against my skin. As the door closes, I catch one last glimpse of her - my beautiful, complicated mother - standing tall and proud despite the tears now flowing freely down her cheeks. The image burns itself into my mind, a bittersweet farewell to the life I've always known.

The driver slides into his seat, and the engine purrs to life. As we pull away from the house, I press my hand against the window, watching as my childhood home grows smaller in the distance. The manicured lawns and wrought-iron gates that once felt like the boundaries of my world now seem laughably insignificant compared to the vast unknown that lies ahead.

I sink back into the plush seat, my mind racing with possibilities. Will Oscar and Zaire's plan work? Or am I truly bound for Moscow and a life I never chose? The uncertainty is both terrifying and exhilarating, a cocktail of emotions that leaves me feeling dizzy and breathless.

As we merge onto the highway, I close my eyes and take a deep breath.

As the car cruises down the highway, my fingers drum nervously against the leather armrest. The weight of everything I've left behind presses down on me, making it hard to breathe. I glance at the driver, his stoic profile revealing nothing. Does he know about Oscar and Zaire's plan? Is he in on it, or just another pawn in this dangerous game?

My eyes dart to the floor of the car, searching for any sign of the promised phone. At first, I see nothing but pristine carpeting. Then, as we round a bend, a glint of metal catches my eye. There, partially hidden beneath the front passenger seat, I spot the edge of a smartphone.

My heart races as I lean forward, feigning the need to adjust my shoe. With trembling fingers, I grasp the device and quickly tuck it into my lap. The driver's eyes flick to the rearview mirror, but he says nothing. I hold my breath, waiting for him to pull over or call my father, but the car continues its steady pace down the highway.

Once I'm sure he hasn't noticed, I power on the phone. The screen flickers to life, displaying an unfamiliar interface. It's a burner phone, I realize, with no personal information or unnecessary apps. There's only one notification: a new message from an unknown number.

I open it, my pulse pounding in my ears. The words on the screen make my breath catch in my throat:

> Put on your seatbelt and hold tight.
> Things are about to get interesting.

A mix of fear and exhilaration courses through me. This is it. The moment of truth. I fumble with the seatbelt, clicking it into place just as the car takes a sharp turn onto an exit ramp. The sudden movement throws me against the door, and I grip the armrest tightly.

The peaceful highway scenery gives way to a maze of industrial buildings and abandoned warehouses. Confusion furrows my brow. This isn't the way to the airport. The driver's knuckles tighten as he grips the steering wheel, his eyes darting between the road and the rearview mirror.

"Where are we going?" I ask, playing my part. The driver doesn't respond. "Hello, I'm talking to you. This isn't the way to the airport."

The driver's eyes flash with anger in the rearview mirror. "Shut up!" he snarls, his composure finally cracking.

But before I can react, the world explodes into chaos. A thunderous crash rocks the car as something slams into us from behind. The impact throws me forward, my seatbelt cutting into my chest as it strains to hold me in place. My head whips back, stars bursting behind my eyes.

We're spinning now, the world outside the windows a dizzying blur of gray and green. I can hear the screech of tires, smell burning rubber and something acrid - gasoline, maybe? My stomach lurches as we continue to rotate, faster and faster.

Then, another impact. This one comes from my side, the metal of the car door crumpling inward with a sickening crunch. The window shatters, showering me with tiny shards of glass that sting my exposed skin. I see the driver lurch forward, the seatbelt that would have stopped his motion gone, and watch in horror as he's thrown from the car through the windshield.

The car, hit from another side, begins to flip. The world

outside the windshield becomes a violent phantasmagoria - pavement, sky, pavement, sky. Each rotation slams me against a new surface - the roof, the door, the shattered windshield. Pain explodes across my body, but there's no time to process it, no time to do anything but try to protect my head as I continue to roll.

One flip. Two. Three. I lose count, my senses overwhelm me, the cacophony of twisting metal, shattering glass, and my own strangled cries. Time seems to stretch and contract, each second feeling like an eternity and yet passing in the blink of an eye.

Finally, the car stops. It comes to a rest on its roof, the frame groaning as it settles. For a moment, everything is still. The only sound is the tick-tick-tick of cooling metal and my own ragged breathing.

I'm hanging upside down, suspended by my seatbelt, which is tightly pressing into my stomach, holding me in place. Blood rushes to my head, pounding in my ears. Every inch of my body screams in protest as I try to move. My vision swims, dark spots dancing at the edges.

Through the broken windshield I can see figures approaching. I can't tell who it is, my thoughts are too fragmented to make sense of anything. The door next to me is ripped open with a screech of protesting metal. A figure crouches down, peering into the wreckage. For a moment, hope flares in my chest. Oscar? Zaire? But as my vision clears, I realize it's a stranger - a man with cold blue eyes and a face like carved granite.

"Well, well. Looks like our little princess survived the ride."

I try to speak, to demand answers, but my tongue feels thick and uncooperative in my mouth. The man's lips curl into a cruel smile as he takes in my battered state.

"Good," he says, reaching into his jacket pocket. "You're worth more alive."

My eyes widen as he pulls out a syringe, its contents a murky amber color. I try to struggle, to pull away, but I'm trapped by the twisted metal and my own injuries. Panic surges through me, lending strength to my leaden limbs.

"No," I manage to croak out. "Please..."

But my pleas fall on deaf ears. The man's hand darts forward, quick as a striking snake. I feel a sharp pinch in my neck, followed by a burning sensation that spreads rapidly through my body.

"Be a good girl, princess. Don't fight what comes next. It'll be easier for you if you don't."

The world begins to tilt and blur around the edges. Colors bleed into one another, sounds becoming muffled and distant. I try to fight against the encroaching darkness, but it's a losing battle. My eyelids grow heavy, each blink lasting longer than the last.

The last thing I see before consciousness slips away is the man's face, those icy blue eyes watching me with a mix of satisfaction and contempt. Then, like a candle being snuffed out, the world goes black.

Chapter 9

OSCAR

THE MORNING SUN filters through the heavy velvet curtains of Father's study, casting long shadows across the antique Persian rug. Zaire and I sit in silence, perched on the edge of leather armchairs that still smell faintly of cigar smoke and brandy. Father's voice, low and intense, drifts from behind his massive mahogany desk as he speaks rapidly into the phone in hushed Russian.

I catch Zaire's eye, and he smirks, mouthing "Uncle Victor" with an exaggerated eye roll. Despite the gravity of the situation, I have to stifle a laugh. Our uncle's flair for the dramatic is legendary within the family.

"Yes, Victor. We have the upper hand now," Father says, a hint of satisfaction coloring his tone. "The situation with my sons and Rossi's heir has given us precisely the leverage we need."

I swallow hard, guilt gnawing at my insides like a hungry rat. This is my fault. If I hadn't asked Zaire to distract Luca so I could talk to Vesper. I glance at my brother, but his face is impassive, almost bored. How can he be so calm? Vesper's life and the future of our family rides on our shoulders today. One wrong move and shit will hit the proverbial fan. Vesper marrying Dmitri is only the start of the cataclysmic shift in power that our uncle has planned. We can't allow that to happen when it means that my father and our family are no longer an asset. He'll have what he wants, Rossi-Petrov heirs. Uncle Victor will have no need for us.

Father's laugh, sharp and sudden, startles me. "Indeed, brother. The Rossis won't know what hit them."

I shift uncomfortably in my chair, the leather creaking beneath me. Father's eyes flick to mine, a warning in their depths. I school my features into neutrality, but my hands are clammy, and my heart races.

Zaire leans over, his voice barely a whisper. "Relax, Oz. You look like you're a sinner stepping foot into a church right now. Keep it fucking together."

Father ends the call with a decisive click. "Boys," he says, leaning back in his chair, "it seems our family's fortunes are about to change. The Rossis have always thought themselves untouchable, but now..." He smiles, a predator's grin. "Now, we hold all the cards."

I force a smile, hoping it doesn't look as strained as it feels. "That's fantastic news, Father."

Father's eyes gleam with a mixture of pride and ambition. "Indeed, Oscar. This is the moment we've been waiting for. With Vesper Rossi as Dmitri's bride, we'll have unprecedented access to both families' operations. The wealth, the power. It's all within our grasp."

Zaire, ever the perfect son, leans forward with an eager expression. "Do we need to prepare to escort Vesper, Father? Ensure her safe passage to Moscow?"

"No need, boys. Your uncle has it well in hand." He waves a dismissive hand. "Your guard duty is over. Victor's men will take care of the transport. The car is already being sent over to the Rossi mansion. "

The irony of his words isn't lost on me. Our guard duty may be over in his eyes, but for Zaire and me, it's only just beginning.

"That's...efficient," I say, struggling to keep my voice steady. "Uncle Victor always was one for thorough planning."

Father chuckles a sound that sends a chill down my spine. "Oh, you have no idea, Oscar. The wheels have been in motion for longer than you can imagine." Father stands, stretching his arms above his head. The sunlight catches on his gold watch, sending fractals of light dancing across the room. "The amount of money that I would have paid to be in the room when Victor calls Antonio. We might even see the explosion from here," he chuckles to himself. "This calls for a celebration. I think I'll open that bottle of Macallan 1926 I've been saving."

As he turns to the liquor cabinet, I exchange a loaded glance with Zaire. My brother's eyes flicker with under-standing, and he gives an almost imperceptible nod. We're on the same page.

"Actually, Father," I say, standing up, trying to keep my voice steady, "if you don't mind, Zaire and I thought we might head into town. You know, celebrate in our own way before school." I force a mischievous grin, hoping he'll assume we're paying a visit to the harem he's always presumed we had at our beck and call.

Father pauses, crystal decanter in hand. For a heart-stopping moment, I think he's going to refuse. But then he chuckles, shaking his head indulgently. "You boys and your escapades. Very well, go on. But remember, we have a family dinner tonight. I expect you both back and presentable by eight. Your mother will be disappointed if you're late. You know how much she misses the two of you when we're abroad."

"Of course, Father," Zaire says smoothly, rising to his feet. "We wouldn't miss it for the world."

As we leave the study, my mind is already racing, formu-lating plans to ensure our success. While I had hoped to be in the car with Vesper as her escort, this doesn't change our plan. It just makes it harder to execute it.

We stride down the marble hallway, our footsteps echoing off the vaulted ceiling. Zaire's face is a mask of calm, but I can see the tension in his jaw, the slight twitch of his left eye that always betrays his anxiety. As we pass the grand staircase, I catch a glimpse of our mother in the drawing room, her delicate hands arranging a bouquet of blood-red roses. She doesn't look up as we pass, lost in her own world of flowers and silence. It's been over a year since she and Father came to our home here in Boston. We'd been left in the care of the staff while they stayed close to Uncle Victor.

The warm summer air hits us as we step outside, carrying the scent of blooming flowers and freshly turned earth. Zaire's black Lamborghini Aventador sits in the circular driveway, a sleek predator among the manicured topiaries. The car chirps as he unlocks it, and I slide into the passenger seat, the buttery leather cool against my skin. Zaire guns the engine, and we peel out of the driveway, gravel crunching beneath the tires. The wrought-iron gates swing open as we approach, and then we're on the open road, the sprawling Petrov estate disappearing in the rearview mirror.

We drive in tense silence, the summer landscape blurring past in a riot of greens and blues. I watch as we pass the turnoff for Saint Jude's, my stomach clenching as I think of the life we're leaving behind. No more lazy afternoons on the quad, no more midnight study sessions fueled by contraband vodka and dreams of the future. But, considering the alternative is Vesper being stuck as Dmitri's heir machine, and us being, well, dead, it's worth the sacrifice. Our world would never survive my uncle gaining this much power. Every other family would be forced to bend their knee to his will. We can't let that happen.

I finally break the silence. "Zaire, we need to talk about the plan."

He nods, his eyes never leaving the road. "I know. This changes things. We need to loop everyone in."

I take a deep breath, organizing my thoughts, while pulling out my phone and connecting it to Zaire's touch screen. Alex picks up immediately.

"Your plan has gone to shit, hasn't it?"

"Yes, and no," I answer. "Victor's men are handling Vesper's transport, not us."

"That complicates things, but it's not insurmountable," Talon chimes in. "We always knew this was a possibility."

"Did you make the drop, Alex?" I ask.

"What drop?"

"Package was delivered with a bow early this morning."

"Is someone going to fucking enlighten me here or are we playing twenty questions," my twin barks back.

"Alex made friends with our uncle's local driver the last time he was in town."

Zaire's eyebrows shoot up. "Seriously? How did he pull that off?"

"Turns out, he used to work for my dad before your uncle snatched him into service for a debt he owed. He's been his personal driver for over two years now when he's state side," Alex adds.

"Which is almost never," Zaire comments. "Why employ someone to drive you, when you have no intention of being here."

I shoot my brother a knowing glare. "You and I both know why."

"Kitty," we answer in unison. Kitty, his mistress, is a Puerto Rican heiress with a geriatric husband on life support. His wife, Katerina, has never stepped foot outside of Russia. Per our father's own admission, she kept his leash short at home. Having a mistress in another country was far easier to conceal. Safer, too, because Aunt Katerina may have just as much blood on her hands as Uncle Victor.

"So, his occasional driver that Alex befriended plays into this shit show situation, how?"

"Alex has been popping by before school to drop off a care package the last couple of weeks just in case we needed access to the car as Uncle Victor got closer to coming to terms with the Rossis."

"Drugs, I'm assuming?"

"Bingo," Alex adds to the conversation. "This morning, I may have 'accidentally' spilled my coffee all over the interior of his car. While he was cleaning it up, he tucked the phone under one of the back seats."

"Clever bastard," Zaire mutters, a hint of admiration in his voice.

"That's not all," He continues, warming to the subject. "I also sabotaged the GPS system. It'll look like it's working fine, but it's actually feeding false data back to Victor's team. They'll think the car is heading straight for the airport even if Vesper manages to deviate from the route."

"We're almost at the warehouse," Zaire remarks. "Get the door open." He ends the call after this last order. Zaire whistles low before glancing over at me. "You've thought of everything, haven't you?"

I shrug, trying to ignore the knot of anxiety in my stomach. "I've had a lot of sleepless nights to plan."

A sly grin tugs at his lips, pulling at the corners in a mischievous display. He teases, "You mean when you weren't playing the charming Romeo and scaling up Vesper's balcony?" I roll my eyes, choosing to ignore his playful jab. My fingers quickly tap out a message on my phone, reaching out to Vesper for some much-needed distraction from this conversation. I barely knew the girl outside of the briefest interactions at school until being thrust into her trajectory this week, but I can't deny that screwing over my family and saving her isn't purely an act of heroism. Despite our brief acquaintance, something about Vesper draws me in like a moth to a flame. I can't resist her magnetic pull. And with Dmitri looming as a potential husband for her, it would be a travesty in more ways than one if they were to marry. My reasons for wanting to save her may be selfish, but I can't help but want her for myself. The few stolen moments we shared in that classroom have ignited a fire inside of me that refuses to be extinguished.

> Be ready. Reset your phone and leave it behind. There's a new one waiting for you in the car.

Zaire takes a sharp left, and suddenly we're on a narrow, potholed road that winds through an industrial district. Abandoned factories loom on either side, their broken windows staring at us like hollow eyes. The car fishtails slightly as we take another turn, and then I see it: our warehouse, a hulking concrete structure covered in graffiti and ivy. The large bay door opens when we pull into the drive. Zaire parks his car, and we both exit, heading towards our work area. The interior of the warehouse is a stark contrast to its dilapidated exterior. Banks of computer monitors cast a blue glow over sleek metal tables covered in maps, documents, and an arsenal that would make our father proud. And there, in the center of it all, stand Alexander and Talon.

Alex is hunched over a laptop, his fingers flying across the keyboard. His usually perfectly styled blond hair is a mess, and there are dark circles under his eyes. Talon, on the other hand, looks like he's gearing up for war.

"Is the safe house online?" I ask Talon as we approach.

"Security is up. All clear." He nods to a couple of bags on the table next to him. "Clothes are in there." Zaire and I both grab a bag, and strip down, discarding the clothes we left with onto the ground and changing into the black t-shirt, and jeans from inside the bag. Zaire leaves his clothes on the ground, but I neatly pack mine away.

"We look like a fucking K-pop group," he remarks at our matching clothes.

"I kind of like it," Talon smiles back at him.

Zaire and I huddle around Alex's workstation, the tension palpable in the air. The warehouse echoes with the hum of servers and the rapid-fire clicking of keys as Alex's fingers dance across the keyboard. Suddenly, his head snaps up, eyes wide behind his thick-rimmed glasses.

"The car just left the Rossi estate,", his voice tight with excitement and nerves.

A collective intake of breath fills the room. This is it. The moment we've been preparing for has finally arrived. Everything has been planned for down to the second. I feel a rush of adrenaline course through my veins, my heart pounding against my ribcage like a caged bird desperate for freedom.

"Alright, people," Talon's deep voice reverberates through the space. "It's showtime."

We move with practiced efficiency, a well-oiled machine born of countless hours of preparation. Zaire and I head for the first car, a nondescript gray sedan that wouldn't look out of place in any suburban driveway. Talon takes the second, a black SUV with tinted windows. Both vehicles carefully selected from an impound lot two days ago, chosen for their unremarkable appearance and easily replaceable parts.

As I slide into the passenger seat of our car, I can't help but marvel at the intricate web of deception we've woven. Talon's meticulous work on swapping the plates, combined with Alex's digital wizardry in wiping them from the impound database, has bought us precious time. It's a delicate house of cards, but it's the best chance we have. Alex appears at the window, handing Zaire two small bundles before running back to Talon. Zaire opens the packages and hands me one. Inside, lies an earpiece. I slip it into place.

"Soundcheck. Everyone good?" Alex asks via the earpiece.

"Who's ready to fuck shit up?" Talon squawks into the receiver.

"I'll take that as an affirmative from Talon. Zaire? Oscar?"

"We hear you," Zaire answers for us.

The warehouse door groans open, revealing the gritty industrial landscape beyond. Zaire guns the engine, and we peel out onto the cracked asphalt, Talon following close behind in the SUV. The morning sun glints off abandoned factories and rusted chain-link fences as we navigate the maze of back streets, keeping our distance from main roads and traffic cameras.

I glance at my brother, noting the hard set of his jaw and the intensity in his eyes. Zaire has always been the more collected one, the ice to my fire. But now, I can see the cracks in his composure, the weight of what we're about to do pressing down on him.

"You okay?"

He nods curtly, eyes never leaving the road. "Just thinking about what comes after. There's no coming back from this, Oz."

The gravity of his words settles over me like a heavy blanket. We're not just risking our lives today; we're burning bridges, cutting ties with everything and everyone we've ever known. Our family, our future, our very identities — all of it will be ash by sundown.

But then I think of Vesper, of the fire in her eyes and the strength in her spirit. I think of the world my uncle wants to create a world where families like ours rule with an iron fist and people like Vesper are nothing more than pawns. The resolve hardens in my chest.

"I know," I say, my voice steady. "But it's worth it. We have to do this."

Zaire's lips quirk up in a half-smile. "You really have fallen for her, haven't you?"

I feel heat rise to my cheeks but don't deny it. There's no point in hiding it from my twin. "She's different. Strong. She doesn't deserve the life they've planned for her."

"None of us do," Zaire mutters, his knuckles whitening on the steering wheel.

We lapse into silence as we approach our first checkpoint. Alex's voice crackles through the earpiece I had forgotten I'd put in.

"I just uploaded the tracking software to each vehicle. You should only have a few seconds delay from my screen with the satellite uplink."

The car's navigation system beeps softly, and I check the screen. "They're heading north," I report. "Looks like they're taking the scenic route."

"Perfect," Zaire mutters. He takes a sharp right, guiding us onto a narrow access road that runs parallel to the highway. We can see the steady stream of traffic to our left, a river of metal and exhaust fumes.

I take the chance to fire off a text to her new phone that Alex stashed in the car.

> Put on your seatbelt and hold tight.
> Things are about to get interesting.

The car's engine purrs as we race along the access road, the scenery blurring into a smear of green and gray. Zaire's eyes are fixed on the road ahead, his hands gripping the wheel with white-knuckled intensity. I keep my gaze locked on the navigation screen, watching the blinking dot that represents Vesper's car as it moves steadily northward.

"Alex, how's it looking on your end?" I ask, pressing a finger to my earpiece.

"All clear so far," he replies, his voice tinged with static. "I've got eyes on the traffic cams and police scanners. Nothing unusual to report."

As we speed along, I can't help but think of Alex back at the warehouse. He'd insisted on staying behind, claiming he could do more good from there. I know he's right — his skills are better utilized in coordinating our efforts and monitoring the digital landscape — but a part of me wishes he were here with us. Still, someone needs to take care of the loose ends, including Zaire's distinctive Lamborghini. Alex had promised to give it a new paint job and swap out the plates before stashing it in a secure location. It's a small comfort, knowing that piece of our old lives will be waiting for us if we make it through this.

Suddenly, the dot on the screen veers sharply to the right. "Shit!" I exclaim. "They're changing direction!"

Zaire curses under his breath, scanning the road ahead for an opportunity to turn. But we're boxed in, concrete barriers on one side and a steep embankment on the other. "I can't turn here," he growls, frustration evident in his voice.

"There's an exit coming up in half a mile," I report, my heart racing. "We can loop back around."

The next thirty seconds feel like an eternity. As soon as we reach the exit, Zaire takes it at breakneck speed, the tires screeching in protest. He executes a flawless U-turn, and we're racing back the way we came, desperate to make up lost ground.

"Talon, what's your status?" I bark into the comm.

"I made the turn," he replies, his usually calm voice tight

with tension. "But there's some kind of accident or construction up ahead. Traffic's at a standstill. I'm stuck."

My stomach drops. "Can you get around it?"

"Negative," Talon grunts. "It's completely blocked. You two need to find another route. I'll catch up when I can."

Zaire nods grimly, already scanning for alternate roads. "On it," he says, taking a sharp left onto a narrow side street.

We weave through a maze of residential areas, the houses blurring past in suburban monotony. I keep my eyes glued to the screen, calling out directions as we go. "Left here. Now right. Straight for two miles."

The suburban landscape gives way to a more industrial area, warehouses and factories looming on either side of the narrow street. Zaire's knuckles are white on the steering wheel, his jaw clenched as he navigates the unfamiliar territory.

"Alex, what's the status of Vesper's car?" I demand, my heart pounding in my ears.

There's a moment of tense silence before Alex's voice crackles through the earpiece. "They've stopped. About two miles ahead of your current position."

Relief floods through me, but it's short-lived. Zaire accelerates, the engine roaring as we tear down the empty street. We're so close. So damn close.

"Wait," Alex's voice cuts through again, panic evident in his tone. "The signal...it's gone. I've lost them."

"What do you mean, you've lost them?" I shout, panic clawing at my throat. "Alex, what the fuck is happening?"

"I don't know!" he yells back, the sound of furious typing coming through the comm. "The tracker just went dark. I'm trying to reestablish the connection, but—."

I don't hear the rest of what he says. My mind is racing, scenarios flashing through my head, each one worse than the last. Vesper captured, Vesper hurt, Vesper...

"Oscar!" Zaire's sharp voice cuts through my spiraling thoughts. "Get it together. We're almost at their last known location."

I force myself to take a deep breath, trying to calm the storm raging inside me. "Right," I manage to say. "Right. Let's just get there."

The next few minutes are a blur of tension and fear. Zaire pushes the car to its limits, taking corners at speeds that would make a professional driver nervous. I keep my eyes fixed on the road ahead, searching desperately for any sign of Vesper's car.

And then we see it.

The world seems to slow down as we round a corner and come face to face with the wreckage. The sleek black town car that was supposed to be transporting Vesper is upside down in the middle of the road, flames licking at its undercarriage. Smoke billows into the air, thick and acrid, stinging my eyes and catching in my throat.

"No," I whisper, the word barely audible over the roar of our engine and the crackling of flames. "No, no, no!"

Zaire slams on the brakes, bringing us to a screeching halt just yards from the burning wreck. Before the car has even fully stopped, I'm out the door, sprinting towards the inferno.

"Vesper!" I scream, my voice raw with desperation. "VESPER!"

The heat sears my skin as I reach the overturned car, the metal groaning and popping. Smoke chokes my lungs, but I push forward, desperate to reach Vesper. Zaire is right behind me, his face a mask of determination and fear. I rush towards the open passenger side door.

"Vesper!" I call out, my voice hoarse and desperate. "Vesper, can you hear me?"

But there's no response. No movement. No sign of life. Shattered glass crunches beneath our knees, and the smell of burning leather and plastic is overwhelming.

"She's not here," Zaire says, his voice tight with disbelief. "Oscar, she's not fucking here!"

I refuse to believe it, continuing to search even as the flames creep closer. "No, no, she has to be here. She has to be!"

But as the seconds tick by and the heat becomes unbearable, the horrible truth sinks in. The back seat is truly empty. Vesper is gone.

Zaire grabs my arm, pulling me back from the wreckage. "We have to go, Oz! This thing's going to blow!"

Numbly, I allow him to drag me away from the burning car. We stagger back, coughing and gasping for fresh air. My mind is reeling, unable to process what's happening. Where is she? How could she just vanish?

The screech of tires announces Talon's arrival. He leaps from his SUV, eyes wide as he takes in the scene before him. "What the fuck happened?" he shouts over the roar of the flames.

"She's not in the car," I manage to choke out, my voice raw and broken. "Vesper's gone."

We've lost. After the promise I made to keep her safe, I've fucking lost her.

Chapter 10

VESPER

THE FIRST THING I notice is the throbbing pain in my head, a relentless pounding that seems to reverberate through my entire body. It's as if a thousand drums are beating all at once. I try to pry open my eyes but find them covered by something thick and dark—a blindfold. Panic tugs at my heartstrings as flashes of broken glass and screeching tires flood my mind.

My attempts to move are met with resistance; my limbs feel heavy and unresponsive. A cold, biting rope digs into my wrists, keeping me restrained. As I take in my surroundings, I realize I am lying on a bed. The sheets beneath me carry an unfamiliar scent, a mix of musty fabric and antiseptic.

With each passing moment, more sensations become apparent. My ribs ache with every breath, and a dull throb pulses through my left leg. Dried blood crusts against the side of my face, causing discomfort as it pulls against my skin.

Desperate for escape, I fight against my bonds with all my might, ignoring the searing pain that shoots through my body. The sound of creaking wood fills the air as I twist and pull on the bed frame, hoping to break free.

But then, a gravelly voice breaks through the silence, startling me. It's close, perhaps just a few feet away. "I wouldn't bother if I were you," the voice says. "Resisting won't help your situation, Ms. Rossi. You might as well get comfortable."

I freeze, my heart pounding in my chest. The voice is unfamiliar, masculine, with a hint of terrifying amusement.

"You're going to be with us for a while," he continues, the sound of a chair scraping against the floor indicating he's standing up. "I'd apologize that the accommodations aren't what you're accustomed to, but, you'll get used to it."

My mind races, desperately trying to piece together the fragments of my memory. Oscar and Zaire—had they betrayed me? Was this their plan all along?

The room falls silent, save for the sound of heavy footsteps circling the bed. I can feel the presence of multiple people. The air feels thick with tension, making it difficult to breathe.

"Oscar?" I whisper, my voice hoarse and barely audible. "Zaire? Is that you?"

A burst of laughter erupts from multiple directions, startling me. It's a cruel, mocking sound that startles me more.

"Oh, that's rich," another voice chimes in, different from the first. This one is higher-pitched, with a hint of a foreign accent I can't quite place. "She thinks we're her little friends."

Confusion washes over me. If not Oscar and Zaire, then who? The realization that I'm in the hands of complete strangers hits me like a bucket of ice water.

Swallowing hard, I gather what little courage I have left. "Who are you?" I ask, my voice trembling despite my efforts to sound strong.

The laughter intensifies, echoing off the walls and seeming to close in around me. It's as if my question are the punchline to some sick joke I'm not privy to.

"Who we are doesn't matter, sweetheart," the gravelly voice from earlier responds, now uncomfortably close to my ear. "What matters is who you are, and what you're worth."

Fear grips me, and I begin to plead, my words tumbling out in a desperate rush. "Please, let me go. I-I won't tell anyone about this. My family—they'll pay whatever you want. Just please, don't hurt me."

A calloused hand roughly grabs my chin, forcing my head up despite the blindfold. "Oh, we know they'll pay," he says, his breath hot against my face. "But why settle for a one-time payout when we can milk this for all it's worth?"

The other voice chimes in again, "That's right, darling. Your life—and that virgin pussy of yours—are far too valuable to just send you back to daddy or your dear fiancé."

My stomach churns at their words, the implications sending waves of terror through my body. I try to pull away, but the hand on my chin tightens its grip.

"You see," the gravelly voice continues, "we're in the business of making money. And you, Ms. Rossi, are going to make us very, very rich."

The realization hits me like a freight train, leaving me breathless and trembling. They're going to traffic me.

"What do you mean?"

"Let me explain," the gravelly voice continues, releasing my chin. I hear him pacing around the room, his footsteps echoing ominously. "You're not just any rich girl, are you? You're Vesper Rossi, the jewel of the Rossi crime family. Do you have any idea how many people would pay a fortune just to have a piece of you?"

The other man chuckles, a sound that makes my skin crawl. "Oh, the bidding war we could start. Rival families looking to humiliate the Rossis, perverts with too much money and a taste for the forbidden, intelligence agencies hungry for insider information."

"And let's not forget," the first man adds, his voice dropping to a conspiratorial whisper, "the ultimate prize - your hand in marriage. Imagine the power someone could wield with you as their bride. The connections. The influence. It's intoxicating."

My heart pounds in my chest, each beat a thunderous reminder of my vulnerability. I try to speak, but my throat constricts, choking back the words.

"But why stop there?" the accented voice muses. "We could auction off different aspects of your life. Your virginity to the highest bidder, your skills and knowledge to another, your future children to someone else. The possibilities are endless."

The room feels like it is spinning.

"And don't think daddy dearest or your Russian prince will save you," the gravelly voice warns. "We have friends in high places: eyes and ears everywhere. One wrong move from them, and you'll disappear forever."

I feel a hand stroke my hair, the gesture mockingly gentle. "But don't worry, princess. We'll take good care of you. Keep you healthy, beautiful...marketable. After all, damaged goods don't sell as well."

Suddenly, I feel a sharp prick in my arm. A needle. Panic surges through me as I realize they're drugging me.

"Sweet dreams, Ms. Rossi," the accented voice says, already sounding distant. "When you wake up, your new life begins."

Chapter 11

TWO YEARS LATER

OSCAR

TWO YEARS. Seven hundred and thirty days of searching, hoping, and coming up empty-handed. Each sunrise brings a renewed sense of determination and each sunset a crushing wave of disappointment. I can't give up. I won't give up. Vesper is out there somewhere, and I'll tear this city apart brick by brick if that's what it takes to find her.

The neon lights of Boston's underbelly flicker and hum as I make my way through the rain-slicked streets. The Second Sons have eyes and ears everywhere, but it's never enough. Every lead fizzles out like a dying ember. But I can't stop. The weight of this guilt sits heavy on my chest, a constant reminder of my failure to protect her.

I pause outside of a seedy bar, its windows clouded with years of grime and cigarette smoke. My reflection stares back at me, a stranger with haunted blue eyes and a perpetual frown. I barely recognize myself anymore. The Second Sons have grown. What started out as a way to save Vesper and our families from Victor Petrov's influence has become our refuge. Even though Victor still hasn't connected the dots of our plan to rescue her, my father had quickly fallen out of favor with our uncle after failing him. With my father out of power, our family fell onto hard times. The opulent estate my parents had loved now belongs to one of our cousins, Victor's new second. With no money of their own and no power, my parents abandoned Boston and returned overseas, leaving Zaire and I to fend for ourselves. Thankfully, we had a nest egg due to some under-ground side work we'd been doing while at the academy. We had a small fortune saved up, and we've managed to grow it to keep us, Alex, and Talon living comfortably.. We may be outcasts and bastards, but we have something that every other heir doesn't, freedom.

"Oscar," Zaire's voice crackles through my earpiece, tinged with exasperation. "It's time to call it a night."

I clench my jaw, frustration bubbling up inside me. "Not yet. I've got one more contact to check."

"Brother," Zaire sighs, and I can picture him pinching

the bridge of his nose, tattoos rippling across his forearms. "It's been two years. We've looked everywhere. She's gone."

"Don't say that," I growl, my hand curling into a fist at my side.

The silence on the other end of the line is deafening. When Zaire speaks again, his voice is softer, laden with a mixture of concern and resignation. "Oscar, we can't keep living in the past. The Second Sons need you here, focused on the present. On our future."

I close my eyes, leaning my forehead against the cool glass of the bar window. Zaire's words cut deep, reopening wounds that have never truly healed. But he doesn't understand. He can't understand the gnawing emptiness, the constant ache of Vesper's absence.

"I'll be back soon," I mutter, ending the call on my earpiece with a tap of my finger before he can argue further.

As I push open the bar door, the stench of stale beer and desperation washes over me. This is where the dregs of society come to forget, to drown their sorrows in cheap liquor, and even cheaper company. But for me, it's another thread in the vast tapestry of Boston's underworld, another potential lead to follow.

I scan the dimly lit room, my eyes adjusting to the haze of smoke that hangs in the air like a shroud. In the far corner, I spot him - Ricky, a grimy fixture in this cesspool of humanity. His eyes dart nervously around the room, never settling on one spot for too long. As I approach, he hunches further over his drink, as if trying to disappear into the sticky surface of the bar.

"Ricky," I say, sliding onto the stool next to him. "We need to talk."

He flinches at the sound of my voice, his fingers tightening around his glass. "I ain't got nothin' for you, Petrov. Now leave me be."

I lean in closer, my voice low and dangerous. "That's not what I heard. Word on the street is you've got some information about the trafficking ring that's moved into town."

Ricky's eyes flick to mine, a flash of fear crossing his face before he schools his features back into a mask of indifference. "Don't know what you're talkin' about."

I slide a thick envelope across the bar, watching as his gaze locks onto it like a starving dog eyeing a scrap of meat. "Maybe this will jog your memory."

His grimy fingers twitch towards the envelope, but I place my hand over it before he can grab it. "Information first, Ricky. Then you get paid."

He licks his lips, eyes darting around the bar once more before leaning in close. The stench of cheap whiskey washes over me as he speaks. "There's a new player in town. Goes by the name of 'The Collector.' Word is, he's got a taste for exotic merchandise."

My stomach churns at his words, bile rising in my throat. The thought of Vesper in the clutches of someone like that...I push the image away, forcing myself to focus. "Where's he operating from?"

Ricky shakes his head. "Nobody knows for sure. But there's talk of a big shipment coming in next week. Big enough that overseas guys are coming in for it. Word is that they have something up for auction that is worth millions."

"Can you get me an invitation to that auction?"

"Look, man, I get information. I don't stick my nose into my boss' business. If I go asking around about an invitation to something above my pay grade, it'll get me killed."

"You're right," I admit, knowing damn well that I don't care if he lives or dies considering he helps get the girls his boss sells. Ricky is a means to an end for me. I find Vesper and his life ends. Plain and fucking simple. The less people like him on Earth, the better. Until then, he's still useful to me.

"Get me an invite, and I'll double this."

I slide the envelope towards him, watching as he snatches it up and tucks it inside his threadbare jacket.

"I'll see what I can do," he answers.

As I stand to leave, he grabs my arm, his eyes wide with fear. "You didn't hear this from me, Petrov. If The Collector finds out I talked..."

I shake off his grip, my voice cold. "No one will know. But if I find out you're lying to me, Ricky, you'll wish it was The Collector coming for you instead of me."

As I step back out into the rain-slicked night, my mind races with the new information. The sex trafficking trade in Boston has exploded over the past year, a festering wound on the city's underbelly. Each new lead, each whisper of a new ring or a fresh shipment of girls, sends a spike of anger inside of me. We've helped as many as we could over the last two years. No matter how many of them we managed to get out, even more were brought in to replace them.. It's an uphill battle we continue to lose.

Vesper lingers in my mind as I walk back to our building. Maybe Zaire's right. Maybe she is gone. Maybe everything that I have done has been for nothing. But, deep down, I think he's wrong. Maybe it's the hope that I can find her and redeem myself for what happened despite what Zaire and everyone else seem to think. Vesper has to be still out there. Because if she isn't, I'm not sure that I can live with myself. It's already hard to face the man in the mirror every morning, knowing that I broke my promise to her and that she may be out there in danger, hurt, or worse because of me. I gave her false hope that marrying my asshole cousin wasn't the end for her. That she could be free. I guess that shit is only in fairy tale books now.

The thoughts of her carry me the rainy twenty blocks home to our warehouse which has a converted penthouse on the top floor. It had been a dump when we bought it. A 1900s brick factory that had closed down long ago. The realtor had it on the market for almost ten years when we made an all cash offer in exchange for our paperwork to disappear after it closed. The agent was more than happy to oblige us. After two years of near constant improvements and renovations in our downtime, it finally feels like home. We have everything we need here.

My clothes are soaked. Water practically pours off of me the second I step inside the building. Making my way to the main elevator, I step inside and hit the button for the top floor.

I step out of the elevator into our penthouse apartment. The carpet muffles my footsteps as I make my way through the dimly lit living room. Talon's absence is palpable; no doubt he's out chasing his latest conquest.

As I pass Alex's office, I catch a glimpse of him through the crack in the door. He's hunched over his desk, bathed in the blue glow of multiple computer screens. His fingers fly across the keyboard, eyes never leaving the monitors. The sound of 'Boots and Blood' by Five Finger Death Punch plays as he works. I consider stepping in, and sharing what I've learned, but I know better when he has music playing while he works. When Alex's in the zone, it's best to leave him be. His playlist acting as a guide to his mood for all of us. The darker the lyrics, the deeper he's into his task. Talon had made the mistake once of stumbling into his office when he was trying to hack into a government database. It wasn't pretty. We all learned a lesson that day. If the singer is screaming his lyrics, it's best to walk away or you might risk stirring the monster inside of him. The last place you want to be is in his playroom in the basement.

The cool night air hits me as I step onto the balcony. Zaire's there, leaning against the railing, his profile illuminated by the city lights. He doesn't turn as I approach, but I know he's aware of my presence. We've always had that connection, an unspoken understanding that goes beyond words.

"You're back earlier than I expected," he says, his voice carrying a hint of surprise and relief.

I join him at the railing, looking out over the glittering expanse of Boston. From up here, the city looks almost peaceful, its darker undercurrents hidden beneath a veneer of twinkling lights and towering skyscrapers.

"Got some new information," I reply, my fingers drumming against the cool metal. "A lead on a big auction coming up. Could be our chance to finally get some real answers."

Zaire turns to face me, his eyes searching mine. "Oscar," he begins, his voice soft but firm. "We need to talk about this. About Vesper."

I feel my jaw clench, my body tensing at the mere mention of her name. "What's there to talk about? She's out there, Zaire. I know it."

He sighs, running a hand through his hair. "It's been two years, brother. Two years of chasing shadows and dead ends. You're not living anymore, you're just...existing."

His words hit me like a physical blow, and I take a step back. "What are you saying? That I should just give up? Forget about her? She's gone because we failed her."

"We did what we could, and it didn't work. We tried. That's more than most can say about the situation."

I turn away, unable to meet his gaze. The city blurs before me as unbidden tears sting my eyes. "You don't understand," I whisper. "I failed her, Zaire. I promised to protect her, and I failed."

I feel his hand on my shoulder, a comforting weight. "You didn't fail her, Oscar. We were all blindsided by what happened. But you can't keep chasing a ghost, Oz."

I shake off Zaire's hand, unable to bear the weight of his concern. My eyes scan the cityscape, searching for something, anything, to latch onto. The neon signs blur into streaks of color, like tears on the face of the night. I can't shake the feeling that she's out there, lost in that sea of lights, waiting for me to find her.

"Every time I close my eyes, I see her face. I hear her voice. She's not a ghost, Zaire. She's real, and she's out there somewhere."

"I got a potential lead tonight." I turn back to face my brother, my hands gripping the railing so tightly my knuckles turn white. "This lead...it's different. There's an auction coming up. Big players from overseas are flying in for it. Whatever they're selling, it's worth millions."

Zaire's eyes widen slightly, a flicker of interest breaking through his mask of concern. "What kind of auction?"

"The kind that deals in 'exotic merchandise,'" I spit out the words, disgust coating my tongue. "It's a whole new operation, run by someone called 'The Collector.'"

I watch as my brother processes this information, his brow furrowing in thought. The tattoos on his arms seem to shift in the dim light, like shadows dancing across his skin. For a moment, I'm struck by how different we look now, despite being twins. While I've remained unmarked, Zaire has embraced the family traditions, his skin a canvas.

"Oscar," he says slowly, "even if this lead pans out, what makes you think Vesper will be there? It's been two years. The chances of her being part of this particular auction..."

"I know it's a long shot," I interrupt, running a hand through my damp hair. "But what if she is? What if this is our one chance to find her? I can't...I won't let it slip away."

The city hums below us, a constant reminder of the life that goes on, oblivious to our struggles. A siren wails in the distance, and I wonder briefly if it's racing towards another tragedy, another life about to be shattered.

"We need to be smart about this," Zaire says, his voice taking on the tone he uses when planning operations. "If this auction is as big as you say, we can't just go in guns blazing. We need intel, a solid plan."

I nod, feeling a surge of gratitude for my brother's unwavering support, even when he doesn't fully agree with me. "I've got a contact working on getting us an invitation. Once we're in, we can gather more information, maybe even identify some of the major players."

Zaire's eyes narrow. "An invitation? Oscar, we can't risk exposing ourselves like that. If Victor finds out we have an operation of our own, we're good as dead. Same for Alex and Talon."

"Victor won't find out," I assure Zaire, my voice low and steady. "We've been careful, brother. As far as he knows, we're off traveling the world like our social media accounts would suggest." Alex had put in a lot of work to throw off Uncle Victor going so far as to sync the location on our phones Victor provides us to mimic the location where we should be at the time. How he did that, I had no fucking idea, but it's been working. You don't mess with a tried and true formula until you need to tweak it. If he only knew just how deeply we were operating in the shadows, gaining influence with some of the less powerful families. The Second Sons is the only thing keeping the playing field even now that he lost his Rossi alliance.

I turn back to the cityscape, my eyes tracing the familiar skyline. The Prudential Tower stands tall and proud, a beacon in the night. To its left, the John Hancock Tower reflects the city lights like a mirror, its glass surface a canvas for the urban glow. These landmarks have become more than just buildings to me; they're silent witnesses to our struggle, and our growth.

"Think about it," I continue, my voice gaining strength. "Two years ago, we were just a couple of outcasts with a crazy idea. Now? We've got a network that spans half the East Coast. The Moretti family in New York, the Caruso in Philadelphia - they're all working with us now. Hell, even the O'Brien in South Boston are starting to come around."

I can see Zaire's reflection in the glass, his face a mixture of pride and concern. "I know we've come far," he admits. "But this auction...it's different. We're talking about major players, Oscar. The kind of people who could wipe us out with a phone call if they found out who we really are."

I turn to face him, meeting his gaze head-on. "That's exactly why we need to be there. To draw out the major hitter. The Collector has something rare to sell."

The night air is cool against my skin, carrying with it the faint scent of the harbor. In the distance, I can hear the low, mournful sound of a ship's horn.

"We've been building this network for two years. Every contact we've made, every favor we've called in...it's all led to this moment. We're not the same scared kids we were when we started this, Zaire. We're smarter, stronger."

I watch Zaire process my words, his eyes scanning the city below us. I can almost see the gears turning in his head, weighing the risks against the potential rewards.

"If this lead doesn't pan out, I'll stop chasing her."

I see the flicker of doubt in Zaire's eyes, the slight tightening of his jaw that tells me he doesn't quite believe my promise. But I can also see the resignation, the willingness to give this one last shot. For me. For us.

"Alright," he says, his voice barely audible above the distant hum of the city. "One last time. But we do this smart, Oscar. No unnecessary risks."

I nod, relief washing over me like a cool breeze.

As we stand there, the city stretches out before us like a glittering canvas. The Charles River snakes its way through the urban landscape, its dark waters reflecting the lights from the buildings that line its banks. In the distance, the iconic Citgo sign pulses with a steady rhythm, a beacon in the night that has guided countless Bostonians home.

The air carries a mix of scents - the briny tang of the harbor, the rich aroma of coffee from the all-night diner down the street, and the faint whiff of exhaust from the cars far below. It's a smell I've come to associate with home, with the life we've built here in the shadows of this city.

I take a deep breath, letting the cool night air fill my lungs. For the first time in what feels like forever, I feel a spark of hope ignite in my chest. It's small, and fragile, but it's there.

"We should bring Alex and Talon in on this," Zaire says, breaking the comfortable silence that had settled between us. "If we're going to pull this off, we'll need all hands on deck."

I nod, my mind already racing with possibilities. "Alex can start digging into The Collector and see if he can find any digital footprints. Talon's contacts in the underground fighting scene might have some useful intel as well."

As if on cue, the sound of the front door opening reaches us, followed by Talon's booming laugh. I can't help but smile; his energy is infectious.

"Speak of the devil," Zaire mutters, a hint of amusement in his voice.

We make our way back inside, the warmth of the penthouse enveloping us like a cocoon. Talon is in the kitchen, his massive frame dwarfing the sleek, modern appliances. He's rummaging through the fridge, no doubt in search of a post-workout snack.

"Anyone want to order delivery?" he calls out, his voice

muffled by the refrigerator door. "There's nothing good in here." He steps back, shutting the fridge, and takes notice of Zaire and me. "Why do you both look so serious? Did someone die? Please say it was Victor."

"We'd be celebrating if that son of a bitch dropped dead, asshole."

"Fair point." Talon comments. "So, what's going on?"

"We've got a lead," I say, leaning against the kitchen island.

"Well, shit, I'll order pizza. Sounds like we have a lot to talk about, and I'm not doing it on an empty stomach."

Chapter 12

VESPER

I DRIFT in and out of consciousness, my mind a hazy fog of disjointed thoughts and fragmented memories. The sterile white walls of my prison blur together, days and nights blending into an endless stream of nothingness. How long have I been here? Weeks? Months? Years? Time has lost all meaning.

The drugs course through my veins, keeping me docile and compliant. When lucidity briefly returns, I'm aware of my body's betrayal - swollen and tender from the constant hormonal assault. They come for me regularly, faceless figures in masks and scrubs, harvesting the precious eggs my treacherous body produces on command. The prick of needles, and the cold touch of medical instruments have become as familiar as breathing.

At first, I fought. I screamed. I clawed. I bit. But my captors were prepared, always one step ahead. Now, I lie here limply as they prod and poke, too weak and broken to resist. The harvesting process is clinical, devoid of any humanity. I'm nothing more than livestock - a living incubator for the precious genetic material they covet.

In a twisted way, I find a sliver of comfort in this clinical violation. At least they're not forcing themselves on me, using my body for their carnal pleasure. The thought of being sex trafficked, actually passed around like a plaything to anyone with enough cash, makes my skin crawl. This sterile harvesting is a mercy compared to that nightmare.

I cling to the hope that my eggs may never result in a child. It's a cold comfort, but it's all I have. The thought of a baby growing somewhere out there, my flesh and blood, never knowing me - it's almost too much to bear. I imagine tiny fingers and toes, eyes that might mirror my own, a smile I'll never see. The phantom weight of a child I'll never hold pressed on my chest, threatening to crush me.

But then I remind myself: maybe it won't happen. Maybe my eggs will fail to fertilize, or the embryos won't implant. Maybe the pregnancies will end early before a real child can form. It's a terrible thing to wish for, but in this hellish existence, it's the kindest outcome I can imagine.

The drugs pull me under again, and I drift into a haze of half-formed dreams. I see myself in another life, cradling a baby, singing lullabies, and feeling the rush of maternal love. But it fades like smoke, leaving me hollow.

When I surface again, the door creaks open, and I brace myself for the familiar routine. My body tenses instinctively, even as my mind remains foggy from the constant stream of drugs. They wheel in the cart, its metal surface gleaming under the harsh fluorescent lights. The tools clink softly, a symphony of impending pain.

As they prep me for the procedure, I catch sight of a new face among the masked figures. His eyes meet mine for a brief moment, and I see a flicker of...something. Pity? Remorse? It's gone in an instant, replaced by the same clinical detachment as the others. But that fleeting connection lingers in my mind, a tiny spark in the darkness. There is something achingly familiar about the curve of his jaw, the set of his shoulders. I struggle to place him, my drugged mind grasping at wisps of a memory that dance just out of reach.

The lead doctor snaps on latex gloves, the sound making me flinch. "Begin sedation," he orders crisply. A cool rush floods my veins as the anesthesia takes hold. Cold gel on my abdomen, the pressure of the ultrasound wand. I've been through this so many times, I could narrate each step. The needle slides in, and I bite back a whimper. No matter how many times they do this, it never stops hurting.

I fix my gaze on the ceiling, counting the tiles to distract myself from the sensation of my body being invaded once again. One...two...three... The familiar face watches silently from the corner, his expression unreadable behind the surgical mask. Four...five...six...

The procedure seems to stretch on forever, each second an eternity of discomfort and violation. Finally, mercifully, I hear the words I've been waiting for: "We're done. Good yield this time."

As the team packs up their equipment, that new face lingers. He hesitates, as if wanting to say something, but then turns and follows the others out. The door clicks shut, leaving me alone with him - the one I've come to think of as The Shadow Man. His voice is deeper than the others, a rich baritone. He's never been present for a harvest before, always lurking on the periphery of my drugged consciousness.

"It's all over now, Vesper," he says, stepping closer to my bedside.

I blink rapidly, trying to clear the fog from my mind. Is this real? Or just another drug-induced hallucination? I've dreamed of this moment so many times, only to wake up still trapped in this nightmare. My heart leaps into my throat, a surge of hope so powerful it's almost painful. Could it be true? Am I finally free of this nightmare? Or is this the merciful death I've been praying for on my darkest days?

I struggle to focus on him through the haze of drugs, willing my eyes to stay open. "What...what do you mean?" I manage to croak, my voice rough from disuse.

The Shadow Man's eyes crinkle at the corners as if he's

smiling beneath his mask. "You've been quite the golden goose, Vesper. More profitable than we ever dreamed possible." His voice drips with satisfaction, making my stomach churn. "And you didn't even have to spread those pretty legs of yours for our clients. Quite the accomplishment."

I feel bile rising in my throat, choking on the implications of his words. How many of my eggs have they sold? How many children might be out there, pieces of me scattered to the wind? The room spins, and I struggle to stay conscious.

"But all good things must come to an end," he continues, his tone almost regretful. "You've served your purpose here. It's time for you to move on."

My heart pounds erratically hope and terror warring within me. Freedom? Or just a different kind of hell?

"Your new owners," he pauses, savoring the words, "well, let's just say they won't be as...accommodating as we've been."

The room tilts sideways, and I fight to keep my eyes open. New owners. The words echo in my mind, each repetition hammering another nail into the coffin of my hopes. I'm not being freed. I'm being sold.

"What..." I lick my dry lips, struggling to form words through the fog of drugs and fear. "What do you mean, 'new owners'?"

The Shadow Man leans in close, his breath hot against my ear. "Oh, sweet Vesper. Did you think this was the worst it could get? That we were the bottom of the barrel?" He chuckles, the sound sending icy fingers of dread crawling up my spine. "There are always darker depths to plummet, my dear. Always someone willing to push the boundaries further."

Tears burn behind my eyes, but I refuse to let them fall. I won't give him the satisfaction of seeing me break. "Why?" I whisper, the single word encompassing a universe of pain and confusion.

He straightens, adjusting his cuffs with clinical precision. "Business, of course. You've outlived your usefulness here, but there's still profit to be made from that pretty body of yours." His eyes rake over me, and I feel stripped bare despite the thin hospital gown. "Your new owners have...shall we say, more diverse tastes. They'll put you to good use, I'm sure."

The implication hits me like a physical blow. No more sterile harvesting. No more clinical detachment. I'll be used in every way imaginable, my body nothing more than a plaything for the wealthy and depraved. The nightmare I've feared all along is about to become my reality.

"Please," I hear myself beg, hating the weakness in my voice but unable to stop. "Don't do this. Just let me go. I won't tell anyone, I swear."

The Shadow Man's laugh is cold and mirthless. "Oh, Vesper," he purrs, his voice dripping with mock sympathy. "You still don't understand, do you? This isn't about what you want. It never was."

His hand falls to my leg, and I flinch at the contact. His

touch is light, almost gentle, but it makes my skin crawl. Slowly, deliberately, he begins to move his hand up my thigh. My muscles tense, every fiber of my being screaming at me to fight, to run, but the drugs have left me weak and sluggish.

"We've treated you so well here, haven't we?" he continues, his fingers tracing lazy patterns on my skin. "Fed you, kept you clean, made sure you were comfortable. Never forced us on you. Never violated you in that way." His hand slides higher, slipping under the thin fabric of my hospital gown. "I've wanted to, though. Oh, how I've wanted to."

I squeeze my eyes shut, willing this to be another drug-induced nightmare. But his touch is too real, too present. "Stop," I whisper, my voice barely audible.

He ignores me, his hand inching ever higher. "Do you know how much you're worth, Vesper? How many men would pay a fortune just to touch you like this?" His fingers brush against my inner thigh, and I bite back a sob. "You're still pure, untouched. A virgin. Do you have any idea how rare that is in our line of work?"

I feel his breath on my face as he leans in close. "I could take you right now," he murmurs. "No one would stop me. No one would care." His hand stills, resting intimately against me. "But I won't. Do you know why?"

I shake my head mutely, tears leaking from the corners of my eyes.

"Because you're merchandise," he says, his voice hardening. "And I don't damage the goods before delivery." He withdraws his hand abruptly, leaving me feeling dirty and violated despite the lack of further touch.

"Your new owners, though?" He chuckles darkly. "They won't be so restrained. They'll use every inch of you, Vesper. They'll break you in ways you can't even imagine."

A sob escapes me, the sound raw and broken in the sterile room. The Shadow Man steps back, straightening his suit as if nothing had happened.

"Enjoy your last night of peace," he says, moving towards the door. "Tomorrow, your real nightmare begins."

Chapter 13

OSCAR

I ADJUST my tie for the hundredth time as our sleek black SUV pulls up to the nondescript warehouse on the outskirts of Boston. The industrial complex looms before us, its corrugated metal exterior a stark contrast to the luxurious vehicles lining the makeshift parking lot. Zaire catches my eye, a silent conversation passing between us. We're here. It's showtime.

"Remember," I mutter under my breath as we step out onto the gravel, "we're the Blackwood brothers tonight. Talon, you're our cousin, Charles, visiting from London."

Talon nods, his usually carefree demeanor replaced by a

focused intensity. "Got it, Oz. Or should I say, Oliver Blackwood? Can I pick out Alex's name?"

"Someone is staying with the car," Alex fires back. "One of us needs to be ready to get us the fuck out of here if and likely when this thing goes south. Plus, there's no hiding me," he gestures at his towering stature, "in a crowd, even with a ridiculous fake name."

"Aw," Talon whines. "I was going to call you Harry Ballsack."

"Not on your fucking life," Alex warns him.

I suppress a smirk. "Let's hope Ricky's intel and these invitations hold up."

Alex, dressed in a suit, casually pulls our SUV up to the main entrance and hops out to open the car, taking his role as our driver seriously. We watch as he's directed away from the entrance and disappears around the back of the warehouse.

As we approach the entrance, I can't help but marvel at the transformation. What was once a dilapidated warehouse has been converted into a high-end auction house for the night. Velvet ropes and burly security guards funnel guests through a checkpoint, their eyes sharp and hands hovering near concealed weapons.

"Invitations and identification, gentlemen," a guard with a neck as thick as my thigh rumbles.

I produce our forged documents with a steady hand, praying that Ricky's work is as flawless as he claimed. The guard scrutinizes them, his face an unreadable mask. After what feels like an eternity, he nods and waves us through.

"If you plan to bid tonight, please proceed to the registration desk for proof of payment," he adds as we pass through a body scanner.

Inside, the warehouse is a study in contrasts. Industrial beams soar overhead, but the concrete floor is covered in plush oriental rugs. Chandeliers cast a warm glow over clusters of the criminal elite, their designer suits and glittering jewelry at odds with our surroundings.

"I'll handle the registration," Talon murmurs, peeling off towards a discreet desk in the corner.

Zaire's eyes roam the room, cataloging exits, and potential threats. "Heavy hitters are here tonight, Oz," he whispers. "I count at least three family heads and a dozen underbosses."

I nod, my own gaze sweeping the crowd. That's when I see him – Dmitri Petrov, my cousin, holding court near the center of the room. My blood runs cold. If he recognizes us, this entire operation goes up in smoke. A pretty little blonde hangs off his arm, beaming up at him.

"Nine o'clock," I mutter. "Our dear cousin has decided to grace us with his presence."

"Got him," Zaire remarks.

Talon joins us a few seconds later with a bidding paddle in his hand. He spots Dmitri immediately. Talon casually shifts, angling his body to block Dmitri's line of sight. "Well, isn't this a lovely family reunion?" he quips, but I can see the tension in his shoulders.

"Are we registered? I ask him.

"We're cleared to bid, but the buy-in is steep. Whatever this exotic merchandise is, just cost one of your uncle's not so secret off shore accounts a ten million dollar deposit."

I turn to Talon, my eyebrows raised in surprise. "How did you get that information?" I ask, keeping my voice low. The constant murmur of the crowd around us provides some cover, but in a room full of criminals, you can never be too careful.

Talon's eyes sparkle with mischief. "Ask Harry Ballsack," he replies with a wink.

"Ask Al…Harry?" I repeat. "He's supposed to be with the car. What's going on?"

Talon leans in closer, his breath warm against my ear as he speaks. "Our boy Harry has been busy. Remember that fancy new smartwatch he's been showing off? Well, it's not just for counting steps and checking his texts."

I feel a mix of admiration and concern wash over me. Leave it to Alex to find a way to be in two places at once. "Go on," I urge, my curiosity piqued.

"That watch? It's a high-tech piece of equipment," Talon explains, his voice tinged with pride. "It's got a built-in scanner that can pick up and decrypt nearby wireless signals. While Harry was 'parking the car,' he managed to intercept some very interesting financial data being transmitted to and from this place. Knowing Dmitri is here…if we find what we are looking for, our uncle will only assume his precious little heir spent the money. None the wiser, and nothing spent from our coffers."

I take a moment to process this information, my eyes scanning the room once more. The opulence surrounding us suddenly seems even more significant. "So, Harry essentially hacked into their system without even stepping foot inside?"

Talon nods, a grin spreading across his face. "Exactly. He's our eyes and ears on the outside, feeding us real-time intel. And let me tell you, the numbers he's seeing? They're astronomical."

"And he's communicating with you how?"

"That's our little secret," he winks.

"What else has he found out?" I ask, my mind already racing with possibilities.

Talon's expression grows serious. "That's the thing. The amount of money changing hands tonight? It's not just about rare artifacts or illegal goods. Whatever's being auctioned off, it's big. Like, 'change the balance of power in the underworld' big."

I feel a chill run down my spine. This is bigger than we anticipated.

"I don't have a good feeling about this, brother, "Zaire remarks. "We're too exposed, and with Dmitri here, we're sitting ducks."

I take a deep breath, feeling the weight of our mission pressing down on me. The temptation to abort is strong, especially with Dmitri's unexpected presence, but I can't shake the feeling that we're on the cusp of something monumental. The air in the warehouse seems to crackle with anticipation, and I'm not about to walk away now.

"We're staying," I announce quietly, my voice firm despite the knot of anxiety in my stomach.

Zaire's eyebrows furrow, a silent question in his eyes. I can see the concern etched on his face, but he trusts my judgment. Talon, on the other hand, looks almost excited by the prospect of danger.

"Alright, but we need to be smart about this," I continue, my eyes darting around the room. "We're going to spread out. Talon, take the bidding paddle. You arrived at the academy after Dmitri left, so he won't recognize you. Mingle, listen, and for God's sake, try not to draw attention to yourself."

Talon grins, taking the paddle with a flourish. "Me? Draw attention? Never," he quips, but I can see the steel behind his playful demeanor. He understands the gravity of the situation.

"Zaire, I want you near the exits. Keep an eye on the security and catalog any changes in their positions or behaviors. If things go south, we'll need a quick escape route."

My brother nods, his posture already shifting as he slips into surveillance mode. "Got it. What about you?"

"I'll be around."

Zaire nods, his posture shifting subtly as he slips into surveillance mode. He moves away, his steps casual but purposeful, blending seamlessly with the other guests.

Left alone, I take a moment to survey the room. The air is thick with anticipation, hushed conversations, and tinkling glasses, creating a symphony of wealth and power. Crystal chandeliers cast a soft glow over the gathered criminals, their faces a mix of excitement and barely concealed greed.

I make my way towards the bar, strategically positioned to overhear conversations without drawing attention. As I wait for my drink, a martini that I have no intention of actually consuming, I catch snippets of whispered exchanges.

"...heard it could change everything..."

"...worth every penny if it's real..."

"...Victor Petrov himself is interested..."

My ears prick up at the mention of my uncle's name. Whatever's being auctioned tonight, it's clear that Victor wants it badly. And that alone is reason enough for us to interfere.

The bartender slides my drink across the polished surface, and I nod my thanks. As I turn, I nearly collide with a statuesque redhead in a shimmering gown. She stumbles slightly, and I reach out to steady her, my free hand grasping her elbow.

"My apologies," I murmur, slipping easily into the role of Oliver Blackwood, charming and slightly aloof.

She looks up at me through long lashes, a coy smile playing on her crimson lips. The redhead's eyes sparkle with interest as she appraises me. "No harm done," she purrs, her voice a sultry whisper. "I'm Natasha. And you are?"

"Oliver Blackwood," I reply smoothly, angling my body

to shield my face from the crowd. I lean in close as if sharing a secret. "I must say, you've saved me from a terribly dull evening. These events can be so...tedious."

Natasha laughs, a tinkling sound that draws the attention of nearby guests. Perfect. I guide her towards a quieter corner, using her as a living shield against Dmitri's potential gaze.

"Oh, I don't know," she says, trailing a manicured finger down my lapel. "I find there's always excitement to be found if you know where to look."

I arch an eyebrow, playing along. "Is that so? And where might one find such excitement, Ms...?"

"Just Natasha," she interjects, her smile widening. "And as for excitement, well...that depends on what you're into, Mr. Blackwood."

I allow a slow smile to spread across my face, all the while scanning the room over her shoulder. Zaire has positioned himself near a fire exit, casually sipping champagne. Talon is engaged in animated conversation with a group of middle-aged men, no doubt charming them effortlessly.

"I'm interested in many things," I murmur, returning my attention to Natasha. "Art, history, the thrill of acquisition..."

She leans in closer, her perfume enveloping me in a cloud of jasmine and something darker, more exotic. "Then you've come to the right place. I hear tonight's offerings are...unprecedented."

Before I can probe further, a hush falls over the crowd. A

distinguished man in a tailored suit takes the stage, tapping a microphone. "Ladies and gentlemen, if you'll please take your seats. The auction is about to begin."

Natasha's eyes light up. "Duty calls," she says with a wink. "Perhaps we can continue this conversation later, Oliver."

I watch her sashay away, mentally filing away her face and name for future reference. As the crowd settles into their seats, I find a spot near the back, close enough to observe but far from Dmitri's line of sight.

The first item up for bid is a newly discovered Fabergé egg, its enamel surface gleaming under the spotlights. The bidding is fierce, with paddles rising in quick succession. It goes for a cool fifteen million to a portly man with a thick Russian accent.

Next comes a set of Romanov jewels, each gem sparkling with history and bloodshed. I watch as Talon raises his paddle once, twice, before bowing out gracefully. The necklace sells for twenty-three million to a severe-looking woman in the front row.

As the auction progresses, I find my attention waning. Priceless artifacts and illicit goods change hands for astronomical sums, but nothing seems to justify the level of secrecy and excitement surrounding tonight's event. I begin to wonder if Ricky's intel was off, if we've risked everything for nothing more than an elaborate, high-stakes yard sale.

But then, just as I'm considering signaling to Zaire that we should cut our losses, the auctioneer's voice takes on a new timbre of excitement. "Ladies and gentlemen, we now come to the pinnacle of tonight's offerings. I assure you, what you are about to see is truly unprecedented."

The crowd stirs, a palpable wave of anticipation rippling through the room. I straighten in my seat, every nerve on high alert. I lock eyes with Talon, who waits for my signal if it's her.

A hush falls over the room as a woman is led onto the stage. Her hands are clasped in front of her, her face hidden behind a black blindfold. A pair of noise-canceling head-phones covers her ears, effectively cutting her off from her surroundings. She's dressed simply in a white shift dress that falls to her knees, her bare feet padding silently across the stage.

My breath catches in my throat. This isn't an object − it's a person. The realization hits me like a punch to the gut.

The woman in the red dress − Natasha − steps up beside her, a predatory smile on her face. With practiced ease, she begins to manipulate the blindfolded woman's body, posi-tioning her like a living doll. She turns her this way and that, showing off her figure to the salivating crowd.

"As you can see," the auctioneer continues, his voice dripping with false charm, "our offering tonight is in peak physical condition. Young, healthy, proven stock with an impeccable pedigree…and a virgin."

The crowd murmurs excitedly, and I can practically see the dollar signs in their eyes. I feel sick.

I scan the crowd, my stomach churning at the hungry

looks on their faces. My eyes land on Dmitri, and I have to stifle a growl. He's laughing, actually laughing, as he watches the woman on stage. The blonde on his arm joins in, her tinkling laughter a discordant note in the tense atmosphere.

I study the girl on stage, my heart pounding in my chest. Her build is rounder than I remember Vesper's being, curves softened by what looks like a deliberate attempt to fatten her up. The long blonde hair cascading down her back is familiar, but without seeing her face, I can't be certain. I strain my eyes, searching for any identifying mark, any hint that this could be her.

The bidding starts at an obscene amount, paddles shooting up across the room. I catch Talon's eye, and he raises an eyebrow, waiting for my signal. But I hesitate, uncertainty gnawing at me. What if I'm wrong? What if this isn't Vesper at all, but some other poor soul caught in this nightmare?

"Five million," a voice calls out, breaking through my reverie.

"Ten million," counters another.

As the bids climb higher and higher, I notice a change in the woman in red - Natasha. Her smile grows wider, more predatory, as she slinks around the blindfolded woman. There's a gleam in her eye that sets my teeth on edge.

"Twenty-five million," someone shouts, and a ripple of excited murmurs sweeps through the crowd.

"Come now, gentlemen," Natasha purrs into a microphone, her voice a silky caress. "Surely you can do better than that? After all, we're not just selling a pretty face here. What we're offering tonight is power. The kind of power that comes with a name. A name that carries weight in our world. A name that opens doors and topples empires."

The crowd murmurs, intrigued. Natasha's grin widens. My blood runs cold. There's only one woman whose name could hold that much sway in our world.

"That's right," Natasha says, reveling in the crowd's growing excitement. "This is none other than Vesper Rossi, the jewel of the Rossi crime family."

The room erupts into chaos. Bids fly fast and furious, the amount skyrocketing to unimaginable heights. I see Dmitri lean forward, his eyes burning with a mixture of lust and greed that makes me want to tear him apart with my bare hands. But I can't move. I'm frozen in place, my eyes locked on Vesper. Now that I know it's her, I can't look away.

She's alive. She's really fucking alive.

Zaire materializes at my side, his voice low and urgent.

My heart pounds in my chest as I watch the bidding war unfold. The room spins around me, a dizzying blur of greed and depravity. I feel Zaire's presence beside me, solid and reassuring, but it does little to quell the storm raging inside me.

"Oz," Zaire whispers urgently, his breath hot against my ear. "We need to move. Now."

I nod, my eyes never leaving Vesper's form on the stage. She stands there, blind and deaf to the world around her, unaware that her fate is being decided by the highest bidder.

The sight of her, vulnerable and exposed, ignites a fire in my chest that threatens to consume me.

"Fifty million!" Talon's voice rings out, clear and confident. The crowd gasps, heads turning to locate the source of such an outrageous bid.

I see Dmitri's eyes narrow, his gaze sweeping the room. It's only a matter of time before he spots us. We need to act fast.

"Z," I murmur, my voice barely audible over the commotion. "Get to Alex. Tell him to be ready. We're going to need a quick exit."

Zaire nods, melting into the crowd with practiced ease. I start to make my way towards the exit, but I stop. I can't leave her. Not again. I turn, watching the bidding war continue.

"Sixty million!" Another voice calls out, and I recognize the thick Russian accent as one of Victor's associates.

Talon counters immediately. "Seventy million!"

The air in the room grows thick with tension, the excitement palpable. I can see the greed glittering in Natasha's eyes as she stands next to Vesper, her hand possessively placed on the small of her back.

I watch, my heart pounding, as the bidding war rages on. The numbers climb higher and higher, each new bid eliciting gasps and murmurs from the crowd. But amidst the frenzy, one thing stands out to me like a beacon in the night: Dmitri isn't bidding. Not one single bid.

My cousin, the man who's supposed to marry Vesper,

sits there with a smug smile on his face, whispering occasionally to the blonde on his arm. It's as if he knows something we don't, and that realization sends a chill down my spine.

Talon, however, is in his element. He stands tall, his face a mask of calm determination as he squares off against two representatives from other European families. I recognize them vaguely - one from the Moretti clan of Italy, the other from the Durand family in France. They were also in the running for the marriage alliance with the Rossis, and now they're fighting tooth and nail for Vesper.

"One hundred and fifty million," the Moretti man calls out, his voice strained with the effort of maintaining composure.

"One seventy-five," counters the Frenchman, sweat beading on his brow.

Talon doesn't miss a beat. "Two hundred million," he announces, his voice ringing clear through the warehouse.

The room falls silent for a moment, the sheer magnitude of the bid sinking in. I can see the other bidders wavering, their resolve crumbling in the face of such astronomical sums.

But then, just as I think it's over, the Italian finds his second wind. "Two twenty-five," he croaks out.

Talon's eyes flash, and I can almost see the wheels turning in his head. He takes a deep breath, and I hold mine, waiting.

"Two hundred and fifty million dollars," Talon declares, his voice steady and sure.

The silence that follows is deafening. The auctioneer looks around the room, his gavel poised in the air. "Two hundred and fifty million going once...twice..."

I dare to hope, my eyes fixed on Vesper's still form on the stage. She hasn't moved throughout this entire ordeal, unaware that her fate hangs in the balance.

"Sold!" The gavel comes down with a resounding crack that seems to echo through my very bones.

Chaos erupts. Two burly men in black suits rush towards Talon, ushering him behind the stage. I watch him go, my heart in my throat. This is it. We've done it.

I feel a hand on my arm and turn to see Zaire. His face is grim, but there's a glimmer of triumph in his eyes. "Time to go," he says, pulling me towards the exit.

Chapter 14

TALON

THE TWO BURLY men usher me backstage, their grip on my arms unnecessarily tight. My heart races, not from fear, but from the adrenaline coursing through my veins. I just bid 250 million dollars on a woman I barely knew, and now I am being led like a prized bull to the slaughter.

As we round the corner, I catch sight of the woman in the striking red dress who had been orchestrating this whole twisted affair on stage. She stands there, cool as ice, her perfectly manicured nails tapping away at a tablet. Not a hint of emotion crosses her face as she looks up at me, as if selling human beings is just another day at the office for her.

"Congratulations on your...acquisition...Mr.?" she purrs, her accent thick, but one I cannot place.

"Blackwood. Charles Blackwood." The casual way she refers to Vesper as a "purchase" makes my skin crawl, but I force myself to remain composed. I'm deep in the lion's den now, and one wrong move could jeopardize everything. Instead, I plaster on my most charming smile, the one that had gotten me out of more than a few sticky situations. "I don't think we've been properly introduced, Miss?"

"Natasha," she purrs. The way she says her name sends prickles of dread through my body.

"I'm eager to finalize this transaction and be on my way."

She raises a perfectly arched eyebrow. "Patience, Mr. Blackwood. We must ensure the payment clears and all the necessary paperwork is in order before we can release your purchase to you."

My eyes dart around the cramped backstage area, searching for any sign of Vesper. But she is nowhere to be seen. The knot in my stomach tightens. Where had they taken her?

"I understand," I say, keeping my voice level despite the growing unease. "But I'd like to inspect my purchase now if you don't mind. Make sure she's as pristine as you claim. You know how fluorescent lighting can distort certain.. damages."

Natasha's lips curve into a cold smile. "All in due time,

Mr. Blackwood. For now, if you'll follow me, we have some forms for you to sign."

As she leads me towards a makeshift office, I can't help but marvel at the surreal nature of it all. Here I am about to sign papers as if I were buying a car or a house, not a human being. The absurdity of it all would be laughable if it weren't so damn terrifying.

Natasha's demeanor doesn't change as she slides the documents towards me. There's not even a flicker of emotion in her eyes as she points out where to sign. It's clear that for her, this is just another transaction, no different from selling a piece of jewelry or a rare painting.

"The payment is being processed as we speak," one of the guards informs us, his voice a low rumble. I force myself not to outwardly sigh in relief. Of all the accounts for Alex to skim, we'd gotten lucky it was one of Victor's. The bastard had way too much money, but in this situation, it worked out in our favor.

I scan the documents before me, trying to absorb every detail without appearing too interested. The legalese is dense, filled with terms like "transfer of ownership". There is a page of medical records as well.

"As you can see on her medical records, she has been given a long-lasting contraception injection prior to her sale. There is also a certified letter from her owner's physician outlining her physical evaluation at the time of sale." Natasha points to a line toward the top of the page that reads "confirmed intact hymen."

"I'll need you to sign here to accept your purchase as stated on the medical record."

My stomach churns as I force myself to sign page after page, each signature feeling like a betrayal to everything I believe in, but at least, the name on her ownership papers isn't my real name. That, I can live with.

As I flip through the stack, a name catches my eye: Johan Mikeal. I commit it to memory, along with a few others that stand out - names of shell companies and offshore accounts. Every bit of information could be crucial later.

Just as I'm about to sign the final page, a small addendum at the bottom catches my attention. "What's this?" I ask, tapping the paper with my index finger, trying to keep my tone casual.

Natasha leans over, her perfume - something expensive and cloying - invading my senses. "Ah, yes. That is a special breeding clause," she explains, her voice devoid of any emotion. "Miss Rossi's previous owners wish to maintain rights to her harvested eggs, and any living offspring she may produce."

The words hit me like a punch to the gut. I struggle to keep my face neutral, even as rage boils beneath the surface. "Breeding clause?" I repeat, fighting to keep my voice steady. "I wasn't aware this was part of the deal."

Natasha's lips curl into a cold smile. "It's a standard procedure for acquisitions of Miss Rossi's caliber. Her genetic makeup is quite valuable, you see. The clause ensures that her previous owners retain rights to any potential future progeny."

The longer she talks, the sicker it makes me feel. I knew that shit like this happened in our world, but seeing it first hand is another beast all together. The casual way she discusses Vesper's reproductive rights as if she were nothing more than a prized mare, makes me want to flip the table and burn this whole place to the ground. But I can't. Not yet. Not if I want to get Vesper out of here safely.

"I see," I manage, swallowing hard. "And what exactly does this entail for me, as her new...owner?"

"Oh, it's quite simple," Natasha replies, her manicured nails tapping against the document. "Should Miss Rossi become pregnant during your ownership, you would be required to notify her previous owners. They would then have first rights to any resulting children." Jesus fucking Christ. It's as if I am buying a heifer for breeding stock.

My mind reels at the implications. This isn't just about Vesper anymore. It's about potential innocent lives, treated as nothing more than commodities before they're even conceived.

"And if I refuse to agree to this clause?" I ask, testing the waters.

Natasha's eyes harden, the first real emotion I've seen from her. "Then I'm afraid we cannot proceed with the sale. The breeding clause is non-negotiable."

I nod slowly, pretending to consider my options. In reality, I know I have no choice. If I want to get Vesper out of here, I have to play along, no matter how much it sickens me. With a heavy heart and a forced smile, I nod. "Very well. I understand."

I sign the final page, my signature feeling like a death sentence. The weight of what I've just agreed to settles on my shoulders like a lead blanket. But I can't dwell on it now. I have to stay focused.

"Excellent," Natasha purrs, gathering the documents with practiced efficiency. "Now, let's confirm the transfer of funds, shall we?"

We wait in tense silence as one of the guards makes a phone call. The minutes stretch like hours, each tick of the clock echoing in my ears. Finally, the guard nods, his face impassive.

"The funds have cleared, ma'am," he announces.

Relief floods through me, but I keep my expression neutral. "Wonderful," I say, infusing my voice with just the right amount of enthusiasm. "Now, if you don't mind, I'd like to see my purchase."

Natasha's lips curl into a cold smile. "Of course, Mr. Blackwood. Right this way."

She leads me down a narrow corridor, the click of her heels on the concrete floor echoing ominously. We stop in front of a nondescript door, and Natasha produces a key card, swiping it with practiced ease.

The door swings open, and my breath catches in my throat. There, in the center of the room, sits Vesper. She's perched on a simple metal chair, her posture rigid and uncomfortable. A black blindfold covers her eyes, and I can see the outline of bulky headphones beneath her cascade of blonde hair.

I want nothing more than to rush to her side, to rip away the blindfold and headphones, to tell her that everything will be okay. But I can't. Not with Natasha's piercing gaze boring into my back.

"Well?" Natasha prompts, her voice laced with amusement. "Aren't you going to inspect your purchase?"

I swallow hard, forcing myself to approach Vesper with calculated nonchalance. I circle her slowly, taking in every detail. The curve of her neck, the slight tremor in her hands, the way her chest rises and falls with each measured breath. She's scared, I realize, but she's doing her damnedest not to show it.

"She's exactly as advertised," I manage, keeping my voice level. "I'm pleased."

Natasha nods, a satisfied smirk playing at the corners of her mouth. "Excellent. Now, Mr. Blackwood, would you like her gift-wrapped for the journey home?"

I blink, caught off guard by the question. "Gift-wrapped?" I repeat, unsure of what she means.

"Yes, it's a service we offer for long-distance transport," Natasha declares. "I find that it makes traveling together a bit easier."

I hesitate for a moment, unsure of what "gift-wrapped" could possibly mean in this context. But I can't risk showing any hesitation or confusion. I need to maintain my facade as a seasoned buyer in this twisted world.

"Yes, of course," I reply smoothly, forcing a smile. "Gift-wrapped would be perfect."

Natasha's eyes gleam with a cold satisfaction that sends a chill down my spine. She snaps her fingers, and one of the guards hands her a small case. My heart races as she opens it, revealing a syringe filled with a clear liquid.

"What's that?" I ask, trying to keep my voice steady.

"Just a little something to make the journey more comfortable," Natasha explains, approaching Vesper with practiced ease. "It's perfectly safe, I assure you. She'll be out for about six hours - plenty of time for you to get her settled and on your way home. We can provide you with an extra dose if your journey is a bit longer. "

Before I can protest, Natasha swiftly injects the contents of the syringe into Vesper's neck. I watch in horror as Vesper's body goes limp almost instantly, her head lolling to the side.

"There we are," Natasha says, stepping back. "All wrapped up and ready to go."

I clench my fists at my sides, fighting the urge to lash out. The casual way they're treating Vesper, as if she's nothing more than a package to be shipped, makes my blood boil. But I force myself to remain calm, to play the part of the satisfied customer.

"Excellent," I manage, my voice tight. "Is there anything else?"

Natasha tilts her head, considering. "We do recommend having a tracker placed before leaving. Just as a precaution, you understand. Some of our clients find it helpful."

I shake my head firmly. "That won't be necessary. My team will handle any tracking once we're in the car."

Natasha raises an eyebrow but doesn't push the issue. "As you wish, Mr. Blackwood. Now, shall we get your purchase ready for transport?"

I watch, my stomach churning, as two guards lift Vesper's unconscious form from the chair. They handle her with an unsettling efficiency, securing her wrists and ankles with padded restraints before wrapping her in a thick, dark blanket.

"Standard procedure," Natasha explains, noticing my gaze. "It ensures a smooth transition from our care to yours."

I nod, not trusting myself to speak. Seeing Vesper like this would have kill Oscar. I know how badly he wanted to be the one to do this, but it's better this way. I barely know her and seeing her bound and drugged is nearly too much for me to bear. Oz wouldn't have lasted two seconds without blowing our cover.

"Your driver is waiting at the rear entrance," Natasha informs me, leading the way as the guards carry Vesper. "I trust you'll find everything to your satisfaction."

As soon as the cold night air hits my lungs, I see Alex standing by the SUV we'd arrived in with the back driver's side door open. The guard places Vesper's limp body inside before stepping back and allowing Alex to close the door behind her. He shifts to the other side of the car, waiting for me to join her.

"Thank you again for your purchase, Mr. Blackwood," Natasha purrs, her cold smile never quite reaching her eyes. "If you find yourself unsatisfied in any way, please don't hesitate to let me know. I assure you, resale will be no issue at all."

The casual way she talks about reselling Vesper as if she were nothing more than a defective appliance, makes bile rise in my throat. I swallow hard, forcing a smile that feels more like a grimace. "I'm sure that won't be necessary, but I appreciate the offer."

With a final nod to Natasha, I round the back of the SUV and climb into the back passenger side, my heart pounding so loudly I'm sure everyone can hear it. The leather seat creaks beneath me as I settle in next to Vesper's still form. She looks so vulnerable wrapped in that dark blanket, her face partially obscured by her blonde hair. I resist the urge to reach out and brush it away, to check if she's breathing. I can't show any concern, not yet. Not until we're safely away.

I wait for Alex to slide into the driver's seat.

"Get us the fuck out of here," I quietly order him. He pulls away from the curb nonchalantly and waits until we're a few miles down the road to speed up.

Vesper stirs slightly beside me, a small moan escaping

her lips. Without thinking, I reach out to steady her, my hand hovering just above her shoulder.

"How long until we reach the safe house?" I ask Alex, my voice tight with tension.

"Twenty minutes, maybe thirty if we need to take a more circuitous route," he replies, his eyes never leaving the road.

"Where's Oz and Zaire?"

"They found their own ride. They'll meet us there."

The car takes a sharp turn, and Vesper's body shifts against mine. Even unconscious, there's a tension in her frame, as if some part of her is still fighting, still aware of the danger. I adjust the blanket around her shoulders.

I watch Vesper's chest rise and fall with each shallow breath, my own heart racing in tandem. The streetlights cast fleeting shadows across her face as we speed through the night, each mile taking us further from that hellish auction house. Her blonde hair looks dull in the dim light of the car's interior. I resist the urge to smooth it back from her forehead, to offer some small comfort even in her drug-induced sleep.

Alex weaves through traffic, his knuckles white on the steering wheel. I count the minutes, each one feeling like an eternity. Fifteen minutes. Twenty. Twenty-five. Finally, we turn onto a quiet suburban street, the houses dark and silent at this late hour.

As we pull into the driveway of a nondescript two-story beach house, I spot Zaire's imposing figure waiting on the front porch. His face is a mask of concern and barely contained rage as he strides towards the car.

"How is she?" he asks as soon as I open the door, his voice a low growl.

"Unconscious," I reply, my throat tight. "They drugged her before we left. Some kind of sedative."

Zaire's eyes flash dangerously. "Those bastards," he mutters, then turns to Alex. "Oz called in a favor. There's a doctor waiting inside."

"How'd he get a doctor here at this time of night in the middle of fucking nowhere?"

"She owes us a favor. Her daughter was the one who was attempting to extort that politician's son."

I nod, relief washing over me. "Good thinking. Alex, can you sweep her for trackers before we take her in? I wouldn't put it past those fuckers to have planted something on her."

Alex nods grimly, producing a small device from his pocket. He runs it carefully over Vesper's still form, paying extra attention to her neck and the backs of her ears. After a tense minute, he shakes his head. "She's clean. No trackers."

"Thank fuck," I breathe, then turn to Zaire. "Can you carry her in? I don't trust myself right now."

Zaire doesn't hesitate. With gentle hands that belie his imposing stature, he lifts Vesper from the car, cradling her against his broad chest. Her head lolls against his shoulder, and a strand of her blonde hair catches on the scar on his neck. The sight makes my chest ache.

We make our way into the house. The doctor, a middle-aged woman with kind eyes and a no-nonsense demeanor is waiting for us in a bedroom that's been hastily converted into a makeshift exam room.

"Put her on the bed," she instructs Zaire, already moving to check Vesper's vitals. Zaire lays Vesper down with utmost care, removing the restraints binding her. His hands linger for a moment before he steps back. Oz stands in the corner of the room, his gaze unwavering. His face is dangerously unreadable.

I watch anxiously as the doctor examines Vesper, her movements precise and practiced. She gently lifts Vesper's eyelids, shining a small penlight into each eye. "Pupils are equal and reactive," she murmurs, more to herself than to us. "That's a good sign."

The doctor's hands move efficiently, checking Vesper's pulse, her breathing, and even her skin tone. I find myself holding my breath as if my own stillness could somehow contribute to Vesper's well-being. The room is thick with tension, broken only by the soft rustle of the doctor's movements and the steady beep of a portable heart monitor she's attached to Vesper's finger.

"I'm going to draw some blood," the doctor announces, reaching for her bag. "We'll need to run some tests to make sure there are no unexpected complications from whatever they gave her."

I wince as the needle pierces Vesper's skin, a drop of crimson welling up before the vial begins to fill. The sight of her blood makes this all feel more terrifyingly real. What have we gotten ourselves into?

"Her pulse is strong," the doctor says, her voice calm and reassuring. "But she's slightly dehydrated. I'd recommend starting an IV if you have the supplies."

Oz nods silently, his eyes never leaving Vesper's face. He moves to a cabinet in the corner, retrieving an IV bag and tubing.

As the doctor sets up the IV, I can't help but marvel at Vesper's strength. Even unconscious, there's a resilience about her that's palpable. Her chest rises and falls in a steady rhythm, her face peaceful despite the ordeal she's been through. I find myself studying the curve of her jaw, the sweep of her eyelashes against her cheeks, committing every detail to memory.

"Without more advanced diagnostic equipment, there's not much more I can do right now," the doctor says, stepping back from the bed. "She seems stable, but I'd strongly recommend bringing her into my office tomorrow for a full workup. We need to know exactly what they gave her and what long-term effects it might have."

I nod, my throat tight. "Of course. Whatever she needs."

The doctor turns to Oz, her expression serious. "I'll call you as soon as I have the blood test results. In the meantime, keep her hydrated and monitor her breathing. If anything changes, anything at all - call me immediately."

As the doctor leaves, Alex and Zaire follow her out, their hushed voices fading down the hallway. I linger for a moment, my eyes fixed on Vesper's still form. Oz remains rooted to his spot, his gaze never wavering from her face.

I feel a strange mix of relief and tension coursing through my veins. We got her out, but at what cost? The memory of signing those papers, of agreeing to that horrific breeding clause, makes my stomach churn. I run a hand through my hair, exhaling slowly.

"I'll take the first watch," Oz says quietly, his voice breaking the silence. He moves to sit in the chair beside the bed, his movements careful and controlled.

I nod, knowing there's no point in arguing.

"Call me if anything changes," I say, my voice sounding hoarse even to my own ears.

Oz nods, his eyes still fixed on Vesper like she'll disappear again right in front of him again.

Chapter 15

VESPER

I'M FLOATING, drifting through a haze of colors and shadows. The drugs coursing through my veins paint vivid pictures in my mind, beautiful and terrifying all at once. One moment, I'm soaring above the glittering skyline of Boston, my blonde hair whipping in the wind, feeling invincible. The next, I'm plummeting into darkness, icy fingers of fear clawing at my chest.

The nightmares come in flashes, memories distorted by the chemicals. I see my father's cold eyes as he tells me of my fate and hear the cruel laughter of the Petrov men as they discuss their plans for me. My wrists burn where rough hands grabbed me, and I can still taste the metallic tang of blood in my mouth from biting my lip to keep from screaming.

As the drug-induced visions swirl around me, a new horror takes shape. I see myself, a shadow of who I once was, trailing behind Dmitri Petrov like a broken doll. My eyes are vacant, my spirit crushed. I watch helplessly as this future version of myself endures unspeakable acts, each one chipping away at my soul until there's nothing left but an empty shell. It changes, flipping to The Shadow Man. The way his hands felt on my legs. His threats. Then, it shifts again, to a white room where I am lying on a hospital bed, legs spread and chained to stirrups, as they steal piece after piece of my body from me until I vanish into nothingness.

Slowly, agonizingly, the fog begins to lift. My senses return one by one, each bringing a new realization. The soft sheets beneath me are unfamiliar, the air heavy with the scent of sandalwood and something darker, more primal. My eyes flutter open, struggling to focus in the dimly lit room. The realization hits me like a punch to the gut.

I've been delivered to my new owner like a package, and now I'm here to be unwrapped and used as he sees fit. My heart races as I try to take in my surroundings, my limbs still heavy and uncooperative.

That's when I see him. A figure standing in the shadowy corner of the room, watching me. I can't make out his features in the low light, but I can feel his eyes on me, watching, assessing. Terror grips me, stealing the breath from my lungs. I want to run, to fight, to scream, but my body won't cooperate. I'm trapped here, helpless, at the mercy of whoever this man might be and whatever he intends to do with me.

I squeeze my eyes shut, willing this to be another drug-induced nightmare. But when I open them again, he's still there. Silent. Watchful. Waiting.

My mind races, searching for a way out of this nightmare. But deep down, I know the truth. There is no escape. This is my new reality, and I have no choice but to face it head-on. Whatever comes next, I'll have to find a way to survive it. To keep my spirit intact, even as fractured as it is.

My mouth is dry, my voice barely a whisper as I croak out, "Who are you? What do you want with me?"

The man takes a step forward, and I instinctively shrink back against the headboard, my body trembling. He stops, holding up his hands in what might be a placating gesture, but I'm too scared to trust it.

"Easy, Vesper," he says, his voice low and surprisingly gentle. "You're safe here. We're not going to hurt you."

We? My eyes dart around the room, searching for other hidden threats. The man seems to sense my panic and takes a small step back.

"I'm the only one in here," he assures me. "The others are outside." He steps closer. Too close. Close enough that I can see him better. He's tall, broad-shouldered. But there's something in his voice, a familiar cadence that tugs at the edges of my memory.

I shake my head violently, pressing myself further

against the headboard. The cool wood digs into my back, grounding me in this terrifying reality. "No, please," I whimper. "Don't come any closer. Don't touch me."

My eyes dart around the room, searching for an escape route, a weapon, anything. The room is sparsely furnished. Only the bed I'm on, a nightstand, and a chair in the corner make up the room. The curtains are drawn, blocking out any hint of the world beyond. I feel like I'm suffocating, trapped in this unfamiliar space with this unknown man.

"Please," I beg, my voice cracking. "Just let me go. I won't tell anyone, I swear. Just please don't hurt me."

The man stops his approach, his hands still raised in that placating gesture. "Vesper, listen to me," he says, his voice steady and calm. "You're not a prisoner here. Look."

He gestures towards my hands and feet, and for the first time, I realize I'm not bound. There are no ropes, no handcuffs, nothing holding me in place except my own fear. I flex my fingers experimentally, half expecting to feel the bite of restraints.

"The door isn't locked either," he continues, nodding towards the exit. "You could walk out right now if you wanted to. But I can't let you leave until I know you're okay."

I stare at him, disbelief warring with hope in my chest. Could it be true? Am I really free to go?

"I don't understand," I murmur, my eyes flicking between the man and the door. "Who are you? Why are you helping me?"

He takes a deep breath, then slowly moves to sit in the chair, putting more distance between us. I feel some of the tension leave my body at this small act of consideration.

"My name is Oscar," he says softly. "You know me."

"No," I whisper, shaking my head violently. "No, you're lying. This is a trick."

"We aren't trying to trick you."

My mind whirls, trying to process Oscar's words. Friends? Outside? I strain my ears, listening for any sound beyond the room, but all I can hear is silence, and the pounding of my own heart. The silence is oppressive, making me feel just as I had with The Shadow Man. "I don't believe you." I think back to The Shadow Man's words. New owners. The horrible, unspeakable things he thought they'd do to my body. "You want to hurt me...like The Shadow Man did."

Oscar's face contorts, a mix of emotions flashing across his features. His jaw clenches, and I see a muscle twitch in his cheek. His eyes, those piercing blue eyes, darken with what I can only describe as barely contained rage.

"The Shadow Man?" he growls, his voice low and dangerous. "Did he...did he hurt you, Vesper?"

I flinch at the intensity in his tone, shrinking back against the headboard. My heart races, and I can feel the panic rising in my chest. I squeeze my eyes shut, trying to block out the memories that threaten to overwhelm me.

"Hey, hey," Oscar's voice softens immediately. When I open my eyes, I see him leaning forward, his hands outstretched but not touching me. "I'm sorry, I didn't mean to scare you. You're safe here, I promise. The Shadow Man can't hurt you anymore."

I want to believe him. God, how I want to believe him. But my fear is too deep, the memories too fresh. I shake my head, wrapping my arms around myself.

"You don't understand," I whisper. "No one can protect me. They'll always find me."

Oscar leans back, giving me space. His eyes never leave mine as he speaks, his voice steady and calm. "Vesper, listen to me. We found you. We got you out. The Shadow Man, the Petrovs, none of them can reach you here. We've made sure of it. Even the doctor said…" he trails off.

The word 'doctor' sends a jolt of panic through me. Suddenly, I'm back in that sterile white room, strapped to a table as faceless figures in white coats loom over me. "No," I gasp, my hands flying to my stomach. "No, no, no. They took them from me again. They took my babies!"

Oscar's brow furrows in confusion. "Babies? Vesper, what are you talking about?"

"My babies," I sob, curling in on myself. "They keep taking them. Every time I close my eyes, they're there with their needles and their knives, and they take my babies away."

The room spins around me, reality blurring with the nightmares that have haunted me for so long. I can smell the antiseptic and feel the cold metal of the stirrups against my skin. My hands clutch at my stomach, desperately searching for the life I know should be there but isn't. The loss is a gaping wound, raw and bleeding, and I can't stop the keening wail that escapes my lips.

Oscar's face swims before me, his blue eyes wide with concern and confusion. He's saying something, but I can't hear him over the roaring in my ears. All I can focus on is the phantom pain in my abdomen, the emptiness where my children should be.

"Please," I beg, my words tumbling out in a frantic rush. "Please don't let them take them again. I can't...I can't lose them again. They are mine, they're all I have left!"

I'm spiraling, lost in a maze of terror and grief. Oscar reaches out, trying to comfort me, but his touch sends me reeling. I lash out, my nails raking across his arm as I scramble away. My back hits the headboard with a thud, but I barely feel it. All I can see are the faceless doctors, their hands reaching for me, ready to tear away the last shreds of my humanity.

"No!" I scream, my voice raw and broken. "Stay away from me! Don't touch me!"

Panic rises like bile in my throat as I back away from Oscar, his soothing words a low growl in my ears, but I don't understand them. The walls of the room seem to be closing in on me, pulsing with my frantic heartbeat as my mind reels with unspeakable terrors.

But then, the door opens, and a figure emerges. My heart races at the sight of someone new, both familiar and terrifying in my state of desperation. In his hand, something glints in the dim light – a syringe. The mere sight of it sends me into a frenzy.

"Get away from me!" I scream, throwing myself off the bed with wild abandon. My legs are weak and unsteady, causing me to crash to the floor in a heap of blankets and limbs. "No more drugs! Please!"

I claw at the ground, trying to crawl away but my body betrays me. The new man moves with lightning speed, before I can react, and I feel the sharp sting of the needle piercing my skin.

"No," I whimper, my struggles growing weaker as the drug takes hold. "Please...not my babies..."

I fight against the haze that threatens to overtake me, struggling to hold onto consciousness but it's like trying to grasp smoke. My limbs grow heavy, and my thoughts become sluggish. In the blurry space between wakefulness and unconsciousness, I hear bits and pieces of their heated conversation.

"...didn't have to do that!"

"She was out of control..."

"We were making progress..."

"She was hurting herself..."

As my vision blurs and my eyelids droop heavily, I catch a glimpse of a tattoo, a phoenix rising from ashes. It's both beautiful and haunting, a symbol of rebirth that comes at a steep price. The image sears itself into my mind as I slip away into drug-induced oblivion, a final anchor to reality before I am consumed by darkness.

Chapter 16

ZAIRE

I BARELY HAVE time to register what is happening before Oscar's iron grip clamps around my bicep, yanking me out of Vesper's room with such force I nearly stumble. The door slams shut behind us, the sound echoing through the empty hallway like a gunshot.

"What the fuck is wrong with you?" Oscar hisses, his blue eyes blazing with a fury I've rarely seen directed at me. His fingers dig into my arm, sure to leave bruises, but I don't flinch. I've endured far worse.

I jerk my arm free, squaring my shoulders as I face my twin. "I did what was necessary."

"Necessary?" He barks out a harsh laugh. "You drugged

her. Again. You're no better than the bastards who took her in the first place!"

His words hit me like a physical blow, and I recoil. "How dare you—"

"How dare I?" Oscar's voice rises, his carefully controlled facade cracking. "How dare you! I told you to stay outside. To let me handle it."

"You call her screaming about missing babies handling it, Oz?"

"I had it under control."

"Didn't seem that way to me," I fire back.

Oscar's jaw clenches, a muscle ticking beneath his skin. I can see the storm brewing in his eyes, the tension coiling in his shoulders. But I'm not backing down. Not this time.

"You're not seeing the truth of the situation, Oz," I spit out, my voice low and harsh. "Whoever had her? They didn't just break her body. They shattered her mind."

The hallway seems to shrink around us, the air thick with unspoken accusations and simmering rage. I can hear my heart pounding in my ears and feel the adrenaline coursing through my veins.

"She's better off a ghost," I continue. "A memory. Not this empty shell of her, screaming about babies that don't exist."

The moment the words leave my mouth, I know I've crossed a line. Oscar's eyes widen, then narrow dangerously. In an instant, his carefully controlled facade shatters completely.

"You son of a bitch," he growls, and then his fist connects with my jaw.

Pain explodes across my face, but I don't stagger. Instead, I let the familiar rush of violence wash over me, welcoming it like an old friend. I lunge forward, tackling Oscar to the ground. We hit the floor hard, the impact jarring my bones.

Fists fly in a flurry of movement. I catch him with an elbow to the ribs and hear the satisfying whoosh of air leaving his lungs. But Oz gives as good as he gets, his knuckles splitting my lip, the taste of copper flooding my mouth.

We roll across the floor, a tangle of limbs and fury. Picture frames rattle on the walls, a vase topples and shatters to the ground. In the back of my mind, I know we're making too much noise, and that someone will come to investigate. But I can't bring myself to care.

"You don't get to decide that!" Oscar roars, pinning me to the ground. His eyes are wild, his perfectly styled hair a mess. "You don't get to write her off like that!"

I buck my hips, throwing him off balance, and reverse our positions. My hands find his throat, not squeezing, just holding. A warning.

"And you don't get to play hero," I snarl back. "Open your eyes, Oz!" I shout, pinning him there. "This isn't a fairy tale. There's no happily ever after here. The sooner you accept that, the better off we'll all be."

For a moment, we're frozen like that, chests heaving,

blood dripping onto the carpet beneath us. The air crackles with tension, with unspoken words and shared history.

Then, from behind the closed door, we hear a muffled whimper. Vesper's voice, small and frightened, calling out for help that isn't coming.

The fight drains out of me in an instant. I release Oscar's throat, rolling off him and onto my back. I stare at the ceiling, my chest heaving as I try to catch my breath. The taste of blood lingers on my tongue, and I can feel a bruise blooming on my jaw where Oscar's fist connected. The silence stretches between us, thick and heavy, broken only by the soft sounds of our labored breathing and Vesper's muffled whimpers from behind the closed door.

Suddenly, footsteps echo down the hallway, growing louder with each passing second. I turn my head, wincing at the movement, to see Alex and Talon rounding the corner. They stop short at the sight of us sprawled on the floor, surrounded by the debris of our fight.

Talon's eyebrows shoot up, his lips quirking into a sardonic smile. "Having a nice chat, are we?" he drawls, his British accent more pronounced than usual.

I grunt in response, pushing myself up to a sitting position. Oscar follows suit, his movements stiff and pained. The fury in his eyes has dimmed, replaced by a weariness that makes him look older than his years.

"Zaire drugged her," Oscar says, his voice hoarse. "Again."

Talon's smile fades, his expression growing serious. He

runs a hand through his shaggy brown hair, loosening it from its man bun. "I see," he says, his tone carefully neutral.

I brace myself for another lecture, another round of accusations. But to my surprise, Talon doesn't immediately condemn my actions. Instead, he sighs heavily, leaning against the wall.

"Look," he says, his eyes darting between Oscar and me. "I'm not saying I agree with what Zaire did, but she's been through a lot. She needs time."

Oscar opens his mouth to argue, but Alex cuts him off with a sharp gesture. "We need to discuss this," he says, his voice low and urgent. "All of us. But not here in the hallway."

As if on cue, another whimper filters through the door. I see Oscar flinch, his hands clenching into fists at his sides.

"What about the babies she keeps mentioning?" I ask, unable to keep the frustration from my voice. "Are we just going to ignore that?"

A heavy silence falls over the group. Talon and Alex exchange a loaded glance, and I feel my stomach drop. There's something they're not telling us.

Finally, Talon speaks, his voice low. "It's not entirely in her head," he admits.

Oscar's head snaps up, his eyes wide with disbelief. "What are you talking about?"

Talon's words hang in the air, heavy and ominous. I feel my blood run cold, a chill creeping up my spine despite the sweat still cooling on my skin from the fight. Oscar and I exchange a glance, momentarily united in our confusion and growing dread.

"Explain," I demand, my voice rough with emotion. "Now."

Talon runs a hand over his face, his usual easy-going demeanor replaced by a grim seriousness that sets my teeth on edge. He takes a deep breath as if steeling himself for what's to come.

"When they took Vesper, it wasn't just about ransom or leverage. They harvested her eggs."

I hear Oscar's sharp intake of breath and see the color drain from his face. My own mind reels, struggling to process the horror of what Talon's saying.

"But that's not all," Talon continues. "They want her living children, too."

"How the fuck do you know this?" Alex asks.

"The paperwork at the auction. They made me sign a breeder's rights agreement. It outlined that should Vesper have kids, they get first rights as her original goddamn breeder."

Oscar's voice cuts through the haze, sharp and accusing. "Why didn't you tell us when the doctor was here?"

Talon's jaw clenches, a flicker of guilt crossing his features before he schools his expression. "I found out just before we extracted her," he admits. "But getting her out was the priority. Those were your own words, Oz. I did what you asked me to do."

"Bullshit!" Oz snarls, surging to his feet. "You should

have told us the moment we got her back. We could have...we could have..."

"What could we have done? The damage was already done. The violation already complete," Talon challenges, pushing off the wall to face me. His brown eyes, usually so warm and friendly, are hard as flint. "Getting her here, getting her safe, that was far more important," Talon continues, his voice softening slightly. "Now that she's here, we can sort it out. Figure out our next move."

Oscar stands slowly, his movements stiff and pained.

"There was a name on the contract. Johan Mikeal. He was listed as the seller."

"Who the fuck is that?"

"No idea, but it's a start. More than we had before we got her back."

"Alex," Oz demands.

"Already on it," he declares, disappearing into the room he'd set up earlier while Oz played night watchmen. The sound of "Boots and Blood" by Five Finger Death Punch comes from the other side of his bedroom door. Unlike the rest of us, Alex has always used music to keep him focused while he worked. The darker the song, the more focused.

Talon's words hang in the air, heavy with implications. I watch as Oscar's face contorts, a mixture of rage and despair battling for dominance. The hallway suddenly feels too small, too confining, as if the walls are closing in on us.

"Oz," Talon says softly, reaching out to place a hand on my brother's shoulder. "I'm sorry. I should have told you sooner. But what's done is done, and now we need to focus on helping Vesper."

Oscar shrugs off Talon's hand, his blue eyes blazing. But before he can unleash another tirade, Talon continues, his voice low and steady.

"And as much as I hate to say it, Zaire did the right thing. Vesper needs time. Time to heal, time to process. We can't push her too hard, too fast. It'll only make things worse."

I blink in surprise, not expecting Talon to come to my defense. Oscar looks equally stunned, his mouth opening and closing wordlessly.

Talon runs a hand through his hair, loosening it further from its man bun. "Look, I know it's not ideal. But right now, the best thing we can do for Vesper is give her space. Let her rest. We'll figure out our next move when she's stronger."

The tension in the hallway is palpable, crackling like electricity in the air. I can see the conflict playing out on Oscar's face, his desire to help Vesper warring with the logic of Talon's words.

Finally, Oscar nods, a short, jerky motion. "Fine," he grits out. "But we're not done discussing this."

Talon's shoulders sag with relief. "Agreed," he says, then glances down the hallway. "I should go check on Alex, make sure he's not tearing the place apart looking for answers."

With a final nod to both of us, Talon turns and strides away, his footsteps echoing in the quiet hallway.

As soon as he's out of sight, the silence between Oscar and me becomes oppressive. I can feel the weight of my earlier words pressing down on me, threatening to crush me under their gravity.

"Oz," I start, my voice rough with emotion. "I'm sorry. About what I said earlier, about Vesper being better off as a ghost. I didn't mean it."

Oscar doesn't respond immediately. He stares at the closed door of Vesper's room, his expression unreadable. When he finally speaks, his voice is low and raw. "You're right, you know," he says, not looking at me. "This isn't a fairy tale. There's no guarantee of a happy ending."

I feel a twinge of guilt in my chest. "I'm sorry," I say again, the words feeling inadequate but necessary. "I saw her like that, and I panicked. I thought I was helping."

Oscar sighs, running a hand through his hair. "I know," he says softly. "But we can't keep making decisions for her, Z. We have to give her a chance to heal, to find herself again."

The weight of everything we've learned in the past few minutes settles over me like a shroud. Vesper's eggs were harvested without her consent. The threat of her future children being taken. It's almost too much to comprehend. All this time that Oz has been looking for her, she's been tortured and harvested like a fucking heifer. The thought of what she's endured creates a coiling snake of rage inside of me. Oz believed, all this fucking time, he believed she was still alive, and I didn't believe him. The guilt for not saving her that he has been carrying for us all dragging him down farther beneath the depths every day she was still gone.

"What do we do now?" he asks, his voice sounding small and lost.

"We wait," I say finally. "We let her rest. And while she does, we plan."

Chapter 17

VESPER

I WAKE WITH A START, my eyes flying open to an unfamiliar ceiling. For a moment, I'm disoriented, unsure of how long I've been asleep. The room is bathed in a soft, golden light that filters through sheer curtains, and I realize with a jolt that I've slept without dreaming for the first time in years. The absence of nightmares leaves me feeling strangely hollow as if a part of me is missing.

Instinctively, I move to stretch my arms, expecting to feel the cold bite of metal against my wrists. But there's nothing. No shackles, no restraints. I blink, wondering if this is some new form of torture – the illusion of freedom. My gaze darts around the room, searching for Oscar's silhouette lurking in the shadows, but he's not there. The room is empty, save for the sparse furniture and the eerie silence that seems to press in on me from all sides.

Heart pounding, I swing my legs over the edge of the bed, my bare feet touching the cool wooden floor. I pause, listening for any sign of movement in the house, but there's nothing. Slowly, I make my way to the door, my hand hesitating on the handle. I take a deep breath and turn it, half-expecting it to be locked. To my surprise, it opens easily.

The hallway beyond is deserted, no guards, no watchful eyes. I move through the house like a ghost, my footsteps echoing in the emptiness. Each room I pass is vacant, devoid of life or any sign of recent occupation. It's as if everyone has simply vanished, leaving me alone in this strange, silent world.

Finally, I reach the front door. My heart is hammering so loudly in my chest that I'm sure it will give me away, even though there's no one to hear it. With trembling fingers, I reach for the handle, expecting at any moment for alarms to blare or for rough hands to grab me. But nothing happens. The door swings open, and for the first time in what feels like an eternity, I step outside.

I take a tentative step forward, then another, my bare feet sinking into the soft grass. The blades tickle my toes, a sensation so foreign and yet so achingly familiar that it brings tears to my eyes. I wiggle my toes, reveling in the cool dampness of the earth beneath them. The heaviness that has weighed on my limbs for so long seems to melt away with each step I take.

I tilt my face upward, closing my eyes against the brilliance of the sun. Its warmth seeps into my skin, chasing away the perpetual chill that has clung to me in my captivity. I spread my arms wide as if I could embrace the entire sky, feeling the gentle resistance of the breeze against my palms. The wind plays with my hair, sending strands dancing across my face and neck in a teasing caress.

A bird calls in the distance, its song clear and sweet. I open my eyes, scanning the trees that border the property. There, perched on a branch, is a small sparrow. It cocks its head at me, curious and unafraid. For a moment, we regard each other. Two free creatures in a world suddenly full of possibility.

I inhale deeply, filling my lungs with the scent of fresh-cut grass and blooming flowers. The air tastes clean and crisp, so different from the stale, recycled atmosphere I've grown accustom. Each breath feels like a gift, a reminder of the life that still pulses within me despite everything.

My gaze falls to my wrists, now bare of the shackles that have been my constant companions. The skin there is pale and marked, a testament to the length of my captivity. I run my fingers over the indentations, marveling at the feel of my skin and the absence of cold metal. The freedom of movement is intoxicating, and I find myself spinning in a slow circle, arms outstretched, simply because I can.

As I turn, the world blurs into a kaleidoscope of colors:

the vibrant green of the grass, the deep blue of the sky, the riot of hues from the flower beds that line the path. It's almost overwhelming after so long in the muted grays and blacks of my prison. I stop, dizzy with the beauty of it all, and sink to my knees in the grass.

I run my hands through the green blades, marveling at their smoothness. On impulse, I lie back, spreading my arms and legs wide as if to make a grass angel. The ground is firm beneath me, solid and real in a way that my world hasn't been for so long. I close my eyes, feeling the gentle caress of the sun on my face, the whisper of the wind in my hair, and the living earth beneath my body.

For a moment, I allow myself to simply exist in this perfect, peaceful bubble. I push away thoughts of the past and fears for the future. I ignore the questions that clamor for attention in the back of my mind. But my moment of peace is shattered as abruptly as it began. A shadow falls across my face, blocking out the sun's warmth. My eyes fly open, my heart leaping into my throat as I see two figures looming over me. Panic surges through my veins, icy and familiar.

"Vesper," a deep voice calls, tinged with concern. "Are you alright?"

I scramble backwards, my fingers digging into the soft earth. The world tilts and spins around me, the colors blurring together in a nauseating swirl. My limbs feel heavy, uncooperative, and a fog seems to settle over my thoughts.

"Shit, Z," another voice hisses. "I think you overdid it with the sedative."

Sedative. The word pierces through the haze in my mind. I wasn't free. This wasn't real. They had drugged me.

I try to stand, to run, but my legs buckle beneath me. Strong arms catch me before I hit the ground, and I find myself staring into a pair of striking silver eyes.

"Whoa, easy there," a deep voice says, hands raised in a placating gesture. "We're not here to hurt you."

I blink rapidly, trying to clear the fog from my mind. The world seems to tilt and spin, colors bleeding into one another. I shake my head, but it only makes the dizziness worse. A cold realization creeps over me.

"You...you drugged me," I accuse, my voice hoarse and unfamiliar to my own ears.

The taller of the two men steps forward, his eyes filled with regret. "I'm sorry that I did that, but you were hurting yourself."

I stare at him, my mind racing to catch up. There's something about those eyes, silver orbs ringed in blue. A memory tugs at the edges of my consciousness, like a half-forgotten dream.

"Z-Zaire?" I whisper, the name falling from my lips before I can even process where it came from.

He nods, a small smile playing at the corners of his mouth. "You remember."

As I look at him, really look at him, more memories

come flooding back. The tattoos snaking up his arms. The way his stare cuts right through you.

As if summoned by his words, memories come flooding back. Zaire Petrov. The second son. The twin. Oscar's brother. My gaze darts to the other man – Talon St. James, his familiar easy smile now taut with worry.

"You were supposed to save me," I say, my voice cracking. "You promised." I shake my head, trying to clear away the last vestiges of the drug-induced fog.

A shadow of pain crosses Zaire's face. "I know. We tried. God, Vesper, we tried so hard. But Oscar-"

"He was the man in my room when you drugged me," I recall.

I stare at Zaire, his words sinking in like stones in a still pond, rippling through my consciousness. The mention of Oscar sends a shiver down my spine, memories of his silhouette in my room flickering at the edges of my mind. Zaire's face softens, his eyes full of an emotion I can't quite place.

"It's probably best if you talk to him yourself and hear it from him."

I open my mouth to protest, but Talon steps forward. "Hey, how about we get some food in you? You must be starving."

As if on cue, my stomach lets out an embarrassingly loud growl. I feel heat rise to my cheeks, but Talon just chuckles, the sound warm and familiar in a way that makes my chest ache.

"I'll take that as a yes," he says, extending his hand to me.

I hesitate, eyeing his outstretched palm warily. Part of me wants to refuse, to maintain this fragile distance between us. But another part, a part I thought long buried, yearns for the contact, for the comfort of a friendly touch.

Slowly, I place my hand in his. His skin is warm, calloused in places, and I can feel the strength in his grip as he helps me to my feet. The world tilts for a moment, my legs still unsteady from the lingering effects of the sedative, but Talon's arm wraps around my waist, steadying me.

"I've got you," he murmurs, his breath warm against my ear.

We make our way back into the house, my bare feet padding softly on the wooden floors. The kitchen is bright and airy, sunlight streaming through large windows that overlook a lush garden. Talon guides me to a chair at the table, his hand lingering on my shoulder for a moment before he moves away.

"Alright, let's see what we've got," he says, rummaging through the refrigerator. "How does grilled cheese sound? With tomato soup?"

The thought of real food, something other than the bland, tasteless meals I've become accustomed to, makes my mouth water. I nod, not trusting my voice.

As Talon busies himself at the stove, the sound of footsteps draws my attention. A man I don't recognize enters the kitchen, his blond hair mussed and eyes heavy with fatigue.

He stops short when he sees me, surprise flickering across his face before it settles into a gentle smile.

"Vesper," he says, his voice rough with sleep. "It's good to see you up. I'm Alex. We've met before, but..." he trails off, running a hand through blonde hair. "I was there when your brother got his ass kicked. Sorry about that."

"Luca?" I breathe, the name catching in my throat. "You've seen my brother?"

Alex's face falls, and I feel my heart sink. "We were trying to find him," I say, memories flooding back. "Before...before everything. You promised you'd help me find him."

Talon sets a steaming plate in front of me, the aroma of melted cheese and toasted bread making my stomach growl louder. But I can't take my eyes off Alex, silently pleading for answers.

"We've been looking," Alex says softly, pulling up a chair next to me. "But Vesper, I'm sorry. There's been no sign of him."

I close my eyes, feeling the weight of disappointment settle over me like a heavy blanket. When I open them again, I find Talon watching me with concern, a bowl of tomato soup in his hands.

"Eat," he says gently, placing the bowl next to my plate. "We can talk more after you've had something."

I nod, suddenly aware of the gnawing emptiness in my stomach. I pick up half of the grilled cheese sandwich, the butter glistening on the perfectly toasted bread. The first bite is like an explosion of flavor in my mouth. The sharp tang of the cheese, the crunch of the bread, the subtle hint of herbs. It's almost overwhelming after so many bland, tasteless meals.

I devour the sandwich in record time, barely pausing to breathe between bites. The soup is equally delicious, rich and creamy, with a hint of basil. I use the remaining half of my sandwich to soak up every last drop, savoring each mouthful. Talon retrieves my bowl and refills it.

"It's okay to ask for more if you're still hungry," he reminds me.

As I eat, I'm acutely aware of the others watching me. Zaire leans against the kitchen counter, his eyes never leaving my face. Talon busies himself cleaning up, but I can feel his gaze flicking to me every few seconds. And Alex sits quietly beside me, his presence both comforting and unsettling.

"You said I saw a doctor. Did they…find anything?"

"Your bloodwork is fine. Outside of the sedative in your system and some elevated hormone levels," Zaire answers flatly.

"What about…?" I mutter, trying to figure out how to ask four men about my reproductive health. I had never talked about stuff like this with anyone. Not even my mother. "What about what they did to me? The Shadow Man, I mean."

"The doctor would need to see you to be sure."

The idea of going back to a sterile white room makes me shiver. Zaire catches my reaction.

"Whether or not you get physically examined is your choice."

"What if I am pregnant?" I blurt out.

"You're not," Talon interjects through gritted teeth. "They gave you a contraceptive injection prior to the auction. There was also a certificate certifying your 'intact' status."

Relief fills me quickly before embarrassment at the fact my captors had a certificate to certify they hadn't defiled me. The thought that all four of them know I'm still a virgin is awkward to say the least.

"I have the file if you want to see it," Talon declares.

"Burn it." The last thing I want to see is a bill of sale for my body. It would make it too real.

I settle into a quiet silence. My soup is no longer steaming in front of me. Talon retrieves the bowl, dumping out the cold soup and replaces it with more from the pot. I focus on eating rather than the swirling, chaotic mess inside of my head.

When I finally set down my spoon, feeling full for the first time in what feels like forever, Alex clears his throat.

"Do you remember much about your time with them?"

Zaire immediately interrupts him. "Now is not the time, Alex. Let her enjoy her fucking meal."

"Studies show that you remember more within the first day or so…"

"I don't give a fuck about what study you've read, jackass. I said no."

"What do you want to know?" I ask, my voice stronger now that I've eaten.

Zaire shifts uncomfortably, exchanging a glance with Talon. Alex takes a deep breath, running a hand through his hair. I'm about to press Alex for more information when the kitchen door swings open. My heart leaps into my throat as Oscar walks in, his piercing blue eyes immediately locking onto mine. The room falls silent, tension crackling in the air like static electricity.

Oscar looks different from how I remember. His hair is longer, brushing his collar, and there's a new hardness to his jaw. A thin scar runs along his left cheekbone, a reminder that time hasn't stood still while I was gone.

"It's good to see you awake." He takes a step towards me, and I flinch involuntarily. Oscar freezes, pain flashing across his face before his expression smooths into an unreadable mask. "About last night," he starts.

"I already apologized," Zaire interrupts.

"I'm glad, but that's not what I was going to say," he looks towards his twin before redirecting back to me. "I want to apologize for startling you. I should never have stayed in your room."

"It's okay."

"No, it isn't," he answers. "You've had your choices stripped away from you for so long, and I did the same fucking thing by staying there. It won't happen again."

"How long?" I ask, the question burning in my throat. "How long was I...?"

Oscar's eyes flicker to Zaire, then back to me. "Two years," he says softly. "You've been gone for two years."

The words hit me like a physical blow. Two years. Two years of my life, gone in what feels like the blink of an eye. I grip the edge of the table, my knuckles turning white as the room spins around me.

"That's impossible," I whisper, more to myself than anyone else. "It can't have been that long."

But even as I say it, I know it's true. The changes in the men around me, the unfamiliarity of my own body. It all speaks to the passage of time. Two years of my life, stolen away.

"What happened?" I demand, my voice rising. "Where was I? Why didn't you come for me sooner?"

Oscar takes another step forward, his hands raised in a placating gesture. "Vesper, I know you have questions. We all do. But now might not be the best time to-."

"Not the best time?" I interrupt, anger flaring hot in my chest. "When is the best time, Oscar? After another two years have passed?"

I push myself to my feet, ignoring the way my legs tremble beneath me. "I want to know everything. Now."

Oscar's jaw clenches, a muscle ticking in his cheek. "It's complicated, Vesper. A lot has changed while you were gone."

"Then un-complicate it," I snap, taking a step towards him. "I deserve to know what happened to me."

For a moment, Oscar looks like he might argue. Then his shoulders slump, defeat written in every line of his body. "You're right," he says quietly. "You do deserve to know. But Vesper, please understand that the truth is going to be painful to hear. Are you sure you're ready for this?"

I straighten my spine, squaring my shoulders despite the trembling in my limbs. The room seems to shrink around me, the air growing thick and heavy. I can feel the weight of their gazes. Oscar's piercing blue eyes, Zaire's silver ones, Talon's concerned stare, and Alex's wary glance. Their silence is deafening, filled with unspoken truths and hidden pain.

"I've survived two years of God knows what," I say, a hint of steel creeping into my voice. "I can handle the truth."

Oscar's eyes cloud with pain as he begins to speak, his voice low and strained. "It was supposed to be simple," he says, running a hand through his hair. "We had everything planned down to the last detail. We were on our way to get you, to bring you to safety."

I lean forward, my heart pounding in my chest as I hang onto his every word. The kitchen seems to fade away, replaced by the vivid images Oscar's words paint.

"We were so close, Vesper. But when we got there, all we found was the wreckage of your car. It was a nightmare.

The vehicle was completely destroyed, twisted metal and shattered glass everywhere. And you were gone."

I feel the blood drain from my face as I remember flashes of that day. The screech of tires, the sickening crunch of metal, and the world spinning out of control. My hands begin to shake, and I grip the edge of the table to steady myself.

"We searched for you," Oscar says, his blue eyes intense with desperation. "For two years, we turned over every stone and followed every lead. We never stopped looking, Vesper. Never."

Zaire steps forward, placing a hand on his brother's shoulder. "It was like chasing a ghost," he adds. "Every time we thought we were close, you'd slip through our fingers again."

"Then, about a week ago," Talon interjects, his face grim, "we got word about an auction. A secret, high-stakes event for the elite of the underworld."

My stomach churns as I begin to piece together what they're saying. "An auction," I repeat, the words tasting bitter on my tongue. "For people?"

Oscar nods, his jaw clenched tight. "We didn't know for sure if you'd be there, but it was the best lead we'd had in months. We couldn't pass it up."

"So, you...bought me?" I ask, my voice trembling with a mix of gratitude and horror.

"We couldn't let anyone else get their hands on you," Zaire says fiercely. "We had to bring you home. It was the only way."

I close my eyes, trying to process the flood of information. Two years of my life are gone in what feels like the blink of an eye. Two years of captivity, of fear, and pain, and loneliness. All the while, these men had been searching for me, never giving up hope. But a nagging thought tugs at the back of my mind, a question I'm almost afraid to ask. I open my eyes, fixing my gaze on Oscar.

"My family. Did they...did they even try to look for me? My father wanted this alliance so badly. Badly enough he bowed down to your uncle's demands, as you said he would. He wouldn't just let me disappear without at least trying…"

The silence that falls over the room is deafening. Oscar and Zaire exchange a look that speaks volumes.

"Vesper, there's no easy way to say this," Zaire begins, his eyes never leaving mine. "Your father...he's dead."

The words hit me like a physical blow, knocking the air from my lungs. I stumble backward, my legs hitting the chair behind me. I grip the back of it, my knuckles turning white as I struggle to process what I've just heard.

"Dead?" I repeat, the word turns to dust on my tongue. "How? When?"

Oscar takes a step towards me, his hand outstretched as if to offer comfort, but he stops short. "It happened about a month after you disappeared," he says softly. "He was gone, and your Uncle Mario took his place. Our uncle told us that he took his own life out of the grief of losing you."

"My father would never do that. Never," I fire back. My

mind reels, images of my father flashing before my eyes. His stern face, his rare smiles, the weight of his expectations always heavy on my shoulders. I think I loved him once, but that fleeting moment was gone a long time ago. Just like him now. "That can't be true."

"We doubt that it is the truth, but we have no way of verifying it."

"And...and my mother?" I ask.

"She fled as soon as your father died. The last we heard, she went back to her family in Russia."

The room spins, and I grip the wooden back, my knuckles turning white as I struggle to process this new information. My mother is gone. Fled back to Russia, leaving behind the remnants of our shattered family. The thought pierces my heart like a shard of ice, cold and sharp.

The words hit me like a tidal wave, threatening to sweep me away. "She abandoned me?" I whisper, my voice cracking with disbelief.

Talon steps forward, his warm brown eyes filled with sympathy. "Vesper," he says gently, "the entire world thought you were dead. Your parents...they even held a memorial service for you not long before your father died. We were there."

A memorial service. They had mourned me, buried an empty casket, and moved on with their lives while I was still out there, still fighting, still hoping for rescue. Tears well up in my eyes, hot and stinging. I try to blink them away, but they spill over, coursing down my cheeks in silent rivers. My chest heaves with silent sobs as the full weight of my loss crashes down upon me.

My family, the people who were supposed to love me unconditionally, to move heaven and earth to find me had simply accepted my death and moved on. While I was trapped in a living nightmare, they had continued with their lives, leaving me behind like a discarded memory.

But these four men - Oscar, Zaire, Talon, and Alex - they had never stopped searching. For two years, they had fought for me when my own flesh and blood had not. The realization is both comforting and devastating. I wrap my arms around myself, trying to hold the pieces of my shattered world together.

A thought hits me. "My engagement to Dmitri…"

"You don't need to worry about him right now."

I feel a gentle hand on my shoulder, and I flinch. Zaire recalls his hand immediately. "Shit, I wasn't thinking. I'm sorry."

"It's okay," I mutter. "The last two years…the only time someone touched me was to take something away from me. I don't know how to process touch as anything else."

"Can I try something?"

I hesitate, my heart pounding. Every instinct screams at me to run, to hide, to protect myself. But Zaire's eyes are soft, concerned. Not like theirs. I nod, barely a movement.

Zaire reaches out slowly, telegraphing his intentions. His hand hovers over my shoulder, giving me time to pull away.

I don't. I can't. I'm frozen, caught between terror and a desperate longing for gentle human contact.

His fingertips brush my skin, and I gasp. My body goes rigid, muscles clenching, preparing for pain. Memories flash through my mind—rough hands, cruel grips, bruising force. I squeeze my eyes shut, willing the flashbacks away.

But Zaire's touch remains light, warm. He doesn't grab, doesn't hurt. Just rests his palm on my shoulder, a steady presence. Seconds tick by, each one an eternity. Gradually, almost imperceptibly, the tension in my body begins to ebb.

I focus on my breathing, on the soft fabric of my shirt beneath his hand, on the faint scent of pine that clings to him. The present slowly reasserts itself, pushing back the shadows of the past.

My eyes flutter open. Zaire is still there, patient and calm. His thumb moves in small, soothing circles. The motion should be terrifying, but instead, it's...comforting. A tear slips down my cheek as I realize it's the first time in two years that touch hasn't meant pain.

"You're safe," Zaire murmurs. "I've got you."

And for the first time in a long time, I start to believe it might be true.

Chapter 18

VESPER

AFTER AN EMBARRASSINGLY LONG time of Zaire touching my shoulder, testing my limits of touch, I excuse myself and step out onto the weathered porch, the old boards creaking beneath my feet like a mournful lament. The midday sun beats down, harsh and unforgiving, much like the truths I've just been forced to swallow. I sink onto the rickety swing, its rusted chains groaning in protest, and let my gaze wander over the overgrown yard.

Wildflowers push through cracks in the concrete path. It's a far cry from the opulent Rossi mansion I once called home, yet at this moment, it feels more real than anything I've known in the past two years.

Two years. The words echo in my mind, each repetition a fresh wound. Two fucking years of my life gone. Gone, like my family now. Father's dead. Mother is God knows where. Luca is still missing.

A terrifying thought sinks into my mind. What if Luca was with The Shadow Man, too? What if they were...the thought of my brother enduring what I had makes my stomach retch. I barely make it to the edge of the porch before I can't hold it back. The acrid taste of bile burns my throat as I heave into the overgrown bushes, their leaves trembling with each violent spasm. My fingers grip the splintered wood of the porch railing, knuckles white with strain. The sound of retching must have carried because suddenly the screen door slams open behind me. Oscar's footsteps thunder across the porch, and I feel his warm hand on my back, rubbing soothing circles. I stiffen under his touch, and he withdraws his hand.

"Vesper, are you alright?" His voice is laced with concern, but it only makes me feel worse.

I straighten up, wiping my mouth with the back of my hand. "I'm fine," I snap, hating how weak I sound and how helpless I feel.

Zaire appears in the doorway, his gaze taking in the scene. There's something in his gaze, a flicker of understanding that makes my chest tighten. He looks at Oscar and nods slightly, some unspoken communication passing between the twins.

"I'll get you some water," Oscar says, retreating into the house.

Zaire steps onto the porch, his presence solid and grounding. "Want to take a walk?" he asks, his voice low and calm. "Might help clear your head."

I glance down at my bare feet, toes curling against the rough wood. "I don't have any shoes," I mutter, embarrassed by how unprepared I am for even the simplest things.

Without a word, Zaire disappears into the house. He returns moments later with a pair of well-worn boots, setting them down in front of me. "They might be a bit big, but they'll do."

I slip them on, the leather soft and warm against my skin. They smell faintly of pine and motor oil, an oddly comforting scent. As I stand, Zaire offers his arm, not insisting but simply making it available if I need it.

For a moment, I hesitate. Then, swallowing my pride, I loop my arm through his. Together, we descend the creaky steps and set off down the overgrown path, leaving behind the beach house and the bitter taste of my fears, if only for a little while.

As we walk, the tall grass brushes against my legs, tickling my skin through the fabric of my jeans. The path is narrow, barely visible, a testament to how rarely it's used. Wildflowers dot the landscape, splashes of purple and yellow amidst the sea of green. Their sweet scent mingles with the earthy aroma of damp soil and sun-warmed grass.

The ground beneath our feet gradually changes from soft earth to gravel, crunching with each step. I can hear it now, a rhythmic whisper growing louder with each passing moment, the sound of waves lapping against a shore. The salty tang of sea air fills my lungs, sharp and invigorating.

Zaire's arm is warm against mine, his steady presence a silent comfort as we navigate the uneven terrain. I steal a glance at him, noticing how the sunlight catches the dark rings in his eyes, making them seem to glow. His face is set in concentration, jaw clenched slightly as if he's deep in thought.

We round a bend, and suddenly, the world opens up before us. The grass gives way to a rocky shoreline, jagged stones of various sizes scattered across the beach. The water stretches out to the horizon, a vast expanse of deep blue meeting the lighter hue of the sky. White-capped waves roll in, crashing against the larger rocks with a thunderous roar before retreating, leaving behind a frothy residue.

Zaire guides me carefully down a natural stairway formed by flat stones, his hand on my elbow to steady me. The boots, slightly too big, slap against the rocks with each step. We pick our way across the beach until we reach the water's edge, where the pebbles are smooth and gleaming, polished by countless tides.

I bend down, picking up a flat stone and turning it over in my hand. It's cool to the touch, its surface marbled with streaks of gray and white. Without thinking, I fling it towards the water, watching as it skips once, twice, three times before sinking beneath the waves.

"Nice throw," Zaire comments, his voice barely audible over the crash of the waves.

I turn to look at him, and our eyes meet. There's something in his gaze, an intensity that makes my breath catch in my throat. He's watching me closely, his eyes roaming over my face as if searching for something. I wonder what he sees - a broken girl, trying desperately to piece herself back together? Or something else entirely?

The wind whips my hair around my face, and I tuck a strand behind my ear, suddenly self-conscious under his scrutiny. "What?" I ask, my voice coming out harsher than I intended.

Zaire shakes his head slightly, a small smile tugging at the corner of his lips. "Nothing," he says softly. "It's good to see you out here. Away from everything. Oscar threw a lot at you all at once. Hearing all of that had to be hard."

I let out a long, shaky breath, my eyes fixed on the horizon where the sea meets the sky. The vastness of it all makes me feel small, but, strangely, not insignificant. "It was hard," I admit, my voice barely audible over the rhythmic crash of waves. "But..."

I pause, searching for the right words. The salt-laden breeze caresses my face, carrying with it the calls of distant seabirds. I close my eyes for a moment, letting the sounds and smells of the ocean wash over me. When I open them again, I find Zaire watching me intently, his silver eyes patient and understanding.

"My entire life has been dictated to me since the beginning," I continue, the words tumbling out like the tide rushing to shore. "Who I could be friends with, what I could wear, how I should act. Even my future was mapped out for me: a marriage to Dmitri, a life confined within the gilded cage of the Petrov family."

I bend down, picking up another smooth stone. It's cool weight in my palm grounds me as I speak. "And then...the last two years." My voice catches, and I have to swallow hard before continuing. "I had no choices again. None. They were all made for me, by...by him."

The stone flies from my hand, arcing through the air before plunging into the water with a satisfying plop. Zaire remains silent, giving me space to find my words.

"But you and Oscar...you gave me a choice," I say, turning to face him fully. The wind whips my hair around my face, and I push it back impatiently. "You could have kept me in the dark, protected me from the truth. But you didn't."

Zaire nods slowly, his gaze never leaving mine. "It was your right to know," he says simply.

I laugh, a short, bitter sound that's quickly swallowed by the crash of waves. "My right? Do you know how foreign that concept is to me? To have rights, to have choices?"

I start pacing along the water's edge, my borrowed boots leaving deep imprints in the wet sand. Each step feels like a small act of defiance against the life that was planned for me. "It was a lot to take in, and I'm still processing it all. The truth about my father, about Luca, about everything that's happened while I was...away."

I stop abruptly, turning to face Zaire again. He's watching me with an intensity that should make me uncomfortable, but instead, it makes me feel seen. Truly seen, perhaps for the first time in my life.

"But it's the first time someone has given me a choice," I say softly. "The first time in so long that I've felt like...like a person, not a pawn. Even though it hurts, I'm grateful for the truth," I finish.

Zaire nods, his eyes softening with understanding. We stand in silence for a moment, the rhythmic crash of waves filling the air between us. A gull cries overhead, wheeling against the cerulean sky, its wings catching the sunlight like polished silver.

I take a deep breath, the salty air filling my lungs, and turn to face Zaire fully. "Can I ask you something?" The words come out hesitantly, my voice barely audible over the ocean's roar.

He raises an eyebrow, a silent invitation to continue. The wind ruffles his dark hair, longer than his brother's, and I find myself momentarily distracted by the way it curls slightly at the nape of his neck.

"What happened after I was taken?" I ask, the question hanging heavy in the air between us. "With Dmitri, I mean."

Zaire's jaw tightens, a muscle twitching beneath the skin.

He turns away, bending to pick up a smooth, flat stone. With a practiced flick of his wrist, he sends it skipping across the water's surface; one, two, three, four times before it sinks beneath the waves.

"It was chaos," he says finally, his voice low and gravelly. "Uncle Victor blamed your father, said the Rossi's had orchestrated your disappearance to break the engagement. Your father, of course, denied it vehemently. He accused the Petrovs of being behind it all."

I close my eyes, imagining the chaos that must have ensued. The shouting matches, the threats, the barely contained violence simmering beneath the surface of forced civility. When I open them again, Zaire is watching me, his eyes filled with a mix of concern, and something else I can't quite place.

"The alliance was broken," he continues, running a hand through his hair. "Shattered, really. Both families retreated to lick their wounds and plot their next moves. It was tense, to say the least."

I nod, processing this information. The wind picks up, whipping my hair around my face, and I tuck it behind my ear impatiently. "And Dmitri?" I ask, almost afraid to hear the answer. "What happened to him?"

Zaire's lips twist into a wry smile, devoid of any real humor. "Unfortunately, my dear cousin is still very much alive," he says, a hint of bitterness creeping into his tone. "Last we heard through the grapevine, he's engaged."

My heart skips a beat, though I'm not sure why. It's not like I harbored any real feelings for him.

"Engaged?" I repeat, the word tasting strange on my tongue. "Who's the unlucky girl?"

Zaire shakes his head, his eyes scanning the horizon as if searching for answers in the endless expanse of sea and sky. "We don't know," he admits, his voice tinged with frustration. "After everything that happened, Victor cut off our father for failing to deliver you. Without Victor's backing, they took what money they had and fled overseas. We haven't heard from them since."

"So, you're outcasts," I murmur, more to myself than to Zaire. "Like me."

I feel his presence shift beside me, his warmth radiating through the space between us. When I turn to look at him, his expression is intense, a fire burning behind those silver eyes.

"No," he says firmly, his voice low and resolute. "We're the Second Sons."

The term hangs in the air between us, heavy with a meaning I don't yet understand. I raise an eyebrow, silently urging him to explain.

Zaire takes a deep breath, his gaze sweeping across the rugged coastline before settling back on me. "After every-thing fell apart, the four of us - Oscar, Talon, Alex, and me - we banded together to make our own family."

He bends down, picking up another smooth stone and turning it over in his hands as he speaks. "We were all second sons, you see. Never destined to inherit, always living in the shadows of our older brothers or cousins. But we saw an opportunity in our shared experiences, in our desire for something more than what our families had planned for us."

With a practiced flick of his wrist, he sends the stone skipping across the water's surface. One, two, three, four, five times it bounces before disappearing beneath the waves.

"We created a safe haven," he continues, his voice taking on a note of pride. "A place for the second sons of family mafias around the world. Those who wanted to forge their own paths."

I listen, mesmerized, as Zaire paints a picture of their organization. The wind dies down as if nature itself is leaning in to hear his words.

"We operate differently from traditional families," he explains. "No strict hierarchies, no blind loyalty to a single leader. We make decisions together, pool our resources and skills. We're attempting to build a network that spans continents, Vesper. A network we can use to protect our own, to right wrongs, to challenge the old ways of doing things."

"That network is how you found me," I say, a hint of wonder in my voice. The realization settles over me like a warm blanket, comforting yet somehow overwhelming.

Zaire's eyes soften, a mix of emotions flickering across his face. "Actually," he says gently, "it wasn't the network that found you. It was Oscar."

I blink, surprised. "Oscar?"

Zaire nods, his gaze drifting out to sea. He never stopped looking for you, Vesper. Not for a single day."

The words hit me like a wave, threatening to sweep me off my feet. I turn away, staring at the horizon where the sky meets the sea in a hazy, indistinct line. The wind picks up, carrying with it the briny scent of seaweed and the distant cry of gulls.

"Two years," I whisper, more to myself than to Zaire. "He searched every day for two whole years?"

"Every lead, every rumor, every whisper," Zaire confirms, his voice low and steady. "He chased them all down, no matter how unlikely. When the rest of us were ready to give up hope, Oscar refused. He said he could feel it in his bones that you were still out there, still alive."

I close my eyes, overwhelmed by the enormity of Oscar's dedication. The wind whips my hair around my face, tendrils of it sticking to my salt-dampened cheeks. I shiver, suddenly aware of how cold I've become.

Zaire notices, his brow furrowing with concern. "The sea breeze is picking up. You're cold," he observes, already shrugging off his jacket. "We should head back to the house."

He drapes the jacket over my shoulders, its warmth and weight grounding me against the turbulent thoughts swirling in my mind. The leather is soft, worn from use, and it carries his scent; a mixture of sandalwood, leather, and coffee.

"Just...a few more minutes," I plead, my eyes fixed on

the horizon where the angry sky meets the restless sea. "Please."

Zaire regards me for a long moment, his silver eyes searching my face. Then, his expression softens, and he nods. "Of course," he says, his voice gentle yet firm. "It's your choice, Vesper. It's always going to be your choice from now on."

Chapter 19

OSCAR

I PACE the hallway outside Vesper's room, my eyes darting to her closed door every few seconds. The black cat clock above the kitchen sink ticks away, each tick is a reminder of how long she's been in there. Hours since she returned from a walk with my brother.

Zaire leans against the wall, his tattooed arms crossed over his chest. His usual smirk is absent, replaced by a furrowed brow that matches my own concern. "Oz, you need to relax. She's fine. Let her sleep."

"I can't relax, Z. It's been hours." I run my hand through my hair, probably messing it up beyond repair. "What if something's wrong?"

Zaire pushes off the wall, his tattoos shifting with the movement. "Nothing's wrong, Oz. She's just tired. Considering what she's been through, it's amazing she can sleep."

I want to believe him, but the knot in my stomach won't let me. The image of Vesper and Zaire returning from the beach keeps replaying in my mind. Her blonde hair had been windswept, cheeks flushed from the salty air. And her smile...God, that smile. It was like the sun breaking through storm clouds, bright and unexpected. A smile she had bestowed on him. Not me. She gave him something so precious that it's killing me inside not to be the one to receive it.

She'd barely looked at me as she breezed past, disappearing into her room with a soft click of the door. That was hours ago, and I've been wearing a path in the hallway carpet ever since.

"You should have seen her out there, Oz," Zaire says, his voice softer now. "It was like watching a caged bird fly for the first time.

I clench my jaw, trying to swallow the bitterness rising in my throat. "And you were the one to witness it."

Zaire's eyes meet mine. "It wasn't about me, brother. It was about her."

I nod, but the jealousy still gnaws at me. I'm the planner, the strategist. I should have thought of taking her to the beach, of giving her a moment of peace amidst all this chaos. But it was Zaire, with his impulsive nature and devil-may-care attitude, who had given her what she needed.

He'd been so close to giving up on her, while I...I gave up my entire life for the last two years to find her.

"I wish I could have seen it," I admit, leaning against the wall opposite Vesper's door.

Zaire's lips purse. A serious look crosses his face. "You will, Oz. This isn't a competition, you know. She needed air, and I gave it to her."

I raise an eyebrow at him. "She needs you now, huh?"

"For fucks sake, Oz. She came to me. Did you expect me to shove her away? After what she's been through? You should be glad she's opening up to someone."

"I am, it's just. I thought it would be me."

"It still can be," Zaire says, stepping closer to me. "Give her time."

"You mean give you more time to take my place."

"I will never take your place. Would it be so bad if she needs both of us? All of us? Her entire life as she remembers is gone now. She has no one, but us."

Just then, we hear a soft rustling from behind Vesper's door. I straighten immediately, every nerve on high alert. But the door stays closed, and silence falls again.

"She's fine," Z remarks. "Probably just turning over in her sleep. Now come on, let's grab something to eat. You look like you're about to pass out. Food might improve your mood."

I hesitate, my eyes still fixed on Vesper's door. Part of me wants to stay, to be here the moment she appears. I'm about to protest when the front door swings open, revealing Talon laden with grocery bags. His shaggy brown hair is pulled back in its usual man bun, and he's wearing that easy grin that makes everyone instantly like him.

"Honey, I'm home!" he calls out, his voice echoing through the house. "And I come bearing gifts!"

Zaire and I exchange a glance before moving to help him. As we unload the bags, I can't help but notice the ridiculous amount of ice cream cartons.

"Talon," I say, pulling out yet another pint, "did you buy out the entire frozen dessert section?"

He shrugs, that golden retriever smile still plastered on his face. "What? I didn't know what kind she likes, so I got...options." Even in the smallest details, he's trying to make her comfortable, to give her a sense of familiarity.

Zaire snorts, peering into one of the bags. "Options? Mate, you've got nine different flavors here. Nine!"

"Better safe than sorry," Talon replies, unfazed. "We've got classic vanilla, chocolate, strawberry, mint chip, cookie dough, rocky road, butter pecan, coffee, and what the hell is this? Lavender honey?"

I can't help but chuckle, shaking my head. "You're ridiculous, you know that?"

Talon winks at me, his easy demeanor lightening the mood. "That's why you love me, Oz."

As we finish unpacking, Talon starts pulling out pots and pans. "I'm thinking pasta for dinner. Something hearty but not too heavy. How's that sound?"

Before we can answer, Alex walks in, his face etched with

fatigue. He nods at us before collapsing onto one of the kitchen stools, setting his closed laptop on the table in front of him.

"Any luck?" I ask, even though I can already guess the answer from his expression.

Alex shakes his head, running a hand through his blond hair. "Nothing. I've been through every database I can access, called in favors from contacts across three continents. He's a ghost or…"

"Or what?" I press, leaning forward.

"Or he doesn't exist," Alex finishes, running a hand through his hair. "At least, not under that name."

A chill runs down my spine. It's not unusual for people in our world to operate under aliases, but this level of anonymity is unsettling.

Talon pauses in his dinner preparations, his usually cheerful face serious. "That can't be good, right? I mean, someone has to know something about this guy."

"You'd think so," Alex says, his voice low. "But whoever he is, he's good at covering his tracks. Too good."

The kitchen falls silent, save for the sizzle of whatever Talon's cooking on the stove. The implications of Alex's words hang heavy in the air. If Johan isn't real, then who sold Vesper? And why use a fake name?

"So, we're back to square one," I mutter, frustration bubbling up inside me.

"Not necessarily," Talon interjects, stirring something that smells deliciously of garlic and herbs. "We could ask

Vesper. She might remember something, anything that could give us a lead."

I feel my jaw clench involuntarily. The thought of putting Vesper through more trauma makes my stomach churn. "Her memory is foggy at best," I explain, trying to keep my voice level. "She spent the bulk of the last two years sedated. If she remembers something, there's no telling if it's real or something that happened in her head."

The kitchen falls silent again, save for the soft bubbling of Talon's pasta sauce. I can see the wheels turning in everyone's minds, searching for a solution, a thread we haven't pulled yet.

"What about the egg harvesting?" Zaire asks suddenly, his eyes intense. "Could we try that route? Maybe they were sold."

The words hit me like a punch to the gut. The egg harvesting. It's a lead we haven't fully explored yet. The thought of Vesper's eggs being sold, of potential children out there somewhere, makes me feel sick. But it's a possibility we can't ignore.

"It's worth looking into," I admit. "But we'd need to be careful. If word gets out that we're asking questions about black market fertility clinics, it could tip off whoever's behind this."

Alex nods, already pulling out his laptop. "I'll start digging, see if I can find any unusual transactions, or new clinics popping up in the last two years." As Alex starts typing furiously, I lean back against the counter, my mind racing. The house suddenly feels too small, too confining. The walls seem to close in, reminding me of all the ways we're trapped - by our families, by our pasts, by this impossible situation.

I glance towards Vesper's closed door again, wondering what she's dreaming about. Is she reliving the horrors of the past two years? Or is she finally finding some peace in sleep?

Talon's voice breaks through my thoughts. "Dinner's almost ready. Should we wake her up?"

I hesitate, torn between wanting to see her and wanting to let her rest. Zaire shoots me a look, reminding me of our conversation earlier. "Let's give her a few more minutes," I decide. "She needs all the rest she can get."

As Talon begins plating the pasta, the rich aroma of garlic and tomatoes filling the air, I can't help but marvel at the strange family we've become. A group of second sons and a stolen daughter, all trying to navigate this dangerous world we were born into.

As we settle around the kitchen table, the sound of soft whimpers breaks through the quiet. My head snaps toward Vesper's door, heart racing. The whimpers grow louder, transforming into muffled screams.

"Vesper!" I'm on my feet in an instant, bolting to her room. I throw open the door, the others close behind.

Vesper thrashes on the bed, tangled in sweat-soaked sheets. Her long blonde hair is matted to her face, tears streaming down her cheeks. "No, please...stop!" she cries out, her voice raw with terror.

I rush to her side, hesitating for a moment before gently grasping her shoulders. "Vesper, wake up. It's just a dream."

Her eyes fly open, wild and unfocused. For a terrifying moment, she doesn't seem to recognize me. "No. No. No. Don't touch me." Then clarity floods her gaze, followed quickly by shame. She curls into herself, body shaking with silent sobs.

"It's okay," I murmur. "You're safe now."

Zaire appears on her other side, his usual cocky demeanor replaced by genuine concern. "We've got you, sweetheart," he says softly, placing a comforting hand on her back. She leans into him, burying her face into the crook of his neck. The sight of her seeking comfort in my brother is almost too much to bear.

Talon hovers in the doorway, his face a mask of worry. "I'll get some water," he says, disappearing down the hall.

As Vesper's sobs subside, she pulls away slightly, wiping at her face. "I'm sorry," she whispers, voice hoarse. "I didn't mean to..."

"Don't apologize," I interrupt gently. "You have nothing to be sorry for."

She nods, but I can see the doubt in her eyes. Talon returns with a glass of water, which she accepts gratefully. As she sips, I notice the tremors in her hands.

"Do you want to talk about it?" Zaire asks carefully.

Vesper shakes her head, then pauses. "I was back there. In that room. But this time, it wasn't just me. There were children. My children. They were taking them away, and I couldn't...I couldn't stop them."

The room falls silent, the weight of her words hanging heavy in the air. I exchange a glance with Zaire, both of us thinking about our earlier conversation about the egg harvesting.

"It was just a dream," I say, trying to keep my voice steady. "No one's going to take anything from you ever again. We won't let them."

She offers a weak smile, but I can see the fear lingering in her eyes. "What if...what if it wasn't just a dream? What if they really did...?"

"We'll figure it out," Talon says firmly, stepping closer. "Whatever happened, whatever they did, we'll deal with it."

I watch as Vesper's cheeks flush with embarrassment, her gaze dropping to the tangled sheets. The vulnerability in her eyes tugs at my heart, and I wish I could erase every painful memory from her mind.

Talon, ever perceptive, notices her discomfort. He steps forward, his easy smile returning. "Hey, don't worry about it. We all have nightmares sometimes. Just last week, I woke up screaming because I dreamt I was being chased by a giant slice of pizza."

Vesper looks up, confusion replacing embarrassment. "A pizza?"

"Oh yeah," Talon continues, warming to his story. "It was terrifying. All that cheese, threatening to smother me.

And don't even get me started on the pepperoni. Those things were like ninja stars."

A small giggle escapes Vesper's lips, the sound like music to my ears. It's been so long since I've heard her laugh.

"And then," Talon says, gesturing wildly, "just when I thought it was all over, the crust started singing opera…in Italian. Which, let me tell you, is not as romantic as it sounds when it's coming from a homicidal pizza."

This time, Vesper's laugh is fuller, her green eyes crinkling at the corners. The sound fills the room, chasing away the lingering shadows of her nightmare. I can't help but join in, Zaire's deep chuckle harmonizing with Talon's infectious guffaw.

As our laughter subsides, I notice Vesper's stomach growl softly. "Hey," I say gently, "are you hungry? Talon made pasta, and I'm pretty sure he bought out an entire ice cream shop for dessert."

Vesper's eyes widen slightly. "Ice cream?"

"Nine flavors," Zaire chimes in, smirking. "Our golden boy here couldn't decide, so he got them all."

Talon shrugs, unabashed. "What can I say? I'm a man of many tastes."

She nods, a hint of shyness creeping back into her expression. "I...I could eat."

"Great!" Talon exclaims, clapping his hands together. "I made enough to feed an army. Or, you know, five people with varying degrees of emotional trauma and questionable eating habits."

We make our way to the kitchen, where Alex has already set the table. The aroma of garlic and herbs fills the air, making my mouth water. Vesper hesitates for a moment before taking a seat, her eyes darting around as if seeking permission.

"Go ahead," I encourage her, pulling out a chair. "Dig in."

We settle around the table, and I can't help but marvel at the scene. Just days ago, we weren't sure if we'd ever see Vesper again, let alone share a meal with her. Now here we are, passing bread and ladling out pasta as if it's the most normal thing in the world.

Vesper takes a tentative bite of the pasta, and her eyes widen. "This is delicious," she says, looking at Talon with newfound respect.

He grins, clearly pleased. "See? I told you guys my cooking would win her over."

"To be fair, you actually had me at ice cream."

I watch as Talon springs up from the table, his enthusiasm palpable. He practically bounces to the freezer, pulling out pint after pint of ice cream. The colorful containers create a rainbow of frozen delights as he arranges them in front of Vesper with a flourish.

"Your choices, milady," he announces with an exaggerated bow. "From the classic to the exotic, we have it all."

Vesper's eyes widen, a childlike wonder spreading across her face. She leans forward, examining each flavor with careful consideration. To my surprise, she reaches for the lavender honey.

"Excellent choice," Talon beams, his grin threatening to split his face in two. He turns to Zaire, waggling his eyebrows triumphantly. "See that, Z? I told you the fancy flavors were a good idea."

Zaire responds with a raised middle finger, but I can see the amusement dancing in his eyes. "Yeah, yeah, don't let it go to your head, golden boy."

Talon just laughs, grabbing a spoon and handing it to Vesper with a flourish. "Your implement of ice cream destruction, my lady."

Vesper accepts the spoon with a shy smile, and I watch as she carefully removes the lid. The pale purple ice cream inside looks almost ethereal, tiny flecks of lavender visible in the creamy swirls.

She takes a small spoonful, closing her eyes as she tastes it. For a moment, the kitchen is silent, all of us waiting with bated breath for her reaction. When she opens her eyes, there's a spark there that I haven't seen in years. "It's...amazing," she breathes, already going in for another bite.

Talon whoops, pumping his fist in the air. "Score one for Team Talon! Who's the ice cream king now, huh?"

As Talon distributes the ice cream, I lean back in my chair, watching the scene unfold before me. Vesper's face is alight with childlike joy as she savors each spoonful of the lavender honey concoction. Zaire and Talon flank her on either side, their usual bravado softened into something gentler, more protective.

Alex joins in, his earlier fatigue momentarily forgotten as he samples each flavor, offering comical commentary on the merits of each. The kitchen is filled with laughter and warmth.

I should be happy. I am happy, in a way. Seeing Vesper smile and hearing her laugh. It's more than I dared hope for just a few days ago. But there's an ache in my chest, a gnawing feeling that I can't quite shake.

Zaire catches Vesper's eye, and they share a private smile. It's subtle, barely there, but it speaks volumes about the connection they forged during their beach walk. I remember Zaire's words from earlier: 'It was like watching a caged bird fly for the first time.' The image burns in my mind, a reminder of what I missed, what I couldn't give her.

Then there's Talon, with his easy charm and golden retriever energy. He's telling some outrageous story now, gesticulating wildly with his spoon, sending droplets of melted ice cream flying. Vesper giggles, a sound so pure and unexpected that it makes my heart clench. Talon beams at her, clearly thrilled to be the source of her amusement.

I feel a pang of guilt for the jealousy course through me. This isn't about me. It's about Vesper, about her healing, her safety. She needs this, needs them. Their lightheartedness, their ability to make her forget, even for a moment, the horrors she's endured.

But a traitorous part of my mind whispers, "It should

have been you." I've spent the last two years searching for her, planning, strategizing, sacrificing everything to bring her home. In my darkest moments, I'd imagined our reunion. I dreamed of how I'd be the one to make her feel safe, to bring that light back into her eyes.

Instead, I find myself on the outside looking in. I watch as Vesper leans into Zaire's side, her body relaxing in a way it hasn't since we found her. Talon reaches across the table to squeeze her hand, and she doesn't flinch away.

The guilt intensifies. I should be grateful that she's found comfort and that she's beginning to trust again. I am, truly. But the selfish part of me aches to be the one she turns to, the one who can chase away her nightmares.

Maybe I'm not the hero of Vesper's story, but I can still be a part of it. And maybe, just maybe, that's enough.

Chapter 20

VESPER

THE SAND SQUISHES between my toes as Zaire and I stroll along the shoreline, the late afternoon sun casts a golden glow over the beach. The salty breeze tousles my hair, and I can't help but smile as I watch Z's longer locks dance in the wind, framing his chiseled jawline. After sleeping for nearly thirty-six hours, per Zaire and a panicked looking Oscar this morning, I'd ask to go back down to the beach. The waves providing me a sense of calm I never knew could exist in this life. The waves and Zaire.

I walk in silence beside Zaire, letting the rhythmic sound of the waves wash over me. The gentle lapping of water against the shore soothes my frayed nerves, a balm to the tension that's been coiled within me for days. I breathe in deeply, filling my lungs with the briny air, hoping it might cleanse away the lingering tendrils of last night's terror.

Zaire's presence beside me is comforting, a solid warmth that grounds me to reality. His fingers brush against mine as we walk, a subtle reminder that I'm not alone. I steal a glance at him, admiring the way the fading sunlight catches on his dark hair, turning the edges to burnished gold.

"I heard you last night," Zaire says softly, breaking our comfortable silence. "You were having another nightmare."

Heat rises to my cheeks, embarrassment flooding through me. I've tried so hard to keep my nocturnal terrors hidden, to maintain the facade of strength that's expected of me as a Rossi. But of course, Zaire, with his keen perception, would notice.

"You don't have to tell me about it if you don't want to," he adds quickly, his hand brushing against mine in a gesture of comfort.

I take a deep breath, tasting salt on my tongue. "It's okay," I say, surprised by my own willingness to share. "I want to tell you. I need to. I can't bottle this up inside and let it consume me. "

We pause our walk, and Zaire turns to face me, his tall frame blocking the wind.

"It's about The Shadow Man," I begin. The name alone sends a shiver down my spine, despite the warmth of the evening.

Zaire's brow furrows, but he remains silent, giving me

space to continue. I'm grateful for his patience, for the way he seems to understand my need to expel these haunting thoughts. I pause, gathering my thoughts. Zaire's hand finds mine. I flinch. He instantly releases my hand, searching my face.

"Shit, I wasn't thinking," he berates himself.

"Touch isn't easy for me, but…I think I would like to try it again."

Zaire nods, finding my hand again. His calloused fingers intertwine with my own. His touch sets off my fear response instantly. My eyes focus on our skin to skin connection, the panic ebbing a few moments later. I notice him exhale deeply.

"This is okay?"

"I think so." It's weird. Being touched, and not being repulsed by it. I settle into the feeling of his rough skin against mine.

His touch anchors me in a way I cannot explain. We settle back into our walk. The tide splashing on the beach, inches from my bare feet.

"Tell me more about your dream."

"Last night, the dream was different," I admit, my voice trembling slightly. "The Shadow Man...he had a face. It was blurred, indistinct, but familiar somehow. And he wasn't just watching or chasing. He was..." I trail off, struggling to find the words.

"He was what, Vesper?" Zaire prompts gently, his thumb tracing soothing circles on the back of my hand.

I meet his gaze, finding comfort in the depths of his eyes. "He was reaching for you, Z. For Oscar, and Talon. Even Alex. He wanted me, but he wanted the four of you more."

Zaire's brow furrows, his grip on my hand tightening slightly. "What do you mean he wanted us more?" he asks, his voice low and urgent.

I shake my head, frustration bubbling up inside me. "I don't know, Z. It's just...in the dream, he was reaching for you all, trying to drag you into the shadows. I could feel his desperation, his need to possess you." I shudder, the memory of the dream causing goosebumps to rise on my skin despite the warm evening air.

"It's just a nightmare, right?" I ask, hating how small and uncertain my voice sounds.

His expression is thoughtful, almost grave. "Nightmares can sometimes be reality-based, Vesper. Our subconscious has a way of processing trauma and fear, turning them into these vivid dreams."

A chill runs through me, despite the warmth of the evening. "What are you saying, Z?"

He sighs, running his free hand through his long, dark hair. "I'm saying that your experiences, the trauma you've endured. It's possible that your mind is trying to make sense of it all."

My mind races, piecing together fragments of memories and dreams. "Do you think...could my nightmares help find the people who kidnapped me?" The words tumble out before I can stop them, hope and fear intertwining in my chest.

"They could," he admits. "Your subconscious might be holding onto details that your waking mind hasn't processed yet."

Zaire's words echo in my mind, stirring up a whirlwind of thoughts and emotions. Could it really be possible? Are the answers we've been desperately seeking buried somewhere in the recesses of my subconscious? The idea is both thrilling and terrifying.

I close my eyes, trying to delve deeper into my memories. Flashes of shadowy figures and muffled voices dance at the edges of my consciousness, always just out of reach. It's like trying to grasp smoke: the harder I try, the more it slips away.

The frustration builds inside me, a knot of tension in my chest. I want so badly to remember, to piece together the fragments of my ordeal. To know who kidnapped me. Who stole from my body over and over again. Who has my eggs…and what they plan to do with them. My mind races, considering all the possibilities. There has to be a way to access those hidden corners of my mind, to shine a light on the darkness that's been haunting me.

I'm so lost in my thoughts, so focused on the internal labyrinth of my mind, that I don't notice the physical world around me. My foot catches on the edge of a tide pool, hidden beneath the sand and encroaching waves. I feel myself pitching forward, arms flailing as I brace for impact with the wet sand.

But the fall never comes. In an instant, Zaire's strong arms are around me, yanking me back against his chest. The sudden movement knocks the breath from my lungs, and I find myself pressed firmly against him, my back to his front.

Time seems to stand still as I register our position. The solid warmth of his chest against my back, his arms wrapped securely around my waist. I can feel the rapid rise and fall of his breathing, matching my own startled gasps.

"You okay?" Zaire's voice is low and husky in my ear, sending an unexpected shiver down my spine.

I nod, not trusting my voice just yet. The panic I expected to feel at such close contact doesn't come. Instead, I find myself relaxing into his embrace, feeling oddly safe and protected.

Slowly, I turn in his arms to face him, my hands coming to rest on his chest. His eyes search my face, concern clear in their depths. "I'm fine," I finally manage to say. "Just got lost in my head for a moment there."

Zaire's lips quirk into a small smile. "Dangerous place, that head of yours," he teases gently, but I can see the underlying worry in his expression.

I laugh softly, the sound surprising even me. "You have no idea," I reply, realizing that I'm still in his arms and making no move to unlock myself from his embrace.

I find myself studying Zaire's face, my eyes drawn to his

unique gaze. While Oscar's eyes are a piercing blue, Zaire's are the opposite. So pale they are almost silver with a dark ring of dark blue circling the outside of them. It's as if his eyes are a battle between darkness and light.

"Your eyes," I murmur. "They're different."

Zaire's lips curl into a soft smile, a hint of self-conscious-ness flickering across his features.

"It's the only thing that really sets me apart from Oz."

I shake my head, my hands still resting on his chest. I can feel the steady thrum of his heartbeat beneath my palms. "That's not true," I say, surprising myself with the conviction in my voice.

Zaire's brow furrows slightly, a question in his eyes. "What do you mean?"

I take a deep breath, gathering my thoughts. The salty air fills my lungs, grounding me in this moment. "I mean, your eyes aren't the only thing that sets you apart from Oscar. You're so much more than just a twin with different eyes."

His arms tighten almost imperceptibly around me, and I find myself leaning into his warmth. The morning sun casts a golden glow on his skin, highlighting the sharp angles of his face and the softness in his expression.

"You've been my rock, Z," I continue, the words tumbling out before I can second-guess them. "The way you understand my silences, how you seem to know exactly when to push and when to give me space. The gentleness in your touch, even with all those tattoos and that tough exterior."

I trace my fingers along one of the intricate designs on his forearm, marveling at the contrast between the harsh lines of ink and the softness of his skin. "You're patient, and kind, and fiercely protective. But there's a wildness in you too, something untamed that calls to me."

Zaire's breath catches, and I look up to see his eyes darkening with an emotion I can't quite name. The air between us feels charged, electric with unspoken words and possibilities.

"Vesper," he breathes my name like a prayer, his forehead coming to rest against mine. "I—"

Zaire's lips hover mere inches from mine, his warm breath mingling with my own. My heart races, a mix of anticipation and fear coursing through my veins. I want this, I realize with startling clarity. I want to feel his lips on mine, to lose myself in the warmth of his embrace.

But as he leans in, closing that final breath of space between us, my body betrays me. I freeze, every muscle locking into place. My breath catches in my throat, and I feel myself trembling in his arms. It's not fear of Zaire, but a deep-seated panic that rises unbidden from the depths of my subconscious.

Zaire immediately senses the change in me. He pulls back, his eyes searching my face with concern. The loss of his warmth is immediate, and I find myself missing it even as relief washes over me.

"I'm sorry," I stammer, heat rising to my cheeks. Embarrassment floods through me, hot and uncomfortable. "I don't know what happened. I thought I was ready, I want to..." I trail off, unable to meet his gaze.

The gentle lapping of waves against the shore fills the silence between us. The sun has dipped lower on the horizon, painting the sky in vibrant streaks of orange and pink. It's beautiful, but I can barely appreciate it through the haze of my mortification.

"Hey," Zaire's voice is soft, coaxing my eyes back to his face. His expression is one of understanding, not disappointment or frustration as I had feared. "You have nothing to apologize for, Vesper. Nothing at all."

His hand comes up to cup my cheek, his touch feather-light and infinitely gentle. "Remember what you just said about me?" he asks, a small smile playing at the corners of his lips. "That I'm a patient man?"

I nod, leaning into his touch despite myself. His palm is warm against my skin, calloused yet comforting.

"Well, you were right," he continues. "I am patient. Especially when it comes to you." His thumb brushes softly across my cheekbone, wiping away a tear I hadn't even realized had fallen. "We move at your pace, Vesper. Always. There's no rush, no pressure. I'm here, for whatever you need, whenever you're ready."

His words wash over me like a balm, soothing the jagged edges of my anxiety. I take a deep, shuddering breath, filling my lungs with the salty ocean air. "Thank you," I whisper, my voice thick with emotion.

Zaire's smile widens, genuine and warm. "No need to thank me. This is what being there for someone looks like. It's what you deserve."

I feel the heat of embarrassment still burning in my cheeks, unable to shake off the lingering shame of my involuntary reaction.

Zaire's words hang in the air between us, his promise of patience and understanding a balm to my frayed nerves. Yet, I can't help but feel a nagging sense of frustration with myself. I know he's not The Shadow Man or any of the people that hurt me. I am safe with him so why can't I just be normal? Why does my body betray me at every turn? Why can't I allow myself to give in to the feelings I have inside of me?

"I want you to know this, Vesper," he says, his gaze never wavering from mine. "I will never, ever take more than you're willing to give. Your choices, your autonomy; they're important to me. You've had so much taken from you already. I refuse to be another person who tries to control you or make decisions for you."

The sincerity in his voice, the fierce protectiveness in his eyes is almost overwhelming. A tear escapes, trailing down my cheek, but before I can wipe it away, Zaire's thumb gently brushes it aside.

Zaire's thumb lingers on my cheek, his touch impossibly gentle. "No one will ever make you cry again," he says, his voice low and fierce. "I'll kill the man or woman who causes a single fucking tear to fall from your beautiful, emerald eyes."

There's a promise there, a vow of protection that should frighten me given my history, but instead, it makes me feel safe. Cherished, even. I lean into his touch, allowing myself this moment of vulnerability.

But Zaire, perceptive as ever, must sense the lingering tension in my body. His expression softens, a mischievous glint appearing in his eyes. "Hey," he says, his tone lighter now. "I've got a serious question for you."

I raise an eyebrow, curious despite myself. "Oh?"

"Is a hotdog a sandwich or a sub?"

The question is so unexpected, so utterly ridiculous given the heaviness of our previous conversation, that I can't help but laugh. It bubbles up from my chest, surprising me with its genuineness.

"What?" I manage to get out between giggles.

Zaire grins, clearly pleased with my reaction. "You heard me. This is a matter of utmost importance, Vesper. The fate of culinary categorization hangs in the balance."

I shake my head, still chuckling. "You're ridiculous."

"Maybe," he concedes, "but you're smiling. I would ask you a million ridiculous things just to have one of your smiles."

Chapter 21

VESPER

I'M BACK THERE AGAIN, *the screeching of metal and shattering glass piercing my ears. But this time, it's different. Instead of the oppressive darkness closing in, a familiar figure emerges from the wreckage. Oscar. His blue eyes, usually so cool and calculating, are wild with concern as he reaches for me.*

"Vesper!" he calls out, his voice cutting through the chaos. "I've got you. You're safe now."

His strong arms wrap around me, pulling me from the twisted metal that threatens to consume me. The scent of his sandalwood cologne envelops me as he cradles me against his chest. I can feel his heart racing, matching the frantic beat of my own.

The world around us fades away, the carnage of the accident melting into a hazy backdrop. All I can focus on is Oscar's face, his features etched with relief and something else...something that makes my breath catch in my throat.

"I thought I'd lost you," he murmurs, his hand coming up to cup my cheek. His thumb traces my lower lip, and I shiver at the contact.

Without warning, he leans in, closing the distance between us. His lips meet mine in a searing kiss that sets every nerve ending alight. It's passionate, desperate, filled with all the words we've left unspoken. My hands fist in his shirt, pulling him closer as I return the kiss with equal fervor.

The taste of him is intoxicating, a heady mix of mint and desire. His tongue traces the seam of my lips, seeking entrance, and I grant it willingly. The kiss deepens, and I feel as though I'm falling and flying all at once.

Just as I'm about to lose myself completely in the sensations, a jolt runs through me.

My eyes fly open, and I find myself bolt upright in my bed, my heart pounding and my breath coming in short gasps. The dream fades quickly, leaving me disoriented and flushed. I bring a trembling hand to my lips, still feeling the phantom pressure of Oscar's kiss.

I close my eyes, willing my racing heart to slow. The dream clings to me like a second skin, refusing to dissipate entirely. Oscar's touch, his scent, the taste of his lips—it all felt so real, so vivid. I can still feel the ghost of his fingers on my cheek, the warmth of his breath against my skin.

With a frustrated groan, I throw off the silk sheets and swing my legs over the side of the bed. The cool wooden floor beneath my feet helps ground me but does little to quell the fire still burning in my veins. I catch a glimpse of myself in the ornate mirror across the room - flushed cheeks, tousled blonde hair, and eyes bright with a mixture of confusion and desire.

"Get it together, Vesper," I mutter to myself, running a hand through my tangled locks. "It was just a dream."

I move to the closet Talon seems to be filling for me. Between ice cream, and new clothes, he seems to always have what I need without having to ask for it. I settle on a pair of high-waisted black leggings, a white t-shirt, and a pair of flip-flops.

The delicious smell of Talon's cooking wafts through the air, further rousing me from my slumber. Expecting to find Talon at work, I am surprised to find Oscar's bare back facing me as he tends to the stove. His toned physique is accented by the low-slung gray sweatpants clinging to his hips.

I freeze in the doorway, my breath catching in my throat. Oscar's movements are fluid and graceful. The muscles in his back ripple as he reaches for a spatula, his skin golden in the early morning light streaming through the kitchen window. There's an ease to him that I've never seen before, a quiet confidence that radiates from every pore.

My eyes trace the line of his spine, following it down to where his sweatpants sit dangerously low on his hips. I find myself wondering what it would feel like to run my fingers along that path, to feel the warmth of his skin beneath my touch. The thought sends a shiver through me, and I wrap my arms around myself, trying to quell the sudden surge of longing.

Oscar hums softly as he cooks, a melody I don't recognize but find oddly comforting. It's as if I'm witnessing a private performance, a side of him that he keeps hidden from the world. I lean against the doorframe, content to watch this unguarded version of Oscar for as long as I can.

But then, without turning, his voice breaks the spell. "Enjoying the view?" There's a hint of amusement in his tone, and I can almost hear the smirk I know is playing on his lips.

Heat rushes to my cheeks as I realize I've been caught. I open my mouth to respond, but the words stick in my throat. How long has he known I was here? Has he been aware of my presence this entire time?

Oscar turns slowly, his blue eyes locking with mine. There's a spark of something in them, mischief perhaps, or challenge. "It's rude to stare."

I swallow hard, trying to regain my composure. "I was just surprised to see you cooking," I manage to stammer out.

He shrugs, the movement causing the muscles in his chest and abdomen to flex. I force my eyes back up to his face, hoping he didn't notice my wandering gaze. "Talon deserves a break," Oscar says. I step further into the room, drawn by both the delicious smell of whatever he's cooking and the magnetic pull of his presence. "Plus, he's passed out on the floor in Alex's room."

"Take a seat. Want some coffee?"

"Sure?"

He retrieves a mug from the cabinet and pours me a cup. He hands it over to me and goes back to the stove. With practiced efficiency, Oscar slides a perfectly cooked omelet onto a plate, the edges golden and crisp, the center promising a creamy decadence. He sets it before me, the aroma of herbs and cheese wafting up tantalizingly. Our fingers brush as he passes me a fork, and I feel a jolt of electricity at the brief contact. His eyes meet mine for a fleeting moment, a storm of unspoken words swirling in their depths, before he turns away.

"I'll be right back," he murmurs, disappearing down the hallway toward his room. The soft click of his door echoes in the quiet kitchen, leaving me alone with my thoughts and the steaming plate before me.

I stare at the omelet, my appetite warring with the knot of frustration in my stomach. The yellow of the eggs seems too bright, too cheerful for the melancholy that has settled over me. I push the food around with my fork, creating abstract patterns in the creamy surface as if I could divine answers from the swirls and valleys.

Oscar returns, now clad in a fitted black t-shirt that does little to diminish the effect of his presence. He moves with the grace of a predator, all controlled power and fluid motion, as he settles into the chair across from me. The table between us feels like an ocean, vast and impassable.

We eat in silence, the only sounds are the scrape of forks

against plates and the distant crash of waves against the shore. I steal glances at him between bites, trying to decipher the puzzle of his expression. His jaw is set, a muscle ticking there betraying some inner tension. His eyes remain fixed on his plate as if the secrets of the universe are hidden in the folds of his omelet.

As I finish the last bite of my omelet, I find myself staring out the window at the sun-drenched beach beyond. The sand glitters like a carpet of diamonds, and the waves roll in with a hypnotic rhythm, their foam-tipped crests beckoning invitingly. A flock of seagulls wheel overhead, their cries carrying on the salt-laden breeze that rustles the curtains. Oscar clears his throat, drawing my attention back to him. His eyes, usually so guarded, now hold a flicker of something I can't quite place. "Are you going down to the beach with Z today?" he asks, his tone deceptively casual.

There's something in the way he says it that sets my teeth on edge. Is it the slight emphasis on 'Z', or the barely perceptible tightening around his eyes? Whatever it is, it strikes a discordant note in the morning's fragile harmony.

I take a slow sip of my coffee, using the moment to study him over the rim of my mug. The tension in his shoulders, the way his fingers drum an erratic beat on the table, it all speaks of an agitation he's trying hard to conceal.

"I haven't made any plans yet," I reply carefully, setting my mug down with deliberate gentleness. "Why do you ask?"

Oscar shrugs, the movement too studied to be natural. "Just curious. You two seem to have made it a habit."

There it is again, that undercurrent of something. Jealousy? Concern? I can't quite put my finger on it, but it makes me bristle.

"Well," I say, meeting his gaze squarely, "You could go with me."

The words hang in the air between us, a challenge and an invitation rolled into one. Oscar's eyes widen fractionally, surprise flitting across his features before he schools them back into neutrality.

For a moment, I think he might refuse. The silence stretches, taut as a bowstring, filled with unspoken words and half-formed thoughts. Then, just as I'm about to retract my offer, a slow smile spreads across his face, transforming his features.

"I'd like that," he says softly, and suddenly the tension in the room dissipates like morning mist under the sun's warmth.

Oscar rises from his chair, the wooden legs scraping softly against the tile floor. He gathers our plates with practiced ease, the porcelain clinking gently as he stacks them before depositing them in the sink.

"Give me a second to grab my shoes and a hoodie," Oscar says, his voice low and warm. "Then we can head out."

I nod, watching as he disappears down the hallway. In his absence, I find myself drawn to the window, gazing out at the beach beyond. The sand stretches out like a pale golden carpet, meeting the tumultuous blue-gray of the ocean. White-capped waves crash against the shore in a relentless rhythm, sending sprays of foam into the air.

Oscar returns, now wearing a pair of well-worn sneakers and carrying a dark blue hoodie. "Ready?" he asks, a hint of a smile playing at the corners of his mouth.

We step out onto the porch, the wooden boards creaking softly beneath our feet. The air is crisp and salty, carrying the plaintive cries of seagulls overhead. As we make our way down the weathered steps and sandy path through the tall weeds, I can't help but steal glances at Oscar.

I find myself comparing him to his twin. Where Zaire is all sharp edges, Oscar moves with a calm assurance that seems to still the very air around him. Z's presence fills a room, demanding attention, while Oscar's is more subtle – a quiet strength that you don't notice until it envelops you completely. The wind ruffles his dark hair, shorter than his twin's, emphasizing the sharp lines of his jaw and cheekbones.

The sand shifts beneath our feet as we reach the shore-line, the grains cool and damp in the morning air. I wrap my arms around myself, a shiver running through me as a particularly strong gust cuts through my thin shirt. Oscar glances over, concern etching lines around his eyes.

Without a word, he shrugs off his hoodie, revealing a sliver of toned abdomen as his shirt rides up. He holds it out to me, his expression softening. "Here," he says, his voice low and warm. "You look cold."

I hesitate for a moment before accepting the offered garment. As I slip it on, I'm enveloped in warmth that goes beyond mere physical comfort. Oscar's scent surrounds me — a heady mixture of sandalwood and sea salt. The hoodie is far too big, the sleeves falling past my fingertips, but I've never felt more secure.

"Thank you," I murmur, nestling deeper into the soft fabric. Oscar's eyes linger on me, a strange mix of emotions swirling in their depths. For a moment, I think he might say something, but instead, he simply nods and turns back to the sea.

Oscar's presence beside me is steady and constant, his stride matching mine effortlessly. The wind has tousled his hair, giving him a boyish charm that softens his usually serious demeanor. I find my gaze drawn to the strong line of his jaw and the curve of his neck disappearing into the collar of his t-shirt.

After a while, Oscar breaks the silence. "So, what do you usually do out here with Z?" His tone is carefully neutral, but I catch the slight tensing of his shoulders as he mentions his brother's name.

"We talk, mostly," I reply, watching a seagull dive into the waves. "Usually about nonsense. Yesterday, we had a heated debate about whether a hot dog is a sandwich."

I expect Oscar to laugh, but when I glance over, his expression is tight, his eyes fixed on the horizon. The jealousy I'd sensed earlier is now palpable, radiating off him in waves.

"Oscar," I say softly, reaching out to touch his arm. He flinches slightly at the contact but doesn't pull away. "Why does it bother you so much? Me spending time with Zaire?"

He tries to brush it off, shaking his head with a forced laugh. "It doesn't. Why would it?"

But I press on, determined now. "Don't do that. Don't lie to me. I've seen the way you look when Z and I come back from our walks. The way you withdraw. Why?"

Oscar's face darkens, a storm brewing in his eyes. He pulls away from me, taking a few steps back. "Drop it," he says, his voice low and tight with barely contained emotion. "It's nothing. Forget I asked."

I follow him, my feet sinking into the sand as I try to keep up with his now longer strides. "Oscar, wait!" I call out, frustrated by his evasion. "Talk to me, please!"

He whirls around suddenly, his eyes blazing with an intensity that takes my breath away. "You want to know why?" he asks, his voice low and tight with emotion. "I'm jealous, okay? I'm jealous of what you have with my brother."

I blink, taken aback by his admission. "What?"

Oscar runs a hand through his hair, his frustration evident in every line of his body. "You cling to Zaire like he's your lifeline. You seek him out when the fear creeps in. But it was me, Vesper. I was the one who didn't give up on you. He almost did."

His words hit me like a physical blow, leaving me reeling. Oscar's eyes bore into mine, a tempest of emotions swirling in their depths. His chest heaves with ragged breaths as he struggles to contain the flood of feelings he's kept bottled up for so long. The wind whips around us, mirroring the storm brewing between us.

"Watching you with Zaire and Talon, it kills me." Oscar's eyes meet mine, filled with a desperate longing. "I know it's selfish. I know I should be grateful that you're healing, that you're finding happiness again. But I can't help but feel like I'm losing you all over again. And the worst part is, you don't even know what you mean to me..."

The world seems to still around us, the crashing waves and crying gulls fading into a distant hum. Oscar's words hang in the air between us, heavy with the weight of unspoken truths and forgotten memories. I stand there, my mind reeling, trying to process the flood of information he's just unleashed.

Oscar's eyes, usually so guarded, now shine with a vulnerability that takes my breath away. The intensity of his gaze pins me in place, and I find myself lost in the depths of blue that seem to hold entire universes of emotion.

"I...I don't understand," I stammer. "What do you mean? What I mean to you?"

He takes a step closer, and I can see the internal struggle playing out across his features. His jaw clenches and unclenches as if he's fighting against the words that want to spill out.

"From the moment I saw you at St. Jude's," he begins, his voice low and rough with emotion, "I knew. God, Vesper, I knew you were it for me. You walked into that classroom, and my whole world shifted."

The sand beneath my feet suddenly feels unsteady, and I sway slightly. Oscar reaches out instinctively to steady me, his hand warm and strong on my arm. The touch sends a jolt through me, awakening something deep and primal that I can't quite name.

"But I couldn't let myself have those feelings," he continues, his eyes never leaving mine. "You were untouchable. The Rossi princess, destined for a political marriage to strengthen alliances. And I was just me. A second son with no real power or influence.

Oscar's hand slides down my arm, his fingers intertwining with mine. The contact sends shivers racing up my spine. "I kept my distance because I knew that having you, even for a moment, and then losing you would destroy me. So I watched from afar, content to be in your orbit, even if I could never truly be part of your world."

Oscar's eyes meet mine, a storm of emotions swirling in their depths. "Having to sit across from you, pretending to be my Uncle's obedient nephew when your father told you about your engagement was pure torture. Worse, having to be my Uncle's spy to make sure you were as pure as your father led my uncle to believe."

"Then why did you do it? Why did you risk everything to get me away from Dmitri?"

"Because I am a selfish fucking asshole who would rather rip you away from the family and life you knew than allow you to marry my monster of a cousin. He would have stolen the light out of your eyes," he admits. "I couldn't bear the thought of you being tied to him, being forced into that life. It was unbearable."

I can see the pain etched into every line of his face, feel it radiating off him in waves. My free hand moves of its own accord, reaching up to cup his cheek. Oscar leans into the touch, his eyes fluttering closed for a brief moment.

"That's why you offered to get me out? Because you had a crush on me?"

"A crush doesn't begin to explain the way I feel about you, Vesper. School boy idolizations don't even come close. The lengths that I would have gone to touch you back then. When I stole you away during that fight, my control was carefully leashed. To be so fucking close to you, to touch you, it drove me crazy. I wanted to claim you in that class-room. To take you and ruin you so you would never be able to marry Dmitri. I would have defiled you, my evening star, until your light blinded the world."

Oscar's free hand comes up to cup my face, his touch impossibly gentle. "I know I have no right to feel this way. No right to be jealous of the comfort you find in Zaire or Talon. But every time I see you smile at them, it kills me. Not because I begrudge you finding comfort, but because I know it should have been me. I should have been the one to help you heal, to be there for you. But I failed you, and now I have to live with that guilt every single day."

My heart aches for him, for the pain and guilt he's been carrying all this time. Without thinking, I step closer, closing the distance between us. My free hand comes up to rest on his chest, feeling the rapid beat of his heart beneath my palm.

"Oscar," I whisper, my voice barely audible above the crashing waves.

His eyes widen in surprise, a flicker of hope dancing across his features before doubt clouds them once more. I take a deep breath, gathering my thoughts. The wind tugs at my hair, sending strands dancing across my face. Oscar reaches up instinctively, tucking them behind my ear with a tenderness that makes my heart skip a beat.

"When it mattered most, Oscar, you were there," I continue, my voice growing stronger. "You found me. You saved me. And even now, when I wake up screaming in the middle of the night, terrified and lost. You're always the first one there, anchoring me back to reality. Yes, Zaire and Talon have been there for me. Yes, I have a connection with them. Maybe it's a trauma bond. Maybe it's more. I don't know. But what I do know right now is this, I need you, too."

Oscar's eyes widen, a mix of hope and disbelief swirling in their depths. His hand trembles slightly as it cups my cheek, his thumb tracing a gentle arc across my skin. The touch sends shivers down my spine, awakening nerves I didn't know existed.

"Vesper," he breathes, my name a prayer on his lips. "Is this okay?"

I'm acutely aware of every point where our bodies connect; his hand on my face, mine on his chest, our fingers still intertwined. There's not a single prickle of unease now. His hands feel like home to me, helping me shove down my fear and anxiety.

"Yes. Please touch me."

Slowly, almost imperceptibly, Oscar leans closer. His breath fans across my face, warm and sweet. My eyes flutter closed as the distance between us narrows, anticipation coiling tight in my belly.

When his lips finally meet mine, it's like coming home and stepping into the unknown all at once. The kiss is soft at first, tentative, as if he's afraid I might disappear. But as I respond, pressing closer and parting my lips, something inside Oscar seems to snap.

His arm wraps around my waist, pulling me flush against him. His other hand tangles in my hair, tilting my head back as he deepens the kiss. A low groan escapes him as our tongues meet.

I clutch at his shirt, desperate to eliminate any remaining space between us. Oscar's body is hard and warm against mine.

Oscar breaks the kiss, trailing his lips along my jaw and

down my neck. He finds a particularly sensitive spot just below my ear, and I can't hold back the breathy moan that escapes me. I feel him smile against my skin before he returns his attention to that spot, alternating between gentle kisses and teasing nips.

My head falls back, giving him better access. The sun warms my face as Oscar's mouth sets my body on fire. His hand slips under the hoodie I'm wearing, his hoodie, fingers splaying across the small of my back. The skin-on-skin contact sends jolts of electricity through me.

"Fuck, I've dreamed about this," Oscar murmurs against my throat, his voice low and rough with desire. The sound of my name on his lips in that tone makes me weak at the knees.

His fingers trail up my spine, leaving goosebumps in their wake. I arch into him, craving more of his touch, more of this intoxicating connection.

Oscar captures my lips again, the kiss deep and passionate. His tongue explores my mouth as if he's trying to memorize every detail. I respond with equal fervor, my fingers tangling in his hair, pulling him closer. The world fades away until there's nothing but Oscar, the taste of him, the feel of his body against mine, the sound of our ragged breathing mingling with the crash of waves.

Suddenly, the crunch of footsteps on nearby rocks shatters the moment. I stumble back from Oscar, my cheeks burning as I see Zaire approaching. His long strides eat up the distance between us, and I can't help but notice the way his eyes narrow as they flick between Oscar and me.

Zaire clears his throat. "Well," he says, a hint of amusement coloring his tone, "that was quite a show."

Chapter 22

ZAIRE

"ZAIRE," Vesper starts, her voice hoarse. She clears her throat, trying again. "About what you saw…I mean, Oscar and I, um, well…kissing."

"It's fine." I stroll closer, hands shoved in my pockets, a lazy grin playing on my lips. "Don't look so shocked, Vesper. It's not like this is the first time Oz and I have shared something in our lives. Twins, remember? "

"I don't…I don't understand," she stammers. "You're okay with this?"

I can't help but laugh. "Sweetheart, in our world, you take pleasure where you can find it. Life's too short and too dangerous to get hung up on conventional morality."

I watch Vesper's cheeks flush, her emerald eyes darting nervously between Oz and me. It's adorable, really, how flustered she is. But beneath that embarrassment, I catch a flicker of something else—desire, maybe even a hint of curiosity.

"But you and me? I almost kissed you."

"And?" I tease her. "Who says you have to choose between us?"

The salt-tinged breeze ruffles my hair, carrying the rhythmic sound of waves lapping at the shore. This beach, our beach, where I've walked countless times with Vesper, sharing whispered secrets and stolen glances. And now, here she stands, lips still swollen from my brother's kiss.

Oz leans against a nearby palm tree, arms crossed, that insufferable smirk plastered on his face. It's the same look he wore when we were kids, and he'd beat me at chess or try to talk his way out of trouble. That smug smile ignites a fire in my gut, more potent than any jealousy over Vesper's kiss. Because I know my brother. I know how he operates, how he always has to be first, has to win.

But Vesper isn't a game to be won. She's so much more.

I tear my gaze from Oz and focus on Vesper. Her blonde hair whips around her face in the breeze, and I fight the urge to brush it back, to run my fingers through those silky strands. "You don't owe me an explanation, sweetheart," I say softly, noting how she shivers at the endearment. "What happens between consenting adults is nobody's business but their own."

Vesper's brow furrows, confusion evident in her expressive eyes. "But...aren't you angry? Or hurt?" She shifts uncomfortably, and I can see the guilt etched across her features. It's almost endearing, how she thinks she needs to explain herself to me. As if I haven't known from the moment I met her that she'd be tangled up with both of us eventually.

I chuckle, the sound low and husky. "Angry? No. A little envious, perhaps." I lean in close, my lips nearly brushing her ear as I whisper, "But I meant what I said before. I'm a patient man, Vesper. I can wait."

As I pull back, I catch the way her breath hitches, how her pupils dilate ever so slightly. Oh yes, there's definitely more than embarrassment there. I reach out, brushing my fingers along Vesper's arm. She shivers, and I can't help but smirk. "Cold, sweetheart?" I ask, knowing full well it's not the temperature making her tremble considering she's swimming in one of Oscar's hoodies.

Oscar clears his throat, clearly annoyed at my interruption. Good. Let him stew for a bit. "We should head back," he says, glancing at his watch. "The others will be wondering where we are."

I nod, but my eyes never leave Vesper's face. "You go ahead, Oz. I'll walk Vesper back."

For a moment, I think he might argue, but then he shrugs and starts walking towards the house. As he passes me, he mutters, "Play nice, Z."

I wait until he's out of earshot before turning back to

Vesper. She's staring at the ground, her toes digging into the sand. "Hey," I say softly, tilting her chin up with my finger. "You okay?"

She nods, but I can see the conflict in her eyes. "Zaire, I...I don't know what I'm doing."

I chuckle, pulling her close. "Join the club, sweetheart. We're all just making this up as we go along." I press a kiss to her forehead, inhaling the scent of her shampoo mixed with the ocean air. "But I meant what I said. You don't have to choose."

As we walk, I can't help but steal glances at Vesper. Her steps are hesitant like she's walking on eggshells instead of sand. I know her mind must be racing, trying to make sense of everything that's happened. She's so innocent in many ways despite the world she comes from. A virgin, if the whispers at that godforsaken auction were to be believed. The thought of her being sold like property still makes my blood boil.

"You're thinking too hard," I say, nudging her gently with my shoulder. "I can practically hear the gears turning in that pretty head of yours."

She looks up at me, those green eyes wide and vulnerable. "How can you be so calm about all this?" she asks.

I sigh, running a hand through my hair. "Years of practice, sweetheart. When you grow up in this world, you learn to roll with the punches." I pause, choosing my next words carefully. "But I know it's different for you. You've been sheltered, protected."

Vesper scoffs, a bitter sound that doesn't suit her. "Protected? Is that what you call being groomed for an arranged marriage?"

I wince, regretting my choice of words. "Fair point. I just meant...you haven't had the chance to explore, to figure out what you want."

We've reached a secluded cove, hidden from the view of the main beach. I stop walking, turning to face her. The sun paints her skin in shades of gold and pink, making her look almost ethereal. I resist the urge to reach out and touch her, to see if she's real or just a mirage.

"I see the way you flinch sometimes," I say softly. "When someone moves too quickly, or when a door slams shut. I know you've been through hell, Vesper. And I know your body and your mind aren't always on the same page."

She wraps her arms around herself, suddenly looking small and vulnerable. "Is it that obvious?" she asks, her voice trembling.

I shake my head. "Only to those who know what to look for. Trauma, it leaves its mark, even when the scars aren't visible."

Vesper takes a shaky breath, her eyes filling with unshed tears. "Sometimes I feel like I'm going crazy," she admits. "One minute I'm fine, and the next...it's like I can't breathe. And then there are times when I want...when I feel..." She trails off, her cheeks flushing.

"When your body wants to feel something good, but

your mind won't let you," I finish for her. She nods, looking relieved that I understand.

I take a step closer, close enough to feel the heat radiating from her body, but not touching. "It's okay to want things, Vesper. It's okay to feel desire, to crave touch."

I watch as Vesper's eyes widen, a mix of fear and longing swirling in those emerald depths. She's like a wild animal, poised to flee at the slightest provocation. I keep my movements slow, deliberate, as I reach out to brush a strand of hair from her face.

"Z-Zaire," she stammers, her breath catching as my fingers graze her cheek. "I don't...I've never..."

"Shh," I soothe, cupping her face gently. "I know, sweetheart. And we don't have to do anything you're not ready for."

The rising sun illuminates the beach around us in a soft. The light softens Vesper's features, making her look even younger, more vulnerable. My heart aches for her, for all she's been through, for the innocence that was stolen from her long before she ever had a chance to give it willingly.

"But what if I want to?" she whispers, her voice barely audible over the crashing waves. "What if I want to feel something good? Something that's mine?"

Her words ignite a fire in my veins, but I force myself to remain calm. This isn't about me or my desires. It's about Vesper, about giving her the choice she's been denied for so long.

"Then we take it slow," I murmur, my thumb tracing the

curve of her jaw. "We go at your pace, and if at any point you want to stop, we stop. No questions asked."

Vesper nods, her eyes fluttering closed as she leans into my touch. I can feel her trembling, but whether from fear or anticipation, I'm not sure. Probably both.

"Can I kiss you?" I ask, my lips hovering just inches from hers.

She hesitates for a moment, then nods again. "Yes," she breathes.

I close the distance between us, pressing my lips to hers in a kiss that's soft, gentle, nothing like the heated exchanges I'm used to. Vesper sighs against my mouth, her body melting into mine as if she's finally letting go of some of the tension she's been carrying.

My hands find her waist, pulling her closer as I deepen the kiss. She tastes like salt and sunshine, and I can't get enough. I pull her tighter against me, but she stiffens.

I pull back immediately, searching her face for signs of distress. "Too much?" I ask.

Vesper shakes her head, frustration evident in the furrow of her brow. "No, I...I liked it. I just..." She trails off, struggling to find the words.

"It's okay," I assure her, running my hands up and down her arms soothingly. "Your body and your mind aren't always going to be in sync, remember? It's normal. Do what feels right to you."

I watch as Vesper's internal struggle plays out across her face. Her eyes dart around nervously, never quite meeting mine, and her teeth worry at her lower lip. It's a habit I've noticed before, one that speaks volumes about her anxiety. I want nothing more than to pull her close, to shield her from the world that's hurt her so badly. But I know that's not what she needs right now.

"Hey," I say softly, ducking my head to catch her gaze. "We don't have to do anything else. This isn't a race, Vesper. There's no finish line we need to cross."

She nods, but I can see the frustration simmering beneath the surface. "I know," she whispers. "I just...I hate feeling so broken. So damaged."

My heart clenches at her words. "You're not broken, sweetheart. You're healing. There's a difference."

I take her hand, leading her to a nearby rock formation. We sit side by side, our shoulders touching, watching as the waves crash against the shore. The rhythmic sound is sooth-ing, and I feel some of the tension leave Vesper's body.

"Can I tell you something?" I ask, keeping my voice low and gentle. She nods, her eyes fixed on the horizon. "When I was younger, maybe fifteen or sixteen, I got caught in the crossfire of a deal gone bad and took a bullet to the shoulder."

Vesper gasps softly, her hand instinctively reaching out to touch the spot where the scar lies hidden beneath my shirt. I let her, savoring the warmth of her palm against my skin.

"It wasn't even that serious of an injury," I continue. "But for months afterward, I couldn't stand the sound of fireworks or car backfires. My body would react before my brain could process what was happening. Heart racing, palms sweating, the whole nine yards."

"What did you do?" Vesper asks.

I shrug. "Learned to cope. Found ways to ground myself when the panic hit. But mostly, I just gave myself time. And eventually, it got better."

She's quiet for a long moment, processing my words. When she finally speaks, her voice is thick with unshed tears. "But what if it never gets better for me? What if I'm always like this?"

I turn to face her, taking both of her hands in mine. "Then we'll figure it out together. You, me, Oz, the whole damn Second Sons if that's what it takes. You're not alone in this, Vesper."

A single tear escapes, trailing down her cheek. I resist the urge to brush it away, knowing she needs to feel whatever she's feeling right now. Instead, I just hold her hands, offering silent support as she works through her emotions.

"I want to be able to feel...desire without panic following close behind."

"Considering what I just walked into, I'd say you're figuring it out with Oscar," I offer with a smile.

She blushes at the reminder. "This is so hard to explain. One second, I'm fine. The next, a single touch makes me want to jump out of my skin. I can't control it."

My heart aches for her. I've seen the way she flinches at sudden movements, how she tenses when anyone gets too close. The auction - that godforsaken event where she was sold like property - has left scars that run deeper than any physical wound.

"Vesper," I say softly, reaching out to tuck a strand of hair behind her ear. She leans into my touch, almost unconsciously, and I feel a surge of protectiveness. "There's no timeline for healing. What you've been through...it takes time to process."

I watch as she swallows hard, her eyes shimmering with unshed tears. The rising sun paints her skin in hues of gold and pink, making her look ethereal, untouchable. But I know the reality. She's flesh and blood, vulnerable and strong all at once.

"I just wish I could turn it off sometimes. The fear, the anxiety...it's exhausting."

I reach out, taking her hand in mine. Her fingers are cold despite the warmth of the morning, and I rub them gently between my palms. "I know, sweetheart."

A ghost of a smile flits across her face, there and gone in an instant. "I'm not used to that," she admits. "Having people I can trust."

"Well, get used to it," I tell her, my voice gruff with emotion. "Because we're not going anywhere."

Chapter 23

VESPER

I CLOSE the door to my room, leaning against it with a sigh. The evening's events playing through my mind like a film reel, each moment tinged with a newfound electricity I can't quite explain. Dinner had been a lively affair, filled with easy laughter and playful banter, but beneath it all, an undercurrent of tension thrummed.

I push off the door and pad across the wooden floor to my bed, sinking onto the edge. The soft glow of my bedside lamp cast shadows across the room, creating an intimate cocoon that only intensified my swirling thoughts.

Oscar and Zaire. Zaire and Oscar. I close my eyes, remembering the warmth of Oscar's hand on my lower back as he guided me to my seat at dinner, the brush of Zaire's fingers against mine as he passed me the salt.

I flop back onto the bed, staring up at the ceiling. "What is wrong with me?" I whisper to the empty room. I've never had one guy in my life, and now, I kissed two in a single day. I roll onto my side, hugging a pillow to my chest as I try to make sense of the tumultuous emotions swirling within me. The memory of Zaire's kiss, tender and reverent, sends a shiver down my spine. His touch had been gentle, almost hesitant, as if he feared I might shatter beneath his fingers. And yet, there was an underlying strength there, a promise of protection that made me feel safe in a way I'd never experienced before.

But then there was Oscar. His kiss had been fire and passion, igniting something primal within me. Where Zaire was the calm eye of the storm, Oscar was the tempest itself, wild and unpredictable. I can still feel the ghost of his hands on my waist, the heat of his breath against my neck.

I press my face into the pillow, torn between exhilaration and confusion. How is it possible to feel so strongly for two people at once? They're twins, yes, but they're also individuals, each with their own unique qualities that draw me in like a moth to a flame.

Oscar's quiet strength and thoughtful nature, the way his blue eyes seem to see right through to my soul. Zaire's roguish charm and fierce loyalty. They're two halves of a whole, complementing each other in ways I'm only beginning to understand.

I sit up abruptly, running my fingers through my hair as Zaire's words echo in my mind. 'You don't have to choose,' he had said, his voice low and intense. At the time, I had dismissed it as impossible, a fantasy born of desire and wishful thinking. But now, in the quiet of my room, I find myself wondering...could it be true?

The concept is foreign, almost taboo. Society has always taught us that love is meant for two people, that anything else is wrong or selfish. But as I think about Oscar and Zaire, about the way they move in perfect synchronicity, and the silent communication that passes between them with just a glance, I begin to see the possibility.

Maybe love isn't about choosing one person over another. Maybe it's about opening your heart wide enough to encompass all the love it's capable of giving. The thought is both terrifying and exhilarating, like standing on the edge of a cliff, ready to take flight. Could I really have both of them? Could we create something beautiful and unique, the three of us together?

I lay back down, my mind racing with possibilities. The soft cotton of the sheets whisper against my skin as I shift, trying to find a comfortable position. But comfort eludes me as my thoughts continue to spiral, each scenario more vivid than the last.

I imagine waking up between them, Oscar's steady heartbeat beneath my ear, Zaire's arm draped protectively over my waist. The three of us moving through life as a unit, supporting each other, and loving each other. I picture lazy Sunday mornings filled with laughter and stolen kisses, the aroma of fresh coffee mingling with the scent of their skin. I see Oscar teaching me to dance, his hands guiding me gently as we sway to a melody only we can hear. Zaire watches from the sidelines, his eyes gleaming with a mixture of pride and desire. Later, it's Zaire who pulls me close, his lips hot against my neck as Oscar's fingers intertwine with mine.

The images that flood my senses are so real that I can almost taste them. The roughness of Zaire's stubble against my palm, the softness of Oscar's lips on my forehead. Their voices, a harmony of deep tones that resonate in my very soul. I imagine the way they would look at each other, a bond deeper than blood, strengthened by their shared love for me.

A soft laugh escapes my lips, surprising even myself. Here I am, contemplating a relationship that most would deem impossible or immoral, yet it feels...right. Like pieces of a puzzle finally clicking into place.

I drift off to sleep with these thoughts, a smile playing on my lips as I surrender to dreams filled with silver and blue eyes, and endless possibilities.

But as the night deepens, my pleasant dreams twist into something darker.

The soft glow of my room fades, replaced by harsh fluorescent lights that buzz overhead. The comfort of my bed morphs into the cold, unyielding surface of a hospital gurney. I try to move, but my wrists and ankles are bound by thick leather straps. Panic rises in my throat as I realize I'm back in that sterile, nightmarish place.

The Shadow Man looms over me, his face obscured by darkness despite the bright lights. His presence is oppressive, suffocating. I can feel his gaze roaming over my body, predatory and hungry. This time, it's different. There's no talk of eggs or fertility. The air is charged with a more sinister intent.

"You're mine now," he whispers, his voice like gravel scraping against my ears. His hand, cold and clammy, traces a path down my arm. I shudder, trying to pull away, but the restraints hold me fast.

He leans in closer, his breath hot against my neck. "They can't protect you here," he hisses, and I know he means Oscar and Zaire. In this realm of nightmares, they feel impossibly far away.

The Shadow Man's form seems to ripple and shift, growing larger, more monstrous. His fingers elongate into claws that tear at my clothes. I try to scream, but no sound comes out. The room spins around me, the walls closing in, suffocating me with their sterility.

I feel him pressing against me, a weight that threatens to crush me. His touch leaves icy trails on my skin, each caress a violation. The Shadow Man's laughter echoes through the room, a cacophony of cruel amusement. "You're mine," he repeats, the words burrowing into my mind like parasites. "Body and soul."

I bolt upright in bed, a scream dying in my throat as the remnants of my nightmare cling to me like a cold sweat. The darkness of my room feels oppressive, closing in around me as I struggle to catch my breath. Before I can fully shake off the terror, my door bursts open, and Oscar rushes in, his blue eyes wide with concern.

"Vesper, are you alright?" he asks, crossing the room in long strides.

I nod weakly, but the trembling of my hands betrays me. "Another nightmare," I whisper, hating how vulnerable I sound.

Oscar's expression softens, and he perches on the edge of my bed. "Do you want to talk about it?"

I shake my head, then surprise myself by asking, "Could you...stay with me?"

He hesitates for a moment, then nods, sliding under the covers beside me. As he wraps an arm around my waist, I stiffen involuntarily, the ghost of my nightmare making me flinch at his touch.

"Shh, it's okay," Oscar murmurs, his breath warm against my ear. "You're safe, Vesper. I've got you."

I gradually relax into Oscar's embrace, my body molding against his solid form. The warmth of his chest against my back seeps through my thin nightgown, chasing away the chill of fear. As my breathing steadies, I become acutely aware of every point of contact between us – his arm draped protectively over my waist, his legs tangled with mine, and the unmistakable hardness pressing against my backside.

A shiver runs through me, but this time it's not from fear. I turn my head slightly. "I hate this," I whisper into the darkness. "Every time I close my eyes, I'm terrified of what I'll see. The nightmares...they're relentless."

Oscar's arm tightens around me, and I feel his lips brush

against my hair. "I wish I could take them away," he murmurs.

"I just want to feel something else," I confess, my voice barely audible. "Anything other than this constant dread."

There's a moment of hesitation, and then Oscar's lips find my neck, placing a gentle kiss just below my ear. The touch sends a jolt of electricity through my body, igniting a warmth that spreads from my core. He trails more kisses along my jawline, each one stoking the fire building within me.

I turn in his arms, facing him in the dim light filtering through the curtains. His blue eyes are dark with desire, mirroring the need I feel coursing through my veins. "Oscar," I breathe, "make me feel good. Please. I need to feel something other than fear."

His response is immediate. His lips capture mine in a searing kiss, erasing all thoughts of nightmares and leaving only a burning desire in their wake.

Oscar's weight shifts over me as he gently rolls me onto my back, his lips never leaving mine. The mattress dips beneath us, and I sink into its softness, feeling anchored by Oscar's solid presence above me. His hand trails down my side, leaving a trail of goosebumps in its wake. When he reaches the hem of my nightgown, he hesitates, his fingers playing with the delicate fabric.

"Are you sure?" he whispers against my lips, his voice husky with desire. "I know you're inexperienced. I need to hear with words that you want this."

I nod, unable to form words that he wants as anticipation coils tightly in my belly. Oscar's hand slips beneath my nightgown, his calloused fingers skimming along my thigh. The contrast between his rough skin and my softness sends shivers through my body. His touch is reverent, exploring every curve and dip as if committing it to memory.

As his hand inches higher, my breath catches in my throat. The room feels charged with electricity, every nerve ending hypersensitive to Oscar's touch. When his fingers finally brush against the apex of my thighs, a soft moan escapes my lips. Oscar captures the sound with his mouth, kissing me deeply as his fingers begin to explore my most intimate area. My body stiffens.

Oscar stops, and removes his hand, having caught my reaction. His blue eyes watching me intently.

"I'm okay," I reassure him.

"I felt you stiffen."

"I'm fine. I promise." I nod, trying to convey with my eyes what I can't quite put into words. Oscar's gaze is tender, patient. He waits, his hand resting gently on my hip, giving me time to process. My heart races, not just from desire, but from the conflicting emotions warring within me.

I want this. I want to feel normal, to experience intimacy without the shadows of my past looming over me. But Zaire's face flashes in my mind, unbidden. I remember how I couldn't let him go further, how I pushed him away. The guilt and shame rise up, threatening to choke me.

No. I push those thoughts aside, focusing on Oscar's

warmth, his gentle touch. I'm here, now, with him. I want to move forward, to reclaim this part of myself. I can't keep allowing my nightmares to win. The only way to face my fear is to replace it with something much more powerful.

"I'm fine," I whisper again, my voice stronger this time. I don't mention the turmoil inside, the desperate wish to feel normal. Instead, I reach up, cupping Oscar's face in my hands. "Please, don't stop."

Oscar searches my face for a moment longer, then nods. He leans in, pressing a soft kiss to my forehead, then my cheek, then finally my lips. The tenderness of the gesture nearly undoes me.

As his fingers resume their exploration, I close my eyes, focusing on the sensations. The soft sheets beneath me, the warmth of Oscar's body next to mine, the gentle pressure of his touch. I breathe deeply, willing my body to relax, to let go of the tension and fear.

Slowly, ever so slowly, I feel myself melting into his caress. The ghosts of the past recede, replaced by the present moment. Oscar's fingers move with careful precision, drawing sighs and soft moans from my lips.

I arch into his touch, craving more of the exquisite sensation. Oscar's skilled fingers dance over my sensitive flesh, teasing and stroking until I'm trembling beneath him. The fear and dread that had gripped me earlier dissolve, replaced by a burning need that consumes my every thought.

"Oscar," I gasp, breaking away from the kiss.

"I don't have any condoms," he admits.

"It's okay. I know they gave me a contraceptive shot. Please..."

He understands my unspoken request, slipping a finger inside me with agonizing slowness. The feeling is indescribable – a perfect fusion of pleasure and fullness that has me clutching at his shoulders. Oscar sets a gentle rhythm, his thumb circling my most sensitive spot as his finger moves within me.

I lose myself in the sensations, my world narrowing to the points where Oscar's body connects with mine. The tension builds steadily, a crescendo of pleasure that threatens to overwhelm me. Oscar's lips find my neck, trailing hot kisses along my pulse point as he adds a second finger, stretching me deliciously.

"Let go, Vesper," he murmurs against my skin. "I've got you."

His words, combined with a particularly skillful twist of his fingers, send me over the edge. Wave after wave of pleasure crash over me, and I cry out Oscar's name as my body shudders beneath him. He holds me through it all, his touch gentle yet grounding as I ride out the aftershocks.

As the last tremors of pleasure subside, I open my eyes to find Oscar gazing down at me, his expression a mix of awe and desire. He starts to withdraw his hand, but I catch his wrist, holding him in place.

"Don't stop," I whisper, my voice hoarse with need. "Please, Oscar. I want more."

He searches my face, his blue eyes intense in the dim light. "Vesper, we can stop here. There's no rush-."

I cut him off with a kiss, pouring all my longing and desperation into it. When we break apart, both breathless, I cup his face in my hands. "I've never made a choice in my life, Oscar. You're the first choice I want to make."

His eyes soften, and he leans down to press his forehead against mine. "Are you sure? We can wait if you're not ready."

I shake my head, my fingers trailing down his chest. "I don't want to wait. I want to feel you. All of you."

Oscar's response is a low groan. He captures my lips in a searing kiss, his body pressing me deeper into the mattress. I can feel the hard length of him against my thigh, and a thrill of anticipation courses through me.

With trembling hands, I tug at the hem of his shirt. Oscar breaks the kiss long enough to pull it over his head, revealing an expanse of toned muscle and smooth skin. I run my hands over his chest, marveling at the warmth radiating from him.

Oscar's fingers find the straps of my nightgown, sliding them down my shoulders with agonizing slowness. His lips follow the path of the fabric, leaving a trail of fire in their wake. When the gown pools around my waist, I resist the urge to cover myself, instead reveling in the way Oscar's eyes darken as he takes in the sight of me.

"You're beautiful," he murmurs, his voice thick with emotion. "So damn beautiful."

His hands and mouth explore every inch of newly exposed skin, leaving me gasping and arching beneath him. When his lips close around a sensitive peak, I cry out, my fingers tangling into his hair to hold him close.

Oscar lavishes attention on my breasts, alternating between gentle kisses and teasing nips that have me squirming with need. His hand slides down my stomach, dipping between my legs once more. I'm already slick with arousal, and his touch sends sparks of pleasure shooting through me.

Just as I'm about to tumble over the edge, Oscar withdraws his hand. I whimper at the loss, but then I feel something else pressing against me, hot, hard, and much larger than his fingers.

"Oscar," I plead, my hips rocking against his hand. "I need you. Please."

His eyes meet mine as he hooks his fingers in the waistband of his sweatpants. "Are you absolutely sure, Vesper? We can stop at any time."

In response, I wrap my legs around his waist, pulling him closer. "Yes," I breathe. "I'm sure."

Oscar nods, his expression a mix of desire and tenderness. He sheds the last of his clothing, and I can't help but stare at his naked form, a work of art sculpted from marble. He positions himself between my thighs, the blunt head of his arousal pressing against my entrance.

"This might hurt a little," he warns, his voice strained

with the effort of holding back. "Tell me if you need me to stop."

I nod, bracing myself for the pain I've heard so much about. Oscar pushes forward slowly, stretching me in a way I've never experienced before. There's a moment of sharp discomfort as he breaks through my barrier, and I gasp, my nails digging into his shoulders.

"Breathe, Vesper," Oscar murmurs, staying perfectly still. "Just breathe through it."

I focus on his voice, on the warmth of his skin against mine, and gradually, the pain subsides. In its place, a new sensation blooms, a delicious fullness that has me craving more. I roll my hips experimentally, drawing a groan from Oscar.

"You feel incredible," he whispers, his forehead resting against mine. "So tight, so perfect."

Encouraged by his words, I move again, and this time Oscar responds, pulling back slightly before pushing in deeper. The friction sends sparks of pleasure through my body, and I moan, arching into him.

Oscar sets a gentle rhythm, each thrust slow and deliberate. His eyes never leave mine, watching for any sign of discomfort. But all I feel is an ever-building pleasure, a warmth that spreads from where we're joined to the tips of my fingers and toes.

As my body adjusts to his size, the initial discomfort fades entirely, replaced by a burning need for more. I wrap my legs tighter around his waist, urging him deeper.

"Faster," I plead, my voice barely recognizable to my own ears. "Please, Oscar."

He obliges, increasing his pace. The room fills with the sound of our mingled breaths and the soft creaking of the bed. Oscar's hand slips between us, his fingers finding that sensitive bundle of nerves, and I cry out at the dual sensation.

The pleasure builds higher and higher, a tidal wave threatening to crash over me. Oscar's thrusts become more erratic, his breathing ragged against my neck. "Come for me, Vesper," he groans. "Let go. I've got you."

His words, combined with a particularly deep thrust, send me over the edge. The world explodes, pleasure radiating from my core in pulsing waves. I cry out Oscar's name, clinging to him as I ride out the most intense orgasm of my life.

Oscar follows me over the precipice moments later, his body tensing above me as he finds his release. He collapses onto me, his weight settles on top of me, and I feel a sense of completeness I've never known before. His breath is warm against my neck, our bodies still intimately joined. For a long moment, we simply lie there, basking in the afterglow of our shared pleasure.

When Oscar finally lifts his head, his blue eyes meet mine, filled with a tenderness that makes my heart ache. He brushes a strand of hair from my face, his touch impossibly gentle. "Are you okay?" he asks softly.

I nod, unable to find words to express the swirl of

emotions coursing through me. Joy, contentment, a hint of lingering pleasure, and something deeper – something I'm not quite ready to name.

Oscar carefully withdraws from me, and I wince slightly at the loss. He immediately looks concerned, but I shake my head, offering him a reassuring smile. "I'm fine," I whisper. "Just a little sore."

He leans down to place a soft kiss on my forehead. "That's normal. Wait here."

I watch as he slips out of bed, admiring the play of muscles beneath his skin as he moves. He disappears into the en-suite bathroom, returning moments later with a warm washcloth. With infinite care, he cleans between my thighs, his touch clinical yet somehow still intimate.

When he's done, Oscar tosses the cloth aside and slides back into bed, gathering me into his arms. I curl against him, resting my head on his chest. The steady thump of his heartbeat beneath my ear is soothing, grounding me in this moment.

"How do you feel?" Oscar asks, his fingers tracing lazy patterns on my bare shoulder.

I consider the question, taking stock of my body and emotions. "I feel different," I finally say. "But in a good way. Like I've crossed some invisible threshold."

Oscar's chest rumbles with a soft chuckle. "That's one way to put it."

I tilt my head to look up at him, suddenly struck by a wave of vulnerability. "Was it okay? For you, I mean."

His expression softens, and he cups my cheek in his hand. "Vesper, it was perfect. You're perfect."

Relief washes over me, and I lean into his touch. "I'm glad," I murmur. "I was worried I might disappoint you."

Oscar's arms tighten around me. "Never," he says fiercely. "You could never disappoint me."

His hand cups my cheek, tilting my face up to meet his gaze. In the dim light, his blue eyes are soft with an emotion I'm not quite ready to name. "What are you thinking?" he asks.

I consider deflecting, but the vulnerability of the moment compels me to honesty. "I'm thinking about how glad I am that it was you," I admit. "That my first time was with someone who cared enough to make it good for me."

Oscar's expression softens further, and he leans in to brush his lips against mine. "You deserve nothing less," he murmurs. "You deserve the world, Vesper."

His words stir something deep within me, a longing for more than just physical pleasure. But before I can examine the feeling too closely, Oscar is moving again, his lips trailing a path down my neck.

"You know," he says between kisses, "there's still so much more I want to show you."

A shiver of anticipation runs through me. "Oh?" I breathe, arching into his touch.

Oscar's response is a wicked grin that sets my pulse racing. "Oh yes," he purrs, his hand sliding down my body.

"The night is young, and I intend to worship every inch of you."

As his fingers dip between my thighs once more, igniting sparks of renewed desire, I surrender myself to the promise of his touch. The world outside my bedroom ceases to exist. There is only Oscar, his hands, his lips, and the exquisite pleasure he coaxes from my body again until exhaustion takes us both under.

Chapter 24

OSCAR

I WAKE to the soft warmth of Vesper's body curled against mine, her golden hair splayed across my chest like strands of sunlight. For a moment, I simply breathe her in, savoring the delicate scent of jasmine that clings to her skin. It's still surreal, waking up next to her like this in my bed. Vesper could have chosen anyone, but she chose me.

My fingers trace lazy patterns along her bare shoulder, marveling at the softness of her skin. In sleep, her face is peaceful, free from the weight of family expectations and mafia politics. I want to freeze this moment, to live in it forever. Just Vesper and me, tangled in these sheets, the rest of the world fading away.

But life has other plans. A sharp knock on the door shatters our bubble of tranquility. Vesper stirs slightly but doesn't wake. I press a gentle kiss to her forehead before carefully extricating myself from her embrace. She deserves her rest after everything she's been through.

I tug on my discarded sweatpants, not bothering with a shirt as I pad towards the door. Opening it reveals Talon, his hair pulled back in its signature man bun, an amused smirk playing on his lips.

"What do you want?"

"Trust me, I didn't want to knock on this door at all, but I drew the short straw. The last thing I want to see is your dick in a compromising position."

I roll my eyes, leaning against the doorframe. "Sorry to disappoint. Next time I'll be sure to answer the door naked just for you."

Talon clutches his chest dramatically. "Be still my beating heart. But seriously, man, we've got news."

The playful atmosphere dissipates instantly, replaced by a tense alertness. "What kind of news?"

Talon's expression turns grim. "We think we've got a lead on who might have sold Vesper's eggs. We're meeting in the kitchen." As Talon turns to leave, he pauses, glancing back at me. "Should we wake Vesper up for this?"

The question hangs in the air, heavy with implications. I consider it carefully, weighing the pros and cons. Leaving her in the dark would be easier, sparing her from immediate worry. But it would also take away her choices, her agency in a situation that directly affects her. The thought leaves a bitter taste in my mouth.

"Yes," I decide firmly. "She deserves to know."

Talon nods in agreement, a flicker of respect crossing his features. "Alright. We'll be in the kitchen when you're ready."

As he disappears down the hallway, I turn back to the bedroom. Vesper is still curled up in the sheets, her golden hair a tangled halo around her head. The sight of her makes my heart clench with a mixture of love and protectiveness.

I sit on the edge of the bed, my hand gently brushing her cheek. "Vesper," I murmur, my voice low and soft. "Wake up, love."

Her eyelids flutter, those mesmerizing green eyes slowly focusing on me. "Oz?" she mumbles, her voice thick with sleep. "What's wrong?"

"Talon came by. There's news about your eggs." I watch as awareness floods her features, sleep falling away in an instant.

She sits up, the sheet pooling around her waist. "Give me a minute. I'll be right there."

I nod, pressing a kiss to her forehead before standing. "We'll be in the kitchen."

A few moments later, Vesper joins us, her hair a beautiful mess and wearing nothing but my discarded t-shirt. It hangs loose on her frame, ending mid-thigh, and my breath catches at the sight. Even now, in the midst of chaos, she's breathtaking. Zaire notices, glancing my way with an eyebrow arched. I shake my head, putting that conversation on the back burner.

She pads into the kitchen, her bare feet silent on the cold tile. The others fall quiet as she enters, all eyes turning to her.

Vesper takes the open chair next to Alex as he types away on his computer. The soft blue glow of the screen illuminates his face, casting shadows that accentuate the sharp angles of his cheekbones. Z and I settle in behind her, my hand instinctively finding its way to her shoulder. She leans into my touch, a barely perceptible gesture that speaks volumes.

The kitchen is eerily quiet, the usual morning bustle replaced by a tense anticipation. Even Talon, normally a whirlwind of energy, is unnaturally still, his fingers drumming a silent rhythm on the countertop. The scent of fresh coffee hangs in the air, a jarring contrast to the gravity of the moment.

Alex clears his throat, his fingers pausing over the keyboard. "I've managed to track down a sale of what I believe to be Vesper's eggs," he begins, his voice low and controlled. "The transaction took place last year."

I feel Vesper stiffen under my hand, her breath catching. Z shifts closer, his presence a silent pillar of support.

"They used a fertility clinic in New York for the implantation," Alex continues, his eyes flickering between the screen and Vesper's face. "The clinic would have records of the patient."

"So how do we get the records?"

"We need to take a road trip," Talon declares.

"The clinic is about four hours away, give or take traffic. Two of us could go, and be back before dinner," Alex suggests.

"Alex and I should go," Zaire volunteers. "If that clinic deals with stolen eggs, they'll have security. That's Alex's department."

I shake my head, tension coiling in my gut. "Splitting up isn't a good idea. It leaves us exposed." The words taste bitter on my tongue, memories of past close calls flashing through my mind. "We're safer together. We've been lucky so far. If anyone from that auction found out who we really are it could bring a lot of trouble to our door step. Trouble we aren't prepared for."

Talon's brow furrows, his usual carefree demeanor slipping away. "But we need those records, Oz. Every moment we wait is another moment someone could be out there with Vesper's—"

"I know," I cut him off, my voice sharper than intended. I take a breath, forcing myself to soften my tone. "I know the stakes. But rushing in half-cocked could blow everything."

"Taking her with us isn't an option either. So, it's either Alex and I go to the clinic, get the information, and come back; or we all go, put Vesper at risk, and hope we all come back."

The weight of Zaire's words hangs heavy in the air. I feel the tension radiating from Vesper, her body coiled like a spring beneath my hand. My gaze locks with Z's, a silent conversation passing between us. His silver eyes are filled with determination and a hint of something else—worry, perhaps, or a flicker of the same protective instinct that courses through my veins.

I know he's right. We don't have a choice. The need to uncover the truth about Vesper's eggs outweighs the risk of splitting up. It's a calculated gamble, but one we have to take. The alternative—leaving Vesper in the dark about her own body, her own future is unthinkable.

"Alright," I concede, my voice rough with reluctance. "You and Alex go. But you stay in constant contact. If anything feels off, you bail immediately. No heroics, no risks. Got it?"

Zaire nods, a ghost of a smile touching his lips. "When have I ever been the reckless one, brother?"

The tension in the room eases slightly, Talon even managing a snort of laughter. "That would be me, thank you very much."

As the group disperses to prepare for the impromptu road trip, I catch Vesper's eye. She gives me a small nod, her green eyes filled with a mix of gratitude and determination. I know she understands the weight of this decision, the risks we're all taking for her.

Zaire heads towards his room, Vesper following close behind. I watch them go, a familiar twinge of jealousy flaring in my chest. It's irrational, I know. Vesper chose all of us, and the bond between her and my twin is as deep and true as the one we share. Still, old habits die hard.

Chapter 25

VESPER

I CAUTIOUSLY ENTER THE ROOM, my heart racing in my chest as I shut the door softly behind me. Zaire is already there, perched on the edge of his bed with his air of quiet strength. Clad in nothing but a pair of sleek black sweatpants that accentuate his sculpted physique. He exudes a magnetic allure that is both mesmerizing and intimidating under the soft glow of the dim lighting. Despite his formidable presence, there's a vulnerable glimmer in his eyes that tugs at my emotions.

"Nice shirt," Zaire said, his voice a low rumble that sends a shiver down my spine. His piercing gaze travels over the oversized garment I'm wearing – Oscar's shirt.

I feel a flush creep up my neck. "I got dressed in a hurry," I stammered, suddenly aware of the fact I had kissed him just yesterday.

Zaire's lips quirk into a half-smile, a mixture of amusement and something darker. "Relax, Vesper. I'm not upset. I knew you'd go to him first." He ran a hand through his dark hair, longer than Oscar's and slightly tousled. "Though I'd be lying if I said I wasn't a little jealous." His honesty catches me off guard. I open my mouth to respond, but he continues, "Patience is a virtue, right?" The wry twist to his words makes my breath catch.

I stand there, frozen, Zaire's words lingering in the charged space between us. The tension is so thick it could be sliced with a blade. Then, a softening in his expression eases the knot in my chest.

"I'm just relieved you've finally chosen for yourself," he murmurs gently. "You've always been tugged in every direction by others' demands. It's high time you acted on your own desires."

I swallow hard, my fingers twisting the hem of Oscar's shirt. The weight of last night's intimacy with his brother hangs heavy between us, unspoken, but palpable. I struggle to find words, my cheeks burning as I remember the tender passion, the whispered promises, and the feeling of finally belonging to someone by my own choice.

"I...um..." I stammer, searching for words that won't come. How do I talk to Zaire about this? About his brother?

The awkwardness is suffocating, and I desperately grasp for a change of subject. "I'm worried about you and Alex," I blurt out, latching onto the pressing concern that's been nagging at me. "The trip to New York...it's dangerous, isn't it?"

Zaire's expression shifts, a flicker of surprise crossing his features before settling into something more serious. He leans forward, elbows resting on his knees, and I can't help but notice the way his muscles ripple with the movement. The intricate tattoos adorning his skin seem to dance in the low light, telling stories I long to hear.

"It could be," he admits. "But, Alex and I know what we're doing. It's not exactly our first break in, Vesper. We'll be fine."

"It isn't?"

Zaire stands, closing the distance between us in two long strides. I step back, my back connecting with the door. He towers over me, his presence both comforting and overwhelming. "Look at me," he says softly.

I raise my eyes to meet his, getting lost in that captivating silver gaze. His hand comes up to cup my cheek, and I lean into his touch instinctively. His touch is gentle, but I can feel the strength in his calloused fingers. I shiver, not from fear, but from the intensity of his gaze and the electricity that seems to crackle between us.

"Vesper," Zaire begins, his voice low and husky, "you need to understand something. My hands. They aren't clean. None of ours are."

I swallow hard, feeling the weight of his words settle in my chest. His thumb traces my cheekbone.

"I've done things," he continues, "things that would make normal people lose their grip on reality. I've seen horrors that haunt my dreams, committed acts that would turn your stomach."

The raw honesty in his voice makes me tremble.

"But walking into danger to help you?" A small, sad smile tugs at the corner of his lips. "I'll do it again and again, without hesitation."

His words hang in the air between us, heavy with unspoken promises and barely contained passion. I can feel the heat radiating from his body, see the pulse beating rapidly at the base of his throat. The scar there catches the dim light, a silvery reminder of the dangerous life he leads.

"Why?" I whisper, my voice barely audible even in the quiet room.

Zaire's hand slides from my cheek to the back of my neck, his fingers tangling in my hair. He leans in closer until I can feel his breath fanning across my face.

"You know why."

My heart pounds so loudly I'm sure he can hear it. The air between us is charged, crackling with tension and unspoken desire. I'm acutely aware of every point where our bodies are almost touching; his hand in my hair, his chest mere inches from mine, our lips a breath apart.

"I know you chose Oscar," Zaire continues, his voice rough with emotion. "And I respect that. But I need you to know that I'm here. Always. Whether it's to protect you from the monsters out there or the ones in your own head."

I close my eyes, overwhelmed by the intensity of his words and the storm of emotions they stir within me. When I open them again, I see a vulnerability in Zaire that I've never witnessed before. It's like looking at a different person - not the hardened, tattooed enforcer of the Petrov family, but a man bearing his soul.

"Zaire, I-" I start, but he gently presses a finger to my lips, silencing me.

His free hand comes up to cup my cheek, his thumb tracing my cheekbone. The gentleness of his touch contrasts sharply with the darkness of his words. "Those monsters in your head? I'll be their nightmare. I will stand between them and you until they bow down to you as their Queen."

My breath catches in my throat as Zaire's words wash over me. The intensity in his eyes, the raw emotion in his voice, it's all too much. I feel myself drowning in the depths of his gaze.

Before I can form a coherent thought, Zaire closes the minuscule distance between us. His lips crash against mine with a passion that ignites every nerve ending in my body. This isn't like any kiss I've experienced before, not the tender exploration with Oscar, not the fumbling attempts of my youth. This is a claiming, a branding of my very soul.

His hand slides from my cheek to tangle in my hair, gripping firmly but not painfully. The other arm wraps around my waist, pulling me flush against his bare chest. I can feel the heat of his skin through the thin fabric of Oscar's shirt, the rapid beating of his heart echoing my own.

Zaire kisses me like a man starved, like I'm the air he needs to breathe. His lips are insistent, demanding, yet there's an underlying tenderness that makes my knees weak. I taste the faintest hint of whiskey from dinner last night on his tongue as it sweeps across my lower lip, seeking entrance. I grant it without hesitation, moaning softly as the kiss deepens.

My hands, which had been frozen at my sides, come to life. They explore the expanse of his muscled back, tracing the ridges and valleys of his scars, feeling the stories etched into his skin. Each touch seems to fuel the fire between us, and Zaire growls low in his throat, the sound vibrating through my entire being.

He breaks the kiss only to trail his lips along my jaw, down the column of my throat. When he reaches the sensitive spot where my neck meets my shoulder, he nips gently, then soothes the sting with his tongue. I gasp, my head falling back against the wall, giving him better access.

"Vesper," he murmurs against my skin, his voice rough with desire. "Moya koroleva."

The possessiveness in his tone sends a shiver down my spine. I'm dimly aware that this is dangerous, that I'm playing with fire. But in this moment, with Zaire's arms around me, his lips on my skin, I can't bring myself to care.

He captures my lips again, this time with a gentleness that contrasts sharply with the earlier passion. It's a kiss full of promise and of unspoken devotion. His fingers trace delicate patterns on my lower back, leaving trails of fire in their wake. I arch into him, wanting, needing, to be closer.

When we finally part, both of us breathing heavily, I feel as though the weight of the world lifts away. Zaire rests his forehead against mine, his eyes closed, his breath fanning across my face.

A rap comes from the door. "Leaving in ten, Z," Talon's voice says from the other side.

Zaire's eyes flutter open, meeting mine with an intensity that steals my breath away. Without a word, he leans in and captures my lips once more. This kiss is different; slower, deeper, filled with a longing that makes my heart ache. His hands cradle my face as if I'm something precious, his thumbs caressing my cheeks with a tenderness that belies the strength in his calloused fingers.

When he pulls away, I feel bereft, cold in the absence of his warmth. Zaire steps back, his gaze never leaving mine as he moves toward his closet. I watch, transfixed, as he peels off his sweatpants, revealing long, muscular legs adorned with intricate tattoos that disappear beneath his boxer briefs.

He pulls on a pair of dark jeans that hug his thighs, then reaches for a black t-shirt. As he lifts his arms to put it on, I can't help but marvel at the play of muscles across his back and the way his tattoos seem to shift and dance with each movement. The shirt slides down, covering the canvas of his skin, and I find myself mourning the loss.

Zaire turns back to me, now fully dressed but somehow

looking just as dangerous as he did half-naked. He grabs a leather jacket from a hook on the wall, shrugging it on with casual grace. The action is so mundane, yet there's an undercurrent of lethal efficiency in every move he makes.

He crosses the room to me in three long strides, backing me against the door once more. His hands come to rest on either side of my head, caging me in, but I've never felt safer.

"I'll be back," he murmurs, his voice low and intense. "Nothing will keep me from coming back to you, Vesper."

I shiver at the fervor in his words, the absolute conviction in his eyes. Zaire leans in, pressing a kiss to my forehead that feels like a blessing and a promise sealed in flesh.

"Wait for me," he whispers against my skin.

Then he's gone, slipping past me and out the door with a final smoldering look that burns itself into my memory. I'm left leaning against the door, my heart pounding, my lips tingling, and the ghost of his touch lingering on my skin.

Chapter 26

ALEX

THE ROAD STRETCHES OUT before us, a ribbon of asphalt cutting through the lush New York landscape. Zaire's hands grip the steering wheel, his knuckles white with tension. The playlist I'd curated for our impromptu road trip fills the car with a mix of classic rock and indie tunes, a futile attempt to lighten the mood. The four hour drive passes quickly despite the silence from Zaire.

"The clinic should be up here on the right."

The clinic finally appears, a nondescript building nestled between a laundromat and a convenience store. Zaire pulls over a few blocks away, finding a spot with a clear view of the entrance.

We sit in silence, watching the steady stream of people entering and exiting the clinic. The late afternoon sun casts long shadows across the street, painting everything in hues of orange and gold. It's almost beautiful if you can ignore the fact that we're here on a potentially dangerous mission.

I pull out my phone, fingers flying across the screen as I text Oscar.

> At location. Clinic closes in 1 hr.
> Waiting and watching.

As I wait for a response, I can't help but observe the scene before us. A young couple exits the clinic, their faces etched with worry. An elderly man shuffles in, leaning heavily on his cane. A harried-looking woman juggles a crying toddler and a diaper bag as she hurries inside.

It's strange, seeing this slice of normal life when our world is anything but. These people have no idea that two members of a powerful crime family are sitting just a few yards away.

My phone buzzes with Oscar's reply:

> Good. Keep eyes open. Be safe.

"Oz knows we made it."

"Good," Zaire responds. He's back to whatever LaLa land he's been letting his mind race off to before I can even take another breath. Normally, he's all business, but there's something about him right now that is piquing my curiosity.

What better time to poke the Russian bear than when you're alone in a car with him? At least, I will have witnesses if he kills me here in the car.

"So," I begin, trying to keep my tone light, "you and Oz, and Vesper. That's quite the triangle you've got going on there."

Zaire's grip on the steering wheel tightens if that was even possible. "It's not a triangle, Alex," he growls, his voice low and rough.

I can't help but chuckle, despite the gravity of our mission. "Oh, I'm sorry. Is it more of a straight line? Or wait, given Vesper's involvement, maybe it's a V-shape?"

Zaire shoots me a glare that could have melted steel, but I catch the hint of a smirk tugging at the corner of his lips. "You're an ass, you know that?"

"It's part of my charm," I quip, turning down the music slightly.

"You and your computer are practically married with three kids, asshole. How did you figure it out?"

"Come on, Z. I'm not blind. The way you two look at her, the tension when you're all in the same room. It's like watching a soap opera but with more guns and tattoos. Plus, she did walk out of her room wearing one of Oscar's shirts then she beelined it to your room after our meeting this morning. Stevie Wonder could have seen this coming."

A muscle in Zaire's jaw twitches, and I knew I'd hit a nerve. "It's complicated," he finally says, his voice low.

"Complicated?" I echo, raising an eyebrow. "That's the

understatement of the century. You're in love with the same woman as your twin brother, who happens to be formerly engaged to your cousin. It's like a Russian nesting doll of drama. Apparently, Petrovs have the same taste in women. Well, one woman."

Zaire's grip on the steering wheel tightens again, and for a moment, I think he might actually punch me. But then, unexpectedly, he lets out a short, bitter laugh.

"You're not wrong."

"So, how is this going to work? Are you guys like taking certain days? Is there a schedule? You get her every other day, weekends, and holidays?"

"Oh, shut up," Zaire groans, but I can see the tension in his shoulders easing slightly. "It's not like that. We're figuring it out."

"Figuring it out?" I can't help but snort. "What's there to figure out? You're both sleeping with her, right? Or is it more of a 'look but don't touch' situation with one of you?"

Zaire's knuckles go white on the steering wheel again. "Alex, I swear to God..."

"Okay, okay," I hold up my hands in mock surrender. "I'm just trying to understand the logistics here. I mean, do you guys have some sort of time-share agreement? Mondays, Wednesdays, and Fridays for you, Tuesdays, Thursdays, and Saturdays for Oz? Or is it more of a spontaneous thing?"

"Oh! I know! You guys probably have one of those fancy

color-coded Google calendars, right? 'Vesper Time' in red for you, blue for Oz..."

"For fuck's sake, Alex," Zaire growls, but I catch the underlying hint of amusement in his voice. "It's not a goddamn timeshare. We're all adults here, and we're making it work."

"Making it work, huh?" I muse, tapping my chin thoughtfully. "Wait a minute. Is Talon mixed up in this too? I mean, he's been hanging around a lot lately, and he's got that whole 'golden retriever with a dark side' thing going on."

Zaire's reaction is immediate and visceral. His face contorts into a mix of surprise, anger, and is that a hint of jealousy? "What? No! Talon's not. I mean, he's not." He trails off, looking uncomfortable.

I raise an eyebrow, intrigued by this new development. "Oh? You seem awfully flustered by that idea, Z. Something you're not telling me?"

Zaire takes a deep breath, his jaw clenching. "Look, it's Vesper's choice, alright? Who she lets into her bed, I mean. We don't control her. She's her own person."

"Whoa, whoa, whoa," I hold up my hands, genuinely surprised. "Are you saying there's actually a possibility that Talon's involved? I was just joking, but is he?"

"No," he immediately fires back. "I think it's just Oz and I."

I can't help but burst into laughter, the sound filling the car and drowning out the music. "Holy shit, Z. You're telling me that not only are you and Oz sharing Vesper but there's a chance Talon's in on this too? This isn't a love triangle anymore, it's a whole damn love...square?"

Zaire's knuckles are practically glowing white on the steering wheel now. "It's not like that, Alex."

"Seriously, Z. How do you deal with it? Knowing that the woman you love is also with your brother? And potentially Talon? I mean, that's got to be rough."

"It's not about me. It's about her. Plain and simple."

"But Vesper," he starts.

Zaire cuts me off abruptly, his voice sharp. "Enough, Alex. We're not here to discuss my love life."

"You mean your love square."

"Enough," he snarls.

I open my mouth to protest, but the words die on my lips as I catch sight of movement at the clinic's entrance. A middle-aged woman in scrubs exits, her keys jangling as she locks the door behind her. The last rays of sunlight glint off her name tag, but we're too far away to make out the name.

"Look," I whisper, unnecessarily. Zaire's already laser-focused on the scene before us.

We watch in tense silence as the woman makes her way to a beat-up Honda Civic parked a few spaces down from us. She fumbles with her purse, pulls out her car keys, and climbs in. The engine sputters to life, and she pulls out of the parking lot, disappearing around the corner.

The street falls eerily quiet. The convenience store's neon sign flickers to life, casting a sickly green glow over the empty sidewalk. A stray newspaper tumbles across the asphalt, driven by a gust of wind. The laundromat's windows are dark, the only movement inside the hypnotic spinning of a lone washing machine.

"That's our cue," Zaire mutters, reaching for the door handle. "Did you hack the alarm system?"

"You wound me." I show him my phone with the system's live feed on the screen. "They won't even know we were here."

"Good, let's go."

The weight of what we're about to do settles over me like a heavy blanket. Breaking and entering, theft of medical records, it's not exactly a typical Tuesday night activity, even for us.

As we step out of the car, the cool evening air hits me, carrying with it the scent of freshly cut grass and distant barbecue. It's such a normal, suburban smell that it feels almost absurd given what we're about to do.

We move quickly and quietly across the street, sticking to the shadows cast by the buildings. Zaire leads the way, his movements fluid and purposeful. I follow, trying to mimic his grace but feeling more like a lumbering elephant in comparison.

As we reach the clinic's door, Zaire pulls out a small leather case from his jacket pocket. The lock picks inside glint in the dim light as he selects two slender tools.

"Keep watch," he murmurs, crouching down to work on the lock.

I turn my back to him, scanning the street. The world seems to hold its breath. No cars pass, no pedestrians wander by. It's as if the universe is conspiring to give us this moment of uninterrupted criminal activity.

Behind me, I hear the soft click of the lock giving way. Not a single alarm goes off audibly. Zaire's hand reaches back, pulling me with him as he opens the door.

"Told you I hacked it."

As we slip inside the darkened clinic, the antiseptic smell hits me like a wall. My eyes adjust quickly to the dim emergency lighting, revealing a maze of corridors and closed doors. Zaire nods towards the reception area, and I make a beeline for the computer terminal while he starts searching the rooms.

I slide into the receptionist's chair, wincing at the soft squeak it makes in the silence. My fingers fly over the keyboard, bringing the system to life. The login screen glows an eerie blue in the darkness, casting strange shadows across the desk, which is cluttered with patient pamphlets and half-empty coffee mugs.

"Come on, baby," I mutter, cracking my knuckles before diving into the system. It's more secure than I expected for a small-town clinic, but nothing I can't manage. Lines of code scroll across the screen as I work my magic, each keystroke bringing me closer to breaching their defenses.

Time seems to stretch and compress as I work, the world narrowing down to just me and the computer. I'm vaguely aware of Zaire's footsteps echoing through the clinic, doors opening and closing as he searches.

Finally, after what feels like hours but is probably only about twenty minutes, I'm in. "Gotcha," I whisper triumphantly, allowing myself a small fist pump.

I hear Zaire's footsteps approaching just as I start digging through the patient records. "Any luck?" I ask without looking up.

"Found the storage room, but it's locked," he replies, his voice tight with frustration. "Some kind of keycard system. What about you?"

"Just got in," I say, fingers still flying across the keyboard. "Give me a sec."

I pull up the records for the date and time I had previously uncovered, scanning through the entries. My heart races as I spot a familiar name.

"Holy shit," I breathe. "Zaire, look at this."

He leans over my shoulder, his breath warm on my neck as he reads the screen. "Is that?"

There in black and white on the computer screen is a file named Rossi.

"Open it," Zaire demands, his voice a harsh whisper in the stillness of the clinic.

My fingers tremble as I click on the file, my heart pounding so loudly I'm sure Zaire can hear it. The screen flickers, and suddenly we're staring at a treasure trove of medical records, each one a damning piece of evidence.

"Jesus Christ," Zaire mutters.

The file is a minefield of medical jargon, but certain phrases jump out at me like neon signs: "oocyte retrieval," "controlled ovarian hyper-stimulation," "in vitro fertilization." My stomach churns as I scroll through the records, each entry more damning than the last.

"Look at this," I say, pointing to a series of entries. "There's at least...six, no, seven separate retrieval procedures listed here."

Zaire's grip on my shoulder tightens, his fingers digging into my flesh. I barely notice the pain, too engrossed in the horrifying details unfolding before us.

As I delve deeper into the records, a pattern emerges. After each retrieval, there are notes about fertilization attempts, all ending in failure. Even the clinical language in the files can't mask the underlying frustration evident in the doctors' notes.

"None of them worked," I murmur, a mix of relief and dread washing over me. "They couldn't create viable embryos."

But then, as if the universe decided we hadn't been punched in the gut enough tonight, I stumble upon a file from ten months ago. My blood runs cold as I read the physician's notes.

I continue scrolling, my heart pounding in my chest. "Wait...look at this one."

The file opens, revealing a set of physician's notes. My eyes widen as I read aloud, "Two viable embryos created. One male, one female."

"They did it," Zaire breathes, his voice a mix of horror and disbelief. "They actually fucking did it."

I scan through the rest of the notes, my mind racing. "It says here they were cryopreserved. Stored for future use."

"Future use," Zaire spits out the words like they're poison. "Like they're talking about spare parts, not human lives."

I lean back in the chair, running a hand through my hair. "This is beyond fucked up, Z. I mean, we knew it was bad, but this is next level shit."

"Wait," I say, squinting at the screen. "There's more. It looks like they've got a specific location for the cryopreservation tank. Didn't you say you found a cryopreservation room?"

"Yeah." Zaire's eyes widen. "Are you saying they might still be here?"

I nod, my fingers flying across the keyboard. "According to this, they're stored in Tank B3, Rack 7, Positions 4 and 5.

"Can you get that door open?"

I crack my knuckles, a grim smile on my face. "That almost hurts."

It takes a few minutes of furious typing and some creative coding, but I finally hear the telltale click of an electronic lock disengaging. "We're in," I announce. I shove out of the desk chair. "Lead the way."

Zaire spins on his heels, heading down the hallway, making a left and then a right until we come upon a large metal door. The sign on the door 'Cryogenic Storage -

Authorized Personnel Only.' I look over to the keypad, where a green light shines from the top of it. "It's unlocked."

I try the handle, and it opens with a soft click. Inside, the room is filled with large, cylindrical tanks, each emitting a soft hum. The air is noticeably colder here, our breath visible in small puffs.

"Which one is B3?" Zaire asks, scanning the labels on the tanks.

I spot it in the corner. "Over here," I call, moving towards it.

As we approach the tank, I can't help but quip, "You know, I'm starting to regret skipping all those science classes at the academy. Any idea how to work this thing?"

Zaire shoots me a look of half exasperation and half amusement. "Just find the right rack, smartass."

I spot a pair of thick, padded gloves nearby and pull them on. The cold hits me immediately as I open the tank, a cloud of icy vapor billowing out. I reach in, my movements slow and careful as I search for Rack 7.

"Got it," I mutter, pulling out the rack. My heart is pounding as I scan the positions. "4 and 5...4 and 5..."

But as I reach the spots where the embryos should be, my blood runs cold. The slots are empty.

"Zaire," I say. "They're not here."

"What do you mean, they're not here?" Zaire demands, peering over my shoulder.

I gesture to the empty slots. "I mean, they're gone. Positions 4 and 5 on Rack 7, they're empty."

Zaire's face contorts with disbelief and frustration. "No, that can't be right. Maybe we got the location wrong. Check again, Alex."

We carefully replace the rack and close the tank, the soft hiss of escaping vapor filling the silence between us. I shed the gloves, tossing them to the ground. The cold air clings to our skin as we hurry back to the reception area, our footsteps echoing in the empty hallways.

I slide back into the chair, my fingers dancing across the keyboard with renewed urgency. The blue glow of the screen illuminates our faces, casting eerie shadows across the room. I pull up the file again, double-checking every detail.

"Look," I say, pointing to the screen. "It's right here. Tank B3, Rack 7, Positions 4 and 5. That's exactly where we looked."

Zaire leans in, his eyes scanning the information. I can see the muscles in his jaw working as he processes the implications. "Fuck," he mutters, running a hand through his hair. "How is this possible? Where could they have gone?"

"I don't know, Z," I reply, scrolling through the file for any additional information. "There's no record of a transfer or...wait, what's this?"

I click on a small icon at the bottom of the page, and a new window pops up. It's a log of access to the file, showing who viewed it and when. My eyes widen as I scan the list.

"Zaire, look at this. Someone accessed this file three days ago. Someone with high-level clearance."

Zaire's eyes narrow as he reads the name. "Dr. Ivanov? Who the hell is that?"

I'm about to run a search on the name when a sound from outside freezes us both in place. It's the unmistakable crunch of tires on gravel, followed by the soft thud of a car door closing.

Zaire and I lock eyes, panic flaring between us.

"Shit," I hiss, my fingers flying across the keyboard. "We gotta go."

I pull out a thumb drive from my pocket and start downloading everything I can. The progress bar crawls across the screen, each second feeling like an eternity as the sound of footsteps grows closer.

"Come on, come on," I mutter, willing the files to transfer faster.

Zaire moves to the window, peering through the blinds. "Local police by the looks of him," he whispers. "He's got a flashlight out like he's doing his rounds.."

My heart hammers in my chest as I watch the progress bar. 95%...96%...97%...

The footsteps are right outside now. I can see the beam of a flashlight sweeping across the parking lot through the gaps in the blinds.

98%...99%...

The door handle jiggles.

100%.

I yank the thumb drive out, barely remembering to shut down the computer. Zaire is already at the back door, gesturing frantically for me to follow.

The cool night air hits my face as we burst out of the back door, adrenaline coursing through my veins. My fingers are still clenched tightly around the thumb drive, the weight of the information it contains feeling impossibly heavy.

We sprint across the parking lot, our footsteps echoing in the quiet night. The moon hangs low and full in the sky, casting long shadows that seem to reach for us as we run. My lungs burn with each breath, the taste of fear metallic on my tongue.

Zaire leads the way, his movements fluid and purposeful, like a predator on the hunt. I follow, trying to match his grace but feeling more like a lumbering bear in comparison. The gravel crunches under our feet, each step sounding like a gunshot in the stillness of the night.

We reach the car, and Zaire practically dives into the driver's seat. I scramble in beside him, my heart pounding so hard I can feel it in my throat. The engine roars to life, and we peel out of the parking lot, tires squealing against the asphalt.

As we speed down the empty streets, the reality of what we've just done begins to sink in. We broke into a medical clinic. We stole confidential patient information. We uncovered a secret that could change everything.

"We need to call Oz," Zaire says, breaking the tense

silence. His voice is tight, controlled, but I can hear the undercurrent of worry.

I nod, fumbling for my phone. My hands are shaking slightly as I pull up Oscar's contact, the blue light of the screen harsh in the darkened car. I hit the speaker button, and it starts to ring.

One ring. Two. Three. Each one feels like an eternity.

Finally, Oscar's voice fills the car through the phone's speaker. "Are you on your way back? You both good?"

"We're fine," I rush to assure him, glancing at Zaire. "But Oz, we found something."

"They created viable fucking embryos from Vesper's eggs."

The silence on the other end of the line is deafening. When Oscar finally speaks. "How many?"

"Two," Zaire replies, his tone grim. "One male, one female. But that's not all."

I watch as Zaire's expression darkens, his brow furrowing as he continues. "They're gone, Oz. The embryos. They were supposed to be in cryo-storage at the clinic, but when we checked, the slots were empty."

Oscar's sharp intake of breath crackles through the speaker. "What do you mean, gone? How is that possible?"

"We don't know," I chime in, leaning closer to the phone. "But we did get a name. Someone accessed the file three days ago. A Dr. Ivanov."

The name hangs in the air between us, heavy with

implications. Zaire's eyes meet mine for a brief moment, a silent understanding passing between us.

"Oz," Zaire says, his voice taking on a determined edge, "we may need to stay longer than we planned. We need to find this doctor and figure out what happened to those embryos."

The silence that follows is thick with tension. I can almost hear the gears turning in Oscar's head, weighing the risks against the potential rewards.

"Agreed," Oscar finally says, his voice firm. "We can't leave without answers. But be careful. If someone moved those embryos, they might be expecting company."

Zaire nods, even though Oscar can't see him. "We'll be careful. We'll start digging into this Dr. Ivanov first thing in the morning."

"Good," Oscar replies. "I'll work my contacts, see if I can find any information on our end. And guys, watch your backs. This just got a lot more complicated."

As we end the call, the weight of our discovery settles over us like a heavy blanket. The rhythmic hum of the car's engine and the soft whoosh of passing vehicles are the only sounds that break the tense silence.

I lean back in my seat, my mind racing with possibilities. Who is Dr. Ivanov? Where are the embryos now? And most importantly, what does this mean for Vesper?

Chapter 27

VESPER

I BLINK AWAKE, disoriented and groggy, my heart sinking as I realize I'm alone in my bed. The sunlight streaming through the curtains tells me it's well into the morning. Memories of last night's revelations flood back, and I bolt upright, suddenly wide awake.

Hastily, I throw on a pair of worn jeans and a soft, oversized sweater, not bothering with makeup or even running a brush through my tangled blonde waves. My bare feet pad silently across the hardwood floors as I make my way to Zaire's room, hope and dread warring in my chest.

The door creaks open to reveal an empty, perfectly

made bed. My stomach clenches. Where are they? Why aren't they back yet?

Trying to quell the rising panic, I move to Oscar's door, my knuckles rapping against the solid wood before I push it open.

"Oz?" I call out, my voice rough from lack of sleep.

Oscar doesn't answer. My heart races as I step fully into his room, the plush carpet soft beneath my bare feet. The sound of running water grows louder, punctuated by occasional splashes. I approach the bathroom door, my hand hovering uncertainly before I rap my knuckles against the sleek wood.

"Oscar?" I call again, louder this time.

His voice, muffled by the shower's spray, finally responds. "Come in, Vesper."

I hesitate for a moment, then turn the handle. A wave of warm, humid air washes over me as I enter. The bathroom is filled with steam, the mirror is completely fogged over. The shower enclosure is frosted glass, but I can make out Oscar's silhouette behind it.

Oscar's silhouette shifts, and the glass door slides open, revealing his muscular form glistening with water droplets. His piercing blue eyes lock onto mine, a mix of concern and something darker swirling in their depths.

My breath catches in my throat as Oscar steps out of the shower, water cascading down his chiseled body. He doesn't reach for a towel, instead holding my gaze with an intensity that makes my skin tingle.

"Join me," he says, his voice low and husky. It's not quite a question, but not quite a command either.

I hesitate for a moment, my heart pounding. Oscar could drag me in there if he wanted to, but instead, I watch him as he patiently awaits my answer. Without saying a word, I peel off my clothes, letting them fall to the tile floor. My answer is unspoken but clear. Oscar's eyes darken as they roam over my exposed skin. He extends his hand, and I take it, allowing him to guide me into the shower.

The warm spray envelops us as Oscar presses me against the cool tile wall. His lips find mine in a searing kiss, urgent and demanding. I respond with equal fervor, my fingers tangling in his wet hair. His hands explore my body, leaving trails of fire in their wake.

Oscar breaks the kiss, trailing his lips along my jawline and down my neck. I gasp as he nips at my pulse point, my back arching. The contrast of the cold tiles against my back and Oscar's hot skin pressed against my front.

"Oz," I breathe, my voice barely audible over the sound of the shower.

Oscar's lips continue their journey downward, leaving a trail of heated kisses along my collarbone and between my breasts. My breath quickens as he drops to his knees before me, his strong hands caressing my thighs. He looks up at me, his blue eyes dark with desire, silently asking permission.

I nod, barely able to breathe as Oscar gently lifts one of my legs over his shoulder. His other hand wraps around my waist, steadying me as I lean back against the cool tile wall for support. The warm water cascades over us, creating a cocoon of steam and sensation.

Oscar's tongue traces delicate patterns along my inner thigh, inching closer to where I ache for him. I tangle my fingers in his wet hair, my body trembling with anticipation.

He pulls me towards him, burying his face in my lap. Once his mouth finally makes contact, I gasp, my head falling back against the wall with a soft thud.

"Oh god."

The world narrows to this moment, this sensation. Oscar's tongue works magic, alternating between teasing flicks and long, languid strokes. My fingers tighten in his hair as waves of pleasure crash over me. The steam swirls around us, making everything hazy and dreamlike.

"Oh god," I breathe again, my voice barely audible over the sound of falling water.

Oscar pulls back slightly, his blue eyes intense as they lock onto mine. "Goddess," he corrects me, his breath hot against my sensitive skin. "The only god in this room is you, my goddess."

With that, he dives back in with renewed fervor. I gasp, my back arching as I press myself closer to his eager mouth. My leg tightens around his shoulder, drawing him in deeper. I lean heavily against the wall, grateful for its support as my knees grow weak. Oscar's strong hands grip my hips, holding me steady as he continues his relentless assault on my senses. His tongue swirls and flicks, finding every spot that makes me moan and shudder.

The steam thickens around us, turning the bathroom into our own private sanctuary. Water droplets cling to my skin, mingling with the sweat beading on my forehead. I'm panting now, my chest heaving as Oscar brings me closer and closer to the edge.

"Oz," I whimper, my voice thick with need. "Please..."

He responds by redoubling his efforts, his fingers digging into my hips as he pulls me even closer. The coil of tension within me winds tighter and tighter, threatening to snap at any moment. I'm trembling now, every muscle in my body taut with anticipation.

And then, with one final, perfectly placed stroke of his tongue, I shatter. A cry tears from my throat as pleasure explodes through me, white-hot and all-consuming. My body shakes uncontrollably, held up only by Oscar's firm grip and the unyielding wall at my back.

Oscar doesn't let up, drawing out my pleasure until I'm gasping and oversensitive. Only then does he slowly, reverently, place a final kiss against my inner thigh before rising to his feet. He gathers me in his arms, supporting my trembling body as the warm water continues to cascade over us both.

"I want to worship every inch of your body. You're so beautiful, so perfect."

He lifts me effortlessly, and I wrap my legs around his waist. Our bodies join in a fluid motion, eliciting a moan from both of us. Oscar sets a steady rhythm, each thrust driving me higher. The steam swirls around us, heightening every sensation.

Oscar digs his fingers into my hips, driving the motion between us with increasing intensity. Each thrust sends shockwaves of pleasure through my body, building upon the aftershocks of my previous climax. The steam swirls around us, creating a dreamlike haze that amplifies every sensation.

I cling to his broad shoulders, my nails leaving crescent marks on his skin as I struggle to ground myself in the onslaught of sensations.

"Mark me, my goddess. Make me yours," he demands.

Oscar's lips find mine in a searing kiss, swallowing my moans as he continues to move within me. His tongue mimics the rhythm of our bodies, stoking the fire that burns ever hotter in my core. I break away, gasping for air, my head falling back against the shower wall with a soft thud.

"Look at me," Oscar commands, his voice low and husky.

I force my eyes open, meeting his intense gaze. The blue of his irises is nearly swallowed by his dilated pupils, dark with desire. The vulnerability and raw emotion I see there takes my breath away.

Oscar shifts slightly, changing the angle of his thrusts. A cry escapes my lips as he hits a spot deep inside me that sends sparks shooting through my veins. My legs tighten around his waist, urging him deeper, harder.

"That's it, Vesper," he growls, his breath hot against my ear. "Let me hear you."

His words unlock something within me, and I stop holding back. My cries of pleasure echo off the tiled walls, mingling with the sound of falling water and Oscar's own grunts and groans. The coil of tension in my core winds tighter and tighter, threatening to snap at any moment.

Oscar's movements become more erratic, his control slipping as he chases his own release. One of his hands leaves my hip, sliding between our bodies to find the sensitive bundle of nerves at my center. His skilled fingers work in tandem with his thrusts, pushing me closer and closer to the edge.

Oscar commands, his voice strained with the effort of holding back. "Come with me, Vesper."

His words, combined with a particularly deep thrust and a clever flick of his fingers, send me careening over the edge. My second orgasm crashes over me like a tidal wave, even more intense than the first. I cry out Oscar's name as my body convulses around him, wave after wave of pleasure washing over me.

Oscar follows me over the precipice with a guttural groan, his hips jerking erratically as he finds his own release. We cling to each other, trembling and gasping, as the warm water continues to rain down upon us.

As the last tremors of our shared climax subside, Oscar gently lowers me to my feet. My legs feel like jelly, and I'm grateful for his strong arms supporting me. The warm water continues to cascade over us, washing away the evidence of our passion.

Oscar reaches for the shampoo, and I close my eyes as he begins to massage it into my scalp. His fingers work through my long blonde hair, carefully untangling any knots. The scent of sandalwood fills the steamy air, and I can't help but lean into his touch.

"Turn around," he murmurs, and I comply, letting the spray rinse the suds from my hair. Oscar's hands glide over my body, cleaning every inch with reverent care. It's intimate in a different way than our lovemaking, soft and tender.

When he's finished, I return the favor, my hands exploring the planes and valleys of his muscular form. We take our time, trading gentle kisses and lingering touches until the water begins to cool.

Oscar steps out first, wrapping a fluffy towel around his waist before holding one out for me. I step into his embrace, sighing contentedly as he pats me dry. He presses a kiss to my forehead before leading me back into his bedroom.

I watch as he rummages through his dresser, pulling out a soft, well-worn t-shirt. "Here," he says, holding it out to me. "Wear this instead of your sweater. It's going to be a hot day."

I slip the shirt over my head, inhaling deeply. It smells like him. The fabric falls to mid-thigh, and I can't help but feel a surge of possessiveness at wearing his clothes.

Oscar helps me into my jeans, his fingers trailing along my legs as he pulls them up. Once I'm dressed, he gently turns me around, gathering my wet hair in his hands.

"Let me," he says softly, beginning to twist my hair into a

bun. His fingers work deftly, securing the style with ease. As he finishes, a nagging worry resurfaces in my mind.

"Oz," I begin, turning to face him. "Where are Zaire and Alex? Z wasn't in his room when I checked earlier."

Oscar's expression softens, a mix of concern and something else I can't quite place flickering across his features. He takes my hand, gently guiding me. The plush carpet sinks beneath our bare feet as he leads me to the edge of his bed.

"They found something, didn't they?" I guess.

"Yes. I wanted to tell you last night, but by the time Z had called, you had already fallen asleep. You were sleeping so well that I didn't want to wake you up."

"Zaire and Alex are okay, right?"

"They're both fine. I checked in with Zaire this morning."

A sigh of relief escapes my lips, but the look on Oscar's face tells me there's more he needs to tell me. "What did they find?"

Oscar takes a deep breath, his blue eyes filled with a mix of concern and determination. "Vesper, they found the records from your egg retrievals while you were held captive."

My heart skips a beat, and I feel the blood drain from my face. The memories I've tried so hard to suppress come flooding back. The cold, clinical rooms. The endless injections. The fear and uncertainty that plagued me every moment of my captivity.

Oscar's warm hand envelops mine, anchoring me to the

present. His thumb traces soothing circles on my skin as he continues, his voice gentle but steady. "They attempted to create embryos multiple times, but according to the records, none of them survived until about ten months ago."

I suck in a sharp breath, my mind reeling with the implications. "Ten months ago?" I whisper, my voice barely audible. "What happened then?"

Oscar's grip on my hand tightens slightly, his eyes never leaving mine. "According to the records, two embryos were successfully created at that time. A male and a female."

I struggle to breathe, my mind reeling with the implications. Somewhere out there, frozen in time, are two potential lives. My potential children. Children created without my knowledge or consent, but my flesh and blood, nonetheless.

"Where are they now?" I manage to ask, my throat tight with emotion. "The embryos, I mean."

"They were stored at the clinic," Oscar replies, his grip on my hand tightening slightly. "But, Zaire and Alex checked the tank. They weren't there."

A cold dread settles in the pit of my stomach. "They weren't there?" I repeat.

"Your file was accessed three days ago by a Dr. Ivanov. Does that name ring a bell to you?"

"No," I shake my head. "They never used names, and always had masks on. They had me so sedated, I'm not sure I would have recognized myself if they'd given me a mirror."

"I figured that would be the case," Oscar nods, his

thumb still tracing soothing circles on the back of my hand. "Zaire and Alex are staying in New York. They're trying to track the doctor down."

"How long will they be gone?"

"As long as it takes."

I nod, trying to process this information. Logically, I know Zaire being away is the right thing. They need to be there to track down the doctor, to uncover the truth about what happened to those embryos, my embryos. But a part of me, a selfish, needy part, hates that he's so far away. I miss his presence, his warmth, the way his lips quirk up in that half-smile when he catches me looking at him.

Oscar seems to sense my inner turmoil. He releases my hand and moves to the nightstand, retrieving something from the drawer. When he turns back to me, I see he's holding a sleek, new smartphone.

"This is for you," he says, placing it in my palm. The device feels foreign and heavy in my hand, a tangible reminder of how much my life has changed. "Our numbers are already programmed into it. Zaire has this number. He'll reach out when he can."

I run my thumb over the smooth screen, a lump forming in my throat. It's a lifeline, a connection to the men who have become my world. I clutch it to my chest as if I could somehow hold them closer through this small piece of technology.

"Thank you," I whisper, looking up at Oscar. His blue

eyes are soft with understanding, and I'm struck again by how much I've come to rely on him, on both of them.

The sunlight streaming through the window catches on Oscar's hair, turning it to burnished gold. It reminds me of lazy Sunday mornings and stolen kisses, of safety and warmth. I want to lose myself in that feeling, to forget about the complications and dangers that lurk just beyond these walls.

But I can't. Not when part of me is missing, not when Zaire is out there, putting himself at risk for my sake. Not when there are so many unanswered questions about those embryos, my potential children.

I take a deep breath, inhaling the lingering scent of Oscar's cologne mixed with the fresh, clean smell of his recently showered skin. It grounds me and reminds me that I'm not alone in this.

"He'll be okay," Oscar says, as if reading my thoughts. "Z's resourceful, and he's got Alex watching his back."

I nod, trying to convince myself as much as to acknowledge his words. "I know. I just...I wish he was here. Both of them."

Oscar wraps an arm around my shoulders, pulling me close. I lean into him, drawing strength from his solid presence. "We'll get through this together," he murmurs into my hair. "All of us."

I nod, managing a small smile as I look up at Oscar. His eyes, those piercing blue orbs that seem to see right through me, are filled with warmth and understanding. He leans in, pressing a soft kiss to my forehead before pulling back slightly.

"How about some breakfast?" he suggests, his voice gentle. "I make a mean omelet."

The thought of food makes my stomach growl, reminding me that I haven't eaten since yesterday. "That sounds perfect," I reply, grateful for the distraction.

Oscar stands, offering me his hand. I take it, letting him pull me to my feet. The soft carpet gives way to cool hardwood as we make our way out of the bedroom and down the hallway. The house is quiet, our footsteps and the distant chirping of birds outside the only sounds breaking the morning stillness.

As we enter the kitchen, sunlight streams through the large windows, bathing everything in a warm, golden glow. The polished granite countertops gleam and the stainless steel appliances reflect the light, creating a dazzling display. Oscar moves with practiced ease, pulling ingredients from the fridge and gathering utensils.

I perch on one of the high stools at the kitchen island, watching as he cracks eggs into a bowl with one hand, his movements fluid and confident. The sharp tap of eggshell against the bowl's rim punctuates the peaceful morning air.

Suddenly, a soft 'ding' breaks through the quiet. My heart leaps as I realize it's coming from the new phone Oscar gave me. With slightly trembling fingers, I pull it from my pocket, swiping to unlock the screen.

A text message pops up, and my breath catches in my throat as I read the words:

Missing you, my queen.

It's from Zaire. Four simple words, but they send a rush of warmth through my entire body. I can almost hear his voice, low and husky, whispering them in my ear. A smile spreads across my face, wide and genuine, the first real one since I woke up this morning.

Oscar glances over from where he's whisking the eggs, a knowing look in his eyes. "Let me guess," he says, a hint of amusement in his voice. "Z?"

I nod, unable to wipe the grin from my face. "He says he misses me."

Oscar's lips quirk up in a half-smile, his eyes softening. "Of course he does. You're impossible not to miss, Vesper."

Chapter 28

ZAIRE

I LEAN against the cold brick wall, my eyes fixed on the entrance of the fertility clinic across the street. The New York air is crisp, biting at my exposed skin, but I barely notice. My mind is consumed with thoughts of Vesper and the bombshell we uncovered days ago.

Her embryos. Stored here, in this nondescript building. The knowledge burns in my chest, a mix of anger and protective instinct that threatens to overwhelm me. I clench my fists, willing myself to stay put, to stick to the plan.

Alex shifts beside me, his presence a steady reminder of our purpose. We've been here for days, watching, waiting.

The doctor we've been hunting - this elusive Dr. Ivanov - remains a ghost. Every lead we've followed has led to a dead end, each clue dissolving like smoke through our fingers. He's glued to his phone, scrolling through the screen at a rapid pace.

"Hvar ertu, helvíti?" Alex mutters under his breath.

"Another dead end?" I mutter, not taking my eyes off the clinic's entrance.

Alex shakes his head, his frustration mirroring my own. "Nothing. It's like he never existed. We're missing something, Z," Alex says, his voice low. "Ivanov did not just vanish into thin air."

I nod, my mind racing. The tattoos on my arms seem to itch beneath my jacket, a physical manifestation of my restlessness. "We need to dig deeper. There has to be a connection we're not seeing."

As I speak, my thoughts drift to Vesper. Her fierce green eyes, the way her blonde hair catches the light. The strength she exudes, even in her most vulnerable moments. The thought of anyone using her, manipulating her biology without her knowledge, makes my blood boil.

I hesitate, weighing our options. The tattoo on my neck, an intricate design of intertwining thorns, seems to pulse with each beat of my heart. It's a reminder of the pain I've endured, the battles I've fought. This feels like another war, but one with higher stakes than ever before.

I pull out my phone, desperate for a moment of distraction. As the screen lights up, my breath catches in my throat. There she is my lock screen a snapshot of paradise. Vesper's long, tanned legs stretch out before her, the azure waters of the beach lapping at the shore beyond. The sight of her brings a bittersweet ache to my chest, a longing so intense it's almost physical.

But it's not just Vesper in the photo. Another pair of legs, unmistakably masculine, frame hers. Oscar's. The sight stirs a complicated cocktail of emotions within me. Jealousy burns hot and quick, a flare of possessiveness that I try to tamp down. It's irrational, I know. Oscar is as devoted to Vesper as I am, and I trust him with my life. With her life. Still, I can't help but wish it was my legs in that photo, my skin warmed by the same sun that caresses hers. I imagine the feel of the sand between my toes, the salt-laden breeze ruffling my hair. Most of all, I yearn for the weight of Vesper in my arms, the scent of her hair, and the sound of her laughter.

"You okay?" Alex's voice cuts through my reverie, concern evident in his tone.

I blink, realizing I've been staring at my phone for far longer than I intended. "Yeah," I mutter, clearing my throat. "Just wishing I was there."

Alex's expression softens, understanding flickering in his eyes. He knows what it's like to be torn between duty and desire, between the mission and the heart.

"She's safe with Oscar," he reminds me gently. "And the

sooner we crack this case, the sooner you can get back to your love pentagon."

Ignoring his comment about the complicated relationship between the three of us, I push off the wall, my muscles aching from hours of inactivity. "We need to change our approach," I say, running a hand through my hair. "This waiting game isn't getting us anywhere."

Alex nods, his blue eyes narrowing as he scans the street. "What do you have in mind?"

I take a deep breath, my mind racing with possibilities. The cool air fills my lungs, sharpening my focus. "Alex," I say, my voice low and urgent, "you still got that voice modulator? And the number spoofer?"

Alex's eyebrows shoot up, a smirk playing at the corners of his mouth. He rolls his eyes dramatically, the gesture so familiar it almost makes me laugh despite the tension thrumming through my body. "Please," he scoffs, "It's one of the first things I pack for road trips."

I nod, a plan rapidly forming in my mind. The tattoos on my arms seem to pulse with anticipation as if they can sense the impending action. "I think it's time we stopped waiting for Ivanov to show his face," I say, my eyes darting back to the clinic's entrance. "Let's bring him to us instead."

Alex's eyes light up with understanding. "You want to call the clinic."

"Exactly," I confirm, feeling a surge of adrenaline at the prospect. "If we can't find him, maybe we can smoke him out."

"But you can't call as Ivanov himself. That wouldn't work."

"No, it wouldn't," I admit. "But, think about what Talon said about the auction. The red headed bitch that brokered her deal said that if he was unhappy with his purchase, resale would be no problem. Let's just say that we are unhappy with our purchase. We can leave a message, as Natasha, requesting Ivanov's assistance."

Alex nods, his excitement palpable. "I like it," he says, already reaching for his phone. "I've got everything we need in the car. Let's do this."

We make our way back to the nondescript sedan parked a block away, our steps quick and purposeful. The city bustles around us, oblivious to the high-stakes game we're about to play.

Alex pops the trunk, revealing a treasure trove of tech. His fingers dance over the equipment, selecting what we need with practiced ease. In minutes, we're back in the car, the engine purring to life as Alex sets up the gear.

"Okay," he says, handing me a small, sleek device. "This will modulate your voice. And I've got the number spoofer ready to go."

I take the device, feeling its weight in my hand. I clear my throat, preparing myself for the performance of a lifetime.

"Ready?" Alex asks, his finger hovering over the call button.

I nod, my heart pounding in my chest. The scar on my

neck seems to tingle, a reminder of all we've been through, all we're fighting for. "Let's do this," I say, my voice steady despite the nerves coursing through me.

Alex hits the button. The phone rings once, twice, three times before a crisp, professional voice answers. "Fertility Solutions, how may I assist you today?"

I take a deep breath, feeling the weight of the voice modulator against my throat. When I speak, the words come out in a sultry feminine tone, completely unlike my own.

"Good afternoon," I purr, channeling all the cold authority I imagine Natasha would possess. "This is Natasha. I need to leave a message for Dr. Ivanov."

There's a slight pause on the other end of the line, and I can almost hear the receptionist's posture straightening. "Of course. How may I help you?"

I lock eyes with Alex, who gives me an encouraging nod. "Please inform Dr. Ivanov that I'll be bringing a product by tomorrow for testing. It's unsatisfactory, and I require his expertise to determine its viability."

The receptionist's voice is all efficiency now, the faint sounds of typing in the background. "I'll make sure Dr. Ivanov receives your message right away. Is there a specific time you'd like to come in?"

"After hours. He'll understand. Make sure he's available. This is a matter of utmost importance."

"I'll pass along the message right away."

I end the call, my heart pounding in my chest. For a

moment, neither Alex nor I speak, the weight of what we've just done settling over us like a heavy blanket.

"Well," Alex finally says, breaking the silence. "I guess now we wait."

We make our way back to the hotel, the streets of New York a blur of noise and color around us. My mind is racing, replaying the phone call over and over, searching for any misstep, any detail that might give us away. The call was a gamble, but I had to take it.

We reach our rooms on the third floor. My mind is so lost in thought I nearly walk past them until Alex tugs on the sleeve of my shirt to stop me.

"I'm going to see if I can track any unusual activity at the clinic. Maybe our little message will stir something up." I nod, barely hearing him before Alex disappears to his connecting room next door.

I unlock the door to my room, and step inside. I collapse onto the bed, the adrenaline of the day finally catching up with me. My hand is already reaching for my phone, scrolling through my contacts until I find the one I'm looking for. Vesper. I select video call and hit send. The phone rings once, twice, three times. Each second feels like an eternity. Then, finally, her beautiful face and voice comes through.

"Z? Is everything okay?"

The sound of her voice sends a wave of longing through me so intense it's almost painful.

"It is now that I am looking at your pretty face, moya koroleva."

She smiles, and my heart skips a beat. Even through the screen of my phone, her beauty is breathtaking. The soft glow of what I assume is her bedside lamp casts a warm halo around her golden hair, making her look almost ethereal.

"What are you up to?" I ask, drinking in every detail of her face, from the slight crinkle at the corner of her eyes when she smiles to the faint freckles dusting her nose.

"Just laying on my bed," she replies, shifting slightly. The movement causes her hair to cascade over her shoulder, and I find myself wishing I could reach through the screen and run my fingers through those silky strands.

"Alone?" I can't help but ask, a mixture of hope and jealousy coloring my tone.

Her laugh, light and melodious, fills my ears. "If you're asking about Oz, he's out in the kitchen with Talon working on dinner."

My heart soars at this information. I love knowing she's alone, that for this moment, I have her all to myself. A mischievous grin spreads across my face. "So, you're all alone in that big bed, huh?"

Vesper rolls her eyes, but I can see the hint of a blush coloring her cheeks. "Behave yourself, Z," she chides, but there's no real admonishment in her tone.

"Now where's the fun in that?" I tease, my voice dropping to a lower, more intimate register. "Have you been missing me, moya koroleva?"

She bites her lower lip, a gesture that never fails to drive me wild. "Maybe," she admits softly.

"Maybe?" I echo, raising an eyebrow. "Come on, Vesper. Tell me how much you've been missing me."

She shifts again, and I catch a glimpse of bare shoulder. Is she wearing one of my t-shirts? The thought sends a jolt of desire through me. "A lot," she confesses.

"I see you've been in my closet."

"I might have been," she coyly admits. My breath catches as I take in the sight of Vesper in my shirt, the hem barely grazing her mid-thigh. Her long legs seem to stretch on forever, and I'm struck by an overwhelming urge to trace every inch of them with my fingertips and my lips.

"Is that all you're wearing, moya koroleva?" I ask, my voice husky with desire.

Vesper bites her lip, a gesture that never fails to drive me wild. Her green eyes sparkle with mischief as she looks directly into the camera. "Maybe," she teases, echoing our earlier exchange.

"Show me," I demand, my pulse quickening. "I want to see what you have on under that shirt."

She hesitates for a moment, her teeth worrying her lower lip. Then, slowly, tantalizingly, she lifts the hem of the shirt. Inch by inch, more of her creamy skin is revealed until I catch a glimpse of lace. My breath hitches as I realize she's wearing nothing but a pair of delicate panties beneath my shirt.

"Fuck, Vesper," I groan, drinking in the sight of her. "You're killing me here."

"Alex isn't in the room with you, is he?" she asks.

"No," I tell her. Like I'd let him see what she's put on display for me right now.

My tattoos seem to burn against my skin, matching the fire coursing through my veins. I want nothing more than to be there with her, to feel her skin against mine, to lose myself in her warmth. But for now, this stolen moment will have to be enough.

She smiles, a soft, tender expression that makes me ache to hold her. "You'll be back soon, right?"

"Not soon enough," I grumble.

I swallow hard, my throat suddenly dry. "Touch yourself, Vesper," I say, my voice low and husky.

Her eyes widen, a mixture of shock and intrigue flickering across her face. "Z, I...I don't know if I can..."

"You can," I assure her, my voice gentle but firm. "Touch yourself, Vesper. For me."

She hesitates, her teeth worrying her lower lip. "I...I've never..." she trails off, a blush creeping up her neck.

My heart swells with a mixture of tenderness and desire. "That's okay, moya koroleva. I'll guide you. I'll be right here with you."

Vesper takes a deep breath, her chest rising and falling

beneath my shirt. "Okay," she whispers, her voice barely audible.

"First, prop the phone up so I can see you," I instruct. She complies, adjusting the angle until I can see her face and most of her body. "Perfect. Now, start by running your hands over your body. Slowly. Feel every curve, every dip."

Her hands tremble slightly as she begins to caress herself, starting at her collarbone and working her way down. I watch, mesmerized, as her fingers trace the swell of her breasts through the thin fabric of my shirt.

"That's it," I encourage, my voice thick with desire. "Now, slip your hand under the shirt. Feel your skin."

Vesper's breath hitches as her hand disappears beneath the hem of the shirt. Her eyes flutter closed, her lips parting slightly as she explores her own body.

"How does it feel?" I ask, my own body thrumming with tension.

"Good," she breathes. "Warm. Tingly."

"Focus on those sensations," I tell her. "Let them build. Now, move your hand lower. Trace the curve of your hip down the inside of your thigh."

She follows my instructions, her movements becoming more confident. I watch, entranced, as she arches slightly off the bed, her legs parting.

"That's it, moya koroleva. You're doing so well. Now, I want you to touch yourself through your panties. Feel how warm you are."

Vesper gasps as her fingers make contact. Her eyes fly

open, locking with mine through the screen. The raw vulnerability in her gaze takes my breath away.

"Z," she whimpers, her hips moving almost imperceptibly against her hand.

"I'm right here," I assure her, my voice low and soothing. "You're so beautiful like this, Vesper. So perfect. Now, slip your hand inside your panties. Feel how wet you are for me."

She obeys, her back arching as her fingers explore. I can see the moment she finds her most sensitive spot, her mouth falling open in a silent gasp.

"That's it, moya koroleva," I murmur, my voice low and husky. "Circle your clit slowly. Feel how sensitive it is."

Vesper's breath comes in short gasps, her hips rocking gently against her hand. I can see the pleasure building in her, evident in the flush spreading across her cheeks and the way her free hand clutches at the bedsheets.

"Z," she whimpers, her eyes fluttering open to meet mine through the screen. The raw need in her gaze sends a jolt of desire straight to my groin.

My cock strains against my jeans, desperate for attention. But I ignore it, focusing entirely on Vesper. "You're doing so well," I praise her. "Now, slide one finger inside yourself. Slowly."

She complies, her back arching off the bed as she penetrates herself. A soft moan escapes her lips, and I have to bite back a groan of my own.

"How does it feel?" I ask, my voice rough with desire.

"Good," she gasps. "So good, Z. I wish it was you."

Her words send a fresh wave of lust coursing through me. "Me too, moya koroleva. Soon, I promise. For now, add another finger. Curl them up towards your belly button."

Vesper's eyes widen as she follows my instructions. "Oh," she breathes, her hips bucking involuntarily. "Oh, Z."

"That's it," I encourage her. "You've found your sweet spot. Keep stroking it. Use your thumb on your clit at the same time."

She obeys, her movements becoming more frantic as she chases her pleasure. I watch, mesmerized, as she writhes on the bed, her face a mask of ecstasy. My cock throbs painfully, begging for release, but I ignore it. This moment is all about Vesper.

"You're so beautiful like this. I want you to come for me, Vesper.

Her movements become more erratic, her breathing labored. I can see she's close, teetering on the edge of release. "That's it, moya koroleva. Come for me. Now."

With a cry, Vesper arches off the bed, her body trembling as her orgasm washes over her. I watch, entranced, as wave after wave of pleasure courses through her.

"Z," she gasps, her eyes locked on mine as she comes down from her high. "That was...incredible."

I smile, feeling a mix of pride and overwhelming love for this amazing woman. "You're incredible," I tell her softly.

As Vesper catches her breath, a noise in the background catches my attention. Footsteps, coming closer.

"Vesper? Dinner's ready!" Oscar's voice calls from the doorway, and I watch as Vesper's eyes widen in shock, her hand still between her legs.

"Shit," she whispers, scrambling to sit up and smooth down my shirt. Her cheeks flush a deep crimson, and I can't help but feel a mixture of amusement and possessiveness at the sight.

Oscar appears in the frame, his eyebrows shooting up as he takes in the scene before him. His blue eyes flick from Vesper's disheveled state to the phone propped up on the nightstand, and understanding dawns on his face.

"Oh," he says, a knowing smirk playing at the corners of his mouth. "I see my brother's been keeping you entertained."

Vesper buries her face in her hands, but not before I catch a glimpse of her embarrassed smile. "Oz, I...we were just..."

"No need to explain," Oscar chuckles, holding up his hands. "I know damn well what you two were up to." He turns his gaze to the phone, and I can see the mix of emotions in his eyes; amusement, resignation, and a hint of something deeper, more complex. "Enjoying the show, Z?"

I clear my throat, suddenly aware of how dry my mouth has become. "You know me, Oz. Always making the most of a long-distance situation." Oscar rolls his eyes, but there's no real heat in the gesture. "Take care of her, Oz," I say, my voice low and serious.

He nods, his expression softening. "Always, Z. You know that."

Vesper, having recovered somewhat from her embarrassment, looks between us, her green eyes shining with emotion. "I miss you, Zaire," she says softly.

"I miss you too, moya koroleva," I reply, my heart aching with the truth of it. "I'll be home soon, I promise."

I tell Vesper I have to go, my voice husky with barely contained desire. As I end the call, the image of her flushed and satisfied burns itself into my mind. My body thrums with unreleased tension, every nerve ending on fire.

Chapter 29

VESPER

I WATCH as Zaire's face disappears from the screen, his last smoldering look seared into my memory. My body still thrums with desire, a delicious ache pulsing between my thighs. Oscar moves away from me, his tall frame casting a shadow as he crosses the room to shut my bedroom door. The soft click of the latch echoes in the silence, and I shiver, suddenly aware of how exposed I am.

Oscar turns back to me, his blue eyes darkening with an intensity that makes my breath catch. He stalks towards the bed with predatory grace, his gaze never leaving mine. In one fluid motion, he grasps my wrist and pulls me to my feet, my body colliding with his hard chest.

"Vesper," he growls, his voice low and rough with desire. Before I can respond, his lips crash against mine in a searing kiss that steals the air from my lungs. His hands tangle in my hair, angling my head to deepen the kiss as his tongue explores my mouth with passionate urgency.

When we finally break apart, gasping for air, Oscar's eyes are molten with lust. "I could hear you," he murmurs against my lips, his breath hot on my skin. "From the kitchen. Every little moan, every gasp."

My cheeks flush with embarrassment, but the heat pooling in my core tells a different story. "You and Talon?" I manage to ask, my voice breathy and unsteady.

Oscar nods, a wicked smile playing at the corners of his mouth. "We both could. And let me tell you, it was the sweetest torture imaginable."

His admission sends a thrill through me, a mixture of mortification and arousal that makes my head spin. "I'm sorry, I didn't realize-"

"Don't apologize," Oscar cuts me off, his hand cupping my face. "I liked it. Hearing you seek your own pleasure, knowing what was happening in here..." He trails off, his thumb tracing my lower lip. "Did you like knowing that Talon and I might hear your every gasp, every whimper?"

I should feel mortified, but instead, a fresh wave of arousal washes over me. "Yes," I admit. "I liked it. I liked Z telling me what to do, guiding me. And I liked knowing you might hear me."

Oscar's eyes flash with approval and something darker,

more possessive. His grip on my waist tightens. "Tell me more," he demands softly. "Tell me exactly what you liked, Vesper."

I swallow hard, my heart racing. The words tumble out, fueled by lingering desire and the intoxicating nearness of Oscar's body. "I liked feeling desired, feeling powerful. I liked the way Z's voice got deeper, rougher. The way he praised me. And..." I hesitate, biting my lip.

"And?" Oscar prompts, his thumb brushing across my bottom lip.

"I wished you were watching us both. Watching him pleasure me."

A low growl rumbles in Oscar's chest. He pulls me impossibly close, his arousal evident against my hip. "Careful, solnishko," he warns, using the Russian endearment that never fails to make my knees weak. "You're playing with fire."

I arch against him, relishing the way his breath hitches. "Maybe I want to burn," I whisper, trailing my fingers down his chest.

Oscar's control snaps. In one fluid motion, he lifts me, my legs wrapping instinctively around his waist as he carries me back to the bed. As he lowers me onto the mattress, his eyes lock with mine, filled with promise and barely restrained passion.

"Then let's set the world ablaze," he murmurs, before claiming my lips once more.

Oscar's fingers trail up my inner thighs, leaving a trail of fire in their wake. When he reaches the apex, he groans, feeling the evidence of my arousal soaking through the delicate fabric.

"Christ, Vesper," he breathes, his voice husky with desire. "You're drenched."

Before I can respond, he hooks his fingers into the waistband of my panties and tears them off with a sharp tug. The sound of ripping fabric mingles with my gasp of surprise and arousal.

Oscar's eyes lock with mine as he quickly shoves his jeans down, freeing himself. In one swift motion, he's inside me, stretching and filling me so completely that I cry out in pleasure.

"Fuck," he growls, his hips snapping forward with an urgency I've never felt from him before. This isn't the controlled, measured Oscar I'm used to. This is raw, primal need, and it sets my body ablaze.

He pounds into me relentlessly, each thrust driving me higher. My nails rake down his back as I arch beneath him, meeting him thrust for thrust. The room fills with the sound of skin on skin, our breathless moans, and the creaking of the bed beneath us.

Just when I think I can't take anymore, Oscar shifts us. He sits back on his heels, lifting me effortlessly onto his lap, his cock still buried deep inside me. The new angle sends sparks of pleasure shooting through my core.

"Ride me," he commands, his hands gripping my hips. "Show me how much you want this."

I begin to move, rolling my hips in a sensual rhythm. Oscar's head falls back, a groan escaping his lips as I take control. I increase my pace, chasing my release with single-minded determination.

Oscar reaches over to my discarded phone on the floor, bringing it between us. The camera clicks. He moves his fingers and the sound of text being sent whooshes. A text chimes immediately after before it starts ringing. He answers the call.

"Show me," Z's demands. With a free hand, Oz twists the phone, so I can see the screen. Z's face fills it, his eyes dark with desire as they lock onto mine. My breath catches at the raw hunger in his gaze, even through the digital barrier.

"Show me how well you can ride his cock, moya koroleva," Z commands, his voice a low growl.

I watch, mesmerized, as Z positions his camera. His hand moves into view, wrapping around his thick, hard length. The sight makes my mouth water and my inner walls clench around Oscar.

"How does it feel, Vesper?" Z asks, his voice husky. "Tell me everything."

I moan, rolling my hips in a slow, sensual circle. Oscar's fingers dig into my flesh, guiding my movements. "It feels...God, it feels incredible," I manage to gasp out. "He's so deep, stretching me so perfectly."

Z's eyes darken further, his hand starting to move along his shaft. "More," he demands. "I want to hear every detail."

Oscar thrusts up suddenly, making me cry out in pleasure. "Tell him, solnishko," he growls. "Tell him how wet you are for us."

The dual stimulation of Oscar's cock inside me and Z's intense gaze through the screen is almost too much to bear. My movements become more frantic, chasing the peak that's building rapidly within me.

"I'm so wet," I moan, my head falling back as I ride Oscar harder. "I'm dripping down my thighs, coating his cock. It's...oh God, it's overwhelming."

Z's breath hitches audibly. "That's it, moya koroleva. Let me see how good it feels."

I look back at the screen, meeting Z's gaze as I increase my pace. Oscar's hands guide my hips, lifting me slightly before slamming me back down onto his length. The new angle has his cock hitting that perfect spot inside me with every thrust.

"Fuck," I whimper, my voice breaking. "I'm close. So close."

"Come for us," Z commands, his own movements becoming more erratic. "Let us see you fall apart."

Oscar's thumb finds my clit, circling it with practiced skill. The added sensation is all it takes to push me over the edge. My orgasm crashes over me in waves of white-hot pleasure, my inner walls clenching rhythmically around Oscar's length.

"That's it, solnishko," Oscar encourages, his voice strained. "Use my cock to find your release."

Through the haze of my release, I hear Z's guttural groan, watch as his face contorts in ecstasy. The sight of him coming undone because of me, even from a distance, sends another jolt of pleasure through my oversensitive body.

Oscar follows soon after, his hips jerking erratically as he empties himself inside me with a low, drawn-out moan. His forehead presses against my shoulder, his breath hot and ragged against my skin.

Oscar gently shifts me in his lap, his hands gripping my thighs as he spreads them wider. I feel exposed, vulnerable, but the heat in his eyes and the low growl from Z through the phone sends a shiver of excitement through me. Oscar tilts my hips, angling my body towards the camera, and I can feel his release slowly trickling out of me.

"Look at her, Z," Oscar murmurs, his voice husky with satisfaction. "Filled with my cum and dripping onto the sheets. Isn't she perfect?"

Z's response is a deep, primal growl that reverberates through the phone's speaker. His eyes are dark with renewed lust, drinking in the sight of me. "Fucking beautiful," he rasps.

"Hurry home, brother," Oscar smiles before pressing his finger to the screen, and tossing the phone onto the bed next to us.

I take a moment to gather my thoughts, still breathless from the intensity of what just transpired. "It felt empowering," I finally say, turning to meet his gaze. "Amazing. A little confusing, if I'm being honest. But God, Oscar, I want to do it again."

His eyebrow quirks up, a small smile playing at the corners of his mouth. "Oh?"

I nod, feeling a blush creep up my cheeks. "With Z," I add. "In person."

Oscar's laugh is rich and warm, filling the room. "My, my, solnishko," he teases, pulling me closer. "What happened to the innocent little mafia princess I first met? The one who blushed at the mere mention of a kiss?"

I smack his chest playfully, rolling my eyes. "She discovered the joys of having two incredibly sexy men at her disposal," I retort, unable to keep the grin off my face.

He captures my hand, bringing it to his lips to place a soft kiss on my knuckles. "And what a joy it is to be at your disposal," he murmurs, his eyes twinkling with mirth and affection.

We both dissolve into laughter, the tension of the moment breaking. As our giggles subside, I snuggle closer to Oscar, relishing the warmth of his body against mine. There's still so much uncertainty in our world, so many dangers lurking just beyond the borders of this room. But for now, wrapped in Oscar's arms with the memory of Z's heated gaze still fresh in my mind, I feel invincible.

Chapter 30

ZAIRE

I CAN'T GET the image out of my head. Vesper, all golden hair and flushed skin, riding Oscar like she was born to do it. My brother's hands gripping her hips so hard I could almost see the bruises forming. And me, on my phone, my own hand working furiously as I watched them.

It wasn't how I typically got my kicks but fuck if it wasn't hot as hell. The way Vesper's back arched, the sounds she made as she chased her release. I shift uncomfortably, my jeans suddenly too tight as the memories flood back. As soon as I get back, the first thing I plan to do is steal her away and lock the world out until I've had my fill of her. Until I possess her body, mind, and fucking soul.

"Earth to Z," Alex's voice cuts through my reverie, snapping me back to reality. We're across the street from the clinic, watching the building from our car. I realize I've been staring blankly at the steering wheel for who knows how long.

Alex quirks an eyebrow at me, a knowing smirk playing on his lips. "You seem relaxed," he says, emphasizing the last word with a waggle of his eyebrows. "Good night?"

I clear my throat, trying to regain my composure. "Just thinking," I mutter, not meeting his eyes.

"Uh-huh," Alex says, unconvinced. "And I'm the Queen of England. Spill it. What's got you so distracted? Vesper call you or something."

"Or something," is all I give him.

"You think he's going to show?" I ask, my hand instinctively moving to the gun holstered at my hip.

"I think he'll show. I left it vague enough that he probably thinks Natasha is bringing Vesper back to him. As much money as she just made The Collector, he'll be too tempted not to take the bait."

I nod, scanning the street for any signs of movement. The night is quiet, almost unnaturally so, as if the city itself is holding its breath in anticipation. The streetlights cast long shadows across the pavement, creating pockets of darkness where anything or anyone could be lurking.

Suddenly, a sleek black SUV glides into view, its tinted windows reflecting the dim streetlights. My pulse quickens as it turns down the alley beside the clinic, disappearing from sight. A moment later, a faint glow emanates from the front window of the building, barely visible but unmistakable.

"Showtime," I mutter, my voice low and tense.

I pull out my phone, my fingers flying across the screen as I type out a quick message to Oz: "Target's here. Moving in." I hit send, then turn to Alex. "You ready?"

He nods, his face set in grim determination. "Cameras are down."

"How about our friend from the other night?"

"They're occupied," he assures me. "I downloaded a scanner app. There's an accident off the highway. The New York State Police called in our friend and his buddies to manage the traffic. We're clear for a couple of hours at least."

"Won't that be a problem for us to get the fuck out of here?"

"It's west of our exit. It's fine."

We exit the car silently, our movements fluid and practiced. The cool night air hits my face, carrying with it the scent of rain and asphalt. My senses are on high alert, every nerve ending crackling with anticipation.

As we approach the building, I can't help but think of Vesper. Her face flashes in my mind; determined, fierce, beautiful. I push the thought away and focus on the task at hand. There'll be time for that later, I promise myself. Right now, we have a job to do.

We stick to the shadows, our footsteps barely audible on

the damp pavement. The alley looms before us, a dark maw ready to swallow us whole. I can feel the weight of my gun against my hip, a cold comfort in the face of what's to come.

Alex takes point, his lean frame melting into the darkness ahead of me. I follow close behind, my eyes darting from shadow to shadow, searching for any sign of movement. The faint glow from the clinic's window grows stronger as we near the back entrance.

My heart pounds in my chest, a steady rhythm matching our cautious steps. The air feels thick with tension, charged with the impending violence. As we reach the door, I meet Alex's eyes. A silent understanding passes between us. Whatever happens next, we're in this together.

With a deep breath, I reach for the handle, ready to step into whatever awaits us inside. The metal is cool against my palm. This is it, I think. No turning back now.

I turn the handle slowly, wincing at the faint creak as the door swings open. We slip inside, the darkness enveloping us like a second skin. The air is thick with the sterile scent of antiseptic, undercut by something darker, more metallic. My eyes adjust quickly, picking out the shapes of medical equipment and shadowy corridors.

A voice cuts through the silence, making my heart leap into my throat. "Natasha? Is that you?" It's male's voice, smooth as silk, but with an edge that sends a chill down my spine. "I'm all set up in exam room three. Bring her in."

Alex and I exchange a look. This is our chance. We move silently down the hallway, our footsteps muffled by the worn linoleum. The sound of rustling papers and clinking instruments grows louder as we approach the open doorway of exam room three.

I take a deep breath, steeling myself for what's to come. With a nod to Alex, we step into the doorway, blocking the exit.

The man inside freezes, his hands hovering over a tray of gleaming surgical tools. He's younger than I expected, maybe early thirties, with a shock of dark hair and eyes so dark they're almost black. Built like a linebacker, he towers over the exam table, his white coat stretched tight across his broad shoulders.

For a moment, time stands still. I can see the realization dawning in his eyes, quickly followed by panic. Then, like a coiled spring suddenly released, he lunges for the far side of the room.

We're on him in an instant. I dive low, tackling his legs while Alex goes high, wrapping his arms around the man's torso. The force of our combined weight sends us crashing to the floor in a tangle of limbs and curses.

He fights like a cornered animal, all desperation and raw strength. An elbow catches me in the ribs, knocking the wind out of me, but I hold on, gritting my teeth against the pain. Alex grunts as a fist connects with his jaw, but he doesn't let go.

Together, we wrestle him towards the hospital bed. It's like trying to subdue a bear, all muscle and fury. Sweat beads on my forehead, my muscles straining with the effort. But we have the advantage of numbers and surprise.

With a final heave, we manage to flip him onto the bed. I grab a leather strap hanging from the side, quickly securing one of his wrists while Alex does the same on the other side and then adds a strap across his midsection. The man bucks and thrashes, but the straps hold firm.

Panting, I step back, wiping the sweat from my brow. The man on the bed continues to struggle, his eyes wild with fear and rage. "Who the fuck are you?" he spits, chest heaving. "Where's Natasha?"

I ignore him, turning to Alex. "You okay?"

He nods.

"Natasha didn't call you. We did, asshole."

As my eyes sweep across the room, taking in the clinical surroundings, my gaze lands on the stirrups at the end of the bed. A chill runs down my spine as I imagine Vesper in this very position, vulnerable and exposed. The thought makes my blood boil, but it also sparks an idea.

Without breaking eye contact, I move to the foot of the bed. My hands, steady despite the adrenaline coursing through my veins and reach for his shoelaces. The room falls silent, save for the ragged breathing of our captive and the soft rustle of fabric as I remove his shoes.

"What...what are you doing?" The man's voice wavers, fear creeping in to replace the anger.

I don't answer. Instead, I position his feet in the cold

metal stirrups. I want him to feel exactly what Vesper felt, what all his victims felt.

"How does it feel?" I ask. "To be on the other side? To be the one exposed, helpless?"

His eyes widen, darting between my face and his positioned body. I can see the realization dawning, followed quickly by terror. "Please," he whimpers, all bravado gone. "I'll tell you anything you want to know. Just...don't do this."

I lean forward, my gaze boring into his. "That's exactly what they said to you, isn't it? All those women you violated. They begged, pleaded. And you ignored them."

The man on the bed begins to tremble, tears welling in his eyes. "I...I had no choice," he stammers. "They would have killed me if I didn't comply."

"There's always a choice," I spit back, my hands clenching into fists. "You chose to hurt innocent women. To steal their futures, their dreams. And for what? Money?"

I reach into my pocket, pulling out my phone. The screen glows to life, casting an eerie blue light across the room. The man's eyes widen as I raise the device, his breath coming in short, panicked gasps.

"Smile for the camera," I growl, snapping a photo of his terrified face. I type out a quick message to Oscar, attaching the photo.

My phone buzzes almost immediately. It's Oz, relaying Vesper's response:

Put a surgical mask on him.

I nod to Alex, who moves to a nearby supply cabinet. He returns with a blue disposable mask, the kind used in countless medical procedures. As he approaches the bed, our captive begins to thrash anew, his eyes wild with fear.

"No, please," he begs, his voice muffled as Alex secures the mask over his mouth and nose. "You don't understand. They'll kill me if they find out I've been compromised."

I ignore his pleas, raising my phone once more, I snap another photo. The second flash seems even brighter in the dim room, casting harsh shadows across the man's masked face. My fingers tremble slightly as I hit 'send'.

The wait for a response feels interminable. I can hear my own heart pounding in my ears, feel the cold sweat beading on my forehead. The man on the bed has gone quiet, his chest rising and falling rapidly beneath his white coat as he awaits his fate.

Finally, my phone buzzes. I open the message with shaking hands, my eyes scanning the words once, twice, three times to be sure.

"It's him," I say. "Vesper confirms it. He's The Shadow Man."

The room seems to grow colder, the air thick with the weight of this revelation. I look at the man on the bed, seeing him through new eyes. This isn't just some low-level grunt following orders. This is the monster who's been haunting Vesper's nightmares, the one who's caused so much of her pain and suffering.

"You sick fuck," I snarl, leaning in close. The smell of his fear is palpable, a sour stench that turns my stomach. "Do you have any idea what you've done? The lives you've ruined?" He whimpers behind the mask, tears streaming down his face. But I feel no pity, only a cold, hard rage that threatens to consume me.

"Please, I am innocent. Just let me go!"

My phone buzzes again, and I see Oscar's name flash on the screen. I answer immediately, my voice low and tight. "Oz?"

"She wants to watch, Z," he says, his tone a mix of concern and something darker. "Vesper...she needs to see this."

I hesitate for a moment, torn between protecting her from this brutality and honoring her wish for closure. But I know Vesper, her strength, her resilience. If this is what she needs, who am I to deny her?

"Alright. Give me a second."

I prop my phone up against a nearby tray of instruments, angling it so the camera captures the full scene. The Shadow Man strapped to the bed, his feet in stirrups, Alex looming over him with cold determination in his eyes. I step back, making sure I'm in frame too.

Oscar's face appears on the screen, and then he's turning the phone to Vesper. The sight of her nearly takes my breath away. Her golden hair is mussed, her green eyes wide and haunted. But there's a fierceness there too, a burning need for justice that makes my heart ache.

"Can you see okay, moya koroleva?" I ask, my voice softening despite the situation.

She nods, her lips pressed into a thin line. "I can see everything," she says, her voice trembling slightly. "Make him pay." Her voice strengthens at her request. The fire I knew was inside of her showing through knowing that the man who hurt her is at my mercy.

The raw pain in her voice ignites something primal within me. "You heard the lady," I growl. "But, first, we need to have a little chat."

I lean in close, my face inches from his masked visage. "Let's start simple. Who were the buyers for Vesper's eggs?"

His eyes dart frantically between Alex and me, sweat beading on his forehead. "I...I don't know," he stammers. "Natasha oversaw all that. I just did the procedures."

"Bullshit," I snarl, slamming my hand down on the metal tray beside him. The instruments rattle, and he flinches. "You expect us to believe you were just some mindless grunt? Try again."

He shakes his head vigorously, eyes wide with panic. "I swear, it's the truth! Natasha brought her when she was ripe, I did the egg retrieval, and they left. I swear."

"He's lying," Vesper's voice cuts through the noise. "The place they kept me. He was there. He visited."

"For her hormone injections," he fires back. "That's it."

"And where would that have been exactly?"

"I can't tell you that. They'll kill me," he pleas.

"If you think you're walking out of here still drawing breath, you're delusional."

I glance at Alex, who's watching the exchange with cold detachment. He gives a subtle nod, and I know we're on the same page. This scumbag isn't going to crack easily.

"Alright," I say, straightening up. "If that's how you want to play it."

I step back, giving Alex room to move. He approaches the bed slowly, deliberately, a scalpel glinting in his hand.

"What...what are you doing?" he whimpers, straining against his restraints.

Alex doesn't respond. Instead, he leans over the man, the scalpel hovering just above the crotch of his dress pants. With precise movements, he begins to cut through the fabric, the soft sound of tearing cloth filling the room.

His pleas grow more frantic as Alex works, cutting through his underwear as well. "Please, stop! I'll tell you whatever you want to know!"

But it's too late. Alex steps back, and I can see the man's exposed flesh, vulnerable and pathetic. The sight fills me with a mixture of disgust and savage satisfaction.

"Now," I say, my voice low and dangerous, "let's try this again. Who were the buyers?"

He's sobbing now, his chest heaving beneath the white coat. "I don't know his real name," he chokes out. "They just went by The Collector, that's all I know, I swear."

I lean in closer, my eyes boring into his. "What did they want with her eggs?"

He swallows hard, Adam's apple bobbing beneath the surgical mask. "I…I didn't ask," he whispers. "They paid triple the usual rate for a viable male embryo. They said she was special. I just did what they wanted me to do."

"The rack with her embryo. It's empty. Where did they go?"

The man's eyes dart nervously between Alex and me, his breath coming in ragged gasps. "The male embryo. It was couriered away as soon as it was frozen. Special handling, top priority. I don't know where it went, I swear."

I feel my jaw clench, anger boiling in my veins. "And the female embryo?"

He swallows hard, his Adam's apple bobbing beneath the surgical mask. "Destroyed," he whispers, his voice barely audible. "Per The Collector's request. They only wanted the male."

The words hit me like a physical blow. I turn to look at the phone propped up on the tray where Vesper's face fills the screen. The devastation in her eyes is palpable, a raw, open wound that makes my chest ache. Her lips tremble, and I can see her struggling to maintain her composure.

The sight of her pain ignites something primal within me. I whirl back to face him, my vision tinged with red. "Where?" I snarl, leaning in close. "Where did they send the male embryo?"

He shakes his head frantically, eyes wide with terror. "I don't know, I swear! They never tell me these things. I'm just the doctor. I don't oversee logistics!"

I can feel my control slipping, rage threatening to consume me. My hands clench into fists at my sides, knuckles white with the effort of restraining myself.

From the corner of my eye, I see Alex move. He reaches for something on the nearby tray, and the fluorescent lights glint off cold, polished steel. A speculum, its curved arms wickedly sharp in the harsh light.

Ivanov's eyes lock onto the instrument, and a whimper escapes from behind his mask. "Please," he begs, his voice cracking. "I've told you everything I know. Please don't do this."

Alex steps forward, his face a mask of cold determination. The speculum hovers over the man's exposed groin, and I can see him trembling, sweat beading on his forehead. Ivanov's sobbing now, tears streaming down his face and soaking into the surgical mask. "I don't know the exact location," he chokes out between gasps. "But I overheard something about a private clinic in Russia."

I look at Alex, our eyes meeting in a moment of shared understanding. Russia. Of course it would lead back there. The word hangs in the air, heavy with implications and unspoken questions. Without a second's hesitation, Alex shoves the speculum into his ass, each click spreading his asshole wide open as he screams.

"I bet that's uncomfortable," I smirk.

"We need more than just 'Russia.' It's a big country, in case you hadn't noticed."

His eyes dart frantically between Alex and me, panic

evident in every line of his face. "I don't know anything else, I swear! Please, you have to believe me!"

Alex gives me a subtle nod before disappearing from the room. For a moment, the only sounds are Ivanov's ragged breathing and the distant hum of medical equipment. Then, a new noise fills the air, the slow, ominous rumble of something heavy being wheeled down the hallway.

The sound grows louder, echoing off the sterile walls until it seems to fill the entire clinic. I watch as his pupils dilating with fear as he strains to see what's coming.

Alex reappears in the doorway, pushing a large, cylindrical container. It's a liquid nitrogen dewar, its metallic surface gleaming under the harsh fluorescent lights. A long, stainless steel hose snakes out from the top, coiling on the floor like some mechanical serpent.

The sight of it sends a chill down my spine, and I'm not even the one strapped to the bed. I can only imagine what's going through Ivanov's mind right now.

Alex maneuvers the dewar into position next to the bed, the wheels squeaking slightly on the linoleum floor. He picks up the end of the hose, examining it with a clinical detachment that's somehow more terrifying than outright anger.

"You know," I say conversationally, as if we're discussing the weather and not about to torture a man, "liquid nitrogen is fascinating stuff. It's so cold that it burns your skin in seconds. Imagine what that would feel like on your most sensitive areas."

Ivanov's eyes are fixed on the hose in Alex's hand, his

chest rising and falling rapidly as he hyperventilates. "Please," he whimpers, his voice muffled by the mask. "I've told you everything I know. I swear on my life!"

I lean in close, my face inches from his. "Your life isn't worth much right now," I growl. "But maybe, just maybe, if you give us something useful, we might let you keep some of your parts intact."

Alex moves closer, the hose hovering menacingly over his exposed groin. I can see goosebumps rising on his skin, whether from fear or the proximity to the frigid container, I'm not sure. Alex twists the knob on the top of the tank, a whooshing sound coming from it as frost begins to form on the hose. Alex hands me the hose. As the liquid spews, I shove the blunt end of the hose into his ass through the speculum.

Ivanov's scream pierces the air, a sound of pure agony that seems to vibrate through my very bones. His body convulses against the restraints, muscles straining as he tries to escape the searing cold invading his most intimate areas. Thick, white fog billows from between his legs, curling around the stirrups and spilling onto the floor like some ethereal waterfall.

The acrid smell of burning flesh fills my nostrils, turning my stomach even as a savage satisfaction courses through me. This is for Vesper, I remind myself. For all the women he's hurt.

I yank the hose free, watching as more fog pours from

his abused orifice. "Start talking," I growl, my hand hovering threateningly over the liquid nitrogen tank.

Ivanov's words tumble out in a frantic rush, punctuated by sobs and gasps of pain. "It was Mario Rossi," he chokes out. "He bought the embryo. Natasha...she arranged it all for him."

The words hit me like a physical blow, stealing the air from my lungs. Mario Rossi. Vesper's own uncle. The man who is supposed to be family. A red haze descends over my vision, rage boiling up from some deep, primal part of me.

Without conscious thought, my hand moves to the tank's controls. I crank it up, unleashing a torrent of liquid nitrogen into the room. The temperature plummets instantly, fog rolling across the floor in thick waves. It swirls around my ankles, climbs up the walls, fills every corner of the room until it's hard to see, hard to breathe.

I can barely make out Alex's form through the dense fog. The temperature in the room plummets, our breath visible in short, sharp puffs. Ivanov's cries grow weaker, muffled by the mask and the ever-thickening mist.

My hand shakes as I reach for my phone, still propped up on the nearby tray. Vesper's face is barely visible on the screen, her eyes wide with a mixture of horror and grim satisfaction. I snatch it up, my fingers numb with cold and shock. "Go to the warehouse," Oscar calls out from my phone. "We'll meet you there."

"We're done here," I growl to Alex, my voice sounding

foreign to my own ears. Without waiting for a response, I turn and stride out of the room, Alex close on my heels.

The hallway feels unnaturally warm after the Arctic chill of the exam room. I can hear the faint, weakening cries of Ivanov behind us, but I don't look back. My mind is a maelstrom of thoughts and emotions, all centered around one devastating fact: Mario Rossi is behind all of this. Vesper's fucking uncle.

"What do we do about him?" I ask Alex once we're outside the room. "We can't exactly leave him on ice. They'll blow the whistle as soon as it opens up tomorrow. You can't exactly miss a frozen ass popsicle in the exam room."

Alex pulls out his phone, firing off a text. "He'll be gone within the hour."

"Do I want to know how?"

"Let's just say I have a friend nearby in the big cat business," he says with a wink. "He's always looking for free meat to feed his tigers."

"How the fuck do you keep making all these friends, Alex?" I ask, shaking my head.

"Message boards," he shrugs nonchalantly. "You can meet all kinds of interesting people online."

Chapter 31

TALON

I CAN'T HELP but grin as I watch Alex and Zaire finish up their handiwork on Ivanov. The sight of the bastard's frozen ass would be almost comical, if it weren't for the gravity of the situation. I've seen some creative torture methods in my time, but a liquid nitrogen enema? That's a new one even for our twisted little family.

"Talon, we need to move," Oscar's voice cuts through my thoughts, sharp and urgent. I turn to see him with his arm around Vesper, her face buried in his chest. My heart clenches at the sight. She's been through hell, and it's not over yet.

"Right," I nod, snapping into action. "I'll get the gear packed up."

I move swiftly, gathering Alex's toys, an assortment of computers and their accessories, and our arsenal of weapons. The weight of the guns is comforting in my hands, a reminder of the power we wield and the protection we can offer Vesper. My father used to joke that I was born with a gun in my hand, and my skills with them would attest that's true.

As I load the car, I can't help but replay Oscar's words in my head. Mario's involvement in Vesper's abduction changes everything. We're exposed, vulnerable. The beach house, our safe haven, might as well have a target painted on its roof. There's no one for miles.

I glance back at Oscar and Vesper, still locked in an embrace. Oscar's usually stoic face is etched with concern, his blue eyes dark with worry. He's whispering something to her, probably reassurances, but I can see the tension in his shoulders. He knows as well as I do that we're far from out of the woods.

"We're ready. I'll drive," I yell to Oscar slamming the trunk shut.

Oscar walks Vesper outside, his arm protectively wrapped around her waist. Her steps are unsteady, and I can see the way she leans into him for support. The sight stirs something primal within me, a mix of protectiveness and a darker, more possessive emotion that I'm not ready to name. Oscar has always been in love with Vesper. It's not shocking that Zaire fell almost as quickly. But, me. I barely knew her. But the longer I'm around her, I can see why the twins fell so fast. Despite everything she has been through, she's still held on to her eternal light. It's no wonder I seem to be gravitating towards her orbit just like they have.

As they approach the car, I open the back door for them. Oscar gently helps Vesper inside, his movements careful and tender. It's a side of him I rarely see, this softness that seems reserved only for her. He slides in next to her, and I watch as she immediately curls into him, her head resting in his lap.

The sound of her muffled sobs fill the car, each quiet gasp like a dagger to my chest. I grip the steering wheel tighter, my knuckles turning white as I fight the urge to reach back and comfort her myself. But this isn't my moment. It's Oscar's, and I respect that, even as jealousy gnaws at my insides.

I turn the key in the ignition, the engine roaring to life. The familiar purr does little to calm my nerves as I throw the car into drive and peel out of the gravel driveway. Rocks spray behind us, a cloud of dust in our wake as we leave the beach house, and the nightmare it now represents, behind.

The tires screech as we hit the main road, and I push the speedometer well past the legal limit. The darkness of the night envelops us, broken only by the occasional streetlight and the glow of our headlights cutting through the gloom. In the rearview mirror, I catch glimpses of Oscar stroking

Vesper's hair, whispering words of comfort I can't quite make out over the rumble of the engine.

Her cries gradually soften, but the pain in those quiet whimpers is no less potent. Each sound twists something inside me, fueling a rage I've been trying to keep in check. I want to turn this car around, go back, and make Ivanov suffer even more for what he's done to her. But I know that's not what she needs right now. What she needs is safety, comfort, and time to heal.

As we speed down the coastal highway, the ocean a dark, ominous presence to our right, I can't shake the feeling that we're being watched. Every set of headlights in the distance sets my teeth on edge. Is it Victor's men? Have they already found us? The paranoia is suffocating, but I force myself to focus on the road ahead.

"How is she?" I ask Oscar, my voice low and rough with emotion.

"She's falling asleep," he replies softly, his hand never ceasing its gentle caress of her hair.

"Do you really think her uncle did this to her? It doesn't make sense. Unless, he knew we were going to stop her from getting to the airport," Oscar offers.

"That's not possible," I argue back. "It's something else. Something we're not seeing."

The miles stretch out before us, an endless ribbon of asphalt disappearing into the night. I settle into the rhythm of the drive, my body on autopilot while my mind races.

The soft hum of the engine and the occasional whisper of tires on the road are the only sounds breaking the heavy silence.

Hours pass, marked only by the changing of the sky from inky black to the muted grays and the pinks of dawn. In the rearview mirror, I catch glimpses of Vesper, still curled up with her head in Oscar's lap. Her face, relaxed in sleep, looks impossibly young and vulnerable. Oscar hasn't moved, his hand a constant, soothing presence on her hair.

As the sun begins to climb higher in the sky, the familiar silhouette of our warehouse looms on the horizon. The worn brick façade and rusted metal roof belie the state-of-the-art security system hidden within its walls. A wave of relief washes over me as I guide the SUV through the concealed entrance, the heavy steel doors grinding shut behind us.

I park in our designated spot, killing the engine. The sudden silence is deafening. Oscar stirs, carefully maneuvering Vesper's sleeping form.

"I've got her," he murmurs, scooping her up effortlessly. "I'll take her up to the penthouse."

I nod, watching as he carries her to the elevator, her blonde hair cascading over his arm like spun gold. The doors close, and I'm left alone in the cavernous garage.

With a sigh, I turn to the task at hand. The trunk is packed to the brim with our gear, and I methodically begin unloading. Each piece of equipment is a reminder of the night's events; the computers Alex used to hack Ivanov's security, the weapons we didn't need to use but were prepared to, the medical supplies we thankfully didn't have to break out.

I'm hauling the last box out when I hear the unmistakable rumble of another vehicle approaching. Tensing instinctively, I relax when I recognize the sleek black Audi pulling into the garage. Zaire and Alex are here.

The car barely comes to a stop before Zaire is out, his face a mask of barely contained fury and concern. He doesn't even spare me a glance as he strides past, making a beeline for the elevator. The doors open as if on cue, and he disappears inside.

Alex emerges more slowly, his usually cheerful face drawn and tired. He moves to help me with the remaining gear, but I wave him off.

"I've got this," I tell him. "You look like hell. Go get some rest."

Alex ignores my suggestion, grabbing a box of his precious tech. His eyes narrow as he peers inside, and I brace myself for the inevitable tirade.

"Jesus, Talon, did you just throw everything in here like a goddamn caveman?" He pulls out a tangle of wires, his face contorting in horror. "This is delicate equipment, not your dirty gym socks!"

I roll my eyes, hefting another box onto my shoulder. "Oh, I'm sorry, princess. Next time we're fleeing a potential mafia war, I'll be sure to pack your toys with silk pillows and rose petals."

Alex mutters something that sounds suspiciously like "Neanderthal" as we make our way to the elevator. The doors slide open with a soft ping, and we step inside. The ascent to our penthouse is smooth, but the tension in the air is palpable.

"So," I begin, desperate to break the uncomfortable silence, "where'd you get the idea for that liquid nitrogen stunt? That was creative, to say the least."

A ghost of a smile flickers across Alex's face, a welcome change from his earlier scowl. "Believe it or not, I saw a video about making ice cream with liquid nitrogen. Got me thinking about other applications."

I can't help but laugh, the sound echoing in the confined space of the elevator. "Only you could watch a cooking video and turn it into a torture method. Remind me never to piss you off when you're in the kitchen."

Alex grins, some of the weariness lifting from his features. "Please, as if I'd waste good nitrogen on your sorry ass. You'd get the dollar store version, maybe some ice cubes down your pants."

The elevator doors open, and we step into the luxurious penthouse. The open-plan living area is bathed in the soft morning light filtering through floor-to-ceiling windows. In any other circumstance, the view of the city skyline would be breathtaking. Today, it just makes me feel exposed.

We make our way to the tech room, Alex's personal sanctuary filled with more screens and gadgets than a NASA control center. As we set down the boxes, I can't help but notice the way his hands linger on each piece of equipment, checking for damage.

"You know," I say, leaning against the doorframe, "for a guy who just turned a man's ass into a popsicle, you're awfully precious about your toys."

Alex shoots me a withering look. "These 'toys' are what keep us alive and off the grid. A little respect wouldn't kill you."

I raise my hands in mock surrender. "Alright, alright. I bow to your superior nerd knowledge. Just don't expect me to start treating your laptops like Fabergé eggs."

He snorts, already engrossed in setting up one of his monitors. "As if you even know what a Fabergé egg is."

"I'll have you know I'm very cultured," I retort, puffing out my chest in mock indignation. "I've seen 'Anastasia' at least twice."

Alex's laugh is genuine this time, a welcome sound after the tension of the past few hours. "Right, because an animated movie is the pinnacle of historical accuracy. Next, you'll be telling me you're an expert on Russian history because you've played Tetris."

I can't help but grin. "Hey, those falling blocks taught me everything I need to know about efficient packing. How do you think I got all your precious gear in the car so fast?"

"Oh, is that why my hard drives are stacked like Jenga pieces?" Alex quips, raising an eyebrow as he pulls out a precariously balanced tower of equipment.

Our banter continues as we unpack, the familiar rhythm

of our friendship providing a much-needed distraction from the gravity of our situation. But even as we joke, I can't shake the nagging feeling of unease that's settled in my gut.

"Alex," I say, my tone suddenly serious, "I need you to run a full security sweep. Check for any breaches, any unusual activity in the past 48 hours. If Mario's involved, we can't be too careful."

Alex nods, his fingers already flying across one of his keyboards. "On it. I'll set up additional firewalls and reroute our digital footprint through a few more proxy servers. It'll slow down our connection, but it'll make us harder to trace."

I clap him on the shoulder, grateful for his expertise. "Good man. I'm going to do a perimeter check, make sure we're locked down tight."

As I leave Alex to his digital fortress, I can't help but feel a twinge of envy. His digital world of code is so much more straightforward than the mess of emotions and loyalties we're dealing with in the real world.

I make my way through the penthouse, checking each window and door, assessing the locks and security systems. It's a routine I've performed countless times, but today it feels different. More urgent. More necessary.

As I pass by Oscar's room, I pause. The door is slightly ajar, and I can't resist peeking inside. The sight that greets me sends a jolt through my system.

Vesper lies on the bed, her golden hair spread out on the pillow like a halo. She looks peaceful in sleep, the worry lines that have marred her forehead for days finally smoothed out. But it's not just her presence that catches my attention.

Oscar sits in a chair pulled close to the bed, his hand gently holding Vesper's. His thumb traces small circles on her skin, a gesture so tender it makes my chest ache.

Zaire stands at the foot of the bed, his usual cocky demeanor replaced by a look of fierce protectiveness. His eyes never leave Vesper's face, as if he's afraid she might disappear if he looks away for even a second. The scar on his neck stands out against his pale skin, a reminder of the dangers we face every day in this life.

I linger in the doorway, unable to tear my gaze away from the scene before me. There's an intimacy to it that makes me feel like an intruder, yet I can't bring myself to leave. The way Oscar and Zaire orbit around Vesper, even in her sleep, speaks volumes about the depth of their feelings for her.

A lump forms in my throat as I watch Oscar gently brush a strand of hair from Vesper's face. His touch is so tender, so reverent, it's almost painful to witness. I've known Oscar for years, seen him in the heat of battle and in the depths of despair, but I've never seen him look at anyone the way he looks at her.

And Zaire, the wild card of our group, stands as still as a statue, his eyes never wavering from Vesper's sleeping form. The tattoos that cover his arms seem to writhe in the dim light, creating a mesmerizing pattern that only adds to the surreal quality of the moment.

I find myself wondering what it would be like to love someone that deeply, that completely. To feel so connected to another person that their pain becomes your pain, their joy, your joy. The intensity of their devotion is almost palpable, filling the room with an energy that's both exhilarating and terrifying.

A part of me yearns for that kind of connection, that sense of belonging. But another part recoils from it, recognizing the vulnerability that comes with opening yourself up so completely to another person. In our world, love is a liability, a weakness that can be exploited by our enemies.

Yet looking at Oscar and Zaire, I can't help but think that maybe it's worth the risk. The way they stand guard over Vesper, ready to face any threat that might come her way, speaks of a strength that goes beyond physical prowess or tactical skill. It's a strength born of love, of unwavering loyalty and fierce protectiveness.

I think about my own feelings for Vesper. The way my heart races when she's near and the overwhelming urge to keep her safe. Is that love? Or just the natural protective instinct of a friend and ally? The line between the two seems increasingly blurred, and I'm not sure I'm ready to examine those feelings too closely.

With one last glance at the trio in the room, I force myself to turn away. The ache in my chest lingers as I make my way back downstairs, each step feeling heavier than the last.

As I reach the main floor, I throw myself into the task of

securing our hideout. I check and double-check every lock, every alarm system. I review the camera feeds, scrutinizing each frame for any sign of unusual activity.

But even as I go through the motions, my mind keeps drifting back to that room upstairs.

Chapter 32

VESPER

I STARE at Zaire's peaceful face, his long lashes resting against his cheeks, his breathing slow and steady. The dim light filtering through the warehouse windows casts shadows across his features, accentuating the sharp line of his jaw and the curve of his lips. My eyes trace the intricate tattoos peeking out from beneath the collar of his shirt.

The weight of Oscar's arm draped over my waist is comforting, grounding me in this moment of surreal calm. I can feel the steady rise and fall of his chest against my back, his breath warm on my neck. It's a cocoon of safety, nestled between these two powerful men who have become my unexpected protectors.

My mind drifts back to the events that led me here, but the memories are hazy, obscured by a fog of grief and shock. I remember fragments; the screech of tires, the low murmur of voices. The rest is a blur, my senses dulled by the overwhelming pain of betrayal.

I shift slightly, and Zaire's brow furrows in his sleep. His arm tightens around me, pulling me closer as if sensing my distress even in his dreams.

The warehouse is quiet save for the distant hum of the city beyond its walls. The smell of metal and leather permeates the air.

I close my eyes, trying to shut out the world and the pain it brings. But behind my eyelids, I see my uncle's face. The ache in my chest threatens to overwhelm me again, but the steady heartbeats of Oscar and Zaire on either side of me function as anchors, keeping me tethered to the present.

Ivanov's words echo in my mind, a haunting refrain that refuses to be silenced. I can still see his face, contorted with pain and fear, as he spilled the truth like poison from his lips. Not that I pity him. After what he did to me, and likely countless others, he deserved every moment of his fate. But his confession, extracted through means I'd rather not dwell on, has left me reeling.

"It was Mario Rossi," he had gasped. "He bought the embryo. Natasha...she arranged it all for him."

The betrayal cuts deeper than any knife, leaving a wound that I fear may never fully heal. Mario, the man who had bounced me on his knee as a child, who had taught me to shoot my first gun, who had sworn to always protect me; he had orchestrated my downfall. He had ordered the theft of my body. He had ordered the creation of two embryos. The viable male embryo god knows where. Even more cruelly, the destruction of the female embryo. A life that would never draw her first breath.

A sob catches in my throat, threatening to break free. I swallow it down, not wanting to wake the twins, but the pain is like a living thing inside me, clawing at my insides. My hand instinctively moves to my stomach, flat and empty, mourning a child that never was.

She would have had my eyes, I think. Green like spring leaves, flecked with gold. Maybe she would have inherited the Rossi nose, straight and proud. I imagine her tiny fingers, perfect and delicate, grasping my own. The weight of her in my arms, the soft downy hair on her head. I can almost hear her first cry, see her first steps, feel the warmth of her first hug.

I think of all the firsts we'll never share - her first word, her first day of school, her first heartbreak. I'll never braid her hair or teach her to defend herself. I'll never see her grow into a strong, fierce woman who could have changed the world. The future I never knew I wanted has been ripped away, leaving a gaping hole in my heart.

But she'll never take those steps. She'll never cry or laugh or call me 'Mama.' She'll never know the fierce love that I already feel for her, this phantom child who exists only in my shattered dreams. The grief is overwhelming, a tidal wave threatening to drown me. How can I mourn someone who never existed? And yet, the loss feels as real and as raw as if I'd held her in my arms and watched her slip away.

Tears slip silently down my cheeks, soaking into the rough fabric beneath me. I mourn for the life unlived, the potential unrealized. I mourn for the mother I'll never be to her, the love I'll never get to give. The pain is a physical ache, as if a part of me has been carved out, leaving only emptiness behind.

I allow myself to feel the full weight of this loss. To grieve for a child who never drew breath, but who had already claimed a piece of my soul. The injustice of it all threatens to consume me. How someone could play God with life so carelessly, destroying a future as if it meant nothing.

I press my lips together to stifle a whimper, my body trembling with the force of my silent sobs. The warehouse suddenly feels too small, too confining. The air is thick with the ghosts of what might have been, suffocating me with possibilities that will never come to pass.

As I struggle to contain my grief, I feel a subtle shift in the air. The hairs on the back of my neck prickle, and I open my eyes to find Zaire's intense gaze fixed upon me. His silver eyes are filled with concern and something deeper, more primal. He doesn't speak, but his hand moves to cup my cheek, his calloused thumb gently wiping away a stray tear.

With a tenderness that belies his fierce exterior, Zaire

draws me closer. I allow myself to be pulled into his embrace, nuzzling into the solid warmth of his chest. His scent envelops me. It's comforting and intoxicating all at once, and I find myself inhaling deeply, trying to memorize this moment of solace.

My tears flow freely now, soaking into the fabric of his shirt. Zaire's arms tighten around me, one hand cradling the back of my head, while the other traces soothing circles on my lower back. He murmurs soft words in Russian, the lyrical cadence of his native tongue washing over me like a balm.

Behind me, I feel Oscar beginning to stir. His arm tightens around my waist for a moment before relaxing. Without a word, Zaire shifts, his movements fluid and graceful despite his size. In one smooth motion, he scoops me into his arms, cradling me against his chest as if I weigh nothing.

I cling to him, my fingers curling into the soft material of his shirt as he carries me away from Oscar, who is sleeping soundly again. My tears have slowed, but my breath still comes in shuddering gasps. Zaire's heartbeat is strong and steady beneath my ear, a rhythmic counterpoint to my ragged breathing.

We move through the warehouse, past stacks of crates and forgotten machinery, until Zaire pushes open a heavy metal door with his shoulder. The room beyond is sparsely furnished but undeniably his. The walls are adorned with intricate sketches. I recognize his artistic hand in the bold lines and delicate shading. A well-worn leather jacket is draped over a chair.

Zaire sets me down gently on the bed, the mattress dipping beneath our combined weight as he sits beside me. His eyes, usually so guarded, are open and vulnerable as they search my face. I can see the pain reflected there, mirroring my own.

"Vesper," he says, his voice low and rough with emotion. "I promised you no one else would make you cry."

His words, meant to comfort, only serve to open the floodgates once more. Fresh tears spill down my cheeks, and I can see the anguish in Zaire's eyes. "Tell me what to do, moya koroleva. Give your monster a purpose. I'll do anything to not see you in so much fucking pain."

"Make it go away. Make the pain go away, Zaire. I can't…I can't breathe."

Zaire's eyes darken at my words, a storm of conflicting emotions swirling in their depths. His jaw clenches, the muscles in his neck tightening visibly. For a moment, he's utterly still, like a predator poised to strike. Then, with a gentleness that belies his fierce exterior, he cups my face in his hands.

"Vesper," he breathes, his voice husky and strained. "You're hurting. You're not thinking clearly. We don't have to rush into this."

His thumb traces the curve of my cheekbone, wiping away a stray tear. The tenderness of the gesture contrasts sharply with the raw hunger I can see simmering beneath the surface of his control. It makes me ache for him even more.

I reach up, running my fingers along the sharp line of his jaw, feeling the slight rasp of stubble against my skin. "I need you. I need to feel something other than this pain. Make me forget, even if it's just for a little while."

Zaire's breath hitches, his pupils dilating until only a thin ring of blue remains. His hands slide down to my shoulders, gripping tightly as if to anchor himself. "You don't know what you're asking for, moya koroleva," he growls, the endearment slipping out almost unconsciously. "There are ways to make the pain recede, Vesper. Ways I know intimately. But it's not simple, and it's not for everyone." He pauses, his gaze intense as it locks with mine. "I'm what's called a Dom. It means I take control, provide structure, and offer a different kind of release. But it also means I bear the responsibility for your well-being, your pleasure, your pain."

His words send a shiver down my spine, a mix of fear and something else, something electric. "What does that mean?" I whisper, my voice barely audible even in the quiet room.

Zaire's hand comes up to cup my cheek, his touch gentle despite the calluses on his fingers. "It means you would be my submissive. You would give yourself over to me, trust me to guide you, to push your limits, to give you what you need — even if it's not always what you think you want."

He leans in closer, his breath warm against my ear. "I would worship every inch of your body, learn every sound you make, every shiver, every gasp. I would take you apart piece by piece and put you back together again. I would be your anchor in the storm, your safe harbor."

His words paint vivid pictures in my mind — images of hands bound, skin flushed, pleasure so intense it borders on pain. I can almost feel the ghost of a touch trailing down my spine, the whisper of silk against my skin.

"But it's more than just physical," Zaire continues, his voice a low rumble that I feel as much as hear. "It's about trust, about letting go completely. It's about finding freedom in submission, peace in surrender. When you're with me, you won't have to think, won't have to decide. You'll just feel."

He pulls back slightly, his eyes searching mine. "I would take care of you, anticipate your needs before you even know them yourself. But I would also challenge you, push you to your limits and beyond. It can be intense, over-whelming even. But the release, the catharsis — it's unlike anything else. I'll consume you, possess you entirely. Are you sure that's what you want?"

The heat in his gaze sends a shiver down my spine, igniting a fire low in my belly. I meet his eyes unflinchingly, letting him see the desperation, the need burning within me. "Yes," I breathe. "I want all of you, Zaire. Every dark, dangerous part. I trust you."

"You need a safe word."

The concept isn't entirely foreign to me, but hearing it from Zaire's lips sends a shiver down my spine. He continues, his voice taking on a softer edge. "If you use this word, everything stops. No questions asked, no matter what's happening. It's your lifeline, your way out if things become too much. Choose something you'll remember easily, something that has no connection to what we're doing. It should be a word that won't come up accidentally."

I think for a moment, my mind racing through possibilities. Finally, I settle on one. "Sunflower," I say, thinking of the bright yellow blooms that used to grow in the garden under my window.

Zaire nods, a flicker of approval in his eyes. "Sunflower," he repeats, committing it to memory. "Remember, moya koroleva, this word gives you all the power. Use it, and everything stops immediately. No consequences, no judgment. Do you understand?"

I nod again, more firmly this time. "I understand, Zaire."

His hands move to my shoulders, squeezing gently. "Good. Now, tell me your safe word one more time."

"Sunflower" I say, my voice stronger now.

"And you'll use it if you need to, won't you, moya koroleva?"

I nod again, my breath catching in my throat at his proximity.

"I need to hear you say it," Zaire growls, his grip tightening slightly.

"Yes," I breathe.

"Let's begin, moya koroleva," he breathes, his voice

husky with desire. His calloused hands caress my thighs, leaving a trail of goosebumps in their wake. My breath catches in my throat as he leans in, his warm breath ghosting over my sensitive skin. "We'll start slow. Don't move," he commands, his silver eyes locking onto mine. "Keep your hands on the bed, and don't you dare look away."

I nod, my heart racing as I obey, gripping the sheets tightly. His lips brush against my inner thigh, his stubble scratching deliciously against my skin. He works his way up slowly, torturously, placing open-mouthed kisses along my flesh.

"Z," I whimper, my hips instinctively arching towards him.

He pulls back slightly, a wicked grin playing on his lips. "Did I say you could move, moya koroleva?" His voice is stern, but his eyes dance with mischief.

I bite my lip, shaking my head.

"Good girl," he purrs, rewarding me with a gentle nip to my inner thigh. "Now, stay still and let me worship you properly."

His talented mouth resumes its exploration, and I fight to keep my eyes open, to keep watching him as he'd commanded. As he finally reaches my center, I gasp, my fingers twisting in the sheets. Zaire's tongue dances over my most sensitive areas, and I struggle to obey his earlier command to stay still.

"Z, please," I beg.

He pauses, his hot breath teasing my sensitive flesh. "What do you need, moya koroleva?" Zaire's voice is husky, dripping with desire.

"You," I breathe, my body trembling with need. "Please, I need you."

His large finger shoves aside my panties, a low growl rumbles in his chest as he dives back in, his tongue circling my clit with expert precision. My back arches involuntarily, a moan escaping my lips as waves of pleasure wash over me. Zaire's strong hands grip my thighs, holding me in place as he works his magic.

His tongue flicks and swirls building me higher and higher. I can feel the tension coiling in my core, my release tantalizingly close. My fingers twist in the sheets, knuckles white with the effort of staying still. Zaire's eyes, dark with lust, never leave mine as he pushes me closer to the edge.

Just as I'm about to tumble over, Zaire pulls away. I whimper at the loss, my body aching for completion. "Not yet," he growls, his voice rough with arousal. "On your knees, now."

I comply immediately, my legs shaky as I position myself before him. Zaire kneels, towering over me, his muscled chest heaving with each breath. His tattoos seem to ripple in the dim light, a work of art brought to life.

"Open your mouth," he commands, his hand cupping my chin. I obey, looking up at him through my lashes. "Good girl," he praises, his thumb tracing my lower lip. "Now, show me how much you want it."

I hesitate for a moment, my inexperience suddenly overwhelming. Zaire's eyes soften as he notices my uncertainty. "It's okay, moya koroleva," he murmurs, his voice gentle. "I'll guide you. Just take it slow."

With trembling hands, I reach for his zipper, fumbling slightly as I free him from his jeans. His length springs forth, impressive and intimidating. I swallow hard, my mouth suddenly dry.

"Start with your hand," Zaire instructs, his voice husky. "Wrap your fingers around the base."

I do as he says, marveling at the contrast between the soft skin and the hardness beneath. Zaire hisses in pleasure, his hand coming to rest on the back of my head.

"Now, use your tongue," he continues. "Lick from base to tip, like it's the most delicious ice cream cone you've ever tasted."

Tentatively, I follow his directions, my tongue tracing the prominent vein along his shaft. The taste is unfamiliar but not unpleasant; salty and musky. His fingers tangle in my hair, encouraging me.

"That's it, moya koroleva," he groans. "Now, take the tip into your mouth. Be careful of your teeth."

I part my lips, taking him in slowly. The weight of him on my tongue is strange but exciting. I look up at Zaire, seeking approval, and find his eyes blazing with desire.

"Fuck," he breathes. "Your swollen lips wrapped around my cock. It's going to undo me, Vesper."

His words send a thrill through me, emboldening me to

take him deeper. I hollow my cheeks, sucking gently as I bob my head, following the rhythm Zaire sets with his hand in my hair.

"Use your hand too," he instructs, his voice strained. "Stroke what you can't fit in your mouth."

I comply, my hand working in tandem with my mouth. Zaire's breathing grows ragged, his hips starting to move slightly. I gag a little as he hits the back of my throat, but his murmured praises encourage me to keep going.

"You're doing so well, moya koroleva," he groans. "Your mouth feels incredible."

His words spur me on, and I redouble my efforts, alternating between long, slow strokes and quick, shallow ones. Zaire's grip on my hair tightens, his control slipping. His breath catches, and he gently pulls me off him. His eyes, dark with desire, lock onto mine. "As much as I'd love to see my cum staining those perfect lips," he growls, his voice husky, "I want to be inside you when we both find our release."

A shiver runs through me at his words, anticipation coiling low in my belly. Zaire's hand cups my cheek, his thumb tracing my swollen lips. "Take off your shirt and your panties." I do as he says. My body on full display for him now.

"Turn around," he commands softly. "Hands and one knee on the edge of the bed."

I comply, my body trembling with need as I position myself as instructed. The cool air of the room kisses my heated skin, raising goosebumps along my exposed flesh. I feel vulnerable, exposed, but the weight of Zaire's gaze on me is electric.

Zaire settles in behind me, his large hands gripping my hips. I can feel the heat radiating from his body, the brush of his tattoos against my skin as he leans over me. His lips find the sensitive spot where my neck meets my shoulder, and he places a searing kiss there.

"Are you ready for me, moya koroleva?" he murmurs against my skin.

I nod, unable to form words as desire courses through me. Zaire's hand slides between my legs, his fingers exploring my slick folds. "So wet for me," he groans, his voice thick with arousal.

Slowly, torturously, Zaire pushes himself inside me. I gasp at the stretch, the feeling of fullness overwhelming. He pauses, allowing me to adjust to his size. His hands caress my sides soothingly, his lips peppering kisses along my spine.

"You feel incredible," Zaire breathes, his voice strained with the effort of holding still. "So tight, so perfect. Mine."

When I push back against him, silently begging for more, Zaire takes the cue. He begins to move, his thrusts slow and deep at first. Each movement sends sparks of pleasure shooting through me, and I moan, my fingers twisting in the sheets.

Zaire's pace gradually increases, his hips snapping against mine with increasing urgency. The room fills with the sounds of our pleasure; skin against skin, breathless moans, and whispered endearments in Russian that I don't understand.

One of Zaire's hands leaves my hip, sliding up my back to tangle in my hair. He tugs gently, arching my back and changing the angle of his thrusts. The new position hits a spot deep inside me that has me seeing stars.

"Z," I gasp, my voice barely recognizable. "Oh god, right there."

"That's it, moya koroleva," Zaire growls, his thrusts becoming more forceful. "Your pretty little pink cunt was made for my cock."

His hand releases my hair, gently wrapping around my throat instead. His fingers splay across my skin, not cutting off my air, but applying just enough pressure to send a thrill of excitement through me. The feeling of his palm against my racing pulse is intoxicating, a reminder of the power he holds over me in this moment.

Zaire's thrusts become harder, more insistent. Each snap of his hips drives me forward, and I struggle to maintain my balance. My back arches further, pushing my ass more firmly against him, taking him even deeper. The new angle has me gasping, spots dancing behind my eyelids as pleasure courses through every nerve ending.

I can feel how close he is, his cock pulsing inside me, growing even harder with each thrust. His breathing is ragged, hot against my neck as he buries his face there, inhaling deeply. Just as I think he's about to let go, Zaire suddenly stills. A low, animalistic growl rumbles through his chest, vibrating against my back. "No," he says, his voice rough with desire and determination. "Not like this."

He releases his grip on my throat, his hand sliding down to rest on my collarbone. "The first time I fill you," he pants, "I want those beautiful emerald green eyes to watch me spill inside of you. To see me, your monster, chasing away your demons."

Before I can process his words, Zaire is moving. He pulls out of me, leaving me feeling achingly empty, and I whimper at the loss. But then his strong hands are on me, pulling me from the bed with an urgency that takes my breath away.

He spins me around to face him, his silver eyes dark with lust. In one fluid motion, he jerks me upwards, and I instinctively wrap my legs around his hard stomach. His hands fall to my ass, large and calloused, cradling me with a strength that makes me feel weightless.

Zaire's eyes lock onto mine, intense and burning with desire. "Ready, moya koroleva?" he asks, his voice a husky whisper.

I can only nod, my ability to form words lost in the haze of pleasure and anticipation. With a grunt of satisfaction, Zaire thrusts up into me, burying himself to the hilt in one powerful movement.

The sensation is overwhelming. In this position, he feels impossibly deep, stretching me in ways I never thought possible. I cry out, my nails digging into his shoulders as I cling to him.

Zaire's hands on my ass guide my movements, lifting me up and then pulling me back down onto him. The muscles in his arms flex with each motion, the intricate tattoos rippling across his skin. I'm mesmerized by the sight, by the raw power he exudes.

"Look at me," Zaire commands, his voice rough. "I want to see every expression on your beautiful face as I fuck you."

I force my eyes to meet his, and the intensity I find there nearly undoes me. His gaze is hungry, possessive, filled with a need that matches my own. As he thrusts up into me again, I watch his pupils dilate, his jaw clench with the effort of maintaining control. The room fills with the sound of skin on skin, our breathless moans and whispered curses. Zaire's pace is relentless, each thrust driving me higher and higher. I can feel my release building.

"Oh god," I moan.

"That's it, moya koroleva," Zaire growls, his voice husky with arousal. "Let me hear you. Let me see how good I make you feel. Wake up the whole fucking penthouse."

I can feel the coarse hair on his chest rubbing against my sensitive nipples adding another layer of sensation to the overwhelming pleasure.

My head falls back, exposing my throat to Zaire's hungry gaze. He takes advantage, leaning in to nip and suck at the delicate skin there. I know he'll leave marks, but I can't bring myself to care. In this moment, I want nothing more than to be claimed by him, to wear the evidence of our passion.

"Eyes on me," Zaire commands, his voice rough.

With effort, I lift my head, meeting his intense gaze. The silver of his eyes is nearly swallowed by his dilated pupils. I feel exposed, vulnerable under his scrutiny, but also incredibly powerful. The way he's looking at me, like I'm the most precious thing in the world, makes me feel invincible.

His command, coupled with a particularly deep thrust has my orgasm crashing over me like a tidal wave, pleasure exploding through every fiber of my being. I cry out Zaire's name, my voice echoing off the warehouse walls as waves of ecstasy roll through me. My inner walls clench around him, pulsing with the force of my release.

Through the haze of my climax, I see Zaire's face contort with pleasure and determination. His jaw clenches, the muscles in his neck straining as he fights to maintain control. His eyes, dark with lust, never leave mine, watching intently as I come undone in his arms.

As the aftershocks of my orgasm ripple through me, Zaire's pace becomes frantic, almost punishing. His hands dig into the soft flesh of my ass, fingers pressing so hard I know they'll leave marks. But the pain only adds to the pleasure, grounding me in this moment of pure sensation.

"Fuck, Vesper," he grunts, his voice strained. "You feel so fucking good."

"Cum for me, Z," I whisper, my lips brushing against his ear. "I want to feel you."

My words seem to break the last of his control. With a guttural roar, Zaire slams into me one final time burying himself to the hilt. I feel him pulsing inside me, his release hot and intense. His arms tighten around me, crushing me to his chest as he rides out his orgasm. Wrapped in Zaire's strong arms and filled with the evidence of his passion, I feel safe. The pain and betrayal that led me here seems distant, pushed aside by the intensity of what we've just shared. My monster has indeed chased away my nightmares replacing them with a different kind of dream.

Chapter 33

OSCAR

I WAKE TO AN EMPTY BED, the sheets still warm but vacant where Vesper should be. It doesn't surprise me. I knew Z wouldn't be able to resist stealing her away for some alone time. Not after watching her ride my cock a few days ago. She'd been through so much since then, but when it came to chasing her demons away, Zaire seemed to excel at it. Her pain calling to his darkness.

Stretching, I roll out of bed. The morning light filters through the half-drawn curtains casting long shadows across the hardwood floor. I pad to the bathroom, shedding my boxers as I go.

The hot water cascades over me, washing away the last

vestiges of sleep. As I soap up, my mind wanders to Vesper; her silky blonde hair, those piercing green eyes that see right through me, the way her body fits perfectly against mine. A familiar warmth stirs in my groin, but I push the thoughts aside. There'll be time for that later.

Toweling off, I pull on a pair of well-worn jeans and a soft gray henley. The smell of coffee lures me out to the kitchen, where I find Zaire standing shirtless at the counter, his back to me. The intricate tattoos that cover his skin seem to shift and dance as he moves, a living tapestry of ink and muscle.

"Morning, brother," I say, leaning against the doorframe.

Zaire turns, a steaming mug in each hand. A knowing smirk plays at the corners of his mouth. "Sleep well, Oz?" he asks, holding out one of the mugs.

I accept the offered coffee, inhaling the rich aroma. "Well enough," I reply, taking a sip. "Though I noticed my bed was a bit emptier this morning than when I fell asleep."

Zaire's smirk fades, replaced by a somber expression that sends a chill down my spine. He sets his mug down, running a hand through his tousled dark hair. "Oz," he says, his voice low and serious, "I couldn't just lie there and watch her break again."

I feel my chest tighten. "What happened?"

Z leans against the counter, his tattooed arms crossed over his bare chest. "I woke up around dawn. She was between us, crying silently. It was like she was trying not to wake us, but she couldn't hold it in anymore."

The image of Vesper, our fierce, beautiful Vesper, crying alone in the darkness makes my heart ache. I set my coffee aside, suddenly no longer interested in its warmth.

"I couldn't bear it, Oz," Zaire continues, his eyes distant. "I couldn't watch her retreat back into that shell she was in when we first brought her here. You remember how she was?"

I nod, remembering all too well the hollow-eyed, barely responsive woman we'd brought to the beach house.

"She was crying like she was in mourning," Z says. "I think everything's finally hitting her. Finding out her uncle had a hand in this fucked-up plan, that he'd actually purchased her male embryo and destroyed the female one. It's messing with her head in ways we can't even imagine."

I close my eyes, feeling a wave of anger and helplessness wash over me. "Fuck," I mutter. "Where is she now?"

Zaire's smirk returns, a glint of satisfaction in his eyes. "Asleep in my bed," he repeats, emphasizing each word with a hint of pride.

I feel a twinge of jealousy, quickly followed by guilt. This isn't about me, or Zaire, or our own desires. It's about Vesper. Still, I can't help but notice the way Z's chest puffs out slightly, his chin lifting in that subtle way it does when he's feeling particularly pleased with himself.

"Z," I begin, my voice low and measured, "we need to talk about what's going on between us and Vesper."

The morning light streaming through the kitchen window catches on Zaire's hair, highlighting the subtle variations in its dark hue. He runs a hand through it, mussing it further, and leans back against the counter. The muscles in his arms flex as he crosses them over his chest

"What's there to talk about?" he asks, his tone nonchalant but with an underlying defensiveness I know all too well.

I take a deep breath, inhaling the rich aroma of coffee that still hangs in the air. "We can't keep dancing around this, Z. The way we feel about her, the way she feels about us. It's complicated. And with everything she's going through, we need to be careful."

Zaire's eyes narrow slightly. "Careful? What we need to do is be there for her, Oz. In whatever way she needs us."

"I know that," I say, trying to keep the frustration out of my voice. "But we also need to make sure we're on the same page. That we're not...competing or making things more confusing for her."

Z pushes off from the counter, taking a step towards me. I can see the tension in his shoulders, the way his jaw clenches slightly. "As long as she's happy," he says, his voice low and intense, "that's all that matters. If she wants me, she can have me. If she wants you, she can have you. If she wants both of us..." He trails off, letting the implication hang in the air between us. "Fuck, if she wants someone else, too. It's her decision. I'll love her no matter what she chooses for herself."

I feel a rush of heat at his words, images flashing through my mind that I quickly try to suppress. The three of us together. Tangled limbs. Vesper's cries of pleasure as we take our turns with her. Her skin slick with sweat. "It's not that simple, Z," I argue, even as part of me wants to agree with him.

But Zaire is already brushing past me, his bare shoulder grazing mine as he heads towards the hallway. "It is that simple, Oz," he tosses over his shoulder. "We protect her. We love her. Everything else is just details. Stop overthinking it."

"You're really okay with this?"

Zaire shakes his head, "I am."

As Zaire's words hang in the air, a soft creak from the hallway catches our attention. We both look up to see Vesper watching us, her beautiful form framed by the doorway. My breath catches in my throat at the sight of her.

She's still wearing my oversized t-shirt, the one I helped her into before we all fell asleep last night. The soft, worn fabric drapes over her curves, hem skimming her thighs. Her long blonde hair is tousled from sleep, catching the morning light and giving her an almost ethereal glow. But it's her eyes that truly captivate me. Those piercing green orbs that have seen too much, felt too much.

I can tell she's still reeling from everything that has happened, it all lingers in the shadows behind her eyes. Yet there's a steadiness to her now that wasn't there before. A quiet strength that makes my heart swell with pride and something deeper, something I'm not quite ready to name.

Vesper steps into the kitchen, her bare feet silent on the cool tile. She moves with a grace that belies the turmoil I know still churns within her. As she approaches, I can't help but drink in every detail. The way the shirt slips off one shoulder, revealing a tantalizing expanse of creamy skin. The subtle sway of her hips, the way she bites her lower lip, a habit I've come to recognize as a sign of her gathering courage.

She comes to me first, and I feel my heart rate quicken. Her hand reaches up, cupping my cheek, and I lean into her touch instinctively. Then she's on her toes, pressing her lips to mine in a kiss that's both tender and fierce. It takes all my willpower not to pull her closer to deepen the kiss.

But then she's pulling away, and I watch as she turns to Zaire. My brother's eyes are dark with desire, his body taut with anticipation. Vesper doesn't hesitate; she steps into his space and kisses him with the same intensity she kissed me. I see Zaire's hands twitch at his sides, clearly fighting the urge to grab her, to claim her.

As I watch Vesper and Zaire, something shifts inside me. The jealousy I felt earlier melts away, replaced by a profound sense of rightness. It's as if a puzzle piece I didn't even know was missing has suddenly clicked into place.

Vesper steps back from Zaire, her eyes darting between us, a mix of vulnerability and determination in her gaze. In that moment, I realize that Zaire was right. It doesn't matter if it's complicated. All that matters is her.

She needs us both. Not just for protection, not just for comfort, but for something deeper, something that defies the easy categorization. And I'm okay with that. More than okay.

Zaire's voice, low and tender, breaks the charged silence. "Are you hungry, moya koroleva?" he asks, the Russian rolling off his tongue.

Vesper nods, still looking a bit dazed, caught between sleep and wakefulness. Her stomach growls softly, and a faint blush colors her cheeks.

"I can cook," I offer, already moving towards the fridge. "How about some eggs and bacon? Maybe some of those blueberry pancakes you like?"

A small smile tugs at Vesper's lips, and she nods again, more enthusiastically this time. It's a simple thing but seeing that spark of joy in her eyes feels like a victory.

As I start pulling ingredients from the fridge, I hear the shuffle of feet in the hallway. Talon appears first, his brown hair a disheveled mess, eyes still heavy with sleep. He's followed closely by Alex, who looks marginally more awake but no less rumpled.

"Morning, lovebirds," Alex mumbles, his gaze taking in the scene before him. His eyes linger on Vesper, standing between Zaire and me, wearing nothing but my oversized shirt. A smirk plays at the corners of his mouth. "Quite the love V you've got going on here," he adds, gesturing vaguely in our direction.

Zaire's head snaps up, his eyes narrowing dangerously.

"What's a Love V?" Vesper asks.

Alex starts to open his mouth, but a glare from Z shuts it quickly.

I watch as Zaire gently pulls Vesper onto his lap, his tattooed arms wrapping protectively around her waist. She settles against him with a contented sigh, her head resting on his shoulder.

As I turn back to the stove, flipping pancakes and stirring eggs, I catch Talon's gaze. His eyes are fixed on Vesper and Zaire, an unreadable expression on his face. There's something in the way he watches them, a mix of longing and resignation that makes me wonder what's going through his mind.

The kitchen fills with the sizzle of bacon and the rich aroma of coffee as I finish cooking. We gather around the table, plates piled high with food. For a moment, it almost feels normal, just a group of friends sharing breakfast. But the tension simmering beneath the surface is palpable.

I clear my throat, setting down my fork. "We need to talk about what happened yesterday," I say, my voice low but firm.

The mood shifts instantly. Vesper stiffens in Zaire's lap. Z's arms tighten around her, his jaw clenching visibly.

"What's our next move?" Alex asks, leaning forward, his usual smirk replaced by a look of intense focus.

The question hangs in the air, heavy with implications. We all know the stakes. Vesper's safety, the future of our families, the delicate balance of power we've been trying to maintain.

Suddenly, Talon pipes up, his voice cutting through the tension. "I think I might have an idea about that," he says, his brown eyes glinting with a mix of excitement and apprehension.

We all turn to look at him, curiosity piqued. Talon rarely offers strategic input, preferring to follow rather than lead. But there's a determination on his face now that catches my attention.

"Ivanov implicated Natasha, too," Talon continues, his words measured and careful. "I think she's our next move."

"But how do we get to her? All we know about her is that she was the broker for Vesper." Zaire asks, his fingers absently tracing patterns on Vesper's arm. "We can't just walk up to her and ask her what she knows."

Talon takes a deep breath, his gaze flickering to Vesper before returning to the group. "We invoke the breeding clause," he says. "And set a meeting with her."

My mind races, parsing through the implications of Talon's suggestion. The breeding clause. It's a risky move, but not without merit. It could give us the in we need, a chance to unravel this tangled web of deception and manipulation. I don't hate the idea, but the logistics of it gnaw at me.

"It's not a bad plan," I say slowly, choosing my words with care. "But how do we even contact her? We can't exactly look up 'shady black market baby broker' in the yellow pages."

A ghost of a smile flickers across Talon's face, a spark of

something I can't quite place dancing in his eyes. Without a word, he reaches into his pocket and produces a small, white rectangle. A business card.

"It was in the bill of sale paperwork," he explains, his voice low and steady. "I found it when I was going through everything again last night."

The card is unremarkable at first glance, plain white stock, no name, no contact information. But there, centered on the glossy surface, is a small black square. A QR code.

Before anyone else can react, Alex's hand darts out, snatching the card from Talon's grasp. His fingers move with the practiced ease of a pickpocket, reminding me once again of the skills that make him such a valuable asset to our team.

Alex turns the card over in his hands, examining it from every angle. His brow furrows in concentration, eyes narrowing as he scrutinizes the QR code. "It's not just a link," he mutters, more to himself than to us. "Yeah, I've seen this before. Once you scan it, it initiates a call. Clever. Untraceable."

The tension in the room ratchets up a notch. We're all acutely aware of what this means, a direct line to Natasha, the woman who brokered Vesper's sale. The woman who might hold the key to unraveling this entire conspiracy.

"It's worth a shot," I say, breaking the silence that has fallen over us. "But we need to be smart about this. We can't go in half-cocked."

Zaire nods, his arms tightening almost imperceptibly

around Vesper. "Agreed," he says, his voice rough with emotion. "Talon needs to make the call. She's heard his voice. As much money as they made, it isn't likely she forgot Charles Blackwood."

"Who?" Vesper asks.

"Long story, sweetheart," Talon smirks. "I'll call." Talon takes the card away from Alex and starts to scan it with his phone. Alex stops him before he can hit send.

"Have I taught you nothing," he mutters before shifting from his seat, and walking towards his room. He returns a few minutes later with a black burner phone in his hand. "Always use an encrypted burner phone, Bjáni."

"I have no idea what you just called me, but I think it might have been a compliment."

"It wasn't," Alex declares flatly.

Talon scans the card with the burner phone, his fingers trembling slightly. The tension in the room is palpable as we all hold our breath, waiting. The phone rings once, twice, three times. Just as I'm beginning to think this might be a dead end, a crisp, accented voice answers.

"Доброе утро," the female voice purrs, the Russian rolling off her tongue like silk. "To what do I owe this pleasure?"

I watch as Talon's demeanor shifts. Gone is the easy-going, golden retriever-like friend I know. In his place stands Charles Blackwood, the suave and confident buyer from the auction. His voice, when he speaks, is low and smooth, with just a hint of a British accent.

"Natasha," he purrs, "it's Charles Blackwood. I trust you remember me?"

There's a pause on the other end of the line, and then a low, throaty chuckle. "Mr. Blackwood," Natasha replies, her voice dripping with honey and venom in equal measure. "What a pleasant surprise. How could I forget our most discerning client?"

I watch as Talon's jaw clenches, a flicker of disgust passing over his features before he schools his expression back into neutrality. "Indeed," he says, his tone light but with an undercurrent of steel. "I was just thinking about our last transaction. I must say, I'm quite pleased with my investment."

Natasha's laugh is like broken glass, sharp and dangerous. "I'm so glad to hear it, Mr. Blackwood. Our merchandise is always of the highest quality. How is the little dove adjusting?"

At the word 'merchandise,' I see Vesper flinch as if she's been struck. Zaire's arms tighten around her, his eyes blazing with barely contained rage. I feel my own anger rising, hot and fierce in my chest, but I force it down. We need to stay focused.

Talon's voice remains steady as he replies, "Oh, she's everything I could have hoped for and more. Well worth what I spent, I assure you." His eyes flick to Vesper as he speaks, and I see a silent apology in them. "In fact, I was wondering if we might discuss the possibility of expanding my investment."

There's a pregnant pause on the other end of the line. When Natasha speaks again, her voice has lost some of its syrupy sweetness, replaced by sharp interest. "Expanding? My, my, Mr. Blackwood. You are insatiable, aren't you? What did you have in mind?"

I lean forward, every muscle in my body tense.

Talon's eyes meet mine for a brief moment, a silent understanding passing between us. He takes a deep breath, his fingers drumming lightly on the table as he speaks. "Well, Natasha, I've been giving some thought to the breeding clause in our contract. I believe it's time to explore those options."

The words hang in the air, heavy with implication. I feel my heart rate quicken, knowing we're treading into dangerous territory. Vesper stiffens in Zaire's arms, her face paling slightly. Z's jaw clenches, his tattoos seeming to ripple with tension.

Natasha's voice, when it comes, is filled with predatory interest. "Ah, the breeding clause. How delightful. It's not often our clients take advantage of that particular feature."

Talon's voice remains steady, but I can see the strain in the set of his shoulders. "Yes, well, I believe in maximizing my investments. I'd like to set up a meeting to discuss the details. Perhaps with her previous owners? I'd like to discuss the possibility of buying them out."

There's a pause on the other end of the line, long enough that for a moment I wonder if we've overplayed our hand. When Natasha speaks again, her voice has a sharp edge to it. "I'm afraid that won't be possible, Mr. Blackwood. My client is extremely private and values their anonymity above all else."

I exchange a glance with Zaire seeing my own frustration mirrored in his eyes. We're so close to a breakthrough, but Natasha's words threaten to slam that door shut.

But Talon doesn't miss a beat. "Of course, I understand completely," he says smoothly. "Privacy is paramount in our line of work, after all. Perhaps we could meet with you instead? As their representative, I'm sure you're fully authorized to discuss these matters on their behalf."

Another pause, shorter this time. I can almost hear the gears turning in Natasha's head as she weighs her options. "That would be acceptable," she finally says, her voice carefully neutral. "I have the authority to act on my client's behalf in these matters."

I feel a surge of triumph, quickly tempered by the knowledge that we're far from out of the woods. Talon catches my eye, a ghost of a smile playing at the corners of his mouth. "Excellent," he says. "I'm eager to move forward with this. What does your schedule look like?"

As Talon negotiates the details of the meeting, I find myself marveling at his composure. The transformation from our laid-back friend to this suave, calculating persona is jarring, yet impressive. I watch as he jots down notes on a nearby napkin, his handwriting neat and precise despite the tension thrumming through the room.

"New York, you say?" Talon replies, his voice smooth as

silk. "As it happens, I have business in Manhattan next week. Perhaps we could arrange something then?"

Natasha's voice crackles through the speaker, a hint of satisfaction coloring her words. "Perfect, Mr. Blackwood. I know just the place. There's a charming little restaurant I simply adore. It's called 'Le Petit Oiseau,' quite fitting, don't you think?"

I feel a chill run down my spine at the name. 'The Little Bird, 'it's almost too on-the-nose, a cruel reminder of how Natasha and her clients view women like Vesper. I glance at Vesper, seeing the same realization dawning in her eyes. Zaire's arms tighten around her, a silent promise of protection.

Talon doesn't miss a beat. "Sounds delightful," he says, his voice betraying none of the disgust I know he must be feeling. "Shall we say Tuesday, at 7 pm?"

"Tuesday, at 7 it is," Natasha purrs. "I look forward to our meeting, Mr. Blackwood."

Just as Talon is about to end the call, Natasha's voice cuts through once more, sharp and sudden. "Oh, and Mr. Blackwood? Do bring your purchase with you. I'd love to see how she's progressing."

The room goes deathly still. I feel my heart skip a beat, my mind racing to process this unexpected twist. Vesper goes rigid in Zaire's arms, her face draining of color. Z looks like he's about to explode, his muscles coiled tight with barely contained rage.

Talon, to his credit, doesn't falter. "Of course," he says

smoothly, though I can see the strain in the set of his jaw. "She'll be delighted to join us, I'm sure."

As soon as the call ends, the tension in the room snaps. Zaire jumps to his feet, nearly knocking over his chair in the process. "Absolutely fucking not," he snarls, his voice low and dangerous. "We are not putting Vesper anywhere near that woman."

"I don't think we have a choice. If Talon shows up without her, Natasha will know something is wrong."

"Over my dead fucking body will I put her in that kind of danger."

I stand as well, my mind already racing through possibilities, trying to find a way to make this work without endangering Vesper. "Z, calm down," I say, holding up my hands in a placating gesture. "We need to think this through."

Vesper, who has been silent throughout the entire exchange, suddenly speaks up. Her voice is quiet but firm.

"I'll do it."

Chapter 34

TALON

THE ROOM ERUPTS INTO CHAOS, a cacophony of Russian expletives and English curses mixing in the air like oil and water. I can barely make out individual words as Oscar and Zaire talk over each other, their voices rising with each passing second. It's like watching two storms collide, all thunder and lightning with no room for reason.

I glance at Vesper, expecting to see her shrink back from the verbal onslaught, but she stands tall, her green eyes flashing with a determination that makes my breath catch. She's a fortress, unshakeable even as the twins' argument threatens to tear the room apart.

"Enough!" Vesper's voice cuts through the noise like a

knife, silencing the room in an instant. "I said I'll go with Talon to meet Natasha, and that's final."

The words hit me like a punch to the gut. Natasha. The name alone sends a chill down my spine, images of what that woman has done flooding my mind. She played a part in Vesper's uncle's plan. She is the puppet master behind Vesper's suffering, the architect of her pain. The thought of Vesper being anywhere near her makes my blood boil.

"We have no choice. If we want to see how far down this goes, we need to meet with her, and the only way we can do that is if I go."

Oscar runs a hand through his short, dark hair, his blue eyes stormy with concern. "Vesper, you can't be serious. After everything Natasha's done-"

"I know what she's done," Vesper interrupts, her voice low and dangerous. "I lived it, remember?"

The room falls silent again, the weight of her words hanging heavy in the air. I watch as Zaire's face contorts with rage, his hands balling into fists at his sides. The dark blue ring around his eyes seems to glow with an other-worldly fury.

"Let me go instead," Zaire growls, taking a step towards Vesper. "I'll make that bitch pay for what she did to you."

I can't help but admire his protective instinct, even if I know it's misplaced. Vesper doesn't need our protection, she needs our support.

"You can't," I declare. "I'm the buyer. Not you. Oscar is out because she was flirting with him at the bar before the auction. She's seen his face. The same fucking face you have, jackass. I'm the only option here."

All eyes turn to me, a mix of shock and betrayal on the twins' faces. But Vesper looks at me with something akin to gratitude, a soft smile playing at the corners of her lips.

Zaire's eyes darken, his jaw clenching as he takes a step closer to Vesper. "You don't know what you're agreeing to," he says, his voice low and gravelly. "This isn't just some undercover op. You were sold as a sex slave, Vesper. Natasha will expect you to act like one."

The words hang in the air, heavy and oppressive. I feel my stomach churn, the reality of what Vesper might have to endure hitting me like a freight train. But Vesper doesn't flinch. She stands tall, her chin lifted in defiance.

"I was raised to be controlled and to submit, Zaire," she says, her voice steady and cold. "It's like breathing to me. I've spent my entire life playing the part my family wanted me to play. This is no different."

Her words cut through me like a knife. I've always known that Vesper's upbringing was far from normal but hearing her speak so casually about being controlled...it does something to me that I can't explain.

I want to reach out, to pull her close and shield her from the world that's treated her so cruelly. But I know that's not what she needs right now.

Zaire's face contorts with a mix of anger and pain. "Not anymore," he fires back, his voice rising. "You're not that person anymore, Vesper. You're free now. You don't have to do this."

I watch as Vesper's eyes flash, a storm brewing behind those emerald orbs. For a moment, I think she might lash out at Zaire, but instead, she takes a deep breath, her shoulders relaxing slightly.

"Natasha will have expectations of your behavior," Zaire continues, his voice softer now, almost pleading. "She'll expect complete submission, unquestioning obedience. Are you prepared for that?"

The room falls silent, all eyes on Vesper. I hold my breath, waiting for her response. Part of me hopes she'll back down, that she'll realize the danger she's putting herself in. But another part of me, the part that's come to know and admire Vesper's strength, knows she won't.

"I can handle it," Vesper says finally, her voice filled with a quiet determination.

I watch as Oscar steps forward, his face a mask of concern. "Vesper, I hate to say it, but Zaire's right. You don't fully grasp what they might demand of you." His voice is soft, but there's an edge to it that I've rarely heard. "The things they could ask. There are no limits, no boundaries. Are you prepared for that?"

The words hang heavy in the air, and I feel my stomach twist. Oscar's right, of course. The world we're about to step into is dark, and twisted, with rules that normal society would balk at. I've seen glimpses of it before, but never like this. Never so personal.

Zaire nods, his eyes locked on Vesper. "And it's not just about you, Ves. Talon's a good actor, sure, but pretending to be your lord and master? To demand things of you, to treat you like..." He trails off, unable to finish the thought. "It's not something I think either of you can pull off convincingly."

I feel a flare of indignation at Zaire's words, but it's quickly doused by the cold reality of the situation. He's right. The thought of treating Vesper like a possession, of demanding her obedience. It makes my skin crawl. How could I possibly convince Natasha that I'm capable of such cruelty?

"Natasha will smell the deception a mile away," Zaire continues, his voice low and urgent. "She's been in this game for years. She'll see right through any act we try to put on."

I watch as Vesper's eyes flicker between the twins, her face unreadable. For a moment, I think I see a crack in her armor, a flicker of uncertainty in those emerald eyes. But then it's gone, replaced by that steely determination I've come to admire and fear in equal measure.

"You're both underestimating me," she says, her voice calm but with an undercurrent of steel. "And you're underestimating Talon. We can do this."

I feel a surge of something - pride? fear? - at her words. The faith she has in me is both exhilarating and terrifying. Can I live up to it? Can I be the monster we need me to be for this mission to succeed?

"Vesper," I start, my voice hoarse. "They're not wrong. The things I might have to do, to say. I don't know if I can-"

She cuts me off with a look, those green eyes boring into mine with an intensity that takes my breath away. "You can," she says simply. "Because you have to. Because we have to."

I swallow hard, my throat suddenly dry. Vesper's right, of course. We have to do this. But the thought of what lies ahead makes my stomach churn.

"Teach us. Both of us."

The room falls silent, the tension so thick you could cut it with a knife. Zaire's eyes widen, a mix of shock and something else, fear, maybe?.

"You don't know what you're asking," he says, his voice low and gravelly.

Vesper steps forward, her green eyes blazing with determination. "We do," she insists. "We need to make this convincing, Zaire. You're the only one who can help us."

Zaire hesitates, his gaze flickering between Vesper and me. I can see the internal struggle playing out on his face, the desire to protect warring with the knowledge that this might be our only chance.

"Please," Vesper adds, her voice softer now. "We have to do this."

Zaire looks to Oscar, a silent conversation passing between the twins. After what feels like an eternity, Oscar nods, his face grim.

"Fine," Zaire says, his voice thick with resignation. "I'll do it."

Relief washes over me, quickly followed by a wave of apprehension. What have we just signed up for?

Zaire takes a deep breath, running a hand through his dark hair. "But you need to understand something," he says, his silver eyes intense. "This isn't about barking orders at someone who's submissive. It's more than that. So much more."

The air in the room seems to grow heavier, charged with an electric tension that makes the hair on the back of my neck stand up.

"The only way to truly learn," Zaire continues, his voice low and serious, "is to experience what it feels like. Both sides of it."

"Where did you learn this exactly?" I question. "I doubt there's a book out there on how to be a dom for dummies."

"I learned through experience. As a second son, like you very well know, we have no power. No control over my future. But in the bedroom, I found a place where I could exert control. Where I make the rules."

"So, you just woke up one day and decided to be a dom?" I chuckle.

"No, asshole. It's who I am." His gaze meets mine, unflinching. "I won't lie or sugarcoat it. It wasn't always pretty. I made mistakes, hurt people unintentionally. But, I discovered a piece of me that I needed like a puzzle piece clicking into place. It just works for me."

I glance at Vesper, curious how she's reacting to hearing about Zaire's sexual history. But her face remains impassive, her green eyes focused intently on Zaire as if drinking in every word.

Zaire continues, his voice taking on a reverential tone. "Through those experiences, I came to understand that true dominance isn't about subjugation or cruelty. It's about guidance, protection, and nurturing growth. It's a sacred responsibility."

I turn to Vesper, searching her face for some clue to her thoughts. "And you?" I ask softly. "Why do you...I mean, how can you..." I struggle to find the right words, overwhelmed by the intensity of the moment. Finally, I blurt out, "Why do you allow Zaire to dominate you?"

Vesper's emerald eyes meet mine, an array of emotions swirling in their depths. She takes a deep breath. "All my life. I've craved freedom. I was raised in a gilded cage, every decision made for me, every move scrutinized. I dreamed of the day I could spread my wings and fly."

She pauses, fidgeting with the hem of her shirt. "But the fear and anxiety of what happened before it started to take over. I was on the brink of shutting down again. Zaire helped me. When I submit to him, the world narrows to just us. The fear melts away, replaced by a sense of safety and certainty." Her eyes meet mine again. "It's paradoxical, I know. But surrendering control, even for a little while, I've found a freedom more profound than anything I've experienced. The freedom to be fully present, to feel everything without reservation, to trust completely."

"Are you sure you want to do this?"

My heart skips a beat, the implications of both of their words sinking in. I glance again at Vesper, expecting to see hesitation or fear in her eyes. Instead, I find only steely resolve.

"Whatever it takes," she says firmly.

"Show me," I demand.

Zaire nods, his face a mask of concentration. "Alright," he says, his voice taking on a new tone, deeper, more commanding. "Vesper, come here."

I watch, fascinated and terrified, as Vesper moves towards Zaire without hesitation.

"Kneel," Zaire commands, his voice soft but brooking no argument.

Vesper sinks to her knees in one smooth motion, her head bowed, hands resting palm-down on her thighs. The transformation is startling - gone is the fierce, independent woman I've come to know. In her place is the woman who came to us broken and controlled.

I watch, transfixed, as Zaire circles Vesper's kneeling form. His eyes rake over her, assessing, calculating. When he speaks, his voice is low and smooth, like velvet over steel.

"Good girl," he murmurs, and I see Vesper's shoulders relax infinitesimally at the praise. "You see, Talon? This is what submission looks like. It's not just about following orders. It's about giving away control and putting your trust in that person whole-heartedly." He reaches out, his fingers ghosting over Vesper's hair. She doesn't move, doesn't even seem to breathe. "It's about becoming an extension of your master's will. A perfect reflection of their desires."

My throat goes dry as I watch the scene unfold. There's an intimacy to it that makes me feel like an intruder, yet I can't look away. Zaire's movements are precise, controlled. Every touch, every word seems calculated to elicit a specific response from Vesper.

"Now, Vesper," Zaire continues, his voice taking on a harder edge. "Crawl to him."

I swallow hard, trying to ignore the way my pulse quickens at his words. Zaire nods at me, a silent command to approach. My legs feel like lead as I step forward.

"Now you, Talon," he says, his voice brooking no argument.

I hesitate, my mind racing. How am I supposed to do this? How can I treat Vesper like property? But then I remember why we're doing this. What's at stake. I take a deep breath, steeling myself.

I reach down, my hand hovering over Vesper's head. I can feel the warmth radiating from her skin, see the slight tremble in her shoulders. Gently, I rest my palm on the back of her neck.

"No," Zaire's voice cracks like a whip. "You're not petting a dog, Talon. You're accepting the devotion of your property. Your touch should be firm. Possessive."

I grit my teeth, forcing myself to press down harder.

Vesper doesn't flinch, doesn't move a muscle. Her complete trust in me, in this situation, is both awe-inspiring and terrifying.

"Better," Zaire nods. "Now, command her to rise."

I clear my throat, trying to inject some authority into my voice.

"Stand," I command, my voice sounding foreign to my own ears. Vesper rises gracefully, her movements fluid and practiced. She keeps her eyes lowered, hands clasped in front of her.

Zaire circles us, his gaze critical. "Better, but not enough. Natasha will expect more." He pauses, his blue eyes flickering between us. "She might demand a demonstration of your control over Vesper. Are you prepared for that?"

The words hit me like a physical blow. I feel my stomach churn, a cold sweat breaking out on my forehead. "What kind of demonstration?" I ask.

Zaire's expression hardens. "Anything. Everything. In that world, there are no limits." He turns to Vesper, his voice softening slightly. "Vesper, look at Talon."

She raises her head, those mesmerizing green eyes meeting mine. I see a storm of emotions swirling in their depths; determination, fear, and something else I can't quite name.

"Natasha could demand that you pleasure him," Zaire continues, his words like ice down my spine. "She could insist on watching you submit to his every whim. Are you prepared for that possibility?"

I want to protest, to say that we'd never go that far. But the words die in my throat as I watch Vesper's reaction. Her chin lifts slightly, a spark of defiance flashing in her eyes.

"I am," she says, her voice steady and sure.

Zaire nods, turning back to me. "And you, Talon? Could you give those orders? Could you treat Vesper as nothing more than a plaything for your amusement?"

I feel my jaw clench, a war raging inside me. The thought of using Vesper like that, of reducing her to an object for my pleasure, makes me sick. But I know we have no choice. This is bigger than us, bigger than our comfort or our morals.

"I can try," I manage, hating how weak my voice sounds.

Zaire shakes his head. "Trying isn't enough. You need to believe it, to embody it." He steps closer, his voice dropping to a low, dangerous tone. "In that world, Vesper is yours. Your property. Your toy. You need to own that role, Talon. Completely."

I swallow hard feeling sweat bead on my forehead. Zaire's right, of course. Half-measures won't cut it. Not with someone like Natasha. I take a deep breath, trying to center myself.

"Vesper," I say, forcing steel into my voice. "On your knees."

She sinks down immediately, her movements graceful and practiced. I reach out, tangling my fingers in her hair, using it to tilt her head back. Her eyes meet mine, wide and trusting.

"Touch me," I command, my voice low and husky. "Show me how much you want to please your master."

Vesper's hands glide up my legs, her touch feather-light yet electrifying. I feel my breath catch as her fingers dance along my thighs, inching higher with agonizing slowness. Her eyes never leave mine, a silent challenge burning in their emerald depths.

I feel something shift inside me, a darker, more primal part of myself rising to the surface. My grip in her hair tightens, eliciting a soft gasp from her lips. "Faster," I growl, surprised by the authority in my own voice.

She obeys instantly, her movements becoming more urgent, more desperate. Her hands roam over my body with fervor. I'm acutely aware of the others watching us – Zaire's intense gaze, Oscar's conflicted expression, Alex's calculating stare – but I find I don't care. In this moment, there's only Vesper and me.

"Good girl," I murmur, the praise falling from my lips naturally. I watch as Vesper's eyes flutter closed, a soft moan escaping her. The sound ignites something within me, a hunger I've never felt before.

My free hand traces the curve of her jaw, thumb brushing over her bottom lip. "Open," I command, and she complies without hesitation, her mouth parting invitingly. I lean down, my lips a hair's breadth from hers. "Remember who you belong to," I whisper, before capturing her mouth in a searing kiss.

Vesper responds with a passion that takes my breath

away. Her hands clutch at my shirt pulling me closer as she surrenders herself to the kiss. I lose myself in the taste of her, the feel of her body pressed against mine.

When we finally break apart, we're both breathing heavily. I look down at Vesper, her lips swollen, her cheeks flushed, and I feel a surge of possessive pride. Mine, a voice in my head growls. She's mine.

I turn to face the others, my arm still wrapped possessively around Vesper. "Is this convincing enough?" I ask, my voice rough with desire and a newfound confidence.

Zaire nods slowly, a mix of approval and something darker in his eyes. "It's a start," he says. "But remember, Talon. In that world, she's not just yours to pleasure. She's yours to punish, to push to her limits and beyond. Can you do that?"

I feel Vesper tense against me, and I tighten my hold on her instinctively. The thought of hurting her, even in play, makes my stomach churn. But I know we have no choice. This is the role we have to play.

"I can," I say, forcing conviction into my voice. "Whatever it takes."

I swallow hard, my heart pounding in my chest. I can feel the weight of the others' gazes on us, but I force myself to focus solely on Vesper. Her green eyes are locked on mine, a mix of trust and challenge swirling in their depths.

"Touch me," I command again, my voice low and husky. "Show me your devotion."

Vesper's hands slide up my thighs, her touch sending

electricity through my body. I bite back a groan as her fingers dance along the waistband of my jeans, teasing and exploratory. She leans in, her breath hot against my skin as she nuzzles against my hip.

I feel a primal part of me stirring a side I've kept carefully locked away. It whispers dark promises, urges me to take what's being offered. For a moment, I let it take over, embracing the role I need to play.

My hand tightens in her hair pulling her head back sharply. "Is that the best you can do?" I growl, surprised by the harshness in my own voice. "I said show me how much you want to please me. Use that pretty mouth of yours."

Vesper's eyes widen slightly, a flash of something, excitement or maybe fear, crossing her face before she schools her expression back to one of submissive desire. She leans in again, this time pressing open-mouthed kisses along the line of my hip, her tongue darting out to taste my skin.

I hear a sharp intake of breath from somewhere behind me, Oscar or Zaire, I'm not sure which, but I don't dare look away from Vesper. She's working her way down now, her fingers deftly unbuckling my belt.

"That's it," I murmur, my voice thick with desire. "Show everyone here who you really belong to."

Vesper looks up at me through her lashes, a smoldering heat in her gaze that makes my breath catch. She presses a kiss to the bulge in my jeans, her tongue tracing the outline of my hardening length through the denim.

I'm dimly aware of the others watching us, of the

tension crackling in the air. But all I can focus on is Vesper, the warmth of her mouth, the softness of her skin under my hands, the way she moves with practiced grace and genuine desire.

"Good girl," I praise, my voice rough with need. "You're doing so well for me."

Vesper practically purrs at the praise, her hands working to unzip my jeans. I know we should stop, that we've proven our point, but I can't bring myself to call an end to this. The dark part of me that I've unleashed wants more, wants to see how far Vesper will go to please me.

Just as Vesper's fingers brush against my bare skin, Zaire's voice cuts through the heated atmosphere like a bucket of ice water. "That's enough," he says, his tone clipped and strained.

I blink, struggling to pull myself out of the intoxicating haze Vesper has wrapped me in. My hand is still tangled in her hair, her breath hot against my skin. For a moment, I consider ignoring Zaire, pushing this further, seeing just how far Vesper would go to please me. But then reality crashes back in, and I force myself to step away.

Vesper looks up at me, her green eyes clouded with desire and confusion. I have to clench my fists to keep from reaching for her again.

"Vesper, come here," Zaire commands, his voice rough and urgent.

She hesitates for a split second, her gaze flickering between Zaire and me. Then, with fluid grace, she rises and moves towards him. I watch, a mixture of jealousy and fascination churning in my gut, as Zaire grabs her arm and practically drags her from the room.

The door to Zaire's bedroom slams shut with a finality that echoes through the suddenly silent house. For a moment, we all stand frozen, the air thick with unresolved tension and the lingering scent of arousal.

Then, a dull thud reverberates through the walls, followed by another, and another. The rhythmic pounding against Zaire's bedroom door leaves little doubt about what's happening on the other side.

I feel my face flush, a potent cocktail of embarrassment, jealousy, and lingering desire coursing through my veins. Oscar clears his throat awkwardly, avoiding eye contact with anyone as he mumbles something about needing air and quickly exits the room.

I run a hand through my hair, trying to regain some semblance of composure. But it's impossible to ignore the sounds coming from Zaire's room, the muffled moans, the creaking of the bed, the occasional sharp cry that I know, without a doubt, belongs to Vesper.

I need to get out of here. Need to put some distance between myself and the vivid images my mind is conjuring. Without a word to anyone, I make my way to the bathroom, stripping off my clothes as soon as the door locks behind me.

The shower spray is a welcome distraction, the hot water sluicing over my skin doing little to cool the fire burning inside me. I close my eyes, but all I can see is Vesper, her perfect lips parted in pleasure, those mesmerizing green eyes locked on mine as she touched me.

My hand moves of its own accord, wrapping around my aching length. I stroke myself slowly at first, then with increasing urgency as memories of Vesper flood my senses. The taste of her lips, sweet and intoxicating. The soft gasp she made when I pulled her hair. The way her body responded to my touch, so eager and willing.

My strokes become faster, more desperate. I imagine it's Vesper's hand on me, her delicate fingers wrapped around my shaft, her lips trailing kisses down my chest. In my mind, I can see her kneeling before me again, those captivating green eyes looking up at me with a mixture of desire and submission.

The memory of her mouth, so close to where I needed her most, sends a jolt of pleasure through me. I groan, the sound barely audible over the pounding water. My free hand braces against the shower wall as I chase my release, my hips bucking into my fist.

I think about how it would feel to have Vesper's lips wrapped around me, her tongue swirling and teasing. The way she'd moan around me, the vibrations sending shockwaves of pleasure through my body. How she'd look up at me, those mesmerizing green eyes never leaving mine as she took me deeper.

The pressure builds, a coiling heat in my lower belly. I'm close, so close. I imagine burying my hands in Vesper's silky hair, guiding her movements as she pleasures me. The thought of her surrendering to me completely, giving herself over to my desires, pushes me over the edge.

My release hits me like a tidal wave, pleasure crashing over me in intense pulses. I bite my lip to stifle my cry, my body shuddering as I spill into my hand. For a moment, the world narrows to nothing but the sensation coursing through me and the image of Vesper burned into my mind.

As the aftershocks subside, reality slowly creeps back in. The water, once hot, now runs lukewarm over my sensitized skin. I lean my forehead against the cool tile, trying to catch my breath and calm my racing heart, but those pretty little green eyes are all I can see. Pretty little green eyes that will be the death of me.

Chapter 35

VESPER

THE SLEEK BLACK TOWN CAR, with Alex acting as our driver, glides through the neon-lit streets of Manhattan. I'm hyper aware of every sensation: the cool leather seat beneath me, the faint scent of expensive cologne mingling with the car's new leather smell, and most of all, the scorching trail Zaire's fingers are blazing across my exposed thigh.

My breath catches as his calloused fingertips trace lazy circles on my skin, inching higher with each pass. The slit in my dress, daring even by my standards, leaves little to the imagination. It's a weapon, this dress, as deadly as any gun. A weapon to turn our fictional story into a reality for Natasha. Black silk hugs every curve, the plunging neckline a deliberate distraction. I can feel the weight of their gazes on me: Zaire's touch searing my skin, Oscar's ice-blue eyes carefully assessing, and Talon's warm brown ones filled with barely concealed hunger. It's as if Zaire's lesson unlocked a part of him he'd kept carefully hidden. I wonder if he's replaying that night in his mind too, remembering the way his lips felt against mine, and how far down we'd gone into the scene that we almost stepped over a line I don't remember drawing.

I bite my lip, and Talon's gaze drops to my mouth. The hunger in his eyes intensifies, and for a moment, I think he might reach out and touch me. But he doesn't. Neither of us has dared to cross that line, to acknowledge the crackling tension that now exists between us. It's maddening and thrilling all at once.

Zaire's fingers continue their torturous path up my thigh, and I have to stifle a gasp. I tear my eyes away from Talon's, only to meet Oscar's cool, assessing gaze. He's been watching the entire exchange, his face an unreadable mask. But I know him well enough now to see the calculating gleam in his eyes. He's piecing together the puzzle, noting every lingering look and hitched breath.

The car takes a sharp turn, and I'm pressed against Zaire's solid form. His arm snakes around my waist, steadying me, but also pulling me into his lap. His hard length digging into my ass. It's dizzying, being surrounded by these three men, each exerting their own gravitational pull.

Zaire's lips brush against my ear, his breath hot and heavy as he whispers, "When we get back, I want you in nothing but those heels, kneeling for me." A shiver runs through my body, desire pooling low in my belly. His words paint a vivid picture in my mind, and I can almost feel the cool floor against my bare knees, the weight of his gaze as I look up at him.

I turn my head slightly, meeting his intense gaze. My breath catches in my throat as I see the raw hunger there, barely contained.

Oscar clears his throat, breaking the moment. "We're almost there," he says, his voice low and controlled. But I can see the tension in his jaw, the way his hands are clenched into fists on his thighs. He's affected too, despite his attempts to hide it. "Drop us off a few blocks away from the entrance, Alex."

Talon shifts in his seat, and I catch a glimpse of the bulge in his pants. His eyes meet mine, and there's a challenge there, a dare. I feel my cheeks flush, but I don't look away. Instead, I let my tongue dart out to wet my lips, a deliberate tease. His nostrils flare, and I hear his sharp intake of breath.

As Alex pulls the car to a stop, Zaire's grip on my waist tightens for a moment. He turns my face towards his, capturing my lips in a searing kiss that leaves me breathless.

His tongue teases mine, a promise of what's to come later. When he pulls away, his eyes are dark with desire.

"Don't forget what I said," he murmurs against my lips before gently shifting me off his lap.

I watch as Zaire gracefully exits the car, his tall frame unfolding into the night. The cool air that rushes in makes me shiver.

Oscar steps out next, his movements precise and controlled. He turns back, extending his hand to me. I take it, marveling at how such a simple touch can send sparks racing up my arm. His fingers are cool against my overheated skin as he helps me slide across the seat to take his place next to Talon.

As I settle in, I'm acutely aware of Talon's proximity. The car suddenly feels much smaller, charged with an electric tension that makes my skin prickle. Oscar leans in, his ice-blue eyes meeting mine. There's a softness there that belies his usual stoic demeanor.

"Be careful," he says, his voice low and husky. He presses a gentle kiss to my cheek, his lips lingering for a moment longer than necessary. "Both of you," he adds, his gaze flickering to Talon.

The door closes with a soft thud, and suddenly it's just Talon and me in the back seat. Alex pulls away smoothly, heading towards the restaurant. The silence between us is heavy, laden with unspoken desires and simmering tension.

I can feel the heat radiating off Talon's body. My heart

is pounding so loudly I'm sure he can hear it. I chance a glance at him from the corner of my eye.

Talon is staring straight ahead, his jaw clenched tight. His hands are balled into fists on his thighs, his knuckles white with tension. The streetlights flashing by illuminate his face in intermittent bursts, highlighting the sharp planes of his cheekbones and the fullness of his lips.

I shift slightly in my seat, the movement causing my dress to ride up even higher. Talon's eyes snap to my exposed thigh, his gaze burning a trail up my body until it meets mine. The hunger I see there makes my breath catch in my throat.

"Vesper," he growls, my name sounding like both a prayer and a curse on his lips.

I don't know who moves first, but suddenly we're crashing together. His lips claim mine in a bruising kiss, all the pent-up desire and frustration pouring out. One of his hands tangles in styled hair.

Talon's lips move against mine with a desperate hunger, his tongue seeking entrance. I part my lips, welcoming him in, tasting the faint hint of whiskey. His hand in my hair tightens, angling my head to deepen the kiss. I moan into his mouth, my fingers clutching at his shirt, pulling him closer.

The world outside the car fades away, narrowing down to just us, the heat of his body pressed against mine, the intoxicating scent of his cologne mixed with desire, the way his stubble scratches deliciously against my skin. His other hand slides up my thigh, pushing the fabric of my dress higher, leaving a trail of fire in its wake.

I arch into him, wanting, no, needing more. My hands roam over his broad shoulders, down his chest, feeling the hard planes of muscle beneath his shirt. Talon groans, the sound vibrating through me, igniting sparks of pleasure low in my belly.

His lips leave mine, trailing hot, open-mouthed kisses along my jaw, down my neck. I tilt my head back, offering more of myself to him. His teeth graze my pulse point, and I gasp, my nails digging into his shoulders.

"Talon," I breathe, his name a plea on my lips.

He pulls back slightly, his forehead resting against mine. His breath comes in short pants, matching my own rapid breathing. I open my eyes to find him staring at me, his gaze dark with desire. The intensity I see there makes me shiver.

"God, Vesper," he murmurs, his voice rough with want. "You have no idea what you do to me."

I'm about to respond when I feel the car slow to a stop. The spell breaks as we hear Alex's door open. Reality crashes back in, reminding us of where we are and what we're here to do.

Talon pulls away, his hands gentle as he helps me sit up straight. His fingers brush against my cheek as he wipes away the smeared lipstick from my now swollen lips. The tenderness of the gesture contrasts sharply with the heated passion of moments before, making my heart clench.

"Ready?" he asks, his voice low and steady, the mask of our act sliding into place.

I nod, taking a deep breath to center myself. Talon exits the car first, his movements fluid and controlled. I watch as he straightens his jacket, running a hand through his hair to tame any evidence of our heated encounter.

He comes around to my side of the car, opening the door with a flourish. As I step out, I feel the cool night air against my flushed skin.

Talon reaches into his pocket, retrieving a delicate lace choker. At its center hangs a tiny silver hoop, diamonds glittering in the streetlights.

Talon's fingers brush against my neck as he fastens the choker. The cool metal of the hoop settles against my skin, a constant reminder of the role I'm about to play. I catch my reflection in a nearby window, the diamonds glitter in the streetlight, a delicate contrast to the daring cut of my dress.

"I did some research," Talon murmurs, his breath warm against my ear. "This is expected for someone in your position." His voice catches slightly on the last word, a hint of his true feelings breaking through the mask.

I swallow hard, feeling the slight pressure of the collar against my throat. It's both thrilling and terrifying, a tangible symbol of the dangerous game we're playing. Talon's hands linger on my shoulders, his touch grounding me.

"Remember," he says, his voice low and intense, "no

matter what happens up there, I will protect you. We're in this together, Vesper."

I meet his gaze, seeing the fierce determination in his eyes. For a moment, I allow myself to lean into his strength, drawing courage from his unwavering support. Then, with a deep breath, I straighten my spine and nod.

Talon's demeanor shifts subtly as he offers me his arm. The warmth in his eyes cools, replaced by a calculated charm that would fool anyone who didn't know him as well as I do. I slip my hand into the crook of his elbow, feeling the solid muscle beneath his tailored jacket.

We ascend the steps to the French restaurant, the click of my heels on marble echoing in the night air. The facade is all gleaming glass and polished brass, exuding an air of old-world elegance. As we approach the entrance, the scent of fresh-baked bread and rich sauces wafts out, making my mouth water despite the nerves twisting my stomach.

Talon pushes open the heavy door, ushering me into a world of soft lighting and hushed conversations. Crystal chandeliers cast a warm glow over tables draped in crisp white linen. The walls are adorned with impressionist paintings, and splashes of color that draw the eye.

We approach the host stand, where an impeccably dressed man greets us with a practiced smile. Talon gives his fake name, his voice smooth and confident. I watch as the host's eyes flicker to the choker at my neck, a fleeting look of understanding passing over his features before his professional mask slips back into place.

"Ah, yes, Mr. Blackwood," the host says, his French accent adding an extra layer of refinement to his words. "The other member of your party is already waiting. If you'll follow me, please."

The host leads us through the main dining room, a labyrinth of white-clothed tables and soft candlelight. The air is thick with the aroma of seared meats, delicate sauces, and freshly baked bread. My stomach clenches with a mix of hunger and nerves as we weave between tables, the weight of curious glances prickling against my skin.

We're guided towards the back of the restaurant, where the lighting grows dimmer and the atmosphere more intimate. The host pushes open a heavy wooden door revealing a private dining room. The space is smaller, cozier, with only one table nestled within its dark wood-paneled walls.

As we step inside, a woman sits alone, her posture perfect, one long leg crossed elegantly over the other. Her red hair falls in loose waves around her shoulders, the color vibrant against the muted gray of her tailored pantsuit. As we approach, she lifts a glass of deep red wine to her lips, taking a slow, deliberate sip.

Her eyes, a startling shade of green, lock onto Talon as we near her table. A smile curves her lips, equal parts welcoming and predatory. She stands from the table as we approach. "Charles, darling," she purrs, her Russian accent thick and rich like honey. "How wonderful to see you again."

Talon's hand tightens almost imperceptibly on my arm

as he returns her smile. "Natasha," he greets her, his voice smooth and controlled. "The pleasure is all mine."

I keep my eyes lowered, as I've been instructed, but I can feel the weight of Natasha's gaze as it shifts to me.

I can feel the weight of her scrutiny, probing for any hint of weakness, any crack in the carefully constructed facade. Her eyes linger on the curve of my neck, the swell of my breasts barely contained by the daring neckline of my dress, the expanse of leg exposed by the high slit.

"My, my," Natasha murmurs, her voice a silky purr. "What a lovely collar." Her perfectly manicured fingers reach out, brushing against the choker at my throat. The touch sends an involuntary shiver down my spine.

I keep my eyes lowered, my posture submissive, even as I feel a flare of defiance in my chest. Talon's hand on the small of my back steadies me, a silent reminder of our roles in this dangerous game.

Natasha's lips curl into a smirk as she gestures to the single chair across from her. "Please, Charles, take a seat. We have much to discuss." Natasha shifts back to her seat.

Talon moves towards the chair, his movements fluid and controlled. As he sits, he turns to me, his voice pitched low but carrying an unmistakable command. "Kneel."

I sink to my knees beside his chair, the cold marble floor a shock against my bare skin. The position leaves me feeling exposed, vulnerable, but I force myself to remain still, to embody the role we've crafted so carefully.

"Well-trained," she comments casually to Talon. "I can

see why you wanted to discuss the breeding clause, but before all of that business talk, we should eat."

Natasha snaps her fingers, the sharp sound echoing in the intimate space. A server materializes at her side almost instantly, his crisp white shirt and black bow tie. He opens his mouth, eyes darting to me kneeling on the floor, a question about a chair forming on his lips. But one look at Natasha's arched eyebrow silences him immediately. His professional mask slips back into place, though I catch a flicker of discomfort in his eyes before he averts his gaze.

Natasha's voice flows like liquid silk as she orders in flawless French, the words rolling off her tongue with practiced ease. "Nous commencerons avec les huîtres de Cancale, suivies du foie gras poêlé avec une réduction de vin rouge. Pour le plat principal, le filet de bœuf Wellington, saignant, bien sûr. Et n'oubliez pas une assiette de fromages pour terminer."

Natasha turns to Talon, her lips curving into a smile that doesn't quite reach her eyes. "And what about the wine, Charles darling? Do you have a preference?"

Talon doesn't miss a beat. His voice is smooth and confident as he responds, "I believe a 1982 Château Lafite Rothschild would pair wonderfully with your selections, Natasha. If the sommelier has it available, of course."

I can almost see Natasha's ears perk up at the mention of the prestigious and incredibly expensive wine. Her smile widens, revealing perfect white teeth. "Excellent choice," she purrs, a note of genuine approval in her voice. She turns back to the server. "You heard the man. And do be a dear and have it decanted immediately."

The server bows slightly, murmuring, "Bien sûr, madame," before disappearing as silently as he had appeared.

"I must say, Charles, your taste in wine is as impeccable as your taste in other areas." Her gaze flicks briefly to me, still kneeling silently beside Talon's chair.

The soft clink of crystal against the marble tabletop draws my attention, though I keep my eyes lowered. The sommelier's voice is hushed as he presents the wine, his French accent thick with reverence for the vintage he's about to pour. I hear the delicate pop of the cork being freed from the bottle, followed by the gentle gurgle of wine cascading into the decanter.

Suddenly, I feel a spray of tiny droplets raining down on my exposed skin. The cork must have slipped, sending a fine mist of the precious wine into the air. The rich, heady aroma envelops me, notes of blackcurrant, cedar, and a hint of truffle. It's intoxicating, and I have to resist the urge to lick my lips, to taste the droplets that have landed there.

"Oh dear," Natasha's voice drips with false concern. "It seems your pet has been christened with our wine, Charles. How fitting."

Talon's hand comes to rest on my head, his fingers threading through my hair in a possessive gesture. "Indeed," he replies, his tone casual but with an underlying current of steel. "She wears it well, don't you think?"

I can feel Natasha's eyes on me, assessing, calculating. "Quite," she purrs. "Now, tell me, Charles, how are things progressing with your little project? I trust she's proving satisfactory?"

The sommelier finishes pouring the wine, retreating silently as Talon and Natasha begin their dance of words. I listen, my heart pounding, as Talon spins a tale of my training, of my supposed eagerness to please. He speaks of me as if I'm not there, as if I'm nothing more than a prized pet, and I have to remind myself that this is all an act.

"She's coming along nicely," Talon says, his voice a perfect blend of pride and detachment. "Eager to learn, quick to obey. Of course, there's always room for improvement."

Natasha hums appreciatively. "I find that punishment is almost as sweet as submission."

I feel Talon's fingers tighten slightly in my hair. "It certainly is."

"Ah, there's our first course," Natasha comments. The scent of fresh oysters mingles with the lingering aroma of the wine, making my mouth water.

"Eyes on me," Talon commands softly, and I obey, lifting my gaze to meet his. His expression is impassive, but I can see the warmth in his eyes, a silent reassurance.

He selects an oyster from his plate, bringing it to my lips. "Open," he instructs, his voice low and husky.

I part my lips obediently, my heart racing as Talon tilts the shell. The oyster slides into my mouth, cool and briny.

The delicate flesh practically melts on my tongue, a burst of ocean flavor that makes my taste buds sing. I swallow, savoring the lingering taste of the sea.

Talon's thumb brushes across my bottom lip, wiping away a stray droplet of oyster liquor. The touch sends a shiver through me, and I have to fight to keep my expression neutral. I can feel Natasha's eyes on us, watching our every move with predatory interest.

"Good girl," Talon murmurs, his voice pitched low enough that only I can hear. The praise, though part of our act, sends a thrill through me.

Natasha leans forward, her elbows resting on the table. "She takes direction well," she observes, her tone casual but her eyes sharp. "Tell me, Charles, how does she handle more intense situations?"

Talon's hand moves to the back of my neck, his fingers playing with the clasp of the choker. "She's quite resilient," he replies, a hint of pride coloring his voice. "Aren't you, pet?"

I nod, keeping my eyes locked on Talon's face. "Yes, Sir," I murmur, my voice soft and demure.

Natasha's laugh is low and throaty. "Charming," she purrs. "I do hope you'll allow me to evaluate her limits myself, Charles. Her owners were quite clear about allowing someone else to play with their toy, so to speak."

The tension in the room ratchets up a notch, and I feel Talon's fingers tighten slightly on my neck. "Perhaps," he says, his tone noncommittal. "But let's not get ahead of ourselves, Natasha. We have business to discuss first, don't we?"

"Of course, darling. Business before pleasure, as they say." I steal a glance as she raises her wine glass in a mock toast. "To fruitful negotiations."

Talon raises his glass, the deep ruby liquid catching the candlelight as he mirrors Natasha's toast. "To fruitful negoti-ations," he echoes, his voice smooth as velvet. The crystal glasses clink together, the sound ringing out in the intimate space of the private dining room.

"Now then," Talon begins, setting down the decanter with a soft clink. His fingers absently stroke the back of my neck as he speaks, a gesture that could be seen as possessive or comforting, depending on the observer. "I believe we have some matters to discuss regarding your clients' interests."

"Ah yes, the breeding clause. I must say, Charles, your interest has certainly piqued their curiosity." Her voice drop-ping to a conspiratorial whisper. "They're quite intrigued by your enthusiasm for this particular asset."

I feel Talon's fingers tighten slightly on my neck, a barely perceptible tension that only I can detect. His voice, however, remains perfectly controlled. "And have they considered my offer?"

I hear Natasha takes another sip of wine, drawing out the moment. The silence stretches between them, filled only by the muted strains of classical music filtering in from the main restaurant.

"They are open to negotiation," she finally says, her words carefully measured. "However, they do have one small stipulation before we can discuss numbers."

Talon's hand stills on my neck, fidgeting with the lace collar around my neck. "Oh?" he prompts, his tone neutral but with an underlying current of interest.

Natasha sets down her wine glass, her manicured nails tapping a soft rhythm against the stem. "They wish to harvest her eggs again," she states. "Upon successful creation of viable embryos, their insurance policy, so to speak, they would be willing to enter into more concrete negotiations."

Talon brings his wine glass to his lips, taking a measured sip before responding. His face remains impassive, but I can feel the tension coiled in his body, like a spring ready to unwind.

"I see," he says, his voice smooth as polished marble. "And what exactly would this procedure entail?"

"Nothing too invasive, I assure you," she purrs, her Russian accent thickening slightly. "We have a discreet clinic that we've used for similar procedures in the past. State-of-the-art facilities, top-notch medical staff."

I steal another glance as she pauses, reaching for an oyster. With practiced elegance, she brings it to her lips, tipping the shell and letting the briny morsel slide into her mouth. I watch as she savors it, her eyes closing briefly in pleasure.

"Of course," she continues after swallowing, "we understand the value of privacy in these matters. We have a doctor on staff who would be more than willing to make house calls for the necessary hormone injections."

Talon's hand moves from my neck to my hair, his fingers threading through the strands. "Hormone injections?" he prompts, his tone casual but probing.

"Yes, to stimulate egg production," she explains, swirling the ruby liquid gently. "It's a standard part of the process. The injections would be administered over a period of about two weeks, followed by the retrieval procedure itself."

I feel Talon's fingers tighten slightly in my hair. His voice, however, remains perfectly controlled. "And the retrieval? What does that involve?"

"It's a minor outpatient procedure," Natasha assures him, her tone almost bored, as if discussing something as mundane as a dental cleaning. "Performed under light sedation. The eggs are harvested transvaginally using an ultrasound-guided needle. The whole process takes less than an hour." The thought of being put under again sets my fear and anxiety on edge.

I'm safe. Talon would never allow her to take me. I remind myself of that over and over again until my mind finally relaxes. Talon must notice as his fingers loosen their grip in my hair.

She takes another sip of wine, her green eyes never leaving Talon's face. "Of course, there would need to be a period of abstinence before and after the procedure. We wouldn't want to compromise the quality of the harvest, after all."

I can almost feel Talon's mind working, processing this information and calculating our next move. His thumb traces small circles on my scalp, a soothing gesture that grounds me amidst the clinical discussion of my body.

"And this abstinence period," Talon inquires, his tone casual, "how long are we talking about?"

"Typically, we recommend abstaining for at least a week before the egg retrieval and two weeks after," she replies. "We understand the inconvenience this might pose. Rest assured, the price would reflect that.

The server appears silently at their side, replacing the empty oyster platter with the next course. The rich, heady aroma of seared foie gras fills the air, mingling with the lingering scent of the sea and the complex bouquet of the wine.

Talon's fingers trail down to the nape of my neck, his touch sending a shiver down my spine.

"We could begin the hormone treatments within the week," she says. "The entire process, from start to finish, would take approximately three to four weeks."

Talon's hand moves to my shoulder, his touch both possessive and reassuring. "I see," he murmurs, his tone thoughtful. "And what guarantees do we have regarding her safety and well-being throughout this process?"

A flash of something, surprise, perhaps, or respect, flickers across Natasha's face before her mask of cool professionalism slips back into place. "We take the utmost care with all our assets, Charles."

I notice a slight tremor in his hand, barely perceptible to anyone who didn't know him as well as I do. His foot begins to bounce slowly beneath the table, the vibration traveling through the floor to where I kneel.

My heart races as I realize Talon is losing his grip on his carefully constructed facade. The tension in the room is palpable, thick enough to cut with a knife. I desperately want to reach out, to offer some form of comfort or reassurance, but I'm trapped in my role as the submissive pet. Helplessness washes over me as I struggle to think of a way to steady him without breaking character.

"What do you say, Mr. Blackwood?"

His hand slides from my shoulder to cup my face, drawing me forward slightly. The movement is gentle but firm, a clear statement of possession. I can feel the tremor in his fingers, the barely contained rage simmering just beneath the surface.

"You see," Talon continues, "Vesper isn't just an asset. She's not a commodity to be traded or harvested. She's mine."

As he speaks, I notice a flash of white moving behind Natasha. At first, I think it's just another server, their crisp uniform blending into the elegant decor of the restaurant. But there's something familiar about the way this figure moves, a fluid grace that sets my nerves on edge.

"You forget yourself, Charles," she hisses. "This isn't a

negotiation. It's a courtesy. The eggs will be harvested, with or without your cooperation."

Talon's laugh is cold and sharp, like shattered glass. "Oh, Natasha," he says, shaking his head. "The last thing I would ever do is hand Vesper over to you or your clients."

My eyes snap towards her. Rage contorts Natasha's features, transforming her face into a mask of fury. She opens her mouth, no doubt to unleash a torrent of threats, but before she can utter a word, the white-clad figure behind her moves with lightning speed.

A hand darts out, gripping Natasha's shoulder with bruising force. In the same fluid motion, a syringe plunges into the crook of her neck. Natasha's eyes widen in shock and fear, her mouth working silently as the drug takes effect.

"Nighty night, cunt," Talon seethes, his voice dripping with satisfaction as Natasha slumps forward in her chair, her forehead hitting the table with a dull thud.

My heart racing, I peer up at our unexpected savior. To my shock, I see Alex, dressed impeccably in a server's uniform. His usually stoic face is alive with grim satisfaction as he smoothly pockets the now-empty syringe.

"Excellent timing, as always, Alex," Talon says, rising from his chair. He reaches down, offering me his hand. "We need to move. We'll take the Red Russian bitch to go."

Chapter 36

ALEX

I WATCH as Zaire and Oscar carry Natasha down the narrow stairs, her limp body swaying between them like a rag doll. The familiar musty scent of the basement hits me as we descend, mingling with the metallic tang of fear that seems to emanate from our unconscious guest.

My playroom, as the guys jokingly call it, awaits us at the bottom. The fluorescent lights flicker to life, casting an eerie glow across the plastic sheets hanging from the ceiling. They rustle softly as we move past, the sound oddly reminiscent of whispered secrets.

The room is a masterpiece of efficiency and horror. Stainless steel gleams from every surface, cold and unforgiving. The drains in the floor, strategically placed, promise to wash away any evidence of the night's activities. I've always appreciated their silent efficiency.

In the center of it all stands the pièce de résistance, a mortuary table. Its surface polished to a mirror shine, an altar to my craft, ready to receive its latest offering. Zaire and Oscar hoist Natasha onto it, her red hair spilling over the edge like molten lava.

"She's heavier than she looks," Zaire grunts, rolling his shoulders. The movement makes the tattoos on his arms seem to writhe in the harsh light. His eyes meet mine, a mix of anticipation and something darker swirling in their depths.

Oscar, ever the pragmatist, is already adjusting the plastic sheeting, sliding the hooks along their tracks with practiced ease. "You want full coverage tonight, Alex?" he asks, his voice low and controlled. Unlike his twin, Oscar's unmarked skin seems to absorb the light, making him look like a shadow given form.

I nod, my fingers trailing along the edge of the table. The cold metal grounds me, focuses my thoughts. "Yes," I reply, my voice sounding distant even to my own ears. "We don't know how messy this is going to get."

As Oscar finishes arranging the plastic and Zaire checks Natasha's restraints, I feel a familiar thrill run through me. This is my domain, my stage. And tonight, I have quite the performance ahead of us.

"Start playlist," I call out to the virtual assistant I have programmed for my playground. The haunting melody of "Just Pretend" by Bad Omens fills the space, providing a shield against the demons that haunt my thoughts during such tasks.

I stride towards the surgical table, my footsteps echoing in the cavernous room with the music. The array of instruments laid out before me glint under the harsh fluorescent lights, each one a promise of pain and revelation. Scalpels of various sizes, their edges wickedly sharp, rest beside delicate scissors designed for precise cuts. Tweezers of different lengths and grips are neatly arranged, ready to pluck and probe.

My eyes linger on the rib extractors, their cruel curves a testament to the depths of human ingenuity when it comes to inflicting suffering. Each tool has its purpose, its moment in the dance I'm about to choreograph. But not yet. Not quite yet.

Instead, my hand reaches for a syringe, its glass barrel filled with a clear liquid that seems to pulse with potential energy. Adrenaline. The key to unlocking our guest's consciousness and ushering her into our world of pain.

As I lift the syringe, I hear two sets of footsteps coming down the stairs. The footsteps grow louder, and I turn to see Talon descending the stairs, Vesper in tow. She's still wearing that slip of a black dress from the restaurant, the fabric clinging to her curves like a second skin. The sight of her makes my breath catch, a mixture of desire and something darker stirring in my chest. An odd feeling considering my longest relationship with either sex didn't last more than satisfying my itch. But, with Vesper, there's something different. Something that I can't explain with pain or computer code.

As they reach the bottom, the harsh fluorescent light catches on the diamond circlet collar adorning Vesper's neck, causing it to sparkle. My eyes are drawn to her legs, where the faint shadows of bruises are visible on her knees, a testament to her prolonged kneeling at Talon's side earlier.

Vesper's eyes widen as she takes in the room, her gaze darting from the plastic-draped walls to the gleaming instruments on the tray beside me. I can almost see the realization dawning in those green orbs, the understanding of what this place truly is. Her chest rises and falls rapidly, her breath coming in short, sharp gasps.

Zaire and Oscar move toward her, their movements fluid and predatory. They flank her, creating a living barrier between Vesper and Natasha. I watch as they lean in, their lips barely moving as they engage in a hushed conversation. Vesper's eyes flick between them, her expression a mix of fear and is that intrigue?

Oscar's hand comes to rest on the small of Vesper's back, his touch light but possessive. Zaire, ever the more aggressive of the two, reaches up to trace the line of her collar with a tattooed finger. I can see the shiver that runs through Vesper at his touch, her pupils dilating slightly. Oscar's eyes meet mine over Vesper's shoulder, a silent question in their depths. I nod almost imperceptibly, granting permission for whatever they have planned.

I hear the snippets of the conversation. "Let her stay," I order. If anyone in this room deserves to see this, she has the most right to witness this.

I turn back to Natasha's prone form on the table, the syringe still in my hand. "Let's wake her up."

I position the needle over Natasha's heart, feeling the weight of everyone's eyes on me. With practiced precision, I plunge the syringe into her chest, the needle sliding through flesh and muscle until it finds its mark. I depress the plunger, watching as the clear liquid disappears into her body.

For a moment, nothing happens. Then, like a bolt of lightning animating a corpse, Natasha's body jerks violently. Her eyes fly open, wide and unfocused, as she gasps for air. Her chest heaves against the restraints, her back arching off the cold metal table. The sound that escapes her throat is primal, caught somewhere between a scream and a sob.

I step back, allowing Talon to move forward. His presence fills the room, commanding and intimidating. Natasha's wild eyes lock onto him, and I see a flash of recognition followed quickly by confusion.

"Charles?" she croaks, her voice raw and disbelieving. "Charles, what's happening? Where am I?"

Talon doesn't respond immediately. Instead, he circles the table slowly, like a predator stalking its prey. His golden-brown eyes never leave Natasha's face, drinking in her fear and disorientation.

"Now, now, Natasha," he finally says, his voice smooth as silk but edged with steel. "Let's not play games. You know very well who I am and why you're here."

Natasha struggles against her bonds, the metal cuffs biting into her wrists and ankles. "I don't understand. Charles, please, what's going on?"

I move to the tray of instruments, selecting a scalpel. The weight of it in my hand is comforting, familiar. I begin to make shallow, precise cuts along Natasha's arms, following the lines of her veins. She whimpers at each touch of the blade, her eyes darting between Talon and me.

I continue my work, the scalpel dancing across Natasha's skin with practiced precision. Each cut is a work of art, shallow enough to avoid major blood loss but deep enough to elicit gasps and whimpers from our guest. She begs me to stop with each pass, but her pleas fall on deaf ears. The room fills with the metallic scent of blood, mingling with the antiseptic smell of the basement.

Talon looms over Natasha, his presence overwhelming in the confined space. "Charles, please," she begs again, her voice trembling. "I don't understand what's happening. Why are you doing this?"

A dark chuckle escapes Talon's lips. "Oh, Natasha," he says, his voice dripping with mock sympathy. "Charles Blackwood doesn't exist. He never did."

I watch as the realization dawns on Natasha's face, her eyes widening in horror. The fear in her expression is intoxicating, and I find myself pausing in my work to savor it.

"The day you sold Vesper to me," Talon continues, his voice hardening, "you started a countdown clock. Did you really think you could traffic the daughter of a crime family and get away with it?"

Natasha's breath comes in short, panicked gasps. "I didn't know. Please, you have to believe me. I was just following orders!"

I can't help but laugh at her pathetic attempt at innocence. "Orders?" I interject, my scalpel hovering over her thigh. "And I suppose those orders included stealing from Vesper's body too, didn't they? Tell me, Natasha, how many times did you harvest from Vesper? How many eggs did you steal from her body while she was drugged and helpless?"

I watch as Natasha's face pales, the last vestiges of her facade crumbling. She opens her mouth, but no sound comes out. Like a fish out of water gasping for air. I grip the scalpel tighter, my knuckles whitening around the steel. The anticipation builds within me, a dark tide rising.

"You took from Vesper. Now it's time we take from you."

I make the first deep cut along her abdomen, relishing her scream. The blade parts flesh and fat, revealing the glistening layers beneath. Blood wells up, trickling down her sides in crimson rivulets. I work methodically, opening her up like a grotesque flower blooming in reverse.

But I don't stop. I can't stop. I imagine Natasha's hands on her, violating her, stealing pieces of her very essence. My cuts become deeper, more frenzied.

"How many?" I growl, pressing the scalpel against her quivering flesh. "How many eggs did you take?"

Natasha's eyes are wild with terror. "I...I don't know! Dozens, maybe. I lost count!"

The admission sends a fresh wave of fury through me. I contemplate removing her uterus right here, right now, without anesthesia. Let her feel a fraction of the violation Vesper endured. But no, that level of torture would have to wait. We need her coherent, able to feel every ounce of pain we inflict.

Instead, I reach for a pair of forceps. With practiced precision, I clamp down on a nerve bundle near her hip. Natasha's back arches off the table, a guttural scream tearing from her throat.

"That's for every time you touched her," I snarl, twisting the forceps. "For every egg you stole, for every dream you shattered."

Natasha writhes on the table, her restraints clanking against metal. "Mercy," she gasps between screams. "I didn't have a choice!"

I laugh, the sound hollow and cruel. "There's always a choice, Natasha. You chose wrong."

I continue my work, alternating between shallow cuts and deep, burning pain. Each incision is a question, each twist of the forceps a demand for information.

As I work, I'm acutely aware of Vesper's presence behind me. I wonder what she's thinking, seeing her tormentor laid bare and broken. Is she satisfied? Horrified? I don't dare glance at Vesper. If I did, I know this would all be over in an instant. One look at her face, whether it showed horror, satisfaction, or worse, pity, and I'd lose my nerve. I'd slice Natasha's femoral artery, and we'd have nothing but a bloody mess and no answers.

Instead, I focus on my work, letting the familiar rhythm of cut and question guide me. The scalpel becomes an extension of my hand, dancing across Natasha's flesh and muscle with brutal precision. Each incision is a work of art, a masterpiece painted in shades of crimson and pain.

The room fills with the sounds of Natasha's screams, punctuated by the soft drip of blood hitting plastic. The air grows thick with the metallic scent of iron, mingling with the acrid tang of fear and sweat. It's a heady mixture, one that threatens to overwhelm my senses if I let it.

Leaving her open abdomen behind for now, I move to Natasha's left hand, carefully separating skin from muscle. The delicate bones of her fingers are exposed, gleaming white against the red of her flesh. With surgical precision, I begin to remove her fingernails, one by one. Each extraction elicits a fresh scream, raw and primal.

Talon's voice cuts through the haze of blood and pain, his tone sharp as the scalpel in my hand. "What does Mario Rossi want with Vesper's embryos? What was his part in all of this?"

Natasha's eyes, wild with agony, dart between us. Her lips move, but only a strangled whimper escapes. The pain has pushed her beyond words, beyond coherent thought. I can see the struggle in her face, the desperate attempt to cling to consciousness even as her body begs for the sweet release of oblivion.

I press the scalpel against her cheek, letting the cold steel kiss her tear-stained skin. "Answer him," I growl, my voice low and dangerous.

But it's too late. Natasha's eyes roll back, her body going limp on the table. The constant stream of screams and whimpers cuts off abruptly, leaving the room in an eerie silence broken only by the soft drip of blood onto plastic.

Talon leans in, his golden-brown eyes narrowed. "Is she dead?"

I press my fingers to Natasha's neck, feeling for a pulse. It's there, weak but steady. "Nope, just out cold," I report, a mix of disappointment and anticipation coloring my voice. "The pain overtook her."

Oscar steps forward, frustration etched across his features. "We didn't get anywhere," he spits, running a hand through his dark hair. "All this, and we're no closer to answers."

I turn to him, a slow smile spreading across my face. It's not a kind smile, there's nothing kind about this room or what we're doing. "Don't worry, Oscar. I can keep her alive." I gesture to the array of medical equipment lining the walls. "I'm just getting started."

My eyes roam over Natasha's unconscious form, my mind already racing with possibilities. The human body is a marvel of evolution, capable of enduring far more than most people realize. And I intend to push those limits to their breaking point.

I move to a nearby cabinet, pulling out vials of various drugs. Stimulants to keep her awake, painkillers to take the edge off just enough to keep her coherent, and other, more exotic compounds that blur the line between science and torture.

"We'll let her rest for now," I say, preparing a cocktail of drugs in a syringe. "When she wakes up, we'll be ready. And believe me, she'll talk."

I inject the mixture into Natasha's flesh, watching as the clear liquid disappears into her veins. It won't wake her yet, but it will ensure she doesn't slip too far away from us.

Chapter 37

VESPER

I STAND at the edge of the plastic curtains, my heart pounding in my chest as I take in the sight before me. The basement's dim lighting casts eerie shadows across Natasha's prone form, strapped to the cold metal table like a sacrifice on an altar. The air is thick with the metallic scent of blood and the sharp sting of antiseptic, a nauseating cocktail that makes my stomach churn.

Hours have passed since we were all down here, since I witnessed the brutal interrogation that left Natasha in this state. The penthouse above is silent now, its occupants likely lost in uneasy dreams or restless contemplation. But sleep eludes me, my mind a tempest of conflicting emotions and half-formed plans.

I take a tentative step forward, the plastic rustling softly around me. Natasha's chest rises and falls in shallow, erratic breaths, the only sign that life still clings to her battered body. Her face, once beautiful and haughty, is now a canvas of bruises and dried blood. I feel a pang of something. Pity? Guilt? Or perhaps a chilling recognition that in this world, in this life, any one of us could end up on this table.

My fingers twitch at my sides, itching to do something, anything. But what? Tend to her wounds? End her suffering? Alert the others? Each option carries its own set of consequences, rippling out into futures I can barely comprehend.

I think of Oscar, his warm embrace still lingering on my skin. What would he say if he knew I was down here? Would he understand this inexplicable pull I feel towards our enemy? Or would his eyes harden with that calculating look I've come to both admire and fear?

A soft moan escapes Natasha's lips, barely audible but enough to make me flinch. Her eyelids flutter, and for a heart-stopping moment, I think she might regain consciousness. But she remains lost in whatever dark realm her mind has retreated to.

I take another step closer, my reflection ghostly in the polished surface of the medical equipment surrounding the table. My hand reaches out, hovering inches from Natasha's battered face. To touch her would be to acknowledge her humanity, to forge a connection I'm not sure I'm prepared for.

"I thought I might find you down here."

I freeze, my hand still hovering above Natasha's face, as Alex's voice cuts through the silence like a blade. "It's funny, isn't it?" he murmurs, his breath warm against my ear. "How the people who hurt you the most bring on the heaviest pangs of guilt."

My heart leaps into my throat, adrenaline surging through my veins. I hadn't heard him approach, too lost in my own tumultuous thoughts. The basement suddenly feels smaller, more claustrophobic, with his presence looming behind me.

I turn slowly, my eyes adjusting to the darkness beyond the harsh circle of light surrounding Natasha's makeshift medical bay. Alex stands there, a shadow among shadows, his expression unreadable in the gloom. The faint scent of his cologne, sandalwood and something distinctly masculine, mingles with the antiseptic air.

"I'm not feeling guilty," I lie, the words tasting bitter on my tongue. But even as I say them, I know it's not entirely true. The sight of Natasha, broken and vulnerable, has awakened something in me, a reminder of our shared humanity that I've tried so hard to bury.

Alex takes a step closer, and I resist the urge to back away. His eyes, dark and intense, search my face. "Aren't you?" he challenges softly. "Then why are you down here,

Vesper? Why stand vigil over the woman who stole from your body over and over again, and sold you?"

I swallow hard, my mind racing for an answer that won't betray the turmoil inside me. The plastic curtains rustle softly around us, like whispers in the night, and Natasha's labored breathing provides a haunting backdrop to our conversation.

"I needed to see," I finally admit. "To understand."

Alex nods slowly, as if he expected this answer. He moves past me, his shoulder brushing mine, sending an involuntary shiver down my spine. He stands over Natasha, studying her with a clinical detachment that both impresses and unsettles me.

"Understanding is dangerous in our world, Vesper," he says, his fingers ghosting over the edge of the metal table. "It leads to hesitation. And hesitation..." He trails off, leaving the consequences unspoken but painfully clear.

I watch him, noting the tension in his shoulders, the way his jaw clenches. There's more here than just a warning there, I realize. There's experience speaking, hard-won and bitter.

"Have you ever felt it?" I ask, surprising myself with my boldness. "That guilt? That connection to someone you're supposed to hate?"

Alex turns to me, and for a moment, I see a flash of something raw and vulnerable in his eyes. It's gone in an instant, replaced by his usual guarded expression.

Alex's eyes bore into mine, a storm of emotions swirling in their depths. For a moment, I think he might not answer, might retreat behind the walls he's so carefully constructed. But then he speaks, his voice low and rough with remembered pain.

"My mother," he says, the words hanging heavy in the air between us.

I feel my brow furrow in confusion. "Your mother?" I repeat, trying to make sense of this unexpected revelation.

Alex nods, his gaze drifting back to Natasha's unconscious form. "I feel guilty," he continues, "because I didn't kill her sooner."

My breath catches in my throat. The basement suddenly feels colder, the shadows deeper. I search Alex's face, looking for any sign that this is some sort of sick joke, but find only grim resolve.

"I don't understand," I whisper, my voice sounding small and lost in the vastness of this terrible confession.

Alex turns back to me, his eyes now burning with an intensity that makes me want to step back. But I hold my ground, drawn in by the raw honesty of this moment.

"My mother," he says, each word deliberate and heavy, "was the Butcher of Selfoss."

The name hits me like a physical blow. I've heard whispers of the Butcher, a serial killer whose brutality shocked even the hardened members of our world. But to hear Alex claim such a monster as his mother...

"Her body count would shock you, Vesper," Alex continues, his voice eerily calm. "Men, women, children, no one was safe from her artistic endeavors."

I feel bile rising in my throat, but I force it down. "How..." I begin, but the words fail me.

Alex's laugh is bitter, devoid of any humor. "How did I not know? Oh, I knew. I always knew." He runs a hand through his hair, a rare display of agitation. "She was training me. Grooming me to follow in her footsteps."

The horror of what he's saying washes over me in waves. I think of my own childhood, of the subtle and not-so-subtle ways my family prepared me for this life. But this is something else entirely.

"I thought that's how you were supposed to love," Alex says. "To hurt, to create beauty from pain. It took me years to understand how wrong it all was."

I reach out, my hand hovering just above his arm, unsure if touch would be welcome at this moment. "Alex, I'm so sorry," I breathe, the words feeling woefully inadequate.

He looks at me then, really looks at me, and I see the scared little boy hiding behind the hardened exterior. "I was fifteen when I finally put an end to it," he says. "Fifteen years old, and I had to kill my own mother to stop the monster she'd become. Before she had a chance to make me in her image. "

I feel my breath catch in my throat as the full weight of Alex's revelation settles over me. I look at him, really look at him, and see him anew. The precise, calculated movements.

The unflinching gaze when faced with violence. The meticulous attention to detail in his 'playroom.'

"That's why," I whisper, my voice barely audible over Natasha's labored breathing. "That's why you know how to do the things you do."

Alex's eyes meet mine, a flicker of surprise crossing his face before it's quickly masked. "What do you mean?"

I take a deep breath, steeling myself. "What you did to Ivanov." The memory of that night flashes through my mind, the clinical precision with which Alex had extracted information, the way he'd wielded pain like an artist's brush. "She trained you to be a weapon, didn't she? The finger of God to wipe the Earth clean of those she deemed unworthy."

A mirthless chuckle escapes Alex's lips. "Finger of God," he repeats, shaking his head. "That's poetic, Vesper. But no, I was to be her masterpiece. Her magnum opus."

He moves away from Natasha's prone form, pacing the small space like a caged animal. The dim light catches the planes of his face, casting sharp shadows that make him look almost skeletal.

"You've seen my work, Vesper," he continues, his voice low and intense. "The precision. The control. But what you don't see is the struggle. Every. Single. Time."

I watch him, transfixed, as he runs a hand through his hair, leaving it disheveled. It's such a human gesture, at odds with the monster he's describing.

"She taught me to find beauty in suffering," Alex says,

his words dripping with disgust. "To see the human body as a canvas, pain as my palette. But she also taught me control. Precision. How to keep someone alive and coherent through unimaginable agony."

I feel my stomach churn, but I force myself to listen. To understand.

He turns to me, his eyes blazing with an intensity that both terrifies and captivates me. "Every time I step into that room, every time I pick up a tool, I feel her ghost over my shoulder. Urging me to go further, to indulge in the artistry she tried to instill in me."

I take a step towards him, drawn by the raw vulnerability in his voice. "But you don't," I say softly.

Alex shakes his head. "No, I don't. But the temptation is always there. Like a voice inside my head."

I swallow hard, my mind reeling from Alex's confession. The weight of his words hangs heavy in the air, mingling with the antiseptic scent and the soft, rhythmic beeping of the medical equipment. I find myself taking a step closer to him, drawn by some inexplicable force.

"How?" I whisper, my voice barely audible. "How do you keep yourself from going over the edge?"

Alex's eyes meet mine, and I see a storm of emotions swirling in their depths. For a moment, he's silent, and I can almost see the war raging within him, the constant battle between the man he's chosen to be and the monster his mother tried to create.

"Because," he says finally, his voice low and intense, "the world needs monsters like me to balance the scales."

I furrow my brow, trying to understand. Alex continues, his words coming faster now, as if a dam has broken.

"There are true monsters out there, Vesper. People who inflict pain for pleasure, who destroy lives without a second thought. And sometimes, the only way to fight that kind of evil is with a controlled version of it."

He runs a hand through his hair, leaving it even more disheveled. "I use the skills she taught me, yes. But I use them with purpose. To protect. To gather information that saves lives. To maintain a balance in our world that keeps the truly depraved in check."

I watch him, transfixed by the raw honesty in his voice, the vulnerability etched across his features. In this moment, I see Alex as I never have before, not just as the skilled interrogator or the dangerous enforcer, but as a man constantly walking a knife's edge between light and darkness.

"It's a choice," he continues. "Every single time, it's a choice. To use these abilities for a greater purpose. To be the monster that hunts other monsters."

I open my mouth to respond, but before I can, a low moan cuts through the air. We both turn, startled, to see Natasha stirring on the table. Her eyelids flutter, and her fingers twitch against the restraints.

The moment shatters, reality crashing back in around us. Alex's expression hardens, the vulnerability I'd glimpsed moments ago vanishing behind his usual mask of cool detachment. He moves swiftly to Natasha's side, checking her vitals with practiced efficiency.

"She's starting to wake up," he mutters to himself. "She needs a higher dose." Alex starts to shift to find another syringe, but I stop him. His blue eyes locking on mine.

I reach out, my hand gently grasping Alex's arm. "Wait. I need to talk to her."

Alex's piercing blue eyes lock onto mine, searching my face with an intensity that makes my breath catch. For a moment, I think he might refuse, might remind me of the danger, of the foolishness of showing mercy to our enemies. But something in my expression must give him pause.

"Vesper," he says, his voice low and tinged with concern, "I can't leave you alone with her. It's too risky."

I open my mouth to protest, but he continues before I can speak.

"However," he says, his tone softening slightly, "if you'll allow me to stay, I can wake her up for you. You won't have to wait."

I hesitate, weighing my options. The thought of being alone with Natasha is both terrifying and oddly compelling, but Alex's presence offers a safety net I'm not sure I'm ready to do without. After a moment's deliberation, I nod.

"Okay," I whisper. "Wake her up."

Alex nods, his movements precise and controlled as he reaches for a small vial and a syringe. The glass gleams dully in the dim light as he expertly fills the needle. I watch, mesmerized, as he approaches Natasha's prone form.

With a gentleness that surprises me, Alex tilts Natasha's head to the side, exposing the pale column of her neck. The needle slides in smoothly, and I see his thumb depress the plunger, sending whatever concoction he's prepared coursing through her veins.

As promised, Alex steps back, moving out of Natasha's immediate line of sight. He positions himself near the plastic curtains, a silent sentinel ready to intervene if needed. The air in the basement feels thick with anticipation, the soft beeping of the medical equipment the only sound breaking the tense silence.

Moments pass, feeling like an eternity, before Natasha's eyelids begin to flutter. A soft moan escapes her lips, her brow furrowing as consciousness slowly returns. I find myself holding my breath, my heart pounding in my chest as I watch her struggle back to awareness.

Finally, her eyes open fully, unfocused at first, then gradually sharpening as she takes in her surroundings. The realization of where she is, of what's happened, dawns on her face in stages – confusion, fear, and finally, a desperate, wild hope as her gaze lands on me.

"Vesper," she croaks, her voice raw and broken. "Oh God, Vesper, please."

I swallow hard, steeling myself against the wave of emotion threatening to overwhelm me. Natasha looks so different from the composed, dangerous woman I've known – vulnerable, desperate, human.

"Please," she continues. "You have to help me."

"Help you?" The words taste bitter on my tongue, memories of betrayal and pain flooding my mind. "Like you helped me, Natasha?"

Her eyes widen, a flicker of shame crossing her battered features before desperation takes over again. "Vesper, I'm sorry. I'm so sorry. You have to understand, I didn't have a choice."

I feel my jaw clench, anger and pity warring within me. The dim light of the basement casts long shadows across Natasha's face, emphasizing every cut and bruise. Her once-proud demeanor is shattered, replaced by a raw vulnerability that tugs at something deep inside me.

"There's always a choice," I say, the words coming out harsher than I intended. But even as I say them, I think of the impossible decisions I've faced, the moral gray areas I've had to navigate in this world of ours.

Natasha's eyes fill with tears, glinting in the harsh fluorescent light. "You're right," she whispers, her voice cracking. "And I'm making a choice now. Please, Vesper. Help me escape. Release me. I can disappear, I swear I'll never bother you or anyone else ever again."

I feel Alex's presence behind me, a silent reminder of the consequences of mercy in our world. But there's something in Natasha's plea that resonates with me, a desperation I understand all too well.

I take a deep breath, steeling myself for what I'm about to do. "I will help you, Natasha," I say, watching hope bloom in her eyes. "But first, you have to do something for me."

"Anything," she breathes, relief evident in every line of her body.

I lean in closer, my voice low and intense. "Tell me the truth. All of it. Why did my uncle want my embryo? Only then will I even consider releasing you."

Natasha's eyes dart nervously to Alex, still lurking in the shadows, before returning to me. I can see the calculations running behind her eyes, weighing her options, considering how much to reveal.

"Vesper, I-" she starts, but I cut her off.

"No more lies, Natasha. No more half-truths or manipulations. If you want my help, I need complete honesty. This is your one chance."

The basement falls silent save for the soft hum of medical equipment and Natasha's ragged breathing. I can feel the weight of this moment, the potential consequences of what I'm offering. But I need answers, and I'm willing to take this risk to get them.

Natasha's voice trembles as she speaks. "It wasn't supposed to be like this, Vesper. I was desperate."

I lean in closer, my heart pounding in my chest as I wait for the truth I've been seeking for so long.

"Your uncle and aunt," Natasha continues, her eyes glistening with unshed tears, "they wanted a child so badly. An heir. They tried for years, but miscarriage after miscarriage. It was destroying them."

I feel my breath catch in my throat, memories of hushed conversations and my aunt's tear-stained face flashing through my mind.

"Your uncle, he was obsessed. He couldn't accept that he might not have a biological heir to continue the family legacy. So, he reached out, used his connections to find an agency in Russia. That's where he found me."

Natasha's words paint a vivid picture in my mind. I can almost see it, the sterile clinic, the air thick with desperation and hope. My uncle, his face etched with determination, signing papers and making promises.

"I was young, naive," Natasha continues, her voice cracking. "The money they offered so much money. It was more than I could ever dream of. Enough to change my life, to help my family. All I had to do was carry a child for nine months."

I feel a chill run down my spine, the pieces starting to fall into place. "But something went wrong," I whisper, prompting her to continue.

Natasha nods, her eyes distant as if lost in the memory. "They had one chance left. One small, precious embryo. Their last hope for a biological child. The day of the transfer came, and I remember lying there, so nervous I could barely breathe."

Her words transport me to that moment, the cold exam table, the hum of medical equipment, the palpable tension in the air.

Natasha's words hang in the air, heavy with the weight

of her confession. I feel my heart pounding in my chest, each beat echoing in my ears as I process the implications of what she's saying.

"The doctor's face," Natasha continues, her voice barely above a whisper, "I'll never forget it. The way his eyes widened, the color draining from his cheeks. He muttered something in Russian, his hands shaking as he turned to the nurse."

I can see it all so clearly in my mind's eye, the sterile room, the harsh fluorescent lights, the panic spreading like a virus through the medical staff.

"Stop the thaw!" Natasha's voice cracks as she reenacts the moment. "But it was too late. The embryo, your aunt and uncle's last hope, it was gone. Too late to preserve it, and no one they could implant it into."

My breath catches in my throat. I think of my cousin, no, not my cousin at all, the child I grew up with, played with, loved fiercely. The heir my uncle had pinned all his hopes and dreams on.

"What happened next?" I ask, my voice sounding strange and distant to my own ears.

Natasha's eyes meet mine, filled with a mixture of guilt and desperation. "We lied," she whispers. "All of us. The doctor, the nurses, your uncle...me. We agreed to keep it a secret. To pretend the transfer had been successful."

I feel my knees weaken, and I grip the edge of the metal table to steady myself. The cold steel grounds me, reminding me of where I am, of the gravity of this moment.

"Nine months," Natasha continues, her words coming faster now, as if a dam has broken. "Nine months of living a lie. Of feeling my baby grow inside me, knowing I'd never be able to keep them. He'd bring his wife to visit me. She'd touch my belly, beaming with happiness about the life growing inside of me. All the while, I was dying inside knowing it wasn't their baby. It was mine."

I close my eyes, overwhelmed by the flood of emotions coursing through me. Anger, pity, confusion, they swirl together in a dizzying cocktail.

"The day she was born," Natasha's voice breaks, tears now flowing freely down her cheeks. "God, Vesper, she was so beautiful. So perfect. I held her for just a moment before they took her away. Before I had to hand her over to your uncle and pretend she wasn't mine."

The basement suddenly feels too small, the air too thick. I struggle to breathe, my mind racing with the implications of this revelation. The cousin I've known my whole life, the heir to our family's empire, is actually Natasha's child. A child born of deception and desperation.

"Why?" I manage to choke out. "Why are you telling me this now?"

Natasha's eyes lock onto mine, filled with a fierce, desperate love. "Because she's in danger, Vesper."

I feel the world tilt beneath my feet, Natasha's words echoing in my head like a deafening bell. "What do you mean, she's in danger?" I demand.

Natasha's eyes dart nervously to Alex, still lurking in the

shadows, before returning to me. "Your uncle," she says, her voice trembling, "he made a deal. A terrible, unthinkable deal."

My heart pounds in my chest as I lean closer, desperate to hear every word. "What kind of deal?" I ask, though a part of me already knows the answer, a cold dread seeping into my bones.

"He..." Natasha swallows hard, her eyes glistening with unshed tears. "He brokered a deal to trade you for Bianca."

The words hit me like a physical blow, knocking the air from my lungs. I stumble back, gripping the edge of the metal table to keep from falling. "What?" I gasp, my mind reeling.

Natasha nods, her face a mask of anguish. "Dmitri," she whispers, "he wanted Bianca. He's always wanted her. But her father...he was the second son. Victor would never have allowed it."

The pieces start to fall into place, a horrifying picture forming in my mind. "So, they made me disappear," I breathe, the truth of it settling over me like a suffocating blanket.

"Without you," Natasha continues, her words coming faster now, "Mario could make his move. And he did. God help me, Vesper, he did."

The basement swims before my eyes, the harsh fluorescent lights blurring into a hazy glow. I can hear Alex moving behind me, but his presence feels distant, unreal.

"Bianca," I whisper, thinking of the girl I've known my

entire life, the cousin I've loved and protected. "She's not...she's not a Rossi at all?"

Natasha shakes her head, tears now flowing freely down her cheeks. "No," she says softly. "She's not. The alliance. It's all a farce, Vesper. A lie built on lies."

I close my eyes, overwhelmed by the flood of emotions coursing through me. Anger, betrayal, confusion, they swirl together in a dizzying cocktail. Everything I thought I knew, everything I believed about my family, my place in the world – it's all crumbling around me.

"There's more," Natasha says, her voice barely audible over the pounding of blood in my ears.

I look up at her, not sure I can bear to hear anything else. But I nod, silently urging her to continue.

Natasha's words hang in the air, heavy and suffocating. I feel my world tilting on its axis, reality warping around me as the full implications of her confession sink in. But there's more, I can see it in her eyes, a final, terrible truth waiting to be unleashed.

"Victor," Natasha whispers, her voice barely audible over the hum of medical equipment, "he had a condition for the alliance. For Bianca."

I feel my breath catch in my throat, a cold dread seeping into my bones. "What condition?" I ask, though a part of me already knows the answer, a horrifying suspicion taking root in the darkest corners of my mind.

Natasha's eyes meet mine, filled with a mixture of guilt and desperation. "An heir," she says, the words falling from her lips like poison. "A male heir to continue the Petrov and Rossi bloodline."

The basement seems to spin around me, the harsh fluorescent lights blurring into a nauseating kaleidoscope. I grip the edge of the metal table, my knuckles turning white as I struggle to process this new information.

"But Bianca," I start, my voice sounding strange and distant to my own ears, "she's not...she's not even a Rossi. How could she..."

And then it hits me, a realization so profound, so earth-shattering, that for a moment I forget how to breathe. The room goes silent, the constant beep of monitors fading away as my mind races to connect the dots.

"Me," I whisper, the word barely audible. "They needed me."

Natasha nods, tears streaming down her face. "You're the only biological Rossi female, Vesper. The only one who could provide what Victor wanted."

The truth crashes over me like a tidal wave, threatening to pull me under. Every strange occurrence, every unexplained medical procedure, every moment of confusion and fear over the past two years— it all suddenly makes horrifying sense.

"My eggs," I breathe, feeling nauseous. "That's why they...that's why you..."

I think back to the countless times I'd woken up groggy and disoriented, to the unexplained bruises and the vague memories of medical equipment. It hadn't been just once or twice – they'd been harvesting my eggs repeatedly, building up a stock for their twisted plans. But, if I am the mother… who was the father?

"Who donated the sperm?"

Natasha's face grows pale.

"Dmitri," I gasp.

"Yes," she admits. "Victor had to ensure his bloodline so he had Dmitri's sperm banked a long time ago. Just in case. Once the embryos were created, and deemed viable, Mario took the male and destroyed the female. They implanted it…"

"When did they do the transfer?" Maybe there is still hope to keep my son from them. To take back what was stolen from me. "Tell me who is carrying my son."

Natasha's eyes meet mine, filled with a mixture of pity and fear. She swallows hard, her throat working visibly before she speaks. "Vesper," she says, her voice trembling, "Bianca gave birth over a month ago."

Chapter 38

VESPER

I STAND THERE, frozen, as Natasha's words echo in my mind like a twisted, haunting melody. The world around me blurs, and I feel as if I'm drowning in a sea of betrayal and lies. My cousin…not my cousin. My uncle and Bianca. The architects of my torture. A son...my son, born from pain and deceit.

My legs give way, and I sink to the floor.

"Vesper," Natasha's voice breaks through the fog, laced with concern and regret. But I can't look at her. Can't bear to see the face that now represents years of lies.

I wrap my arms around myself, trying to hold the pieces of my shattered reality together. The memories of those two years of torture flood back, more vivid and painful than ever. Each scar on my body now tells a different story, not one of random cruelty, but of calculated manipulation by those I trusted most.

"A son," I whisper, the words foreign on my tongue. A child born from the union of deception and brutality. My mind races, conjuring images of a faceless boy with my eyes and the monster's smile. Does he know about me? Does he wonder why his mother abandoned him?

The weight of this revelation crushes me, and I struggle to breathe. The carefully constructed walls I've built around myself since my return crumble, leaving me exposed and vulnerable. Tears I've held back for years finally break free, cascading down my cheeks in a torrent of anguish and rage.

Through the haze of my pain, I hear footsteps approaching. The sound echoes off the tile floors, growing louder with each passing second. Suddenly, the room fills with a whirlwind of movement and voices.

Zaire is there in an instant, his strong arms enveloping me. His familiar scent surrounds me as he pulls me close. I feel the steady thrum of his heartbeat against my cheek.

"What the fuck happened?" Oscar's voice booms through the room, his usual calm demeanor shattered by the scene before him. His blue eyes, normally so controlled, now blaze with a fury I've never seen before.

Talon stands beside him, his hands clenched into fists, his normally cheerful face twisted with concern and anger.

The tension in the room is palpable, thick enough to choke on.

Alex, his face ashen, steps forward. His voice trembles as he recounts the horrifying truth, the years of lies, the betrayal of my uncle and Bianca, the existence of a son born from my suffering. With each word, Oscar's face grows darker, the veins in his neck pulsing with barely contained rage.

As Alex finishes, a roar of pure, unadulterated anger tears from Oscar's throat. It's a primal sound, filled with pain and promises of vengeance. In three long strides, he reaches Natasha.

Time seems to slow as Oscar's hands grasp Natasha's head. There's a moment of terrible stillness, and then, a sickening crack echoes through the room. Natasha's body crumples, lifeless, onto the table.

Zaire tries to shield my eyes, his large hand covering my face, but it's too late. Through the gaps between his fingers, I see everything. The violence, the finality of it all, burns itself into my retinas. I should feel something, horror, perhaps, or satisfaction, but I'm numb, lost in the storm of my own emotions.

"Take her upstairs," Oscar commands Zaire, his voice low and dangerous. His eyes, when they meet mine, are filled with a mixture of fury and tenderness that makes my heart ache.

As Zaire lifts me into his arms, I catch a glimpse of Talon. He stands guard at the door, his normally jovial face set in grim lines. His eyes meet mine for a brief moment, conveying a silent promise of protection.

Zaire carries me up the staircase, his steps sure and steady, as he makes his way through the living space of the penthouse until he reaches his room, kicking open the door. He lays me gently on the plush comforter, the material cool against my feverish skin. He searches my face desperately. "Vesper," he pleads, his voice cracking with emotion. "Please, say something. Anything."

But words elude me. My mind is a maelstrom of fractured thoughts and raw emotions, each fighting for dominance. It's too much. Too much pain. Too much fear. Too much of everything.

Zaire's warm hand cups my cheek, turning my face towards his. "Come back to me, Vesper," he whispers, before pressing his lips to mine. The kiss is gentle yet insistent, filled with a desperation that threatens to break through the fog enveloping my mind. I feel the warmth of his breath, taste the hint of whiskey on his tongue, but it's not enough to anchor me to reality.

A shadow falls across the room as Oscar appears in the doorway. The soft glow from the bedside lamp catches the crimson droplets on his hands, hands that had just ended a life with terrifying ease. His presence fills the room, a storm barely contained within human form.

"Vesper," Oscar's voice is low, controlled, but I can hear the undercurrent of worry. He approaches the bed, his movements measured and careful, as if afraid of startling me.

His blue eyes, usually so calm and calculating, now swirl with a tempest of emotions; anger, fear, and something deeper, more primal. He reaches out, his bloodstained hand hovering inches from my face, not quite touching.

The door creaks open once more, and Talon slips in. His usual easy grin is nowhere to be seen, replaced by a grim determination. He moves to the foot of the bed, his presence solid and reassuring.

"Hey there, sweetheart," Talon's voice is gentle. "You're scaring us a bit here. How about you come back to the land of the living, yeah?"

But their words wash over me like waves on a distant shore. I'm adrift in an ocean of pain and betrayal, the revelations of the day threatening to pull me under. My son, a living, breathing piece of me out there in the world.

Zaire's composure begins to crumble as he watches me, his eyes darting frantically between my face and the other men in the room. His breathing becomes ragged, chest heaving with each labored inhale. The muscles in his jaw clench and unclench, a visible manifestation of his internal struggle.

"Fuck, fuck, fuck," he mutters, running his hands through his hair, tugging at the dark strands. "This isn't happening. This can't be fucking happening."

Oscar steps closer, placing a steadying hand on his

brother's shoulder. "Z, you need to calm down. We can't help her if we're falling apart ourselves."

But Zaire shakes off Oscar's touch, whirling to face him. His eyes, usually a mirror image of his twin's, now blaze with a wild, almost feral intensity. The ring of blue in his eyes seems to glow in the dim light, giving him an other-worldly appearance.

"Calm down?" Zaire's voice rises, bordering on hysteria. "How the fuck am I supposed to calm down when she's like this?" He gestures wildly towards me, his movements jerky and uncontrolled. "It's worse than when we found her, Oz. At least then she was fighting, screaming, showing some sign of life. This...this is like she's gone. Like they've taken her away again, right in front of our eyes!"

Oscar's face pales at the comparison, his own composure slipping for a moment. He glances at me, and I see the fear flickering in his eyes. "You're right," he admits quietly, "but losing our shit isn't going to bring her back."

Talon moves closer, his imposing frame casting a shadow over the bed. "He's right, Z. We need to keep it together for Vesper."

But Zaire is beyond reason now. His control, always so tenuously maintained, finally snaps. With a roar of frustration and anguish, he slams his fist into the wall, leaving a sizable dent in the plaster. The sound echoes through the room like a gunshot.

In that moment of chaos, something shifts in Zaire's

eyes. The wild panic recedes, replaced by a steely determination. He turns back to me, leaning in close, his face mere inches from mine.

"Vesper," he growls, his voice low and commanding. It's not the voice of the man I've come to know, but something darker, more primal. "Put your fucking eyes on me. Now."

The force of his words cuts through the fog in my mind like a knife. I blink, once, twice, my gaze slowly focusing on his face. The world around me starts to come back – the worried faces of Oscar and Talon, the soft glow of the bedside lamp, the faint scent of Zaire's cologne.

"There you are, moya koroleva."

They all sigh in relief as my eyes finally focus, the fog lifting from my mind like mist dissipating in the morning sun. Zaire kneels before me, his face a canvas of emotions; relief, fear, and an intensity that makes my breath catch in my throat.

"I thought I lost you," he whispers, his voice cracking with the weight of his words. "We all did."

His hand trembles as he reaches out to cup my face, his touch as gentle as a butterfly's wing against my skin. The contrast between this tenderness and the raw power he displayed moments ago sends a shiver down my spine.

Oscar moves closer, his presence solid and reassuring. The blood on his hands has dried to a rusty brown. His blue eyes, usually so guarded, now shine with a vulnerability that makes my heart ache.

Talon exhales loudly, running a hand through his disheveled hair. The tension in his broad shoulders eases slightly, but his stance remains protective, as if expecting danger to burst through the door at any moment.

The room seems to come alive around me, details sharpening into focus. The intricate patterns on the wallpaper swirl and dance in the soft lamplight. The faint scent of sandalwood and leather fills my nostrils, a comforting reminder of where I am.

"Vesper," Oscar's voice is low, almost reverent. He kneels beside Zaire, his eyes searching mine. "Are you with us?"

I nod slowly, feeling as if I'm moving through molasses. My throat feels dry, words sticking like sand. But I force them out, needing to reassure them, to reassure myself.

"I'm here," I croak.

The relief that washes over their faces is palpable. Talon lets out a shaky laugh, the sound breaking the tension in the room.

"Christ, sweetheart," he says, moving closer. "You scared the living daylights out of us."

I try to smile, but it feels more like a grimace. The weight of everything that's happened, everything I've learned, still presses down on me, threatening to drag me under again.

"Tell me what you need, moya koroleva. Give me a purpose."

As I look into Zaire's pleading eyes, something stirs within me. A spark ignites, growing into a flame that threatens to consume everything in its path. The numbness that had enveloped me begins to recede, replaced by a fierce, burning rage.

"My son," I whisper, my voice growing stronger with each word. "I want my son."

The men exchange glances, a mixture of surprise and determination crossing their faces.

"And I want them to pay," I continue, my hands clenching into fists. "My uncle, Bianca. I want them to suffer for what they've done."

Oscar's eyes harden, a cruel smile playing at the corners of his mouth. "Consider it done, my love."

As I speak, images flood my mind, a little boy with my green eyes and a mischievous smile. I imagine his laughter echoing through the halls of this penthouse, his tiny hand clasped in mine as we walk through the park. The thought of him out there, alone and unaware of his mother's existence, fills me with a desperate longing.

"He must be so beautiful," I murmur, more to myself than the others. "Do you think he has my eyes? Or my smile?"

Zaire's grip on my hand tightens. "We'll find out soon enough, moya koroleva. We'll bring him home to you."

The idea of home takes on a new meaning now. It's no longer just a place, but a feeling. The warmth of my son in my arms, the security of these three men surrounding me with their love and protection.

"I want to see the fear in their eyes," I say, surprising

myself with the venom in my voice. "I want them to know what it feels like to be helpless, to have everything they love torn away from them."

Oscar nods, his eyes glinting dangerously. "We'll give you that, Vesper. We'll give you everything."

Chapter 39

OSCAR

I STEP AWAY FROM VESPER, my heart heavy as I leave her in the capable hands of Zaire and Talon. The weight of what I'm about to do settles on my shoulders like a lead blanket. As I move through the dimly lit hallway, the floorboards creaking beneath my feet, I catch sight of Alex emerging from the basement door.

The sight of him stops me dead in my tracks. Alex's shirt is stained with Natasha's blood. His face is a mask of grim determination, but I can see the slight tremor in his hands as he wipes them on a handkerchief. When we'd left him downstairs, there wasn't a drop on him.

"Alex," I call out. He looks up, his eyes meeting mine.

"It's taken care of," he mutters on instinct. "The chemicals are working right now."

"Good," I remark. "But, we need to make a call," I say, closing the distance between us. The metallic scent of blood clings to him, making my stomach churn. "I need you to find the right number."

Alex nods, understanding the gravity of what I'm asking without needing further explanation. We've reached a point of no return, and this call will set in motion events that will change everything.

As we move towards Alex's room where his tech toys live, I can't help but glance back towards the room where I left Vesper. The muffled sounds of Zaire's reassuring murmurs and Talon's soft laughter drift down the hallway. For a moment, I allow myself to imagine a different world—one where we're not caught in this web of violence and deceit.

But that world doesn't exist for us. Not yet.

Alex nods solemnly, his eyes reflecting a mixture of determination and apprehension as we enter his room. Walls lined with monitors cast an eerie blue glow across our faces, the soft hum of multiple computers creating a white noise that seems to isolate us from the outside world.

With practiced ease, Alex slides into his chair, fingers flying across the keyboard. The screens before us come alive with scrolling data, each keystroke bringing us closer to our target. I lean against the desk, my eyes fixed on the digital labyrinth unfolding before us.

"Who am I looking for, Oscar?" Alex asks, his voice barely audible over the rhythmic tapping of keys.

I take a deep breath, the name feeling like lead on my tongue. "Mario Rossi."

Alex's fingers freeze mid-air, his head snapping towards me, eyes wide with disbelief. "Are you sure that's the right move?"

I meet his gaze steadily, the weight of my decision evident in my voice. "It's the only move, Alex. He's taken two years of Vesper's life away from her, and a son. The path to getting her son back starts with him."

Alex holds my stare for a moment longer, searching for any hint of doubt. Finding none, he turns back to his screens, fingers resuming their frantic dance across the keyboard. "Alright," he mutters, "but this is playing with fire, Oz. You know that, right?"

I nod, even though he can't see me. "Sometimes you have to fight fire with fire."

The room falls silent save for the clicking of keys and the low hum of machinery. Minutes stretch like hours as Alex works his digital magic, navigating through encrypted networks and hidden databases. Finally, a triumphant "Got it!" breaks the tension.

Alex swivels in his chair, reaching for a nondescript box on his cluttered desk. From it, he produces a sleek burner phone, its screen dark and lifeless, a blank slate waiting to become the conduit for a conversation that could change everything.

As he hands me the phone, our eyes meet once more. In that moment, I see the gravity of our situation reflected in Alex's gaze. We're about to cross a line, one that we can never uncross. But for Vesper, for her son, it's a risk we have to take.

I take the phone, its weight feeling far heavier than it should. As my thumb hovers over the power button, I can almost hear the gears of fate grinding into motion. Whatever happens next, there's no going back.

With a deep breath, I press the button, ready to set my plan into motion. The phone rings once, twice, three times. Each ring feels like an eternity, the tension in the room thickening with every passing second. On the fourth ring, a gruff voice answers, the sound of it sending a chill down my spine.

"Rossi." The voice is gravelly, laced with suspicion and a hint of irritation.

I take a deep breath, steeling myself for what's to come. "Mario Rossi," I say, my voice steady despite the rapid beating of my heart, "this is Oscar Petrov."

"How the fuck did you get this number?" he hisses.

"I have my ways," I sneer back at him. "We need to meet."

"I'm afraid you've caught me at a bad time. I'm far too busy to entertain outcasts from the Petrov family."

His dismissive tone ignites a fire in my chest. I grip the phone tighter, my knuckles turning white. "Is that so?" I reply, my voice dripping with sarcasm. "Too busy to discuss how you've managed to provide a fraud as a bride for Victor Petrov's son?"

The silence that follows is deafening. I can almost hear the gears turning in Mario's head, his breath catching ever so slightly. When he speaks again, his voice has lost its casual indifference, replaced by a razor-sharp edge.

"What did you say?" he hisses, the threat in his tone unmistakable.

"I think you heard me quite clearly."

"You're treading on dangerous ground, boy," he growls. "Do you have any idea what you're accusing me of?"

I let out a dry laugh. "Oh, I have more than an idea, Mario. I have proof. And I think it's time we had a face-to-face chat about it, don't you?"

"You're playing a dangerous game, boy," Mario growls, but I can hear the undercurrent of uncertainty in his voice.

"Perhaps," I concede. "But it's a game I'm willing to play. The question is, are you willing to risk everything on the chance that I'm bluffing?"

There's another pause, longer this time. I can almost hear the wheels of Mario's mind spinning, weighing his options, calculating the risks. When he speaks again, his voice is low, almost a whisper.

"Where and when?"

"Tomorrow. I'll come to you. It's best we have this

conversation away from prying ears, don't you think? I mean, if I handed off a fake to my uncle, I don't think I would want that kind of information moving through the gossip grapevine."

"Fine. Three o'clock. Come alone."

The line goes dead, Mario's abrupt hang-up punctuating our conversation like a thunderclap. I lower the phone, a mixture of adrenaline and anticipation coursing through my veins. The air in the room feels charged, electric with the weight of what we've just set in motion.

Alex's face breaks into a slow, calculated smile. His eyes dance with a mixture of excitement and apprehension. "We're making our move, huh?" he asks as if speaking any louder might shatter the delicate balance we've just tipped.

I nod, my jaw set with determination. "Yes," I reply, my voice steady despite the storm of emotions swirling inside me. "The first of many."

Alex's fingers are already flying across his keyboard, screens flickering to life with satellite imagery and blue-prints. "I'll get eyes on the Rossi Mansion," he says, his focus laser-sharp. "By tomorrow, we'll know every entrance, exit, and blind spot."

I clap him on the shoulder, a gesture of gratitude and camaraderie. "Good work, Alex. Keep me posted."

Leaving Alex's tech sanctuary, I make my way back through the dimly lit hallway, the floorboards creaking beneath my feet like old bones shifting in their sleep. The warehouse seems to hold its breath, aware of the momentous events unfolding within its walls.

I pause outside Zaire's room, my hand hovering over the doorknob. Taking a deep breath, I steel myself and push the door open.

Zaire is stretched out on his king-size bed, his long frame relaxed against the plush pillows. Vesper is nestled in his arms, her golden hair spilling across his chest like liquid sunshine. The sight of her, safe and protected, sends a wave of relief through me.

Talon has moved to a plush armchair in the corner of the room, his legs draped casually over one arm. His eyes, usually dancing with mischief, are now sharp and alert, watching me intently as I enter.

As the door clicks shut behind me, three pairs of eyes turn to me, filled with questions and expectations. The air in the room shifts, charged with anticipation.

"We're meeting with Mario Rossi tomorrow."

Vesper gasps, her body tensing in Zaire's arms. Zaire's grip on her tightens instinctively, his eyes narrowing as he processes the information. Talon leans forward in his chair, all traces of casualness gone from his posture.

"You've set the wheels in motion," Zaire says, his voice a mix of admiration and concern. "Thanks for including us in the decision."

I nod, feeling the weight of my decision settle on my shoulders like a mantle. "I have," I confirm, my voice steady despite the turmoil inside me. "There's no point in waiting any longer. Not after everything that's happened."

Vesper's eyes, those mesmerizing pools of green that have haunted my dreams for years, lock onto mine. In them, I see a whirlwind of emotions; fear, hope, determination, and something else, something that makes my heart skip a beat.

"Oscar," she whispers, her voice barely audible above the hum of the old air conditioning unit. "What are you planning to do?"

I move closer, kneeling beside the bed so that we're at eye level. Her vanilla scent envelops me, grounding me in this moment. I take a deep breath, steeling myself for what I'm about to say.

"What you asked me to do, solnishko," I reply, using the Russian endearment that feels so natural on my tongue when addressing her. "Your uncle is just the start."

The room falls silent, the air thick with tension and unspoken promises. Zaire's arm tightens around Vesper's waist, a protective gesture that I can't help but appreciate. Talon leans forward, his usually carefree demeanor replaced by an intensity that reminds me why he's such a valuable member of our team.

"Every person who had a hand in taking your son, every individual who profited from your pain, every single one of them will face justice. We'll dismantle their empires brick by brick, expose their secrets, and leave them with nothing but the ashes of their former glory."

Vesper's breath hitches, her eyes glistening with unshed tears. I reach out, gently cupping her face in my hands. "We won't stop until you have your revenge, Vesper. Until your son is in your arms where he belongs."

The room seems to pulse with energy, the air crackling with the intensity of our shared determination. Zaire's eyes meet mine over Vesper's head, a silent agreement passing between us. Talon rises from his chair, moving to stand beside the bed, his presence a solid pillar of support.

"It won't be easy," Talon says, his voice uncharacteristically serious. "We'll be making enemies of some of the most powerful families in the world."

I nod, acknowledging the truth in his words. "I know. But we have something they don't. We have a cause worth fighting for, a purpose that goes beyond power and greed."

Vesper's hand finds mine, her grip tight and desperate. "I'm not sure you should do this. You're risking everything."

I bring her hand to my lips, pressing a gentle kiss to them. "For you, solnishko. I would watch the world burn just to spare you a single second of pain."

"So would I," Zaire adds, pressing a kiss to the top of her head. "You have fought against your nightmares and stitched your soul back together again. I won't let anyone take that away from you."

"Fuck the families," Talon adds in.

"Fuck the families," Zaire repeats. "I promised you, moya koroleva, not another single fucking tear."

Vesper's eyes widen, a mix of emotions swirling in their

emerald depths. Her gaze flicks between me, Zaire, and Talon, her breath quickening. Slowly, she shifts in Zaire's arms, her movements deliberate and graceful. The soft rustle of fabric against skin fills the room as she leans towards me, her golden hair cascading over her shoulder like a waterfall of sunlight.

Her hand, warm and soft, cups my cheek. I can feel the slight tremor in her fingers, betraying the intensity of her emotions. Her lips part slightly, her breath warm against my skin as she draws closer. Time seems to slow, the world narrowing to just this moment, just us.

When her lips meet mine, it's like a supernova exploding in my chest. The kiss is soft at first, tentative, but quickly deepens with a hunger that takes my breath away. Her lips are velvet against mine. My hands find their way to her waist, pulling her closer as the kiss intensifies.

The room around us fades away, the only reality that matters is the feel of Vesper in my arms, the taste of her on my lips. It's everything I've dreamed of and more, a perfect moment crystallized in time.

As we part, both breathless, Vesper's eyes are dark with desire. She turns back to Zaire, who's watching us with a mixture of heat and admiration in his gaze. Without hesitation, she leans in, capturing his lips in a kiss that's just as passionate, just as all-consuming.

Zaire's hands tangle in her hair, holding her close as they lose themselves in each other. The sight of them together, so beautiful and passionate, sends a jolt of electricity through me. It's not jealousy I feel, but a deep, primal satisfaction. This is right. This is how it should be.

From the corner of my eye, I see Talon shift uncomfortably, moving towards the door. But before he can leave, Vesper breaks away from Zaire, her voice husky as she calls out, "Talon, stay. Please."

Talon freezes, his hand on the doorknob. He turns slowly, his eyes seeking mine and Zaire's, a question clear in his gaze. Zaire and I exchange a look, a silent conversation passing between us in a heartbeat.

"She asked you nicely," Zaire says, his voice rough with desire but firm with conviction. "Stay."

I nod in agreement, extending a hand towards Talon in invitation. "You're part of this too, Talon. If you want to be."

Talon approaches the bed, his eyes dark with desire. Vesper reaches out, pulling him close. Their lips meet in a fiery kiss, passionate and urgent. As they part, Vesper's gaze flicks between the three of us, her chest rising and falling rapidly.

"Please," she breathes, her voice husky with need. "I don't know why. Maybe something cracked in my head over the last two years. For the first time in my life, I know what I want."

"What do you want?" I ask her.

"All of you." Her voice is quiet and unsure.

"Are you asking or declaring, moya koroleva? There's a difference."

She carefully considers his question before she smiles. "I want this. All of you. I don't know how any of this will work, but I want this. How does this work…I've never…"

"We'll figure it out as we go." Zaire's eyes darken with understanding. He nods slowly, a predatory smile curving his lips. "Strip, moya koroleva," he commands softly. "Leave only your panties."

Vesper's breath catches, but she obeys without hesitation. She shifts to her feet. Her fingers tremble slightly as she unbuttons her blouse, revealing smooth skin inch by tantalizing inch. The silky fabric whispers as it falls to the floor, followed by her skirt. She stands before us in nothing but a delicate lace bra and matching panties, her skin glowing in the soft light.

Three pairs of eyes drink in the sight of her, tracing the curves of her body with hungry gazes. Vesper's chest rises and falls rapidly, her excitement palpable in the charged atmosphere of the room.

Talon's eyes are wide, his lips parted slightly as he stares at Vesper. A low growl escapes him, almost involuntary. Zaire notices, a smirk playing on his lips.

"See something you like, T?" Zaire asks, his voice low and teasing.

Talon swallows hard, his eyes never leaving Vesper's form. "She's breathtaking," he manages, his voice rough with desire.

Vesper blushes under the intensity of their gazes, her skin flushing a delicate pink. She reaches behind her back, unclasping her bra with practiced ease. As the lace falls away, revealing her perfect breasts, Talon lets out a strangled groan.

"Come here, moya koroleva," Zaire beckons, his voice thick with need.

Vesper moves towards Zaire with a grace that belies her nervousness, her hips swaying hypnotically. Zaire's eyes darken as she approaches, his gaze roaming hungrily over her exposed skin. When she reaches the edge of the bed, he reaches out, his large hands spanning her waist, pulling her closer.

"Beautiful," he murmurs, his voice a low rumble that sends shivers down Vesper's spine. His thumbs trace slow circles on her hips, just above the lacy edge of her panties. "Turn around, moya koroleva. Let us all appreciate you."

Vesper complies, turning slowly. The room is silent save for the collective intake of breath as we drink in the sight of her. The curve of her spine, the swell of her hips, the cascade of golden hair falling over her shoulders. Every inch of her is perfection.

Zaire's hands never leave her body as she turns, tracing the contours of her waist, her hips, her thighs. When she faces him again, his eyes are molten with desire. Without warning, he pulls her onto the bed, eliciting a surprised gasp that quickly turns into a moan as his lips find her neck.

He kisses a blazing trail down her throat, his teeth grazing her collarbone. Vesper arches into him, her fingers tangling in his dark hair. Zaire's hands roam her body, mapping every curve, every dip, as if committing her to memory through touch alone.

His lips travel lower, peppered kisses across her chest before capturing a nipple in his mouth. Vesper cries out, her back arching off the bed as Zaire lavishes attention on her breasts, alternating between gentle kisses and playful nips that leave her gasping.

Zaire's hand slides down Vesper's stomach, his fingers toying with the waistband of her panties. He looks up at her, his eyes seeking permission. Vesper nods frantically, her hips lifting off the bed in a silent plea.

With agonizing slowness, Zaire peels the lace down her legs, revealing her most intimate parts to our hungry gazes. He tosses the garment aside, his hands returning to caress her thighs, spreading them gently.

"Look at her," Zaire says, his voice rough with desire. "Have you ever seen anything so perfect?"

Talon and I can only shake our heads, words failing us in the face of such beauty. Vesper blushes under our collective gaze.

Zaire's eyes lock onto Vesper's, a predatory gleam in their depths. His hands slide up her thighs, thumbs tracing tantalizing circles on her inner legs. Vesper's breath comes in short gasps, her body trembling with anticipation.

"So beautiful," Zaire murmurs, his voice low and husky.

He lowers his head, pressing a soft kiss to her inner thigh. Vesper whimpers, her hips lifting slightly off the bed.

Zaire chuckles, the sound vibrating against her sensitive skin.

"Patience, moya koroleva," he whispers, his breath hot against her core.

He works her with his mouth, alternating between long, languid strokes and quick flicks that leave her gasping. His hands grip her thighs, holding her in place as she writhes beneath him.

Zaire's tongue circles her clit, applying just the right amount of pressure to drive her wild. Vesper's back arches off the bed, a string of incoherent pleas falling from her lips.

"That's it," I murmur, my voice rough with desire. "Let go for us."

As if my words were the key to her release, Vesper cries out, her body tensing as waves of pleasure wash over her. Zaire doesn't let up, working her through her orgasm until she's trembling and oversensitive.

When he finally lifts his head, his lips are glistening with her essence. He looks up at her, a satisfied smirk on his face. "Delicious," he purrs, licking his lips.

Vesper lies there, panting, her skin flushed and glistening with a light sheen of sweat. She looks utterly debauched and incredibly beautiful.

Zaire crawls up her body, pressing kisses to her stomach, her breasts, her neck, before finally capturing her lips in a searing kiss. Vesper moans, tasting herself on his tongue.

As they part, Zaire's eyes find mine, then Talon's. The

look in them is clear; an invitation, a challenge, a promise of more to come.

"Who's next?" he asks, his voice thick with desire and anticipation.

I look at Talon, whose eyes are dark with desire, his chest heaving with each breath. He's been watching intently, his hands clenched at his sides in an effort to maintain control. But the tension in his body is evident, he's like a coiled spring, ready to snap at any moment.

Zaire notices too, a knowing smirk playing on his lips. He turns to Vesper, who's still flushed and panting from her recent climax. "Look what you've done to him, moya koroleva," he murmurs, nodding towards Talon.

Vesper's gaze follows Zaire's, her eyes widening as they land on the prominent bulge straining against Talon's pants. The fabric is stretched tight, leaving little to the imagination.

"He's been so patient," Zaire continues, his voice low and seductive. "Don't you think he deserves a reward?"

Vesper nods, her tongue darting out to wet her lips. She sits up slowly, her movements languid and sensual. Her golden hair cascades over her shoulders, framing her naked breasts.

Talon's breath catches as Vesper's crawls toward the edge of the bed. She stops just in front of him, close enough that he can feel the heat radiating from her body. Her hands hover over his waistband, her eyes seeking permission.

Talon nods, unable to form words. Vesper's fingers make quick work of his belt, the soft clink of metal the only sound in the room. She pops the button of his jeans open, then slowly, torturously, drags the zipper down.

Talon hisses as the pressure on his cock eases slightly. Vesper hooks her fingers into his waistband, tugging his jeans and boxers down in one smooth motion. His erection springs free, hard and proud, the tip glistening with precum.

Vesper's eyes widen appreciatively, her tongue darting out to wet her lips once more. She wraps one hand around his length, her touch feather-light. Talon groans, his hips jerking involuntarily.

"Patience," Vesper whispers, echoing Zaire's earlier words. Her hand begins to move, stroking him with agonizing slowness. She twists her wrist on the upstroke, her thumb swiping over his sensitive head, spreading the moisture gathered there.

Talon's head falls back, his eyes squeezing shut as he fights for control. His hands clench and unclench at his sides, unsure where to settle.

"You can touch me, you know," she purrs. "I want you to."

With a groan, Talon's hands pull her closer. Vesper's lips part, her tongue darting out to taste the glistening tip of Talon's cock. He groans deeply as she takes him into her mouth, her lips stretching around his impressive girth. Her golden hair cascades forward as she begins to bob her head, taking him deeper with each pass. Talon's hands tangle in her silky locks, not guiding, just holding on as if she's his lifeline in a storm of pleasure. His breath comes in ragged gasps punctuated by low moans of appreciation.

The erotic sight before me is too much to bear. My clothes feel constricting, my skin too hot. With trembling hands, I strip, my eyes never leaving Vesper's form. She's a vision of sensuality, her back arched beautifully as she pleasures Talon. She came to us so broken that a part of me worried that she would never regain her strength, but fuck, to watch her as she is right now, it makes all those nightmares I chased away worth it.

I crawl across the bed, the mattress dipping under my weight.

Talon's sole focus is on her that he barely notices me dragging her from the edge of the bed onto her hands and knees. His cock never leaving her mouth for a second. Vesper widens her stance slightly, an invitation I can't resist. My hands find her hips, fingers digging into the soft flesh as I position myself behind her. I run the head of my cock through her folds, coating myself in her arousal. She's so wet, so ready for me. With a groan, I push inside her, reveling in the tight, wet heat that envelops me.

Vesper moans around Talon's cock, the vibrations making him curse softly. The sound spurs me on, and I begin to move, setting a steady rhythm that pushes Vesper forward with each thrust.

The room fills with the sounds of our fucking; skin against skin, muffled moans, and breathless gasps. Zaire watches from the side, his eyes dark with lust as he strokes himself inside his pants slowly.

I increase my pace, driving deeper into Vesper. Each thrust pushes her further onto Talon's cock, taking him deeper into her throat. Talon's grip on her hair tightens, his hips beginning to move in counterpoint to my thrusts.

Vesper is caught between us, filled from both ends, and she's glorious in her pleasure. Her body trembles, small whimpers escaping her occupied mouth as we drive her higher and higher. Her hand reaches out, grasping blindly for Zaire. He shifts closer, understanding her unspoken desire. In one fluid motion, he pulls out his impressive length, already hard and glistening with anticipation.

Vesper's eyes widen at the sight, a muffled moan escaping her lips as she takes in the sight of Zaire's cock. Without missing a beat, she wraps her free hand around him, her delicate fingers barely meeting around his girth.

The contrast is mesmerizing. Her golden skin against Zaire's olive tone, her small hand working his impressive length. She begins to stroke him in time with her movements on Talon, creating a rhythm that has both men groaning in pleasure.

I watch, transfixed, as Vesper alternates between them. She pulls back from Talon with a wet pop, her lips swollen and glistening. Without hesitation, she turns her attention to Zaire, taking him into her mouth with a hunger that makes my hips stutter in their rhythm.

Her tongue swirls around Zaire's tip, tracing the prominent vein on the underside before taking him deeper. All the while, her hand continues to work Talon, her grip firm and sure as she pumps him in long, steady strokes.

The sight before me is intoxicating. Vesper is lost in pleasure servicing two men with an enthusiasm that takes my breath away. Her body moves sinuously between them, her back arching beautifully as she takes me deeper with each thrust.

Zaire's hand tangles in her hair, guiding her movements as she works him with her mouth. His eyes are half-lidded with pleasure, his chest heaving with each ragged breath. "That's it, moya koroleva," he growls, his voice rough with desire. "Just like that."

Vesper moans around him, the vibrations causing Zaire to curse softly under his breath. She pulls back, her tongue flicking out to taste the bead of precum at his tip before turning her attention back to Talon.

Talon's head is thrown back, his strong jaw clenched as he fights for control. Vesper takes him deep, her throat working around him as she swallows. Her hand never stops moving on Zaire, maintaining a steady rhythm that has him panting with need.

The air is thick with the scent of sex and sweat, creating an intoxicating atmosphere that only fuels our desire.

I can feel the tension building in my core, my thrusts becoming more erratic as I chase my release. Vesper's inner walls flutter around me, a telltale sign that she's close too. I reach around, my fingers finding her swollen clit, circling it in time with my thrusts.

Talon's breath comes in ragged gasps, his muscles tensing as he nears his peak. His fingers tighten in Vesper's hair, guiding her movements as she works him with her mouth. "Fuck, Vesper," he groans, his voice strained. "I'm close. Drink me down, baby. All of it."

With a guttural moan, Talon finds his release. Vesper's throat works as she swallows, her eyes locked on his face, drinking in the sight of his pleasure as eagerly as she drinks his seed. Not a drop escapes her lips as she milks him through his orgasm, her tongue swirling around his sensitive tip until he shudders from overstimulation.

Talon stumbles back, his legs weak, collapsing into the chair he occupied earlier. His chest heaves as he catches his breath, a look of sated bliss on his face.

Zaire's eyes meet mine over Vesper's shoulder, a silent communication passing between us. With a slight nod, I understand his intention. Slowly, regretfully, I pull out of Vesper's welcoming heat, eliciting a whimper of loss from her.

Zaire moves with fluid grace, shifting to lean back against the headboard. "Come here, moya koroleva," he purrs, his voice thick with desire. His hands find Vesper's hips, guiding her to straddle him.

Vesper moves eagerly, her body trembling with need. She positions herself over Zaire's impressive length, her eyes locked on his as she slowly sinks down. A long, low moan escapes her as she takes him in, her back arching beautifully as she's filled to the brim.

I watch, mesmerized, as Vesper begins to move. Her hips roll in a hypnotic rhythm, taking Zaire deeper with each downward stroke. The sight of them together is breathtaking.

Zaire's eyes find mine again, and he gives me a slight nod. Understanding floods through me, sending a fresh wave of heat coursing through my veins. My heart pounds as I move into position, straddling Zaire's legs behind Vesper.

"Oscar," Zaire's voice is rough with desire, "show our girl what she's been missing."

Vesper's movements falter, her breath catching as she realizes what's about to happen. She turns her head, her eyes meeting mine over her shoulder. The look she gives me is a heady mix of desire, anticipation, and a hint of nervousness.

I lean in, pressing a soft kiss to her shoulder. "Relax, solnishko," I murmur against her skin. "We've got you."

My hands caress her hips as I position myself behind her. Vesper's breath comes in short, excited gasps as she feels the tip of my cock pressing against her entrance, already stretched around Zaire's impressive girth.

"Breathe, moya koroleva," Zaire murmurs, his hands stroking her sides soothingly. "Nice and slow."

I push forward gradually, giving Vesper time to adjust.

The sensation is indescribable, the incredible tightness, and the heat.

Vesper cries out, her body trembling. "Oh god," she gasps. "It's so much. You're both so big."

I freeze, not wanting to hurt her. "Do you need us to stop, solnishko?" I ask, pressing gentle kisses to her shoulder.

"You can invoke your safe word. You do that and we stop," Zaire adds.

She shakes her head frantically. "No, don't stop. Please. I need this. I need you both. All of you."

Encouraged by her words, I continue to push forward, inch by exquisite inch. Vesper's breath comes in short, sharp pants, her fingers digging into Zaire's shoulders as she adjusts to the intense stretch.

Finally, after what feels like an eternity, I'm fully sheathed inside her. We all pause, panting, overwhelmed by the intensity of the moment. Vesper is sandwiched between us, filled more completely than she's ever been before.

"You're doing so well," Zaire praises, his voice strained with the effort of holding still. "You feel incredible, moya koroleva."

I nod in agreement, unable to form words. The sensation of being inside Vesper, feeling Zaire's cock pressed against mine, is almost too much to bear.

Slowly, carefully, I begin to move. The friction is incredible, sending sparks of pleasure shooting through my body. Vesper whimpers, her head falling back against my shoulder as she's consumed by sensation.

We find a rhythm, Zaire and I moving in tandem. As I pull back, he pushes in, ensuring Vesper is constantly filled. The room fills with the sounds of our collective pleasure, skin against skin, breathless moans, and whispered words of encouragement.

Vesper is lost in a haze of ecstasy, her body trembling between us. Her inner walls flutter and clench around us, drawing groans from both Zaire and me. The sight of her, caught between us, her face contorted in pleasure, is the most erotic thing I've ever seen.

"That's it, moya koroleva," Zaire growls, his voice rough with desire. "Take us both. You're doing so well."

I increase my pace slightly, driving deeper. The change in angle has Vesper crying out, her nails digging into Zaire's shoulders. "Oh god," she gasps. "It's too much. I can't...I can't..."

"You can," Zaire reassures her, his hands cupping her face tenderly. "Let go, moya koroleva. We've got you."

I lean in, my chest pressed against her back, surrounding her completely. "Come for us, solnishko," I murmur in her ear. "Show us how good we make you feel."

With a keening cry, Vesper shatters. Her body goes rigid between us, her inner walls clamping down with incredible force. The sensation is overwhelming, pushing both Zaire and me to the edge.

Zaire's eyes meet mine over Vesper's shoulder, a silent understanding passing between us. With a final, powerful thrust, we both find our release, our cries of pleasure mingling with Vesper's as we fill her completely.

The world seems to fade away, narrowing down to just the three of us, connected in the most intimate way possible. Time loses all meaning as we ride out the waves of our shared climax, our bodies moving together in perfect harmony. We collapse onto the bed in a tangle of limbs, panting heavily. Vesper lies between us, her body still trembling with aftershocks, a look of utter bliss on her face.

Vesper lies between us, her chest rising and falling rapidly as she catches her breath. Her golden hair is splayed across the pillow, tangled and wild from our lovemaking. Her skin glows with a light sheen of perspiration, making her look ethereal in the soft light.

I'm the first to move, pressing a gentle kiss to her shoulder before carefully extricating myself from our tangle of limbs. Vesper whimpers softly at the loss of contact, her hand reaching out blindly for me.

"Shh, solnishko," I murmur, stroking her cheek tenderly. "I'll be right back."

I pad quietly to the ensuite bathroom, my legs still a bit shaky from the intensity of our encounter. The cool tiles feel soothing against my feet as I gather what we need for aftercare. I wet a soft washcloth with warm water, grab a couple of fluffy towels, and return to the bedroom.

Zaire has shifted slightly, cradling Vesper against his chest. His large hand strokes her back in soothing circles, his lips pressed against her temple as he murmurs soft words of praise and comfort. Talon has moved closer, perched on the edge of the bed, his hand resting gently on Vesper's ankle.

I settle back onto the bed, the mattress dipping slightly under my weight. With infinite care, I begin to clean Vesper, the warm washcloth gliding over her sensitive skin. She sighs contentedly, her body relaxing further under my ministrations.

"How are you feeling, moya koroleva?" Zaire asks, his voice a low rumble in the quiet room.

Vesper stirs, her eyes fluttering open. A slow, satisfied smile spreads across her face. "Incredible," she murmurs, her voice husky from use. "I feel whole for the first time in my life."

"Good," Zaire smiles. "Hold onto that feeling, moya koroleva. We're all going to need it tomorrow."

Chapter 40

I LEAN BACK against the plush leather seat, sandwiched between Oscar and Zaire as our sleek black SUV winds through the bustling streets of Boston. The events of last night play through my mind like a fever dream. Oscar's hand rests on my thigh, his touch both possessive and comforting. I glance at him, taking in his sharp profile and the way his blue eyes scan the passing scenery with calculated precision. Last night, those same eyes burned with passion as he mapped every inch of my body with his lips.

On my other side, Zaire's muscular arm presses against mine, his warmth seeping through the thin fabric of my dress. The memory of his calloused hands on my skin, the gentle way he traced my curves despite his rough exterior, sends a flush creeping up my neck.

In the front seat, Alex is behind the wheel while Talon fidgets with his suit jacket, adjusting it to conceal the arsenal he carries in the passenger seat. His brown eyes meet mine over his shoulder, a playful glint dancing in them as if he can read my thoughts. The ghost of his touch lingers on my skin, recalling how he effortlessly lifted me, his strength both thrilling and reassuring.

The four of them fit together in my life like pieces of an intricate puzzle, each filling a void I hadn't realized existed. Oscar, with his strategic mind and unwavering loyalty grounds me. Zaire's fierce protectiveness and hidden tenderness give me a sense of security I've never known. And Talon, with his easy charm and lethal skills reminds me that life can be both dangerous and exhilarating. Though with Alex, I am still trying to figure him out. He'd been so open with me about his past, but he's kept me at arm's length so far.

"You nervous about heading back to the Rossi mansion?" Oscar's voice breaks through my reverie, his tone laced with concern.

I take a deep breath, the scent of leather and cologne filling my lungs. "Yes and no," I reply. "It's strange. That place was never really home, you know?"

The word 'home' feels foreign on my tongue, a concept

I've only recently begun to understand. I look around at the four men surrounding me, each one a pillar of strength in their own right and realize that home isn't a place—it's a feeling.

"I never knew love there," I continue, the words tumbling out before I can stop them. "Not like I have now."

Talon's eyebrows shoot up on in the rear view mirror. "Did you just drop the L-bomb? Should we be planning a group wedding?"

I roll my eyes but can't help the smile tugging at my lips. "Shut up, Talon. You know what I mean."

Zaire chuckles, the sound rumbling through his chest and into my side. "Leave her alone, T. We all know you're just as smitten."

"I would like the record to state that I called the love square," Alex chimes in.

The SUV falls into a comfortable silence as we continue our journey. I watch the familiar streets pass by memories of my childhood flashing before my eyes. The pristine lawns and towering mansions of my old neighborhood feel cold and unwelcoming now.

As we approach the iron gates of the Rossi estate, I feel Oscar's hand tighten on my thigh. I place my hand over his, our fingers intertwining. "It's okay," I murmur, more to myself than to him. "We're here together."

The gates swing open, revealing the sprawling mansion that once held so much power over me. Its imposing facade no longer instills fear in my heart. Instead, I feel a surge of determination. I'm not the same girl who left this place, desperate for escape. I'm stronger now, surrounded by love and loyalty I never thought possible.

Talon's keen eyes sweep across the manicured lawns and ornate fountains, searching for any sign of danger. After a tense moment, he nods, his shoulders relaxing slightly. "All clear," he murmurs, his voice low and reassuring.

"Where are his guards?" I comment, noting the lack of security around the entrance or at the gate when we passed. When this was our family home, Father had a small army to protect our family.

"They're here," Oscar states, scanning the property. "He would never meet with me without them close enough to make himself feel safe, but considering why I called the meeting, he might have sent them away. Secrets like this are hard to keep with so many ears to hear them."

Oscar's hand finds the small of my back as he helps me out of the SUV. The gravel crunches beneath my heels, the sound echoing in the eerie silence that blankets the estate. As I stand, smoothing down my designer dress, an armor of silk and lace, Oscar leans in close, his breath warm against my ear.

"Whatever happens in there, Vesper," he whispers, his blue eyes intense and unwavering, "if anything goes wrong, we'll get you out. No matter what."

The determination in his voice should be comforting,

but instead, it sets my nerves on edge. What does he know that I don't? What are they expecting to happen behind those imposing mahogany doors?

We begin our ascent up the grand marble steps, my footsteps echo against the stone in a rhythm that feels like a countdown. The men form a protective square around me, Oscar to my right, Zaire to my left, Talon and Alex bringing up the rear. Their presence is both comforting and suffocating, a reminder of the danger we might be walking into.

As we approach the massive double doors, I can't help but notice how the brass knockers gleam in the afternoon sun, polished to perfection, just like everything else in my father's world. The perfect facade hiding the rottenness within.

Oscar pauses at the threshold, his hand hovering over one of the knockers. He glances back at us, a mischievous glint in his eyes despite the tension. "Should we knock?" he asks, his tone light but underlined with caution. "Wouldn't want to be rude to our gracious hosts."

Before anyone can answer, Zaire steps forward, his tattooed hand reaching for the ornate handle. Without hesitation, he turns it and pushes the door open. The heavy wood swings inward with an ominous creak that seems to reverberate through my very bones.

"No need for formalities," Zaire growls, his voice low and dangerous. "We're family, after all."

As the door opens wider, revealing the opulent foyer

beyond, I take a deep breath. The familiar scent of lemon polish and old money assaults my senses, bringing with it a flood of memories, some tender, most painful. I steel myself, drawing strength from the four men surrounding me.

We step over the threshold together, a united front entering the lion's den. The click of the door closing behind us sounds like the sealing of a tomb. The entrance looks much the same as it did when I walked out of the door two years ago. The grand foyer stretches before us, a testament to opulence and old money. Gleaming marble floors reflect the soft light from the crystal chandelier hanging overhead, each facet catching and scattering rainbows across the room. The sweeping staircase, with its intricately carved mahogany banister, curves gracefully upward, leading to the second floor where so many of my childhood memories—both cherished and painful—reside.

My eyes are drawn to the top of the stairs, where a familiar gilded frame hangs. But the faces staring back at me are not the ones I expect. Instead of my father's stern visage and my mother's forced smile, I see my uncle's family portrait. A portrait of fucking lies.

My breath catches in my throat as I take in the scene. My uncle stands tall and proud, his hand resting on the shoulder of his wife, who sits primarily in an antique chair. Bianca sits next to her mother. It's a vision of familial harmony, of strength and unity. But I know better. The portrait is a masterpiece of deception, each brushstroke carefully crafted to hide the rot beneath the surface. A wave of nausea washes over me as I stare at this visual representation of my uncle's coup. This is more than just a change in decor—it's a statement. A declaration that the old order has fallen, and a new regime has taken its place.

I feel Oscar's hand on the small of my back, a gentle pressure grounding me in the present. Zaire shifts beside me, his body coiled with tension as if ready to spring into action at any moment. Talon's eyes dart around the room, cataloging every potential threat and exit point.

"Well, I guess some things do change."

As I stand there, surrounded by the men who have become my chosen family, I realize that while the house may look the same, I am not. I am no longer the scared girl who fled this place two years ago. I am Vesper Rossi, and I have returned to reclaim what is rightfully mine.

I lead our group down the familiar corridor. The portraits of Rossi patriarchs lining the walls seem to watch us with judging eyes, their painted gazes following our every move. The air grows heavy with tension as we approach my father's, no, my uncle's, study.

Oscar moves ahead, his hand brushing against mine in a brief, reassuring touch before he steps forward to open the heavy mahogany door. The polished handle gleams under the soft light of the wall sconces, and for a moment, I'm transported back to countless childhood memories of standing before this very door, heart pounding, waiting to be summoned inside.

Oscar pushes the door open, revealing the room beyond.

Talon follows close behind, his eyes scanning every corner, every shadow. I can almost see the gears turning in his head as he assesses potential threats and escape routes.

With Zaire and Alex flanking me, their presence solid and comforting at my back, I step into the study. The scent of leather-bound books and expensive cigars washes over me, so achingly familiar it makes my chest tighten. The room is bathed in the warm glow of the afternoon sun filtering through the floor-to-ceiling windows, casting long shadows across the intricately patterned Persian rug.

My eyes are immediately drawn to the massive mahogany desk that dominates the room. It's the same desk I remember from my childhood, its surface scarred with countless memories. But the man sitting behind it is not my father.

"I thought you said you were coming alone, Petrov," my uncle's gruff voice snarls.

I step out from behind the protective wall of my men and show myself. "Well, when you've been held captive for the last two years, you tend to feel safer in numbers, Uncle Mario," I reply.

He looks up from the papers spread before him, his pen frozen mid-stroke. His eyes widen in shock, mouth falling open slightly as he takes in the sight of me standing before him. For a moment, the carefully crafted mask of the ruthless crime boss slips, revealing a flicker of genuine surprise and fear?

"Vesper," he breathes, my name falling from his lips like

a prayer—or a curse. He quickly composes himself, straightening in the high-backed leather chair that once belonged to my father. "What an unexpected surprise."

I feel a surge of satisfaction at having caught him off guard. It's a rare thing to see Mario Rossi rattled, and I savor the moment, letting the silence stretch between us.

"Uncle," I reply, my voice cool and controlled. I take a step forward, feeling the solid presence of my men behind me. "You look surprised to see me. I wonder why that could be the case."

Mario's lips tighten into a thin line as he rises from his chair, his hands splaying across the polished surface of the desk. "Vesper, my dear, we thought…"

"No," I cut him off, my voice sharp as a blade. "Don't pretend that you haven't known where I've been the last two years."

I take another step forward, my eyes never leaving his face. The room seems to shrink around us, the tension palpable in the air. I can feel the steady presence of Oscar, Zaire, Talon, and Alex behind me, their silent support giving me strength.

"It's funny. The last time I stood in this room," I begin, my voice low and steady, "I was arguing with my father. I stood right here," I continue, moving to stand in the exact spot where I'd faced my father two years ago. "Right here, where I told him I wouldn't marry Dmitri Petrov. That I wouldn't be a pawn in his power games."

I run my fingers along the edge of the desk, feeling the

smooth wood beneath my skin. How many times had I stood on the other side of this desk as a child, barely able to see over its imposing surface?

"He told me I had no choice. That it was my duty to the family. And now look at where we are."

I turn back to face Mario, noting the beads of sweat forming on his brow. "My father is dead, and you've taken his place. And isn't it ironic, Uncle, that the very man my father wanted me to marry is now married to your daughter? But, she's not really your daughter, is she?"

Mario flinches at my words, his composure cracking further. I press on, relishing the way he squirms under my gaze.

"You forget your place, niece."

His words ignite a fire within me, rage coursing through my veins like molten lava. I laugh, a harsh, bitter sound that echoes off the wood-paneled walls.

"My place?" I spit the words out, venom dripping from every syllable. "You dare speak to me about my place?"

I stalk around the desk, my movements fluid and predatory. Mario flinches, I can smell the fear radiating off him in waves, mingling with the scent of his expensive cologne.

"For two years," I continue, my voice low and dangerous, "you let Natasha take everything from me. My home, my family, my dignity. You ordered every violation done to me."

Mario's eyes widen, a flicker of guilt crossing his features before he masks it with indignation. "Vesper, you don't understand-"

"Oh, I understand perfectly," I cut him off, slamming my hands down on the desk. The sharp crack echoes through the room, making him flinch. "You allowed me to be sold like livestock once I'd served my purpose. Tell me, Uncle, how much did my suffering line your pockets?"

He shakes his head vehemently, sweat beading on his upper lip. "No, no, you've got it all wrong. I never-"

"Don't you dare lie to me!" I roar, my composure finally shattering. "I know what you did. Every. Single. Detail."

I lean in close, close enough to see the flecks of gold in his brown eyes, so similar to my father's and yet so different. "I know about your plan for your daughter to take my place as Dmitri's bride. Honestly, that part doesn't bother me. Being married to a monster isn't really where I saw my future heading. For that, I am grateful. But, you had to take it a step further to protect your dirty little secret. You took from me. You created a life from my own body and gave it to your daughter. The daughter who doesn't have a single drop of Rossi blood in her."

Mario's face drains of color, his mouth opening and closing like a fish out of water. I press on, relentless in my assault.

"You stole that innocence from me. Look what you made, Uncle Mario."

I step back from the desk, my anger giving way to a cold, calculated calm. With deliberate grace, I begin to twirl, my dress flaring out around me like the petals of a deadly flower. The movement is slow, controlled, reminiscent of a ballerina in a music box—beautiful, yet mechanical and slightly unnerving.

"What do you want, Vesper?" Mario asks, his voice strained as he watches me spin. His eyes dart nervously between me and the men standing guard at the door. "Money?"

"You cannot buy what you've already sold, Uncle. You see," I continue, my voice steady despite my constant motion, "everything in this room, everything in this house— it all belongs to me. You're just a temporary caretaker, a placeholder."

"Oh, my dear niece," he chuckles, wiping tears from his eyes. "You truly believe you can just waltz in here and take it all back? You're a woman, Vesper. A woman without a family to back her outside of myself and your cousin, and I'll never do that."

His words hit me like a physical blow, but I refuse to let him see how they affect me. I stand tall, chin raised defiantly.

"You're wrong," Oscar's voice cuts through the tension, calm and steady. He steps forward, his presence a comforting warmth at my side. "She has a family."

Mario's eyes dart between us, confusion evident on his face before realization dawns. His lips curl into a sneer as he takes in the protective stance of the men around me, the way Oscar's hand rests possessively on the small of my back.

"I see," he spits, disgust dripping from every word. "So, this is what it's come to, eh? For someone who was so against marrying into the Petrov family, you're still fucking one, aren't you? Tell me, niece, did you spread your legs for all of them, or just the pretty ones?"

The room seems to vibrate with tension, the air crackling with barely contained rage. I can feel the fury radiating off the men behind me, but it's nothing compared to the inferno blazing inside my chest.

"You're no better than a common whore. Selling herself to whatever fool has enough cash to pay for her time," he snarls.

The words have barely left his mouth when a blur of motion catches my eye. Zaire surges forward, his face a mask of pure, unadulterated fury. Before anyone can react, his fist connects with Mario's jaw with a sickening crack.

Mario falls back in his chair, blood trickling from his split lip. Zaire doesn't give him a chance to recover, grabbing him by the lapels of his expensive suit and slamming him against his desk. A stack of papers tumble to the floor as Mario's head connects with the solid wood.

"You don't get to talk about her like that," Zaire growls, his voice low and dangerous. "You don't even get to say her name, you piece of shit."

I watch, frozen in place, as Zaire's hands tighten around Mario's throat. My uncle's eyes bulge, his face contorted in pain.

"Zaire, stop," I order. The same tone that Zaire uses on

me when the weight of our world comes crashing down around me and I lose control. The room falls silent, save for Mario's labored breathing. Zaire's grip loosens, but he doesn't step away. His eyes are dark with rage. I can see the muscles in his jaw working as he fights to control himself.

"Is that why you came?" Mario rasps. "To have one of your paramours kill me for you?"

His words hang in the air, heavy and accusatory. I feel a surge of emotions, anger, disgust, but also a flicker of something else. Pity, perhaps? For a moment, I see my uncle not as the monster he's become, but as the man I once knew. The uncle who used to sneak me extra desserts at family dinners, who taught me how to play chess on lazy Sunday afternoons.

But that man is gone now, replaced by this bitter, power-hungry shell.

I take a deep breath, inhaling the scent of old books and polished wood. Dust motes dance in the golden light, swirling in intricate patterns as if choreographed by an unseen hand. I move closer. I push the memories aside, steeling myself against the tide of emotion threatening to overwhelm me. This man before me may wear my uncle's face, but he is no longer the person I once loved more than my own father.

Leaning down, I bring my face level with his. Our eyes lock, and I see a flicker of fear in the depths of his gaze. Good. Let him be afraid. Let him feel a fraction of the terror I've lived with for the past two years.

"I've learned something about myself since you kidnapped, violated, and sold me." The words hang in the air between us, heavy with the weight of unspoken truths.

Mario's eyes narrow, a mixture of curiosity and apprehension clouding his features. "And what's that, my dear niece?" he asks, his voice hoarse from Zaire's assault.

I take a deep breath, inhaling the scent of his cologne, the same brand he's worn for as long as I can remember. It's a scent that once brought comfort, but now only serves to fuel my resolve.

"I've learned that blood means absolutely nothing," I say, each word precise and cutting. "Blood doesn't determine your family. A family, a real one, doesn't need to share a single drop of it."

As I speak, I feel a shift in the air around me. The men who came with me, Oscar, Zaire, Talon, and Alex, seem to draw closer, their presence a tangible force at my back. I draw strength from them, from the bonds we've forged through trials and tribulations.

"Family," I continue, my voice growing stronger with each word, "is not about shared DNA or family trees. It's about loyalty, trust, and unconditional love. It's about standing by someone's side when the whole world has turned its back on them."

I straighten up, looking down at Mario. The afternoon light streaming through the windows catches the tears welling in my eyes, turning them into liquid gold. But these aren't tears of sadness or fear. They're tears of revelation, of a truth so profound it shakes me to my very core.

"You taught me that lesson, Uncle," I say, a bitter smile tugging at my lips. "When you betrayed me, when you sold me like chattel, you showed me exactly what family isn't. And in doing so, you set me free to find my own family. One that will soon help me rule from this very seat."

"You'll have to kill me first before you'll put your ass in this seat."

"That can be arranged," I threaten him.

Mario's eyes flicker with a dangerous glint, his lips curling into a devious smile that sends a chill down my spine. He leans back in his chair, a newfound confidence radiating from him despite the bruises forming on his throat.

"Family, family, family," he mocks, his voice a low growl. "You speak so passionately about it, my dear niece. And yet, in all your righteous anger, in all your talk of betrayal and loyalty, you seem to have forgotten someone rather important."

My heart skips a beat, a cold dread seeping into my bones. I struggle to maintain my composure, but I can feel my mask slipping. Mario's smile widens, like a predator sensing weakness in its prey.

"What are you talking about?" I manage to ask.

"Why, your brother, of course, or have you forgotten him so easily?" Mario's eyes glitter with malicious glee, like a cat toying with a wounded mouse. He leans back in his chair, the leather creaking ominously in the tense silence of the study. "Oh yes, your dear brother Luca. The prodigal son, the heir apparent until he wasn't."

I clench my fists at my sides, my nails digging crescents into my palms. The pain grounds me, keeps me from losing myself.

"I happen to know where he is. Well, was," he sneers. "He's been alive and well this entire time," Mario continues, his voice dripping with false sympathy. "A little hard to find, to be honest. Your father made sure of that. But I...well, let's just say I have my ways."

I feel a hand on my lower back, steadying me. I didn't even notice him moving behind me. Oscar's touch, warm and reassuring, anchors me.

"You want to know where he is, don't you, Vesper?" he purrs, his voice silky smooth. "You want to see your dear brother again, to reunite your fractured family?"

I swallow hard, my throat suddenly dry. "What will that information cost me?" I ask, hating how small my voice sounds.

"Smart girl. Never expect anything for free. Maybe my brother taught you something about our world after all." Mario's smile widens, revealing teeth that seem too sharp, too predatory. "It's simple, really. You walk away. You and your companions," he gestures dismissively at the men behind me, "leave this house, leave Boston. You forget about your claims to the Rossi empire, about your misguided quest for revenge. About your son, who is thriving with his mother and father. You disappear, and I'll tell you where to find Luca."

The offer hangs in the air between us, tempting and terrible all at once. I can feel Oscar's hand tighten on my back, a silent reminder of his support. Zaire shifts restlessly behind me, his anger a palpable force. Talon's eyes are darting around the room, no doubt calculating odds and escape routes. And Alex, steady and silent, radiates a calm that helps center me.

I close my eyes for a moment, letting the competing desires war within me. The longing to see Luca again, to hold my brother and know he's safe, is almost overwhelming. But the thought of walking away, of letting Mario win after everything he's done, makes my blood boil.

When I open my eyes again, I see Mario watching me intently, a vulture waiting for its prey to succumb. I straighten my spine, drawing strength from the presence of my chosen family behind me.

"Walk away, and I will give you everything you need to get him back," he doubles down.

I feel Oscar's hand at the small of my back again, the cool metal of a gun pressing against my skin through the thin fabric of my dress. Without breaking eye contact with Mario, I reach behind me, my fingers closing around the grip of the pistol. The weight of it is familiar, comforting even, as I bring it forward.

Mario's eyes widen as the barrel comes into view, his smug expression faltering for the first time. I can see the wheels turning in his head, calculating his odds, searching for an escape route. But there is none. Not this time.

The gun feels alive in my hand, an extension of my will. I can feel every groove of the grip, every minute imperfection in the metal. Time seems to slow, the world narrowing down to just me, Mario, and the weapon between us.

"Tell me where I can find Luca."

My uncle steels his face. "My offer hasn't changed just because you don't agree to the terms. He's better off where he is. Your brother would have ruined this family. The Rossi empire deserved better than a f…" The crack of the gunshot cuts him off, the sound impossibly loud in the confines of the study. For a moment, everything is still, frozen in the aftermath of that single, violent act. A warm spray of my uncle's blood splatters against me from the wound in his shoulder. The tiny droplets seeping into my clothes.

"Fuck!" he roars.

"That," I say, my voice eerily calm over Mario's pained gasps, "was for every night I spent in that hellhole you sent me to. For every time I cried out for help, and no one came."

I move closer, the gun still trained on him. Behind me, I can hear the shuffling of feet as my men adjust their positions, ready to act if needed. But this is my moment, my reckoning.

"You can't do this. I am the fucking head of this family,"

he snarls back with pain lacing every syllable that slips from his lips.

A bitter laugh escaping my lips. "You forget that I am a Rossi, too, and despite what you think, I can take your place just as easily as you stole it from my father."

Mario whimpers, his face pale with pain and fear. Blood drips onto the antique Persian rug. "You fucking bitch…"

I fire again, hitting his other shoulder. My uncle roars in pain again.

"I have a counter proposal. You tell me where my brother is, and I let you live," I pause, allowing a sinister smile to cross my face. I let the weight of my words sink in, watching as the color drains from Mario's face. His eyes dart frantically between the gun in my hand and my face, searching for any sign of mercy. He finds none.

"You wouldn't," he gasps, his voice trembling. "You're not a killer, Vesper. You're not…"

The third gunshot rings out, drowning his protests in a cacophony of noise and pain. Mario's body jerks violently as the bullet tears through his groin spraying a fine mist of blood across the polished mahogany desk. The metallic scent of blood fills the air, mingling with the acrid smell of gunpowder.

His scream echoes off the wood-paneled walls, a primal sound of agony that rattles the foundation of my family home. But I don't flinch. I don't look away. I watch as he writhes in pain, clutching at the bloody mess of where his dick used to be with his already bloodied hand.

"You were saying?" I ask, my voice eerily calm over his pained gasps. "I'm not what, exactly?"

Mario's eyes are wild with fear now, darting between my face and the gun still trained on him. Sweat beads on his forehead, mingling with the tears of pain streaking down his cheeks. He opens his mouth to speak, but only a choked sob escapes.

"I'm going to ask you one more time," I say, raising the gun slightly higher. "Where. Is. Luca?"

Mario's eyes widen as he realizes where I'm aiming now. Right at his cold black heart. His Adam's apple bobs as he swallows hard, a bead of sweat trailing down his neck to disappear into his blood-soaked collar.

"Vesper, please," he whimpers, his earlier bravado completely shattered. "You don't understand. I can't just-"

"Wrong answer," I cut him off, my finger tightening on the trigger.

"Wait!" he screams, throwing up his hands in a pathetic attempt to shield himself. "He was...he was with you," he confesses.

The words hit me like a physical blow, stealing the breath from my lungs. "What?" I manage to choke out.

"Luca," Mario continues, his words tumbling out in a rush now. "He was in the same facility as you. You were together the entire time."

"Where?" I demand, my voice cracking with desperation. "Where is it?"

Mario's eyes flutter, struggling to focus on my face. "The

Collector," he mumbles, blood-stained spittle flying from his lips. "Luca is with The Collector."

"Where?" I press, leaning in closer. "Where can I find The Collector?"

Mario's laugh is a wet, gurgling sound that makes my stomach turn. "You don't find The Collector, Vesper. The Collector finds you."

"Tell me where my brother is," I roar, but the only noise that comes from my uncle's lips is the rasp of one final breath. Taking with it my chance to find my brother.

Epilogue

LUCA

THE ELECTRIC PULSES course through me, sending shockwaves of unwanted pleasure radiating from my core. I grit my teeth, refusing to make a sound as the machine continues its relentless assault on my body. Cold metal presses against my most intimate areas, extracting what it needs with clinical efficiency.

I try to focus on anything else - the stark white walls, the hum of medical equipment, the ticking of a clock somewhere out of sight. Anything to distract from the violation of my body and my pride.

The door opens with a soft click. Polished shoes tap across the tile floor as The Collector enters, a predatory smile playing on their lips. Their eyes rake over my restrained form with open greed.

"Well, well. The mighty Luca Rossi brought so low," they purr.

Rage and shame battle within me.. I glare at them with all the defiance I can muster, even as another pulse racks my body. The Collector just laughs, clearly relishing my helplessness.

"Such spirit," they muse. "The buyers will love breaking it." They turn to adjust some settings on the infernal machine. "Now, let's see how much more we can wring out of you, shall we?"

I close my eyes, steeling myself against whatever is to come. I will endure. I have to, for my family. For revenge.

The Collector eyes gleam with a predatory satisfaction that makes my skin crawl. I try to speak, to demand answers, but the gag in my mouth reduces my protests to muffled grunts. My body is wracked with involuntary spasms, the electrodes attached to my most sensitive areas sending jolts of unwanted pleasure mixed with pain through my entire being.

"Your sister made me a lot of money," The Collector says, their voice dripping with smug satisfaction. "Let's see if the Rossi heir is worth even more."

I glare at them, fury and fear warring within me. What have they done to Vesper? And what do they mean by their cryptic statement? I struggle against my restraints, but it is futile. The machinery hums, continuing its relentless assault on my body, drawing out every last drop as if I am nothing more than a prized breeding animal.

The Collector circles me, their gaze clinical and cold. "You Rossis always did think you were above it all," they muse. "But here you are, reduced to your basest function. It's almost poetic, don't you think?"

I want to spit in their face, to show them that they can't break me. But as another wave of forced pleasure crashes over me, I can't help but wonder how long I can hold out. The shame of my body's betrayal is almost worse than the physical sensations. I had always prided myself on my self-control, on being the strong, stoic heir to the Rossi empire. Now, I am reduced to this, a puppet dancing on The Collector's strings.

The Collector moves closer, their face looming over mine. I can see every pore, every line etched into their cruel features. Their breath ghosts across my skin as they lean in.

"You Rossis always were fighters," they murmur, almost admiringly. "But everyone breaks eventually. I wonder what it will take to break you, Luca?"

* * *

If you're ready to dive deeper into Vesper's story, don't miss the next chapter! Preorder *All The Darkest Truths* now: https://books2read.com/AllTheDarkestTruths

Acknowledgements

To Glen, my endlessly patient husband—you've seen me dive into the dark, twisty minds of fictional criminals and somehow still let me back into our house. Thanks for the snacks, the Coca-Cola, and not asking *too many* questions about all the suspicious Google searches.

To my fierce PR team, Chaotic Creatives—especially Cass and Mads, who seem more invested in Alex than I am. Thanks for insisting I start book 2 immediately (apparently, sleep is optional) and for turning the "Who gets to claim Alex?" debate into an actual blood sport. You two keep me grounded…mostly by tying me to my writing desk.

And finally, to my readers—you're as wild and wonderfully unhinged as this story. I wouldn't have it any other way.

Welcome to the madness...there's so much more to come.
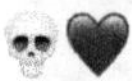🖤

About Avelyn

Meet Avelyn Paige, the creative genius behind thrilling romantic suspense and heart-pounding motorcycle club and mafia romance novels that have conquered the Wall Street Journal and USA TODAY bestseller lists. Nestled in a cozy corner of Indiana, she shares her quaint abode with her hubby and a lively bunch of five furballs.

By day, Avelyn transforms into a cancer research superhero, battling in the realm of science. But when the lab coat comes off, the writing cap goes on, and she dives into a world of passion, intrigue, and leather-clad rebels. An unabashed bookworm from the get-go, Avelyn decided to weave her own tales after a plot twist in her life – losing her dad in 2015. Since then, she's been on a wild ride through imagination and hasn't hit the brakes!

Join Avelyn's Reader Group: Avelyn's Angels

Devil's Queen

* 9 7 8 1 9 6 8 8 0 8 0 1 3 *